DREAM
OF
FREEDOM

Dream of Freedom

MICHAEL PHILLIPS

TYNDALE HOUSE PUBLISHERS, INC.
WHEATON, ILLINOIS

Visit Tyndale's exciting Web site at www.tyndale.com

Also visit the author's Web site: www.MacDonaldPhillips.com

TYNDALE is a registered trademark of Tyndale House Publishers, Inc.

Tyndale's quill logo is a trademark of Tyndale House Publishers, Inc.

Scripture quotations are taken from the *Holy Bible*, King James Version.

This novel is a work of fiction. Names, characters, places, and incidents either are the product of the author's imagination or are used fictitiously. Any resemblance to actual events, locales, organizations, or persons, living or dead, is entirely coincidental and beyond the intent of either the authors or publisher.

Library of Congress Cataloging-in-Publication Data

Phillips, Michael R., date.
   Dream of freedom / by Michael Phillips.
   p. cm. — (American dreams; bk. 1)
ISBN 1-4143-0176-6 — ISBN 0-8423-7776-X (pbk.)
   1. African American women—Fiction. 2. South Carolina—Fiction. 3. Slaves—Fiction. I. Title.
PS3566.H492D74 2005
813'.54—dc22
                                           2004062144

Printed in the United States of America

11 10 09 08 07 06 05
7   6   5   4   3   2   1

Dedication

To my dear friends Hans and Christa Peters, Marlies Borrmeister, and Anke Peters Clemens, with whom barriers of language have prevented the saying of much that draws individuals together in this world, but between whose hearts and mine pulses the greater language of sincere affection. That often-silent tongue of a common humanity and a shared Fatherhood has bound us together for more than 35 years (or, in Anke's case, for a little over half that!). To call them my friends is one of the priceless possessions for which I feel most greatly blessed in this life. Both I and my family have through the years been as kindly welcomed with every courtesy and consideration back to that stately brick farmhouse in Graulingen, Suderburg in northern Germany as we have been into all of their hearts. It was there that Christa, Marlies, and I first began the adventure of a cross-cultural friendship more than three decades ago. To this place of my spiritual foundations I have often returned—for a day or two, a week or two, a month or two—a place far from home where God saw fit to stir the passions of a young man many years ago toward the wonder of a life of obedience to him, and to the vision of communicating that life through the written word. It is there, in a remarkable and peaceful three weeks, that the first draft of this book was substantially written, and to Hans, Christa, Marlies, and Anke it is humbly and warmly dedicated.

CONTENTS

Introduction

*S*ome of you embarking with me on this series will be new readers; others will be old friends. I hope both will find it exciting, as I do, to launch into a new historical adventure together.

The era in which American Dreams is set is a familiar one—the U.S. Civil War. It is a period in our collective past that fascinates us from many perspectives. It is an era of ideas and change and growth, when new trends clashed with old ideals.

It is also an era in which the entire history of our nation comes into focus in a unique way. This history can be seen in the context of the intermingling of three primary ethnic roots—the first Native American settlers who called this continent home long before the rest of civilization even knew it existed, the black African tribesmen and tribeswomen who were transplanted as laborers into a strange new world from their own continent, and the white European races who subdued the other two at first and later had to find a way to include them in an ongoing history that is still being written.

As these three streams of humanity both converged and clashed through the years of the nineteenth century, the globe's newest nation had to discover what the freedom upon which it was founded really meant . . . for all its people.

Into the familiar backdrop of the Civil War, I have chosen to set a story that explores the roots of human unity by asking the fundamental questions: What does freedom mean? How can three ethnic cultures learn to live together and forge a united nation as one new people—a people called *Americans*, a people with diverse dreams and yet who share a single dream: Freedom?

To answer such questions *nationally*, an even more fundamental perspective must also be considered: What do slavery, redemption, and freedom mean *individually*? In a sense, the slavery that once existed in this land is a picture of the bondage that enslaves us all, a slavery from which our "Master" sets us free. Such is the universal story of life, the story I try to retell in all my books. At root it is a story about a Father-Master who frees us from the essential human slavery, which is independence of will . . . slavery to sin and self.

There are those who think the characters of my books are "too good" and their themes too spiritual to offer the "realism" today's market demands. But the characters you are about to meet are types and pictures of that great redeeming Christ-work that has brought freedom to us . . . and to the world. Is it too good to envision a wonderful and perfect Father? I hope not. For if the Lord's redemptive work cannot take root in real people and lead to real goodness of character, we are just playing at Christianity.

The release from the bondage that long ago enslaved the children of Israel in Egypt, and not so very long ago the African blacks of our own land, is an image of the freedom God desires to bring to all men. All redemptions must begin small, one heart at a time, until the whole world sees that freedom *must* be the wave of the future, that bondage to self cannot endure. The light of freedom, and the overpowering Love of the universe must, and *will*, overcome it in the end.

Every book takes on a life of its own. The story that comes to life often dictates the format and structure a book will take. In order to avoid confusion as you begin, therefore, I should tell you that the "Prologue" to each book (entitled "From the Old Books") encompasses all the volumes that follow. Their clues and threads and mysteries will resolve themselves over the course of the entire series—although I'm sure you will unravel many of them before then!—not in just one particular segment of the story. The Prologue will establish the historical context out of which emerged these three great streams of humanity, and will lay the groundwork for the series by providing a sense of the bigger picture of our nation's foundations.

In closing, I will add these thoughts from the Introduction to *Wild Grows the Heather in Devon*, emphasizing that:

> Perhaps even more than any other series of mine which you may have read, [this] truly is a *series*. Hopefully each of its titles will give you a sense of completion and satisfaction. Yet at the same time it will be clear that "the whole story" has not yet been told. The first several books all combine to form a unity which none of the individual titles can achieve on their own. I beg the patience of my readers as the series develops, in the knowledge that the various entrées of a "full-course literary meal" take longer to prepare than they do to consume.

I hope you enjoy our journey together, and our look back at a pivotal time of danger, change, and growth in our nation's history, an era when freedom was a dream that became a reality.

Michael Phillips
Eureka, California

Out of the Unknown Past

1619

*O*n the shores of the Dark Continent a Portuguese merchantman—sailing under the name *Vidonia*—sat in the harbor of a natural bay along a little-known coastline between the mouths of the two rivers of western Sudan. Originally attracted to this region for its gold, a new cargo had, in recent decades, come to dominate the attention of its crew. Onshore the *Vidonia's* captain matched wits and purse with an Arab trader who had arrived overland from the region of the Nile for the same reason as he, to bargain for slaves.

The two traffickers in humanity met in the hut of a local Songhai king, who sat listening to their bids with growing satisfaction. Between the Arab and the European, his supply of rum and other small treasures would last all year. The recent foray to round up and kidnap men, women, and children from tribes less powerful than his own had proved as highly profitable as last year's. He only regretted that he did not have more of his countrymen to sell to the traders.

He motioned an attendant to pour more rum, then returned his attention to the haggling promises of the two foreigners. He did not understand their every word. But he understood more than they thought he did of their occasional asides to one another, and enough to secure for himself a lucrative commission for this transaction in human flesh.

The wooden barracoons behind the hut where the negotiations were in progress held more than a hundred captives who had been abducted from their inland villages over the past three months. They came from a half-dozen tribes, related by blackness of skin but little else. Some were allies, some were bitterest of enemies. But now they were united in common fate.

Among them stood a chieftain of the Ibo tribe, whose Niger river would one day give its name to a portion of the continent he had ruled. Beside him, waiting tall and stoic as he, stood his seven children—three sons and four daughters, ranging in age from twenty-four-year-old son to nine-year-old daughter. Their mother had been killed in the raid that had resulted in their abduction. They would all weep for her in time, each in his own way. For now, however, the shock of capture and fear of what awaited them kept silent rule over their tongues and their hearts.

Stories of the sea raiders had circulated for years among the peoples of the regions of Ghana, Sierra Leone, Senegal, and Gambia. Few who were captured were ever seen again. The tales that returned to their ears contained more hearsay than fact, yet certain threads of truth could be found among them. The islands of the Caribbean where the Portuguese took their cargo had a fearful reputation. But the Arab markets of Zanzibar had worse. If the chieftain's Ibo daughters—taller than many of their cousins of the Negro race and thus attracting the attention of lusting Arab eyes—survived the grueling overland march to Egypt and then Arabia, their only reward would be a place in some eastern harem. Meanwhile, if the chief's sons, also taller and more muscular than their new masters, were bought by the Arab, some would be conscripted to occupy the front lines in the never-ending wars of the Middle East, while others would be taught to capture and plunder their own people to make of them slaves like themselves. In either case, their life expectancy would not be long.

But even the images conjured up in Chief Tungal's imagination were not so inhumane as what would eventually come to the progeny of these Nigerian people and their racial kinsmen from up and down the west of Africa. Centuries from now, the whole world would be outraged by their story. None from their race had yet settled on the continent of that New World which two centuries later would become known for its own unique and cruel form of human bondage. Theirs was a story yet in its infancy, and much suffering would be endured before they were delivered from it.

Over the crude spiked fence Chief Tungal saw the turbaned Arab and the pale-skinned Portuguese captain emerge from the hut, accompanied by the Songhai chief.

The proud captive turned to his seven children. In a voice low and solemn, in an ancient tongue now long forgotten, he spoke to them:

"My sons, my daughters," he said, "we may not see each other again. Plant my words deep in your memory. Look . . . read the sign of the lines of the hand . . . and remember!"

He held up his left hand, palm outward to face them.

"As the five ancient rivers run through our land," he continued, his voice taking on the dignity of the ages, "so does the blood of ancient kings flow through our veins and give power to our limbs. Take strength from the memory of that knowledge. Do not forget the five rivers. Do not forget the land. Wherever you are taken, remember your home. Look to your own hand . . . remember the rivers . . . remember your land . . . remember the old tales. You come from kings and will give birth to kings. None can take that from you. Tell it to your children and their children. Tell them of the rivers and of the land . . . tell all the children after them, that the knowledge remain green."

As he spoke, tears began to trickle from the eyes of his youngest daughter. He stooped down, smiled tenderly, and wiped her soft black cheek with the back of his hand.

A shout behind him broke the tender silence. The two traders approached the barracks to inspect their purchases. Chief Tungal stood, then turned to face them. He cast a proud glance at the pale, bearded captain, then let his eyes wander toward the swarthy, clean-shaven Arab. His fate and the fate of his children lay in the hands of these men. He had met cruelty often enough to know it in any color or race. These men also knew cruelty—he could see it in their eyes. But they were those who inflicted rather than endured it.

The gates swung open. Chief, captain, and Arab walked into the midst of the black crowd. Before Tungal could speak to his children again, they were all swept into a confusing melee as Portuguese captain and Arab merchant inspected, probed, scrutinized, and divided their human plunder between them.

Helplessly the father watched as one son and daughter were herded off with the prisoners of the Arab.

Desperately the terrified son looked back. Tungal stood tall and caught his eye. With anguished heart he raised his hand one final time in the royal blessing. A cruel grip on his shoulder the next instant yanked him away, and his son disappeared from his sight.

With much jostling and bumping, and accompanied by the barking of angry commands, he and those who remained were herded out of the compound in the opposite direction, frightened and trembling, toward the harbor. They paused briefly while each was bound to the hand of another in front and back, then were marched across the gangplank in single file, and finally shoved into the foul depths of the ship's hold, where they were bound more securely.

Many weeks would pass before the sunlight would shine again on their faces . . . *if* they survived the voyage at all.

Slavery was nothing new in the world. It had existed since Old Testament times. The civilizations of Egypt, Greece, and Rome were all built on the backs of slave labor. In all lands and in all cultures, slavery was the price of defeat in battle. Among the blacks of Africa, too, slavery had long been a way of life for warring tribesmen defeated by their enemies. But the modern African slave trade, where men made commerce of captive human flesh, had begun with the export of Negroes out of Africa to the Muslim world.

This trade advanced northward into Europe in the year 1440. In that year, sailing under the flag of Prince Henry the Navigator, Portuguese sea captain Antam Goncalvez captured three Moors along the west coast of Africa. These Moors exchanged their own freedom for ten African

Negroes. Goncalvez took the ten blacks to Lisbon and there sold them for a handsome profit. Initially drawn to Africa for its gold and ivory, Goncalvez now realized there was an easier path to wealth. He returned south, raided several coastal African villages, and sailed back to Lisbon, this time with even more slaves in the hold of his ship.

The European slave trade had begun.

Over the next twenty years nearly a thousand Negroes a year were taken to Portugal and sold. By the end of the century, Portugal was supplying slaves to Spain.

With Columbus' discovery of the New World in 1492, a vast new marketplace for the infant slave trade opened to European conquerors. As settlements formed on the islands of the Caribbean, slaves were imported to work in their fields, plantations, and mines. The sea voyage over the Atlantic from Africa to the Caribbean West Indies, called the Middle Passage, was so inhumane and brutal that up to half the captive slaves to set sail from their homeland did not survive it. By the mid-1500s, the Portuguese, Spanish, and Dutch were all involved in the vigorous and profitable trade.

As the sixteenth century advanced, the newly established European plantations of the West Indies and Spanish colonies in South America supplied steadily increasing quantities of sugarcane, tobacco, and indigo to Europe. These island colonies of the New World paid a premium for strong field hands. The Portuguese, and later the Dutch and English, competed vigorously to supply the growing need for humanity. More and more ships arrived every year along the Guinea Coast, plundering its villages for humanity. As the trade continued to expand, they took advantage of tribal rivalries to purchase captives from victorious local chiefs and kings.

Well might the victims of this tragic oppression look heavenward and wonder, like the Egyptian-imprisoned Israelites of old, if a loving God existed at all. If so, why he had forgotten them. But their Father saw the misery that man inflicted upon man, and held the anguished cry of each slave-child in his own grieved heart. He had not forgotten them, and would send others, his servants, to put an end to their despair.

Tens of thousands of African slaves were bought and sold in the

Caribbean islands of the New World through the 1500s. When the
seventeenth century opened, however, slavery still had not come to the
mainland of the North American continent.

It was accidental irony, not design, that finally brought slavery to
the English colonies.

———

The ship carrying Chief Tungal and his dark-skinned brothers and
children away from their homeland bore for the West Indies of the
Caribbean. There its Portuguese captain hoped to turn a handsome
profit for his cargo with Spanish plantation owners.

Only a week across the Atlantic, however, a violent storm threw
him badly off course. Scarcely had he recovered from it before another
assaulted them, and then a third. Badly damaged, and, too crippled to
right itself, the *Vidonia* was driven far to the north. Its fate, in one of
the tragic twists of history, now lay at the mercy of the winds.

Whether the winds were kind or cruel in blowing them into the
path of another vessel prowling the Atlantic's northern waters would
depend on the color of one's skin.

It was the *Vidonia*'s lookout atop the crow's nest who first saw the
sail on the horizon.

"Ship sighted . . . starboard stern!" cried the sentinel in Portuguese.
"Rouse the captain!"

The captain hurried on deck, spyglass in hand, followed by three of
his men. The grim expression on all their faces moments later told the
story. The flag snapping from the stalking masthead carried no
nation's colors. An unmarked ship could mean but one thing.

Pirates!

"All hands on deck!" called the captain. "Run up every sail . . . roll
out the cannon . . . prepare for battle!"

In its crippled condition, the *Vidonia* could not hope to outrun its
pursuer. The unmarked vessel was a Dutch man-of-war, trim and
fleet, unburdened by cargo and gaining steadily.

In less than an hour, the seasoned crew of Dutchmen could be seen scurrying about on deck making ready for a fight. Gradually the ships drew even.

In the blackness below, Chief Tungal knew nothing of the battle that followed, only that a barrage of explosions, loud as thunder, violently shook the ship. As the sides of the wooden hold groaned, screams echoed from the prisoners trapped in darkness.

Gunfire . . . shouts from above . . . more explosions . . . the sounds of wood cracking and splintering . . . suddenly a flood of light burst upon them. Icy salt water rushed between the decks where Tungal and his fellow captives struggled in vain with the ropes that bound them. The *Vidonia* heaved and began to list to one side.

Screams, more desperate now, rose in every direction from white and black alike. Suddenly a trapdoor opened above them. Strangers, white of skin like their captors but yelling commands in yet another unfamiliar tongue, leaped down into the seething clamor of the bowels of the sinking ship. Frantically, as they were able, they sliced the ropes of those within reach, gathered what rich bundles of ivory they could carry, and urged those they had loosed up on deck. The Africans fortunate enough to be freed, water swirling now above their knees, scrambled after them, desperate to save themselves.

Finding his own ropes dangling loose, Tungal turned back, fighting the flow of escapees. In a loud voice he called to his children. But he could not make his way back below deck against the human tide before a heavy blow knocked him senseless.

As his consciousness returned, Tungal lay rocking gently back and forth in a hammock of hemp. Slowly his vision came into focus. He was staring up at the tarred underside of a wooden deck. The smell and sway of creaking wood told him he was still inside the lower portions of a ship.

With difficulty he tried to pull himself up. Beside him, a pale-skinned foreigner in the next hammock turned toward him and spoke in a strange tongue. Tungal stared back uncomprehending. He glanced about at the empty berths lining the walls, and at the rows of mostly empty hammocks swinging from hooks in the low ceiling.

Where was he, Tungal thought. This was not the ship that had carried him away from Africa. Slowly the events of the attack and the confusion that followed came back to him.

Startled in the midst of his reverie, a small black hand slid over Tungal's arm. He turned, and gasped with astonished delight. His youngest daughter crept beside him. Her two older sisters and two brothers stood behind her! Great smiles spread over the five black faces to see their father's eyes open at last in wakeful recognition. None of them wore ropes or chains.

The white stranger spoke again, though they still did not understand him.

"We are bounde, ye and we twelve immigrants, my goode dark-skinned brother," he said in the English tongue Tungal and his kind would adopt in time as their own, "for the colonie in Virginia called Jamestowne. It is in the New Worlde. We are bounde as servants to worke for our freedom, as will ye, I am thinking."

Their captors and rescuers were not pirates at all, but a ragged crew of Dutch and English smugglers who carried on a fitful trade between the Old World and the New. They had captured the *Vidonia*, but had only managed to bring twenty or so of the Africans on board before it sank and what remained of its crew and cargo was lost. It was the hope of the Dutchmen to purchase fresh supplies from the Jamestown colonists in exchange for their cargo of servants and ivory. The new freight of blacks would perhaps increase their bargaining power. Whether the colonists would want them they had no way of knowing. There had never before been Africans in Jamestown.

Until the ship arrived on the American continent, the African tribesmen and the white servants could do as they pleased.

Tungal did not understand the words. But he understood the man's smile.

For now at least, he and his children were free.

Dispersion

1619–1808

*W*hen the Dutch man-of-war unloaded its goods at Jamestown, the colonists gaped with astonishment and curiosity at the twenty-one blacks walking silently down the gangplank. They had read about the existence of dark-skinned races of men. But never with their own eyes had they beheld their like before.

Though profit-seeking English seamen had eventually become involved in the Caribbean slave trade along with the Portuguese, Spanish, and Dutch, the religiously minded English Puritans who settled along the eastern seaboard of the American mainland would have disdained the very idea of slavery. No Englishman *owned* another human being as his permanent property anywhere in England or in the new English colonies of the Americas. Indentured servitude, on the other hand, was a well-known means by which a man without money might offer his services for a given term of years in exchange for passage to the New World and subsequent freedom. During the period of his service he was provided a home, food, and clothing. After seven, fourteen, or twenty-one years, as the bargain was struck, he was given a sum of money to buy land and start his own life as a free man.

In the negotiations that followed the arrival of Chief Tungal and his fellow Africans, therefore, neither opportunistic Dutchmen nor English settlers considered themselves bargaining for the sale of *slaves*.

The colonists purchased the Negroes, along with the new arrivals from Europe, as temporary servants, to be given the same rights as the indentured whites.

Tungal and his five children and their fifteen fellow Africans stepped onto the soil of the colony known as Virginia, indentured to their new English masters. They were the first permanent Negro settlers on the continent of America. They would not be the last.

Chief Tungal found himself indentured to a Jamestown Englishman by the name of Shaw. Between his scanty grasp of the English tongue and his master's gentle persistence, he was finally made to understand that he would have a house and land of his own if he and his daughter worked for Mr. Shaw for seven harvests. In some bewilderment, though without a great deal of say in the matter, Tungal agreed.

His youngest daughter remained with him and became part of the Shaw family. The other two daughters and two sons went to others in the struggling young colony. As in most cases of indenture, they were fairly and kindly treated as illiterate apprentices who were considered members of the extended household.

Before he could complete his seven years of service, however, Chief Tungal's health failed him. Only his youngest daughter Unanana was with him at the end. His final words in the old tongue, as he laid the royal blessing upon her, pierced the young woman's heart. "You are the last of my own," he said, struggling with great effort, pausing to draw one labored breath after another. "My eyes grow dim. . . . I cannot see the future. I fear you will never return to our homeland. Perhaps your children . . . but you must remember . . . do not forget our heritage."

"I will remember, Papa," she said with tears in her eyes.

"As the rivers run through our land," the weary black chieftain continued in a scarcely audible voice, "the five ancient rivers . . . the blood of ancient kings . . . take strength . . . do not forget the rivers and the old tales . . . the land. You come from . . ."

His voice faded. He struggled to lift his left hand, palm outward. Unanana reached her right up to join it.

". . . the blood of kings flows in my body," said Unanana in a choked voice. "I will remember. I will tell my children of the five rivers, and of the land, and teach them to teach their children."

Tungal smiled weakly and dropped his arm to his side in the bed where he lay. He could pass content into the mystical invisible land of his fathers. He knew the ancient legacy of his people would live on.

By nightfall he was gone.

⤺

To complete her father's indenture, Unanana agreed to work for the Shaws another seven years. Master and Mistress Shaw treated her kindly, helping her learn their English tongue and customs. Before the end of her own indenture, Unanana had married the Shaws' son and had a house to call her own.

From Jamestown, Unanana's brothers and sisters drifted out across the untamed new land. As the indenture of each was complete, with husbands and wives and families, they spread out yet farther in the intervening years. Their sons and daughters and grandsons and granddaughters after them married whites, fellow Africans, and also those from native Indian tribes. They dispersed, intermarried, lost track of their past, and became a new race of *African-Americans*. Memories of their former homeland dimmed. But many taught their children to cling to the fragmentary words their father had taught them as a lasting legacy to their royal ancestry and the former life they had left behind.

Tungal's oldest son Goto traveled north, drawn by a love of the sea, and became a fisherman off the French Canadian coast. His reclusive habits earned him the nickname D'Solitaire. He took a native-born wife late in life from the Algonquin tribe, and passed on his proclivity to solitude to sons and grandchildren. Their seed spread along the northern coast and inland toward the region that would later be known as Quebec.

The next, a daughter called Kabel who came to be called Isobel, married a Frenchman. Their granddaughter moved deep into the French territory in the environs where a town called New Orleans would one day take root, and there her descendents remained, spreading throughout what would later become Louisiana and Mississippi.

The next daughter, Danyawo, found work in a settlement in Pennsylvania, married another indentured African, and adopted the name of their Pennsylvania master, Albright. Her grandson converted to the new Quaker faith under the influence of William Penn, and his sons and daughters drifted south into southern Virginia, westward to Ohio, while some remained in Pennsylvania.

The remaining son, Magoda, who came to be called Moses, grew skilled at smithy work. He traveled widely plying his trade, which he taught to his son, and he to his son after him. Within several generations his descendents had settled in the Indian wilds, and within several more generations his African descendents could be traced from the Carolinas to Georgia, and to the lands future great-grandsons would till for their Alabama masters.

Though each of Tungal's children who had arrived with him at the English settlement all eventually gained their freedom, their descendants were not so fortunate to retain it. Perhaps thinking it in their best interests, many masters simply continued to provide for their blacks as they had, keeping them as servants beyond the originally specified term. The motives of the masters in so doing were not entirely cruel. They saw an extension of the period of service as the most sensible, even humane, way of taking care of a backward and illiterate native people who, in the whites' eyes, were culturally incapable of owning farms and businesses and incorporating into English culture on their own.

By the time the two sons and three daughters of Tungal had lived out their days, the Jamestown colony where they had landed declared all Negroes perpetual servants. Other English colonies followed its example, adding regulations that steadily took away the rights of blacks.

Whatever had been the intent of such changes in the beginning, and as the staunchly religious attitudes of the original Puritans gave way to more self-serving economic and capitalistic motives, more rights continued to be taken from them. Gradually, Virginia's blacks passed from *indentured servants* to *perpetual servants* and finally to *slaves.*

Following what had begun with the Portuguese and Spanish far to the south, the commerce in human flesh expanded and grew profitable in the English colonies as well. Slave ships began to haunt the eastern seaboard with increasing frequency. A new slave market was gradually born that proved even more lucrative than the former marketplaces of Arabia, the West Indies, and that flourishing in the New World's first city, Spanish St. Augustine in Florida.

A travesty in mankind's history had begun.

By late in that same seventeenth century, any African unfortunate enough to land on the shores of the New World, whether in Florida or Virginia, could expect a lifetime of drudgery, the length of which would depend on the strength of his constitution and the benevolence of his master.

As the French spread through the northern provinces of the continent now known as America, as the English continued to populate its middle regions of the Atlantic seaboard, and as the Spanish added to their settlements in the south, each brought its own unique form of European custom and language to displace those of native tribes. Slavery accompanied them all and was soon a fixture of life.

The plight of Africans in the New World grew more deplorable. All pretence of indentured servitude had long since vanished. Even those who managed, through the grace of an occasional benevolent white master, to earn, buy, or inherit their freedom had no guarantee of keeping it.

In Virginia, the descendants of Tungal's youngest daughter Unanana Shaw found small comfort that they bore the white man's name. Indeed, most were now known by the name of their masters. The names and legacies of their own ancestors had disappeared in the fading mists of the past. Their dark skin disguised whatever claims of mixed ancestry they might have raised. They worked the very land

some of their great-great-grandparents had owned. Those few who
recalled stories of their royal heritage shared it with their children and
grandchildren as a slowly fading memory. They said the tales that
came from the lost old books of time were important. Thus they
passed on words they scarcely understood, from father to son and
mother to daughter. Perhaps future generations would find better days
in which again to recall their heritage.

Theirs was a doleful life. Tobacco flourished in the fields of
Virginia. Cotton increased throughout the South as a profitable cash
crop. Plantation owners worked their slaves to the last ounce of their
strength.

Stoically Tungal's descendents endured their miserable lot until the
time came when the dream of freedom would awaken within their
collective soul.

The colonies of the New World went to war in 1776 against their
English forebears, basing their struggle for independence on the bold
pronouncement: "We hold these truths to be self-evident, that all men
are created equal, that they are endowed by their Creator with certain
unalienable Rights, that among these are Life, Liberty and the pursuit of
Happiness." It was a foundation for nationhood, conceived and immor-
talized by landholding and slave-owning Europeans. It would take
successive generations, however, to awaken the national consciousness to
the imperative of the words of the nation's founders to the *all men* of
which the new nation was comprised.

For now there were whites and there were blacks and there were
natives with skins of brown. They were anything but equal.

As the eighteenth century drew to a close, the demand for slave
labor waned. But the invention of the cotton gin in 1793 exploded
the market for cotton throughout the South. Suddenly, with enough
cheap labor, it was a crop to make men wealthy beyond their dreams.
Overnight, it seemed, the slave trade from the shores of Africa mush-
roomed. Slavery, which had till then been far more heavily concen-
trated in Virginia than any other Southern state, now spread toward
Kentucky and Tennessee and Louisiana like a brush fire before a hot
wind. Within a generation its blight bound together the southern

portion of that nation calling itself the United States of America with an economic and cultural grip that would not easily be broken.

The thirteen states that made up the original Union interpreted the words of the Declaration of Independence and the Constitution differently. The northern states, where slavery was neither prevalent nor a serious economic concern, began to ban slavery. The southern states, however, whose economies because of King Cotton had grown dependent on it, declared slavery legal. As the United States was a national government founded on the basis of the rights of states to make the majority of their own laws, so it remained. Each state determined for itself the status and rights of the three races which now comprised their populations—the *European whites,* the *African blacks,* and those of the native tribes now universally called *Indians.* All three were *Americans,* but they cherished distinct and discordant dreams of what that national name meant . . . and should mean.

By the time the nineteenth century opened, an invisible divide existed between North and South. At first it was an economic divide, not particularly a moral one. In the North, freedom for Negroes posed no threat and was simply accepted. In the South, however, where slavery lay as the foundation of a mushrooming plantation-based economy, such freedom was a threat to what gradually came to be called "the Southern way of life." Though some, like Quaker John Woolman, railed against that way of life in the years prior to the Revolution, widespread moral abolitionist outrage against it lay yet decades in the future.

But the divide which was economic at root would grow in time to be a moral and cultural chasm as well. Slowly the voices of men like John Woolman began to cause thinking, conscientious, and spiritual men in every state to lament the existence of slavery. Written or verbal appeals did little, however, to stop the traffic of human flesh or the increasing contempt with which masters viewed their slaves. The only hope of deliverance lay in the hope that the Master of both black and white would stir the hearts and consciences of those with courage enough to stand against it.

Freedom Stirs

1808–1830

*A*mong all the nations of the world, it was England whose national conscience first began to awake to the inhumanity of men owning men and making them beasts of labor.

Persuaded by George Whitefield and others, and at last realizing that the inhumanity had persisted far too long, the British parliament ordered an investigation into slavery in the English colonies of the Caribbean.

The persuasions of such voices of conscience mounted across the Atlantic to join Woolman's and the Quakers' and began to slow the flow of human traffic there as well. Blacks in the northern states of America were increasingly given their freedom. Others managed to purchase it. Many who had fought in the war against Great Britain were rewarded for their service with liberty. But the early cries that would ultimately extend freedom to all, in both Great Britain and the United States, were not at first directed against the institution of slavery itself, but only against the commerce of the slave trade.

In 1808, the U.S. Congress banned further importation of slaves from the Guinea coast. But the decision did nothing to stop the domestic slave trade within the states themselves. Deafened to opposing views by the whir of the cotton gin, southern plantation owners declared "that peculiar institution" of slavery a vital necessity to their economic survival. Supported by the federal government on the basis of states' rights, even most northern politicians went along with the argument.

As a means of keeping their slaves content, and also perhaps in some measure to keep their consciences asleep, spiritually minded southern plantation owners steeped their slaves in the religion of Christianity. If slaves could be Christianized, and taught that slavery was not prohibited in the Bible—indeed, that slaves were instructed to obey their masters—they would be far more likely to remain compliant and obedient.

Through the early decades of the 1800s, however, louder and louder voices publicly deplored the existence of what was increasingly seen as a blot on the national character. Thoughtful northerners came to hate the very thought of such a vile institution. In England and the United States, consciences grew restless. The weight of the mounting power of Evangelicalism began to speak forcefully for abolitionism. The debate grew more and more heated.

Yet . . . what could be done? The nation had been founded on certain principles—states' rights among them, inviolate as freedom itself. The national government was powerless to alter it without a constitutional amendment. Such a drastic change was impossible without support from the southern states. Evangelicals of the South were just as adamantly supportive of states' rights as those in the North were against slavery. Religion, it seemed, was no guarantee of unity. A permanent impasse seemed likely.

But freedom was in the air. The American and French revolutions had set forces in motion throughout Europe and the West that could not be stopped. Gradually the divide between North and South widened.

At the center of the conflict and debate sat a huge, slumbering, silent people of dark skin and African descent. In some eyes it was a tremendous *workforce* and the principal form of economic capital of the South. In other eyes it was an even more powerful *army* . . . if only its potential could be aroused. The descendents of Tungal and his brethren who had endured the Middle Passage in the sixteenth and seventeenth centuries had, by the early years of the nineteenth, grown to nearly a million people, a vast horde of dark Americans slowly coming awake to the stirring of freedom in the world, and to its own destiny as a race.

For many of them, the dream of freedom seemed too distant to imagine. Here and there, however, a few courageous voices began to try to awaken their fellows.

Some, like Boston's David Walker—who began the nation's first black newspaper, *Freedom's Journal,* in 1827 and published a widely distributed and inflammatory booklet in 1829 called *Appeal to the Slaves of the United States*—urged his black brethren to claim their freedom by force.

Deliverer

1831

*A*n uneasy breeze stirred through the sultry Virginia night.

Four dozen or more dark faces, illuminated by the flickering flames of a small bonfire, waited in silence as the preacher they had crept out to hear rose and stood before them. For days, word had been secretly spreading through the slave shanties of the surrounding countryside—here and there men and women quietly singing a few bars of "Steal Away to Jesus," followed by a knowing glance and nod as word of the gathering was invisibly made known.

All knew what the hymn meant, and where the meeting would be held.

Slowly Brother Turner raised a solemn finger. His white eyes flashed in the firelight. His was a mission . . . a holy and prophetic mission.

"Freedom calls, my brothers and sisters," he began. "Listen to my voice, for it is the voice of liberty . . . and it is calling to *you*."

He paused and glanced around at his listeners.

"Are you willing," he continued, "to live subjected to our enemies? Does the call of freedom mean nothing to you? Surely you are brave men. Look around at your wives, your children. Are you not willing to sacrifice yourselves to the heavenly cause of freedom . . . if not for yourselves, for their sakes? The time has come for us to act!"

Everyone listening knew well enough what preacher Nat Turner

meant. When he said the time had come, it was a call to arms, to
demand their freedom by violence. Word of his summons to the
blacks of Virginia had been spreading secretly from plantation to plantation for weeks. Now they heard his plea with their own ears.

He was not the first Negro firebrand to call for freedom. Gabriel
Prosser had led a proposed uprising in 1800. He secretly raised an
army of nearly a thousand and planned to take the city of Richmond
with a three-pronged attack using homemade swords, bayonets,
scythes, and a few guns. Prosser's orders were to kill all whites except
Methodists, Frenchmen, and Quakers. From Richmond, they would
march throughout the entire state until all of Virginia was under their
control. A violent storm interfered with their first attempt, making it
impossible to cross a bridge into the city. Before a second attempt
could be made, the plot was betrayed by two slaves who told their
owner of the plan. Those involved were either hanged or deported.
But Prosser's efforts led to a major debate throughout Virginia about
the advisability of ending slavery. Virginia governor James Monroe,
the later president, spoke with his friend Thomas Jefferson, himself a
slave owner, about what should be done. In secret sessions, the
Virginia legislature brought the matter of abolishing slavery to a
debate, but in the end put off a decision.

Within the next two years, however, all states above the Maryland-
Pennsylvania border—the dividing line between North and South—
with the exception of New Jersey had abolished slavery. The legislatures of Maryland and Kentucky also discussed that possibility,
though, like Virginia, decided against it.

White Virginia businessman George Boxley led another attempted
slave revolt in 1816. But the most highly organized conspiracy of all
was led by Denmark Vesey in 1822. Vesey managed to recruit, by
some estimates, nine thousand to his cause. Their proposed march on
Charleston possessed the complexity of a well-planned military operation, and called for five separate routes into the city, which would be
put to the torch and burned. The planning, however, continued for so
many months that white informants penetrated the plot before the
march began. Vesey and most of his followers were rounded up and

paraded through the city in carts, each seated on the coffin that would hold his body. They were then publicly hanged and their bodies left hanging in a row as a warning against further uprisings.

Prosser, Boxley, and Vesey had all been educated men. But when field hand Nat Turner began to preach to Virginia's slaves in the summer of 1831, he commanded an even wider following. He was one of them. He would lead the fight with his own hands. A spiritual visionary, Turner's passionate rhetoric called for rebellion. His confidence that he was God's prophetic voice to raise America's blacks to a general uprising throughout the South led hundreds to follow him.

Claiming to have discovered the gift of prophecy at the age of three, several years before coming to national prominence Turner declared, "I heard a loud noise in the heavens, and the Spirit instantly appeared to me and said the Serpent was loosened, and Christ had laid down the yoke he had borne for the sins of men, and that I should take it on and fight against the Serpent." He then went on to relate in bloody detail the murders of whites he intended to carry out when the time was right. And now, three years later, he was going about the country-side raising the army to carry out exactly such a mission.

"Those who call themselves our masters," Turner went on to the group listening around the fire, "while draining the lifeblood from us, must meet the judgment, like the Egyptian tyrants of old. You remember the words of our brother David Walker in his *Appeal*. Like him, I tell you it is no more harm for you to kill a man who is trying to kill you, than it is for you to take a drink of water when thirsty. The Serpent must be laid waste and crushed beneath our heel. We have an example in the Good Book. As Moses killed his Egyptian, so too you and I must—"

"'Scuse me, Rev'rund Turner," interrupted a young boy at the front of the group, "but I'se a mite confused."

Surprised by the interruption, Turner squinted in the dim light to make out who had spoken. "What confuses you, boy?" he asked, seeing the child staring up at him.

"I'se confused 'bout who be dose enemies. You be talkin' 'bout dose 'Gyptians, but I ain't neber seen one."

"Hush yo mouf, Zeb. You don' know nuthin'," snapped the boy's mama beside him, enforcing her words with a sharp elbow between the ribs of the twelve year old. Neither she nor her son had ever heard of an ancient chieftain by the name of Tungal, or knew that they had descended from his daughter Danyawo. Yet though the legacy had grown dim, still she had repeated to him many times what she had heard from her own mother, that the lines in her hand stood for the five rivers of the land of her ancestors, and that the blood of ancient kings ran in their veins.

"Let the boy talk," said Turner. "If he must give his life for the cause, he should know the reason for it. What is your name, young man?"

"Zeb, sir . . . Zebediah Albright."

"Well, Zeb," said Turner, "the Egyptians I'm talking about are the cruel white tyrants who keep you and your mama and your sisters under bondage. And their appointed end has come. The Serpent has been loosed and a deliverer shall arise to crush them beneath his heel."

Zeb rubbed his head and looked more confused than ever.

Turner saw that he must speak more plainly. "The time has come when we must fight for our freedom," he said. "Those in power never give freedom willingly. It must be demanded. It must be taken by force. We must take up arms against those who treat us like animals. The first shall be last and the last first."

"You mean . . . fight Massa Travis?" asked Zeb in amazement.

"Not just your master, but every man, woman, and child who participates in the abomination of slavery. We must cleanse the land with their blood."

Zeb's eyes widened in horror. "Not little Miz Emily!" he said. "You don' mean *dere* blood, duz you, Rev'ren' Turner? Not Miz Travis!"

Zeb's mama clamped a firm hand over his mouth. "Hush *up!*" she hissed. "You want yo' voice driftin' up to da big house? Hit's time fo us ter git back."

She stood, yanked him to his feet, apologized to Reverend Turner for the disturbance, and marched into the night toward the slave village.

Gradually the murmur of the preacher's voice died out behind them. But the boy called Zeb could not forget his words. A shudder crawled down his young spine at what the preacher seemed to have said. He edged closer to the big black woman who walked through the blackness ahead of him.

"Mama, he don' really mean what he sez—he don' mean ter hurt Massa and Miz Travis, duz he? He wuzn't talkin' 'bout killin' w'ite folks, wuz he, Mama . . . not Massa Travis, duz he, Mama?"

She stalked on in silence.

"Mama?" repeated Zeb, trotting behind to keep up. Almost at the door of their rough-hewn primitive cabin, she wheeled around and looked him in the eye.

"Don' you know why yo pappy ain't wif us no mo?" she said, her eyes gleaming with the same fire of hatred as the preacher's. "Massa Travis dun sol' him down ter Alabama, dat's why. Duz you know what happened ter yo sister Liz? Miz Travis said she wuz too lazy fo housework an' dun gib her ter Massa Horace. Effen Massa can gib away my husban' an' chillins like dey wuz cattle, I don' hab no feelin' er kindness lef fo dat man. Rev'ren' Turner knows what's right. He's read dat Good Book fo hizself. He's like God's angel, cum ter lead us ter freedom. He be a proffit, dat's what folks be sayin'. Sumtime da proffits ob da Almighty duz fearsum things fo da Lord, an' dis be one er dose times."

Her passion silenced the boy's questions. Meekly he followed her inside and lay down on his pallet. But the preacher's words rang eerily in his ears for hours, and sleep eluded him until only one or two hours before the roosters were beginning to look eagerly toward the dawn.

Before the next light of day the preacher and his followers moved to another midnight meeting at yet another clandestine location. Within a week Nat Turner's slowly mounting army was indeed ready to turn their general's words into actions.

In the middle of the night, led by the firebrand preacher, several

dozen blacks from three or four plantations west of Norfolk, armed
with stolen guns and muskets, a handful of pistols, clubs and knives,
scythes and axes, shovels and pitchforks, and whatever makeshift
weapons they could devise, broke into the house of wealthy widow
Catherine Whitehead. Whether theft or murder was their original
intent, within an hour Mrs. Whitehead, her son, and five daughters
lay brutally massacred on their bedroom floors. The mob, emboldened by the success of their initial raid, and gathering more slaves as
they went, now headed west across the fields toward the Travis plantation.

Zeb Albright came suddenly awake. It was the middle of the night,
that was all he knew. The blackness outside was filled with evil shouts
and strange lights.

He climbed to his feet and shuffled sleepily to the window. What
looked like hundreds of men were running and shouting outside. A
band with torches, shouting and calling for others to join them, was
coming from the direction of the big house. He heard singing, hymns
and loud battle songs, in the midst of the commotion. They were
carrying hoes and shovels and rakes.

A large figure came toward the cabin through the night. Fully
awake by now, Zeb ran to the door as his mother walked up the rick-
ety steps.

"What is it, Mama?" he asked. "What's everybody doin' out at dis
time er night?"

"Zeb, what you doin' up?"

"I couldn't sleep from all da ruckus, Mama. What is it?"

"It's Rev'ren' Turner," she replied. "He an' his angels er mercy, dey
be exactin' da recompense er da Lord's judgment!"

"What dat mean, Mama?"

"Massa Travis be dead, dat's what!" she said, her eyes gleaming in
the night. "Dey's all dead up at da big house!"

Too stunned to say more, Zeb stumbled past her out into the darkness. Shuddering in horror, he watched the throng of rioters march
across the fields to the next plantation. He walked from the porch, but
managed only a half dozen more steps. His stomach lurched, then

again, until everything he had eaten that night for supper lay on the ground at his feet. He could think of nothing but the faces of Master Travis' family. He could not believe they were actually . . . *dead*.

Why did they have to die? Was this the thing they called freedom?

Jubilant slaves everywhere rejoiced at the news. The hand of God had given Reverend Turner and his followers the victory! The triumphant rioters had gone on to the Malone plantation next, singing battle songs of praise, and had burned it to the ground.

God had raised up a new Moses to lead them to freedom!

Blacks everywhere left their shanties to join the rebellion. Before night was over, the violence was spreading throughout Southampton County. Over the next few days Nat Turner and his growing band of slaves swept through southeastern Virginia leaving a wake of bloody triumph behind them. Six to eight hundred black men flocked to the rebellion. Within four days they had murdered more than sixty whites.

Zeb Albright, despite his mama's rejoicing, continued to feel sick at heart. He could think of nothing but the many hours he had spent playing with Master Harold and Master John at the big house. He had crooned over baby Emily. He remembered her tiny white fingers curling around his dark one. Once Mrs. Travis even let him taste lemonade along with her own boys. He didn't care about the color of their skin. They were his friends and playmates. They had never been mean to him. Imagining them lying in their own blood made him gag every time he thought of it.

Troops and militia quickly poured into the region, rounding up, disarming, and arresting hundreds of blacks. Sporadic fighting continued, but soon it was over. The insurrection was snuffed out, long before Nat Turner's dream of a full-fledged rebellion throughout the South could be realized. The militia captured everyone except the ringleader. But Nat Turner had slipped between their fingers.

Weeks passed. A new master arrived. Master Travis's brother was determined to beat his slaves into submission if necessary. Whites everywhere vented their fear and anger by retaliating against their slaves. Zeb's mother, along with the rest, fell into sullen silence,

hoping every day to hear word of their Moses rising out of his temporary defeat to complete their liberation from the Egyptians.

At length news reached them of Nat Turner's capture.

Tension between slaves and masters had never been so high. Zeb
felt the pressure of the new master's eye on him wherever he went and
whatever he did. The master forbade his slaves to speak to each other
during their work. He promised to shoot any slave found outside his
house after dark. The former Master Travis had been kind, thought
Zeb. But they all knew their new master meant what he said.

Nat Turner's dream of freedom had plunged them into a worse
nightmare than before.

⌒

One October morning Zeb Albright sat silently on the floor in the big
house blacking the family shoes like he had done fifty times before.

A rustle across the room drew his attention. He glanced up. There
stood an eleven-year-old girl. He had not seen her this close since her
arrival. With her green eyes and corn-colored hair, she was in his eyes
the prettiest girl he had ever seen.

At sight of him, the girl froze in her tracks, her face as white as her
dress. Zeb's hands halted in the middle of his work. Then he smiled.

Only a moment more the girl stood staring, then suddenly screamed,
spun around, and darted back for the stairs the way she had come.
Gazing after her in confusion, Zeb heard heavy booted feet descending
the stairs. Seconds later the girl's father appeared and with large strides
hurried toward him. New Master Travis wasted no time on words.

"Stand up, boy!" he demanded angrily.

Having no idea what was coming, Zeb did so. The next instant a
blow from the master's fist sent him staggering back against the wall.
A second blow knocked him through the open door. He stumbled
down the steps and onto his back in the dirt outside.

"If you so much as look at my daughter again, I'll kill you," the
master growled as he walked out and looked down from the porch.
He glanced about the yard. "Tie this nigger whelp to the post!" he

shouted to one of his men. "Give him the lash—we'll teach him to show respect to his betters."

The man came over, reached down and laid hold of Zeb by the scruff of the neck, yanked him to his feet, then dragged him toward the barn.

Mrs. Travis, who had heard her daughter's screams and the commotion that followed, now followed her husband outside. "The brutes understand nothing but violence," she said. "I declare I shan't sleep sound in my bed with such demons around."

"The troops hung the murderers weeks ago, Ellen," said Travis. "Last week they finally got Turner himself. He'll hang as sure as the rest."

"That may be, but how do we know they caught them all? That boy there," she said, pointing toward their man hauling Zeb across the ground away from them, "—what if he is one of Nat Turner's protégées?"

They stood a few moments more, then slowly descended the porch and walked toward the barn. Crisp snapping explosions from a leather whip, each followed by a scream of pain, rang in their ears.

"If you are truly concerned, Ellen," said Mr. Travis, "I'll order the boy killed."

They rounded the corner of the barn and stood watching as a few more lashes split the skin of the twelve-year-old back, already lined with blood.

The lady watched as the whip fell two or three more times. She seemed to be mulling over her husband's offer. "Whatever you think best," she said after a moment. "I have to admit, he doesn't look vicious, and has never given me trouble before this. But then I never could tell one of their hideous faces from another, or tell what evil and filth they might be thinking."

She turned and walked back to the house. In fact, she was unconcerned whether the boy lived or died. Her husband watched until he considered the punishment sufficient, then signaled to his man to cut the boy down.

Zeb slumped senseless to the ground in a heap. He had long since

ceased to feel the pain. The bleeding welts on his back had already
begun to swell and ooze. He lay in near unconsciousness, hardly aware
of being dragged to the slave quarters and left on the ground in front
of his house where his mother, returning from the fields, found him
several hours later.

Nat Turner's trial and execution put a stop to further talk of open
rebellion. There would be no promised land for America's black children of Israel. Freedom would not come by Nat Turner's hand. Their
deliverer was dead.

Zeb Albright survived his first whipping. But he bore its scars from
that day till the end of his life. The injustice of the penalty bit far
deeper into his mind than the lash did into his back.

From that day on, Zeb began to change. It might be said that his
road to manhood began with the first sting from Master Travis' whip.
He had crossed those burning sands of pain that generations of slaves
before him had trod, initiated into the company of some of the best
men and women of his race. His natural compassion, his blindness to
the color of one's skin, the guilelessness of his gentle nature, all slowly
gave way to a growing root of hardness in his soul. He had been falsely
accused and unfairly punished. He began to think that a comparison
between the white masters and the taskmasters of Egypt might be
accurate after all. Maybe Ol' Prophet Nat, as he was being called, had
been right all along.

As he pondered the ancient story of the liberated people, however,
recalling the words he had heard that night in the woods around the
fire, he realized that the Israelites had *gone* to the land of milk and
honey, rather than expecting to find it in Egypt. Maybe in the North
he and his mama could find the freedom she yearned for.

Perhaps their best chance lay, not in some new Moses to lead them,
but in *escape*.

Slowly life in the South returned to normal.

Yet what was *normal* now? Whether there would ever be normal again, a great awakening had begun. Nat Turner had stirred the hope of freedom in the souls of America's Negroes . . . and the fear of what that freedom might mean in the souls of the whites who owned them.

The long-slumbering legacy of Tungal and his heirs had begun to stir. The faint scent of freedom was in the air. Nat Turner might be dead, but the memory of his valor was not. As news of his failed rebellion spread from mouth to mouth, eventually every slave village on every plantation from the Texas-Louisiana border to the Mason-Dixon Line knew of that dream and began to hope for a new deliverer to lead them to the promised land of freedom.

The dream lived on, and it would grow. Songs of ancient Egypt and the river Jordan began solemnly to float across the cotton fields of the South in the melancholy tones of rich African harmony. Another day would come. Another deliverer would arise.

But something far different than a dream of freedom began to spread among whites on the plantations of the South—fear of the rising tide of black hope. With *fear* came anger. With *anger* came paranoia. With them all came a new determination that no Nat Turner would ever rise again, and that *nothing* would upset the secure world they had built, or the economic balance of their source of wealth.

The *Southern way of life*—which meant a life based on a "peculiar institution" increasingly out of step with the march of progress in the world—became as sacred in the South as the church.

Yet whites could not help knowing that a great moving and shaking had begun. They were terrified where it might lead. If "Ol' Prophet Nat" was a constant topic of conversation in the slave shanties of the South, memory of his failed rebellion never left the minds of the wealthy plantation owners. Southern leaders came to recognize a new problem that required careful consideration.

Education and spirituality became the new foes that, if allowed to spread through the slave community, could in time destroy the way of life they held sacred. The Turner rebellion had been successful because slaves had been allowed too much education and independence. That would have to stop. They would have to clamp down. They would have to keep the slaves illiterate, and prevent the darkies from getting *too* many spiritual ideas in their heads.

Too much talk of freedom of *soul* inevitably led to talk about freedom of other kinds.

If Virginia had almost outlawed slavery in 1800, it now led the South *against* progress with a series of the harshest prohibitions it could devise—forbidding blacks, whether slave *or* free, to assemble in large groups, to read or write, to preach, to own weapons, to defend themselves, or to leave their plantations without written consent. If Turner's conspiracy had drawn nourishment from the soil of education and religion, Virginia now took care to remove the possibility of such desires finding root in those soils again.

The new laws, however, only increased the desire for liberty. Zeb Albright was not the only one to realize that their only hope lay in escape. The more daring among them began to devise secret routes from the heart of the South that led to the free states and even all the way to Canada. A secret underground human railroad to freedom had begun.

Though their masters controlled every part of their lives, they could not quench the whispers of freedom. Nor could the South's new laws of prohibition slow the mounting cry of liberty.

As he matured into a teenager and began to fill out and grow tall and muscular, a hardness could be seen in Zeb Albright's eyes and face. As the lashes of the master's whip crisscrossed his back with more and more frequency, scars forming upon scars, at last he understood the fire of hatred he had seen as a boy in Nat Turner's eyes.

It was not long before a similar fire began to burn in his.

Three Lives . . . Three Fates . . . Three Futures

1833–1835

$\mathcal{F}$ar west of any plantation house or sign of civilization a bride of less than two years cradled the head of her husband in her lap.

The day had begun as all days in this godforsaken wilderness . . . long miles ahead, nothing to anticipate but endless dust and dry heat, and the knowledge that every step forward took them farther from a life and loved ones she might not know or see again. She had harbored grave doubts about this trek from the outset. But he would have their life together begin with adventure. He had prayed, he said, and the Lord had spoken. They would take God's Word to the outposts of frontier expansion where it was so badly needed, and eventually start a church among the settlers. Reluctantly she had agreed. She also wanted to serve God and teach others about him. She loved her new helpmeet and trusted that he had heard from God. She would accompany him wherever he went.

Her father, however, who had walked with God far longer than both, shared her concern. He was not so easily persuaded that the journey was right. The West was full of dangers —Indians, heat, deserts, hunger, thirst, loneliness. But the son-in-law insisted that through such hardships were God's servants made strong. God had led his people into the wilderness before. They would trust the Lord to protect them, he said. And in the end, the young visionary's arguments carried the day.

But there were other deadly and unforeseen dangers as they set out across the wide young land—drought, scorpions, exhaustion, wolves, madness . . . and rattlesnakes. Indeed, they had seen no Indians. Though the heat had been unbearable, they somehow found sufficient water to keep their containers full and the two oxen healthy. Their prayers, however, had not kept away the fangs whose wounds now scarred her husband's swollen calf. Nor had they been able to prevent the venom from spreading. A few knife slashes at the skin and a tightly bound tourniquet at the knee were not enough. By evening he was unconscious and feverish. She could do nothing but sit in the wagon and hold him, wiping his face with a damp cloth, and pray that God would somehow intervene in the midst of her helplessness.

Nightfall brought no miracle. The black silence advanced. The menacing howls of wolves and doleful coyotes drew closer. Her mind began to wander and she drifted into a waking stupor.

Hot tears dripped from her cheeks and fell on the ghastly white face of the man she loved. How long she sat senseless—her hands chilled from the prairie night, the skin beneath them burning to the touch—gently rocking back and forth as she held him, she had no idea . . . nor when the final flickers of life quietly ebbed away from the head in her hands.

Coming to herself sometime after midnight and beholding that death lay in her arms, her quiet tears gave way to heaving moans of anguish.

"*Oh, God!*" she wailed as the horrible truth at last broke upon her. "*Why! God . . . oh, God!*"

There were no other cries. Words were as useless now as prayers. And none heard the despairing sobs of the young widow save him who stores in his heart every human tear of grief and distress until the day they will be sent back whence they came as tears of joy.

Mercifully she did not have to endure the haunting torments and terrifying sounds of the night. Sleep overtook mental exhaustion. She slumped over in the back of the wagon where she had sat for hours and slumbered dreamlessly.

When she came to herself, the gray light of dawn was spreading over the desolate landscape. A chill of clammy dampness clung to everything. She shivered, trying to bring her brain awake.

Suddenly the reality swept over her that the cold came not from the prairie morning but from the stiff, lifeless form of her dead husband, his head still lying upon her lap. The body that had kept her warm during the long nights until now was solid as ice.

Memory of the previous day overwhelmed her. A momentary glance at his face and her stomach lurched. Sickened and horrified, she struggled from under the ghastly weight of the rigid corpse. She reached the ground, heaved several times, and took a few steps to steady herself. She did not weep. Her tears had been spent the night before. With the light of dawn came the strength given to women to endure.

She stood outside the wagon several minutes and tried to breathe deeply of the morning. She filled her lungs not with the air of courage but of resignation. She would do what she had to do. She would survive, because that's what women did. There was nothing but that. Men dreamed dreams and chased visions. Women survived. The luxury of vision was not given them. She would do what she had to do.

The man in the wagon would probably have wanted her to continue west and live out his dream. But she could not. It had been his dream, not hers. Ministry was the last thing she could think of now. All at once survival itself was paramount. It would take every ounce of courage and stamina she possessed merely to stay alive. If she could manage that, perhaps one day she might think of God again.

She was too devastated to pray. The idea of asking for God's help seemed suddenly strange, distant, foreign, unreal. How could she ask for God's help again? If he had not answered yesterday's desperate pleas, for what else could she ever ask him? What would be the use?

Who was God anyway? If he existed at all, what kind of God was he?

Drawing in another breath, she turned back to the wagon. She must do what had to be done. She would bury him. She would do it alone, and then turn back. The other three wagons could go on, but

she would not. She did not care about being the first white woman to
cross the Rockies, nor to establish the first Christian mission in the
Oregon territory. She would leave that to others. She only hoped that
she could find her way out of this desert of desolation and back to
some form, *any* form, of civilization.

If she did not, and died herself along the way, perhaps it would be a
relief after all.

At this moment of her own trial and tragedy, she knew nothing of
another home across the Atlantic that death would soon visit. Nor
that fate would destine her life to intertwine with one cruelly accused.
She only knew that suddenly she was more alone than ever, and in no
little danger herself.

On the following night, a continent away, a blood-chilling scream
sounded in the blackness of an early, ungodly hour. Trembling and
terrified, a man stole quickly down the darkened upper corridor of a
large, three-story English manor. The terrible echoes died away as he
hurried forward with careful step.

A door partially open at the end of the hall revealed the faint light of
a flickering candle from inside. Hoping to disturb no one else in the
house—though who could possibly sleep after those piercing shrieks?
—he stepped forward, inched the door open, and crept through.

Another dreadful shriek froze him in his tracks. At the sound his
blood turned to ice. The face that met his gaze across the room was
ghostly white, drawn and haggard. Wide eyes stared at him in mingled
horror and revulsion. The uneven light from the candle beside the bed
revealed cheeks sunken and hollow. The expression of the face showed
no fear, only hatred.

In the second or two it took him to take in the confusing scene, the
previous four years swept through his mind in a flash.

He had gone to England as a young idealist to study law, leaving
behind father, mother, and older brother, considering his own prospects for the future in no way connected with the estate of his father's

called Greenwood. He loved England but was understandably lonely. There he met a young woman, beautiful but oddly out of step with the society about her. In her strangeness, he also found a peculiar fascination. Whether he was in love with her was doubtful, but to all appearances she fell in love with him. Her family lavished upon him praises perhaps a little overzealous, indicating clearly enough that they were anxious for the two young people to marry.

Alone, away from home, and swept off his feet by what seemed to be love, he did not discern warning signs inherent in the reluctance of her father and mother for the two to spend time alone together. Thus he did not see the signs of emotional instability, nor learn of the cases of insanity that had plagued the extended family for generations.

They were married, he with high hopes of remaining in England to practice law and make for himself and his new family a happy life. Soon afterward, however, disturbing signs in his wife's mental state began to manifest themselves. Attempting to make the best of it, he gave of his best to her, hoping that no more lay at root of the increasing melancholy than the adjustments of newly married life.

She became pregnant. Instead of happiness, the knowledge turned her yet more moody and withdrawn. Hushed comments and sighs now occasionally escaped the lips of various relatives in his hearing, giving rise to serious concerns. They had seen such behavior before.

Only a few days before this, a son was born. His wife grew weak, delirious, and feverish. Hours ago as he had put her to bed, she was raving and frantic, drifting in and out of consciousness, calling for the baby, then yelling at him and her attendants to take it away.

At last, holding the infant in her arms, she drifted into what appeared to be a peaceful sleep.

Exhausted, he had gone to bed.

Then suddenly, the screams of only moments ago had awakened him.

"You killed him!" screamed the woman, bringing him back to the present crisis. "How dare you show your face in this room!"

In panic he continued toward her. He stooped down and stretched out his arms, but fierce blows at his face prevented closer approach.

"Please . . . please!" he said desperately. "Let me help. I must see if—"

"Help!" she echoed bitterly. "Look what you have done. You're a murderer! Go away. Get out, I tell you! I cannot bear the sight of you! I hate you!"

With uncommon strength for her weakened condition, she flailed at him violently, until at last he succeeded in subduing her fury by the sheer force of his might.

The effort had taxed her. She swooned and fell into a faint. Seconds later he was carrying the prostrate form from the room, shouting to rouse the servants to send for the doctor.

Not until dawn did the house fall quiet. The young husband sank into a chair and stared dully at the floor. He had endured more mental and emotional anguish during the last few months than some men encounter in a lifetime.

A sigh rose up from deep inside him. His shoulders sagged wearily. There seemed no escape from the living nightmare into which he had been plunged. "What can I do?" he whispered to himself. "I have tried everything—loved her to the best of my ability, but no change. Now she thinks I murdered . . ."

A rough, dry sob shook him. "Oh, God," he cried out, forgetting that he did not believe in such a being. "What should I do!"

But he received no answering reply.

A young woman, worlds separated by position, race, and distance from the man and woman who had just faced death, was thinking instead of the *life* stirring in her womb. She sensed the time fast approaching when her little one would enter the world. And at this time of her own woman's glory, she was looking ahead, with a vision even she did not fully comprehend, toward the kind of world her child might someday face.

She glanced about with a deep breath to calm the anxiety from the increasing pains that signaled to her that her time was at hand. Her eyes fell upon the mud floor and crude walls of the place she called home. She could give her baby neither security nor liberty. These Carolina slave quarters were the only home she had ever known.

Faintly she began to whisper to the one yet unborn within her what her own mama had told her many times.

"Honey-chil'," she whispered, "I won' be able ter promise you nuffin much. All I can gib you is da same love my mama gib me, an' da words she tol' me. She took my hand, an' stretched out my fingers, an' say dat our people cum from a place far, far away, an' dat land belonged ter us. Dat's what she say. She say we gots blood what cum frum kings flowin' in us. Dat life be all I can gib you. An'—"

A sharp pain cut her whispered words short. She winced and bent over till it passed.

What kind of future would her baby know, she wondered to herself. Would he or she live and die picking cotton like generations before? Was life really better on plantations up North, like she'd heard? If only the good Lord they sang about would bring his children freedom like they said blacks had there.

Another sharp pain doubled her over. When it had passed, she called to the girl playing just outside.

"Go git Amaritta!" she called. "Go to da kitchen door ob da big house. She'll answer it hersel'. Tell her hit's time an' dat I needs her."

The girl ran off and the expectant mother lay back on the straw of her pillow, closed her eyes, and breathed in and out peacefully.

As she waited for Mistress Crawford's house mammy, who also acted as midwife for the slaves on the plantation, her reflections drifted again to the unborn child now struggling in earnest within her to enter a world of men which was no happy place for those whose skin was black.

That many slaves were related in distant fashion was not something either whites or blacks found unusual. Since the trafficking in slaves from Africa had been ended, plantation owners had to breed their own slaves to keep the supply constantly increasing. As generations passed, it might have been that half or more of the slaves on any large plantation were related in some way. Thus it was that the lady called

Amaritta from the big house, and the young woman about to become a mother, had both descended from old Tungal's son Magado of the Ibo tribe—the only evidence of which, had they known it, would have been the many men of their lineage who had gone by the name Moses. But now it was time for a lineage of women to carry Magado's ancient African progeny into the future . . . a future which to this new mother seemed like a distant dream. She little knew that her own child, despite her paternity, would be one of a bold rising generation that would find the courage to claim that freedom of their heritage for themselves.

In a few minutes she heard footsteps approaching outside. Two more pains had come as she waited. It was with relief that she glanced up as the large house mammy entered.

Amaritta smiled and dabbed at the beads of perspiration on the expectant mother's forehead, then set about to make her comfortable and begin that most ancient and precious work of ministration that one woman can give to another.

Three hours later, a tiny brown daughter was born. Amaritta wiped her dry and handed her to the weary but eager arms of the new mother. Little did the midwife realize that in twenty years she would be handing this same infant her own newborn baby, as one of the first in a new generation of their race, who would grow up to know the freedom they could as yet only dream about.

"She's a beautiful chil,'" said Amaritta. "Wha'chu be fixin' ter call her?"

"Lucindy," the young woman answered wearily, "her name be Lucindy."

She closed her eyes in a peaceful smile. Within minutes, both mother and daughter were asleep.

When she awoke several hours later, she was alone. Her daughter slept on her breast.

The young mother gently reached for the hand of the infant sleeping so close to her. It was scarcely wider than one of her fingers. Tenderly she stroked the tiny fingers and thumb, then gazed at the palm.

"Dere be dose lines ob doze five ol' ribers," she whispered in a voice no one else ever heard. "Dey's tiny an' faint all right, but dey's dere jes' like on my own han'. I been hearin' dat story as long as I been alive. What it means, I ain't so sure, and now here's one mo generashun born ter hear dat ol' story ob dose ribers an dat king from dat ol' land. I'll be tellin' you dose ol' stories in time too, little chil', when you's old enuf ter know what I's sayin'. I don' know why we's sur'pozed ter keep tellin' 'em. Dey say dey's stories from da ol' books—books dat no one's eber seen—da ol' books er freedom when our kin wuz kings in da ol' land. An' so maybe you's da one, my little one, dat'll sumday know what dat ol' book er freedom sez. Maybe you'll be da one dat'll know da freedom er dose ancient kings dey say we all cum from."

She paused and set down the little hand, gazing contented at the sleeping face, then offered her breast to the tiny mouth, which, even asleep, took it eagerly.

"So you drink an' eat an' grow, little Lucindy, chil'," she added, "an' you git strong, so dat when yo' day er freedom cums, you's ready ter fin' it."

Prologue Notes

Out of the Unknown Past

" 'About the last of August came in a dutch man of warre that sold us twenty Negers,' John Rolfe of Jamestown, Virginia, wrote in his record of 1619. They were the first blacks known to have entered a mainland English colony. Although they had been 'sold,' their status was probably that of white indentured servants; if so, they were freed after a fixed period of service.

"Though the original legal status of blacks in Virginia was nebulous, it was quickly given form by legislation and court decisions. A black indentured servant was enslaved for life in 1640 as punishment for running away. His two white companions simply had their term of indenture lengthened. In 1659 the term 'Negro slave' first appeared in legislation designed to encourage the importation of slaves. Finally, in 1662 it was decided that the child of a black woman 'shall be bond or free according to the condition of the mother.' Slavery had become hereditary.

"A 1705 Virginia law broadened and codified the rights of white servants. It also defined the role of black slaves as 'real estate [which] shall descend unto heirs and widows.' If slaves escaped, anyone might legally 'kill and destroy' them. Their masters would then be compensated by the colony—for loss of property.

"Colonists unable to meet their need for laborers with indentured servants increasingly turned to slaves. Between 1670 and 1700 the white population of the English colonies doubled. In the same period the number of blacks increased fivefold." [*Historical Atlas of the United States,* Washington, D.C.: National Geographic, 1993, p. 40.]

"Olaudah Equiano was a Nigerian prince. When he was about ten years old he and his sister were captured and sold into slavery. . . . The children were sold and separated.

"After a long and weary journey overland, the slave traders and the young boy reached a ship that was anchored at sea. Many other Africans were on board the ship. . . . All the captives were chained together. . . . Notes

"When the ship arrived in America, Olaudah was sold to an Englishman. . . . He changed Olaudah's name to Gustavus Vassa . . . but deep inside, Olaudah knew that he was an Ibo prince, the son of an African chief." [Angela Medearis, *Come This Far To Freedom*. New York: Atheneum, 1993, pp. 8–10.]

"African cargo was advertised to British colonists by handbills. Many buyers preferred slaves from particular regions of Africa. . . .

"Chained together by twos at both hands and feet, African men were stacked like firewood—as were women and children—in the dank, filthy holds of slave ships. Overcrowding and lack of sanitation allowed diseases such as smallpox and dysentery to spread throughout the human cargo. Africans who lived through the long voyage survived one terrifying nightmare only to encounter another—life on southern plantations." [*Historical Atlas of the United States*, Washington, D.C.: National Geographic, 1993, p. 41.]

Dispersion

"During the 18th century, the peak of the slave trade, Britain cornered the lion's share of a profitable business. Some 40 percent of slaves sent to the New World were carried in British ships. Most of them were taken to the plantations of the Caribbean; relatively few ended up in mainland North America.

"In the peak years of the 1700s, slave traffic flourished along the coast of West Africa. European traders paid African kings goods and guns in exchange for human cargo to fill their ships. The largest numbers of slaves were by far sent to Portuguese Brazil and the British and French Caribbean. Between 1700 and 1808 only 6 percent were sent to the American Colonies, and, later, the United States." [*Historical Atlas of the United States*, Washington, D.C.: National Geographic, 1993, p. 40.]

"The importation of blacks into the colonies was slow. After the initial twenty arrived in Virginia, several years elapsed before any more were imported. In 1625, there were only twenty-three Negroes in Virginia, and by the middle of the century the black population was only three hundred. Major importations of Negroes did not begin until the last quarter of the century. Just how major the importations were is shown by the fact that Virginia's population in 1708 was listed as twelve thousand Negroes and eighteen thousand whites. By 1756, there were 120,156 blacks and 173,316 whites.

". . . as the black population of the colony grew, Virginians became deeply concerned about the social problem, as it would be called today. When there were two blacks for every three white men in the colony, the enforcement problem became immense, particularly since Negroes in the colony showed a strong tendency toward insurrection. As early as 1663 there was evidence of a conspiracy to rebel. In 1687, a plot was uncovered in which Negroes planned to kill all the whites in the area in a bid for freedom. The colony was rife with rumors of still other plots.

"The Virginia legislature tried to combat the threat of insurrection by stringent laws that severely restricted the rights of slaves, their ability to congregate and travel from place to place, and imposed barbaric penalties for breaking the slave law or the white man's law. Even in Colonial America, slaves and free whites were covered by different laws with radically different punishments. The slave regulations, known as the "Black Codes," were adopted by all the colonies and went through many refinements through the years. The early code of Virginia called for some notable punishments. A slave found guilty of murder or rape was hanged. If he robbed a house or store, a slave was given sixty lashes by the sheriff, then placed in the pillory with his ears nailed to the posts for half an hour. After that, his ears were severed from his head. If the slave's offense was less serious than burglary, he was merely whipped, maimed, or branded." [Robert Liston, *Slavery in America*. New York: McGraw-Hill, 1970, pp. 42–44.]

A note on what "freedom" meant to blacks in the 18th century South:

". . . free people of color ought never to insult or strike white people, nor presume to conceive themselves equal to the whites; but, on the contrary, they ought to yield to them on every occasion, and never speak or answer them but with respect, but, under penalty of imprisonment, according to the nature of the offense." —a Louisiana law. [William Goodell, *The American Slave Code*. New York: American and Foreign Anti-Slavery Society, 1853, reprinted by Arno Press, New York, 1969, p. 357.]

Freedom Stirs

"At the end of the Revolution, the new American government warned the British government against export-ing slaves into the United States. Many states also took legal action to limit or abolish slavery. Virginia in 1778 and Maryland in 1783 enacted laws against bringing slaves into their states to sell. Pennsylvania passed a law for the gradual abolition of slavery in 1780. By 1783, slavery had been abolished in Massachusetts by judicial decision; the Massachusetts courts decreed that the institution was obviously illegal since the state constitution had declared that 'all men are born free and equal.' In 1786, New Jersey passed a manumission act [the right to grant freedom to slaves] and North Carolina imposed a heavy duty on slave imports. In 1787, South Carolina banned the importation of slaves for five years. During this same year, the Continental Congress, acting under the Articles of Confederation, forbade the existence of slavery in the territory northwest of the Ohio River." [L.H. Ofosu-Appiah, *People in Bondage*. Minneapolis: Lerner Publications, 1971, p. 76.]

"The first census, in 1790, reported the slave population at nearly 700,000, with 75 percent in the southern Atlantic states.

"Though all the northern states had abolished slavery or provided for its gradual end [by 1810], 30,000 slaves still worked in fields, homes, and factories. The largest number, 15,017, labored in New York State under the harshest codes in the North.

"Although Virginia still had the most slaves [by 1830], the spread of cotton into Alabama and Mississippi required massive increases of slaves there. The nation's slave population had grown to two million, and in the South more stringent codes were introduced to control and confine them.

"By 1860 nearly four million Afro-Americans remained in bondage, while some 500,000 were free—half of them living in slave states. Most were descendents of manumitted slaves who had been released after the Revo-lution for meritorious service or because sympathetic masters had felt a moral imperative."

"When the legal U.S. slave trade with Africa ended in 1808, domestic trading became big business in the South, where demand was growing as fast as cotton. Finding less profit in owning slaves than in selling them, eastern farmers shipped slaves to the Gulf states. Some walked west with migrating masters, but most were auctioned at centers such as New Orleans, where a slave sold for a third more than in Virginia." [*Historical Atlas of the United States,* Washington, D.C.: National Geographic, 1993, pp. 40–41.]

"The roots of the abolitionist movement lay in the growing power of evangelical Christianity, which was appalled at the wickedness and injustice evident in so many areas of American life. Businesses were rapacious and dishonest, banks misused their customers' money, cities were sinks of iniquity and licentiousness; many Americans drank to excess, denied the rights of women and free blacks, abused the Indians, threatened the Mexicans, talked recklessly of war with Great Britain for a remote portion of territory in the Pacific Northwest. Above all, above everything else, 'the land of the free' denied freedom to millions of human beings whose only crime was the color of their skin. Evangelical Christianity had about it, certainly, a touch of hysteria, and a degree of fanaticism, the hysteria that was so evident in camp-meetings and revivals, the fanaticism that refused to be quiet about the terrible sin of slavery. . .Blacks were the modern prototypes of the 'suffering servant.' Their suffering and servitude brought to the orthodox Christian mind the servitude of the Jews in Egypt, the suffering of Christ on the cross. By sharing, through physical and material sacrifice, the sufferings of the black man and woman, the white Christian might identify himself or herself with the Savior. One thing was clear enough: America stood in desperate need of redemption.

"American reformers worked in virtually every area, but it was as abolitionists that the champions of Chris-tian redemption made their greatest impact. William Jay, the son of John Jay, wrote, 'I do not depend on anyone as an abolitionist who does not act from a sense of religious obligation.'

"Abolitionism was, to be sure, merely a branch of a larger antislavery movement. Anyone who disliked slav-ery and was willing to say so was eligible to join one of the numerous antislavery societies that sprang up in such profusion during the late 1820s and the 1830s. The antislavery movement was, moreover, international, or at least Anglo-American. British middle-class Protestant reformers had been tireless in their efforts to have slavery abolished from the British West Indies, and they made common cause with their American cousins. What became, increasingly, the dividing line in the antislavery movement was 'immediatism' versus 'gradual-ism.' The immediatists declared that no compromise could be made with the institution of slavery. Slavery must be abolished 'immediately,' or, at the very least, its abolition should *begin* immediately. It was not enough to declare that slavery must be *eventually* abolished; 'eventually' sounded more and more like 'never.'" [Page Smith, *The Nation Comes of Age*. New York: McGraw-Hill, 1981, pp. 597-98.]

". . . in 1829 [David Walker] published his pamphlet, *Walker's Appeal*. It was a harsh outcry against the injus-tices done the Black, and an open call to rise up in arms and overthrow slavery. In a year it ran through three editions, terrifying the slaveholders. Georgia offered $10,000 for Walker taken alive and $1,000 for him dead. State after state in the South made it a crime to circulate his *Appeal*, and a crime to teach Blacks to read.

Suddenly, Walker disappeared; some said murdered. . . . [Milton Meltzer, *The Black Americans*. New York: Thomas Crowell, 1964, pp. 14–16.]

"My Beloved Brethren: The Indians of North and of South America—the Greeks—the Irish, subjected under the king of Great Britain—the Jews, that ancient people of the Lord—the inhabitants of the islands of the sea—in the fine, all the inhabitants of the earth (except however, the sons of Africa), are called *men*, and of course are, and ought to be free. But we (coloured people), and our children are *brutes*!! And of course, and *ought to be* SLAVES to the American people and their children forever!! To dig their mines and work their farms; and thus go on enriching them, from one generation to another with our *blood* and our *tears*!!!! . .

"Remember Americans, that we must and shall be free and enlightened as you are, will you wait until we shall, under God, obtain our liberty by the crushing arm of power? Will it not be dreadful for you? I speak Americans for your good. We must and shall be free I say, in spite of you. You may do your best to keep us in wretchedness and misery, to enrich you and your children, but God will deliver us from under you. And wo, wo, will be to you if we have to obtain our freedom by fighting. Throw away your fears and prejudices then, and enlighten us and treat us like men, and we will like you more that we do not hate you, and tell us no more about colonization, for America is as much our country, as it is yours.

"Treat us like men, and there is no danger but we will all live in peace and happiness together. For we are not like you, hard hearted, unmerciful, and unforgiving. What a happy country this will be, if the whites will listen. What nation under heaven will be able to do any thing with us, unless God gives us up into its hand.

"But Americans, I declare to you, while you keep us and our children in bondage, and treat us like brutes . . . we cannot be your friends." [An excerpt from David Walker's *Appeal to the Slaves of the United States*. Milton Meltzer, *The Black Americans*. New York: Thomas Crowell, 1964, pp. 14–16.]

The Deliverer

"Nat Turner died on the gallows, but his ghostly spirit hovered above every southerner. Slaveholder James McDowell told the Virginia legislature the uprising raised the 'suspicion that a Nat Turner might be in every family. . .'"

"Mrs. Lawrence Lewis, niece of George Washington, wrote about 'a smothered volcano—we know not when or where the flame will burst forth, but we know that death in the most horrid forms threatens us. . . .'

"Southern legislatures voted their fears. Since Turner read and preached, laws were passed against black preachers and banning the teaching of slaves. 'To see you with a book in your hand, they would almost cut your throat,' recalled one slave. Laws were passed in many southern states that made manumission [freeing] of slaves almost impossible.

"One Virginia legislator spoke of his goal for slaves: 'We have, as far as possible, closed every avenue by which light might enter their minds. If you could extinguish the capacity to see the light, our work would be completed; they would then be on a level with the beasts of the field, and we should be safe." [William Katz, *Breaking the Chains*. New York: Atheneum, 1990, pp. 119–121.]

"After 1831 the abolitionists began to use railroad terms when talking about runaways. Abolitionists were 'agents' on the Underground Railroad. A runaway slave was called a 'package.' When a slave ran away he was 'taking a ticket on the Underground Railroad.' A man or woman who led a runaway slave to the North was called a 'conductor.' A conductor went into the South to lead slaves north to freedom." [Angela Medearis, *Come This Far To Freedom*. New York: Atheneum, 1993, pp. 28–31.]

"The Underground Railroad was the practical arm of the abolitionist movement. It was a daily, dramatic manifestation of the determination of slaves to be free, free in the face of every hazard, and of the determination of thousands of whites to aid and abet them. The Underground Railroad was the more remarkable in that it ran directly in the face of the American respect for property. Every slave helped to escape by a white man or woman appeared to Southerners, and to many Northerners as well, to be stolen property, and those who aided them no better than bank robbers or burglars. Each theft encouraged among other slaves the hope of being 'stolen,' so that the anology must encompass the notion of an epidemic as well as a theft, a cancerous disease as well as an assault on property. Every single escaped slave made the system tremble." [Page Smith, *The Nation Comes of Age*. New York: McGraw-Hill, 1981, p. 599.]

"From the New England Articles of Confederation in 1643 forward, European masters legally bound themselves to assist in the return of escaped slaves. Slaveholders had this pledge written into the U.S. Constitution and two federal Fugitive Slave acts. Slave-hunting was to be carried out by federal marshals and the U.S. Army if necessary.

"Slaveholders would not tolerate any gap in their defense system. They bitterly resented Native American nations for accepting African Americans into their villages and were furious about an Indian adoption system that drew no color line. . . . the governor of Virginia had the Five Civilized Nations promise to surrender escapees, and in 1726, the governor of New York made the Iroquois Confederacy take the same pledge. . . .

"Along the Atlantic coast and spreading westward through woods and over mountains to the Mississippi, two dark races began to blend and marry. Artist George Catlin, writing in the 1830s, called the children of this mixture [of Negroes and Indians] 'the finest and most powerful men I have ever yet seen.'. . .

"The strongest U.S. coalition of red and black people flowered in Florida around 1776. African runaways from plantations in Georgia became the peninsula's first settlers and were soon joined by Seminoles fleeing oppression. . . . The two dark peoples developed a prosperous and peaceful farming and grazing economy. . . .

"Runaways who reached the North were often pursued by possies who seized and returned them. The 1793 Fugitive Slave Act imposed a $500 fine on any person who harbored or aided an escapee. . . .

"African-American communities in the North and their white friends increasingly defied the law to provide armed assistance to fugitives." [William Katz, *Breaking the Chains*. New York: Atheneum, 1990, pp. 84–85, 97.]

Three Lives . . . Three Fates . . . Three Futures

In 1836, missionary Marcus Whitman and his wife Narcissa Prentiss Whitman traveled west with three others. The two women of the group were the first white women to reach Oregon by an overland route. The five established a mission at Waiilatpu near Fort Walla Walla and went on to establish several other missions in present eastern Washington and Idaho. The Whitmans and eleven of their co-workers were murdered by the Cayuse Indians in 1847, resulting in the American Board of Commissioners for Foreign Missions abandoning its work in the Oregon Territory.

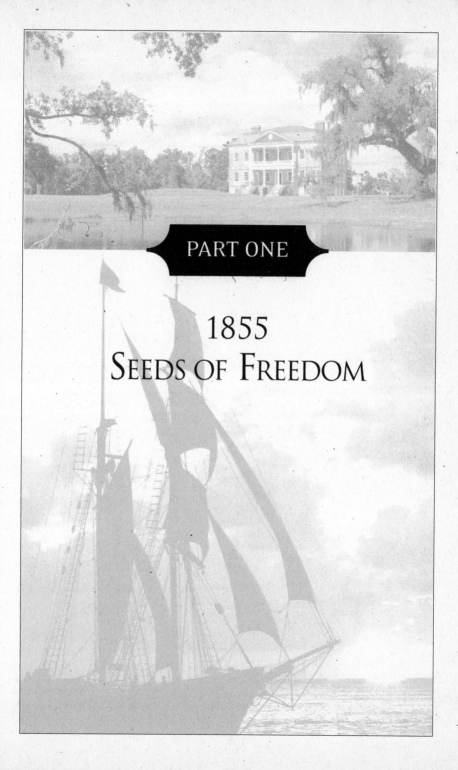

PART ONE

1855
SEEDS OF FREEDOM

One

$\mathcal{A}$ woman with caramel skin, but the rest of whose features gave clear evidence of her African heritage, stole quietly from the hovel she called home and tiptoed away from the slave quarters.

The hour was late and the night quiet. A half-moon illuminated her steps, though she would have been able to find her way even had the darkness been as black as her husband's skin. The stream was less than half a mile away. She could have found it with her eyes closed. They carried their wash this way once a week, and bathed the children more often than that. But on this night all she wanted to do was let the cool water flow over the wounds on her back. It might only stop the stinging for a few minutes. But even such temporary relief would be worth it. The water, however, would not prevent tears continuing to rise, nor quiet the anguish in her heart from the day's events.

She reached the stream safely and paused. No sound other than the gentle gurgle of water met her ears. She glanced around nervously, though she knew from the deathly quiet that she was alone. Then she slipped her dress over her head, dropped it on the ground, and walked barefoot and naked into the stream. Moments later she sat on one of the large submerged stones of the washing pool, where the water reached about four feet, and slowly sank into its depths. The water gently rose up over her shoulders to her neck in wonderfully anticipated relief from the throbs pulsing across the skin of her back.

Twenty-four-year-old Lucindy Eaton was a slave. Whippings were part of a slave's life in South Carolina. She expected no different. But today—hearing that her husband had been sold and that, even as she carried his child, she would probably never see him again—everything had changed.

Today, for one of the first times in her life, she had become angry. Angry enough to speak up, to fight back, and inwardly to curse the white man. Today she had felt the injustice of this way of existence like never before. For today that injustice had suddenly revealed its harsh ugliness in her own life.

The master had ridden into the village while the men were in from the fields eating lunch.

"Caleb!" he called in the voice they all knew and feared. "Caleb Eaton . . . come out here."

Lucindy glanced at her husband with wide eyes of silent terror. "What does he want?" she whispered.

"I don' know," answered Caleb, rising from where they sat on the floor eating. "But you jes' wait here wif da young'uns."

He walked outside, where a dozen or more black faces had already poked out windows, with a few emerging out of their own cabin doors to see what was happening.

"I's here, massa," said Caleb walking bare-chested into the sunlight.

"I can see that, Eaton," said the white man, still seated on his horse, holding the ever-present whip, whose tongue had tasted the flesh of nearly all the men present more than once. "All right, then, get your things—you've been sold."

The words fell like a sentence of doom on the ears of the listening blacks. Dumbfounded, Caleb stood as still as a statue. The number of watchers quickly increased as the master's message spread like an invisible brush fire through the collection of shanties.

The overseer and another white man now rode up behind the master, the latter holding the reins of a riderless horse.

"But, massa," said Caleb after two or three seconds, "I gots me a family, wif anuder chil' on da way. Maybe you ain't herd, but my Lucindy's gwine hab anuder—"

"I know all about it, Eaton," interrupted Master Crawford. "Why else do you think I waited till now? I figured I ought to get myself one more nigger baby out of the bargain."

Low churlish laughter sounded from the two men behind him.

"But, massa . . . Lucindy, she need me. I's work harder effen you likes, an I's—"

A cruel lash on the front of his shoulder silenced him. He staggered back and fell to his knees.

"It's too late for all that, Eaton! That's the trouble with you—your tongue's too long for your own good. I've put up with it long enough."

Crawford turned and nodded to one of his men, who jumped off his horse and dragged the black man to his feet.

"Now either you get in there and get what things you want to take with you, or else we'll take you as you are, without shirts or coat or anything else."

Caleb shuffled back toward the house in a daze, where Lucindy now stood in the doorway watching in stunned disbelief. He could not look into her eyes, but walked past her inside.

Two little children, aged one and three, clung to her legs and dress. A minute or two later, Caleb walked back carrying a small handful of ragged clothes and an extra pair of boots. This time he paused and now sought Lucindy's face. His expression was one of sorrow, grief, and apology for whatever might be his own part in this terrible turn of events.

"Caleb . . . ?" she said in a forlorn tone of question and desperation.

"Where Daddy goin'?" said a young voice at her side.

"Oh, Broan!" said Lucindy, suddenly bursting into tears.

The innocent boy's question jolted Lucindy's brain awake. Even as Caleb stooped to give a tearful good-bye kiss and hug to the three-year-old little boy and his sister—both too young to understand what was happening—she ran out toward the imposing presence of the master where he sat on his horse with growing impatience.

What went through the mind of such a man at sight of her—whether her light skin, or that of any number of his slaves, roused the awareness anywhere in his being that this was his own flesh and blood, his own daughter—it would have been hard to say. If Miles Crawford even thought of that fact, he gave no sign of it. For the purposes of expediency in adding to his stable, in the absence of suitable men, he had fathered fifteen or twenty of his own slaves through the years, but he made no attempt to keep track of them. They represented mere inventory, value on his ledger. If he had paid nothing for them but a few minutes of his time, so much the better.

Lucindy had always been vaguely aware that the master was her father, a legacy or a fate, depending on how one looked at it, that she shared with a dozen of her fellow slaves who were still here. But the fact meant nothing to her. Pity the poor heart to whom the word *father* arouses no thoughts of tenderness and compassion. Before that day, in Lucindy Eaton's mind, it aroused no feelings at all. Ever after, the word filled her with hatred. She knew that some black fathers were kind. Caleb was a good father to Broan and Rebecca. But in her deepest heart, nothing more represented evil to Lucindy's ear than the single word *father*.

"Massa, please!" she cried, running forward and looking up at him with pleading expression. "Dese two young'uns, dey need dere daddy. I's work too, massa. I's do whateber you wants effen you jes' don'—"

"Shut up!" he yelled, as a shove from his boot sent Lucindy sprawling to the ground. "What good can you do me in your condition! Now stand back and get out of our way before you feel the whip along with your man."

He nodded to his overseer again, who now walked toward the house where Caleb knelt on one knee and was talking quietly to the two children. The man took hold of his shoulder and wrenched Caleb viciously to his feet. Keeping a tight grip, he now turned him and shoved him toward the waiting horse.

Lucindy scrambled to her feet and ran toward him. She threw her arms around his neck.

"Caleb . . . Caleb . . . ," she sobbed, kissing his eyes and forehead and cheeks and finally his lips.

But another crack from the master's whip, this time on her back, brought an end to the tearful parting.

She screamed in pain. At her side she felt Caleb's muscles tighten in silent rage. He was a large and powerful man and in an instant could have put all three white men on the ground. But even outspoken slaves like Caleb Eaton learned that to yield to temper never helped, but always made things worse. To fight them now, even to protect his wife's honor, would only insure a worse whipping than the lash she had already received.

"Get up, Eaton!" barked the overseer. "You're not so dumb you need to be told what to put in that saddle!"

Caleb reached for the saddle horn and set his left foot up in the stirrup.

"No!" cried Lucindy, picking herself off the ground and again running toward her husband. But the overseer rudely pushed her away, then shoved the black man up the rest of the way onto the horse's back.

"Mama, Daddy?" babbled the little girl, who had waddled out from the house.

Lucindy swept her daughter into her arms and again approached the awful throne of judgment.

"Please, massa! Look at dis chil'!" she said, holding the one year old up toward her own grandfather. "Dis little girl need—"

"She needs to learn something her mother apparently never did," the white man spat back angrily, "and that is to hold her tongue!"

Again he shoved Lucindy away from the side of his horse with his boot, sending mother and child to the ground. At last his patience had been driven to the extreme.

"Get him out of here," he shouted to his overseer as he dismounted, "while I teach this tramp a lesson!"

"Caleb!" cried Lucindy as the other three horses turned and began clomping away. Caleb glanced behind him with tears blurring his vision.

Lucindy was silenced again by the master's hand. He did not stop this time until the back of her dress was sliced and ripped and soaked

with the blood of a dozen fresh lashes of the cruel leather thongs.
When she came to herself, Caleb was gone and some of the women
were tending to her wounds.

Tears stung Lucindy's eyes at the memory of the cruel parting. She
splashed several handfuls of water from the stream into her face, but
the coolness could not stop the hot burning flow of tears.

"Oh, Caleb . . . Caleb," she whimpered, then began to sob gently.

She knew that if the master or one of his men found her here, away
from the slave quarters, and naked besides, she would probably be
killed on the spot. But she didn't care. Today she had stopped being
afraid. She had hardly felt the master's whip. Even with two small
children to care for, and a third on the way inside her, at this moment
she hardly cared if she lived or died.

She cried for a few minutes. Slowly the tempest of grief passed.

As she sat in the stream, thoughts of the songs they sang about the
river Jordan came back to her. She didn't know how big the Jordan
was. Probably it was a huge and mighty river from the way the songs
told it. She knew she would never see the real river called Jordan
because that was somewhere far away. She didn't even know where it
was. But that river symbolizing the border where people, even blacks,
crossed into the land where all people were free no matter what color
they were—maybe she *could* cross that Jordan one day.

The water continued to flow, and as she sank into a reverie, the
water of that stream became the water of the river Jordan in her
dreams, and a determination rose in Lucindy Eaton's heart that she
would not live the rest of her life only to die in slavery. Somehow she
would make sure her children knew freedom, even if to give it to them
cost their mother her life. Perhaps she would not cross into that land
herself. But like Moses of old she would see them cross into it and
enter into the land of promise.

Who would be her deliverer, she didn't know. How she would get
them to that place where freedom lay on the other side, Lucindy
didn't know. But she would not spend her days and die under the
shadow of the taskmaster's whip. She would see the promised land,

even if she died gazing upon it from afar. But if she died knowing that her children would know freedom, it would be a happy death.

"God," she whispered, "he'p me git ter dat ol' riber, whereber it is, so dat I kin see my chilluns git crossed hit. He'p me, God, fin' dat road ter freedom leadin' ter dat Jordan."

Two

The morning of early April promised warmth.

Spring, arriving a month ago to the plantations of Georgia, Alabama, and Mississippi, had now advanced northward to the verdant growing regions of southern Virginia. Even the hillier portions of the Piedmont Plateau, which diagonally separated the mountainous western half of the state from the eastern Coastal Plain, were beginning to grow warm and fragrant with the budding life of a new season.

A ridge of mountains, however, was not the only thing separating west Virginia from east Virginia. The sympathies of the eastern coast lay with the South. But in the mountains of the west, antislavery sentiment was strong. Virginia was a state destined to feel the brunt of the growing conflict. Neither side would budge an inch from its zealously held convictions.

A woman in a plain blue work dress, one hand raised to shield her eyes from the sun, stood on the porch of an expansive two-story brick plantation house. Her gaze was directed at the figure of her husband across the fields beyond the barn where he was just disappearing into the arbor.

Carolyn Davidson knew why. This was likely to be an important day in his future. Before he set out, he needed to know that he and his God were of one mind.

As she watched him, she glanced about. Nearly everything upon which her eyes fell belonged to them, at least it did until final disposition of the estate was settled . . . green meadows filled with grazing Red Devon cattle, and beyond them ploughed fields sprouting new wheat, tobacco, cotton, and oats.

The pride she felt in what surrounded her was not in possession, even if theirs was more tenuous than it ought to have been, but in stewardship. They worked hard, the land produced, and God prospered the result. If a creed could be said to dictate her outlook on the life of farmer and plantation owner, as well as that of wife, stewardship would certainly be contained within it. Hers had not always been an easy life, but in most respects she was now a woman at peace—at peace with herself, at peace with her God, and at peace with her role in the divine order of things. There was more than that, of course. That she and her husband had both been married previous to meeting one another contributed in no small measure to the difficulties of arriving at her present outlook. Hers had been a hard-won peace, as peace with God and oneself often is. But the contest had yielded much fruit of character, and a deep sense of God's being to sustain her. She held dreams of things she would someday like to accomplish. But she was in no hurry.

The soil here was perhaps not so lush as on the low plains further south and east. But neither was the climate quite so humid or hot. And the rolling landscape, with its scattered woods and forests, offered infinite variety of color. There was no other place on earth she would rather be, she thought as she took in the sight. She had grown up in the northwest of the state where the Allegheny Plateau stretched toward Pennsylvania near the panhandle. But since the day of her marriage twenty years before she had called this place southwest of Fredericksburg home. She hoped to spend the rest of her days here, grow old and die here, and be buried in the small Davidson family plot at the northwest corner of the garden.

Glancing to her right, she squinted imperceptibly. On the clearest of days, the Blue Ridge Mountains might faintly be seen to the west. But not today. On this morning, as on most, the characteristic thin blue haze obscured the horizon from sight.

She brought her gaze back in front of her as she saw her husband emerge from the arbor.

Richmond Davidson had also been thinking about their land on this unseasonably warm morning. His visage, however, revealed a distant look, extending far beyond the boundaries of this land that had been his father's and grandfather's before him. If his life's focus took on more complexities than his wife's, it was not because the intellectual currents of his brain ran more deeply than hers. She was fully his mental equal, an essential sparring partner as they wrestled through issues that confronted them. But his mental shoulders bore the added responsibilities of manhood at a critical time, not only in their lives together, but also in the life of their nation. The time was quickly approaching when he would have to bring politics into his faith, whereas his wife cared little for such thorny issues. "Let men dictate the affairs of state," she said. She cared only about their people whose welfare God had given them to watch over.

Their home stood about two-thirds of the way to the Maryland border from North Carolina. Fate had placed them where they could not ignore the increasing drumbeats of history. When destiny arrived, they would be drawn into the middle of it, the wife as well as the husband.

Difficult decisions were on the horizon. Would those decisions, Davidson wondered, pit him with or against his Virginian peers? If the latter, he was well aware that the cost to his reputation would be high, though that had never been one of his prominent priorities. The internal compass of his conscience was not oriented in a direction that made heroes in the eyes of men, but toward that which made sons and warriors in the invisible conflict of the ages. Right and wrong made up the components of his matrix of life, not what might add to his advantage according to the world's ledger of success. Like his wife, this inner equilibrium of spiritual perspective had not been easily won, nor were the struggles to maintain it altogether past. His was a faith he had to *work* to hold. And the two worked hard together to walk out the life they shared with a tenacity that kept them from dwelling on the griefs and questions of the past.

But though he keenly felt the burdens and responsibilities of his position, and though his own personal demons of doubt occasionally seared the memory of his conscience, Richmond Davidson too was a man at peace with himself, his God, and his place in the world.

The year was 1855.

The Davidsons' beloved Virginia, for two centuries the peaceful foundation stone of the American experiment in democracy—birthplace of Washington, Jefferson, Madison, and Monroe, as well as more recently William Harrison and John Tyler—was feeling the strain of the times.

It was a good and peaceable land. Yet all was not as idyllic as it seemed. Most of Richmond Davidson's fellow plantation owners, even as far north in the state as Spotsylvania County, shared neither his concerns nor his convictions. As the decade had advanced, the issue of slavery had come to dominate national politics as never before. Some of his fellow landowners and farmers ignored developments and decisions in Washington. Their daily lives went on as they had for generations, though their very way of life sat at the eye of the growing storm. Others, like his closest neighbor and boyhood friend, desired to involve themselves in the political fray.

Had it not been for the gold rush in the West, the conflict might have been forestalled, if not indefinitely certainly for some time. But California's admittance to the Union in 1850 as a free state broke what had been a deadlock in the Senate—making sixteen free states and fifteen slave states—tipping the balance of power toward the North. With statehood now eventually inevitable for the territories of Minnesota, Oregon, Kansas, and Nebraska, all of which could well become free states, many of his fellow Southerners viewed the future with alarm. If steps were not taken, it seemed that the South would be forever doomed to a subservient role. Such was not a fate its leaders were prepared to accept.

Which direction would determine Virginia's future as the cadence of approaching conflict grew louder with each passing year?

⌇

"Good morning, my dear," said Davidson, smiling as he walked toward the house.

He was taller than average, perhaps two inches over six feet and of well-proportioned build tending toward slender. His face was angular, with strong chin, wide mouth, narrow lips, and well-defined high cheekbones. His hair was plentiful and unwieldy, with one great clump toward the back permanently standing straight in the air like wild prairie grass, in spite of his wife's most persistent efforts to tame it. Thick and brown in his youth, his crop was now showing the first hints of approaching gray.

"It is nearly time for us to get you to the station," said Carolyn, returning his smile. "You look very nice."

"Thank you, but I am still uncertain whether I should have accepted the invitation."

"Any new eleventh hour revelations?" she asked.

"Only that, as I *did* accept," he replied, "I am to keep the appointment and listen to what they have to say. After that, I'm sure our prayers will become more specific."

"You still have no idea what it could be about?"

"None whatever. But it must be important judging from the names they told me would be present!"

"Will Denton be among them?" asked Carolyn as they walked inside the house together.

"I don't know," replied Richmond. "He was not mentioned, and I am more than a little puzzled by that fact."

"Have you spoken to him about it?"

He shook his head. "I am still hopeful he will be there."

"Maybe such will be the case and all your worries will take care of themselves," suggested Carolyn.

"Perhaps . . . and if not, whatever it is about, he is sure to know of the meeting in time. Denton and my brother always cherished more political ambitions than I."

"You cannot run from your destiny, Richmond. You are one of Virginia's important men."

"A distinction I would give anything to relinquish!" laughed Davidson. "As secondborn, I never expected this."

"But you cannot relinquish it, Richmond. And you know it. If for no other reason than because of your grandfather and father, your name in Virginia's political circles is one that will always bring attention to itself no matter how much you try to shun the limelight. For better or worse, you *are* a Virginian, and you are a Davidson."

"Would that it had been Clifford instead."

"How often have you told me that we cannot second-guess God. You and I of all people know that his purposes extend beyond our limited sight."

Davidson laughed again. "You sound like your father. Ever the preacher's daughter."

"I never had any aspirations to follow in my father's footsteps any more than you did yours," said Carolyn. "Preaching is not suited for women."

"Perhaps, but you *are* wise and our women depend upon you. *I* depend on you." He paused and thought a moment. "I realize that my father's and grandfather's reputations live on in the minds of many," he added. "They assume that I am of a political bent just as they were. So you are right in what you say."

"Then I will just add this and let it go at that—you must do what God places before you to do."

"Of course you are right . . . as always! I will keep an open mind. One never knows what God will do. If my destiny, as you call it, turns out differently than I had anticipated, then I am sure he will prepare me for it."

"I know you will do what he shows you."

"But as you say," added Richmond, "it is time for me to go or I shall miss the train! I'll just run upstairs and say good-bye to Cynthia and Seth and Thomas. Then I'll hitch the buggy and you can take me to the station."

Three

$\mathcal{A}$s Richmond and Carolyn Davidson rode toward town twenty minutes later, they saw a rider approaching on horseback. Davidson slowed their single horse as he and his brother's childhood friend reined in.

"Ho, Denton!" he called. "Out for a morning ride just for the pleasure of it, or does business bring you over the ridge to the west?"

"A little of both, my friend," replied the Davidson's neighbor Denton Beaumont, scion of a family as deeply rooted in Virginia's past as Davidson's. "Good morning, Carolyn," he said, tipping his hat toward Davidson's wife. "Where are you two bound?"

"Into town," replied Carolyn.

"To answer your question, Richmond," Beaumont went on, turning again to his friend, "I apologize for straying onto your land—"

"Please, Denton, do not even say such a thing," interrupted Davidson. "Our land is your land and you are welcome anywhere on it."

A faint expression of irony passed over the horseman's expression, but his words did not betray the reaction. Indeed, the two plantation houses, though technically neighbors, were more than five miles from one another, separated by a low ridge of hills, the highest point of which, known as Harper's Peak, was some 2,400 feet in elevation.

"Thank you . . . you are too generous," said Beaumont. "In fact I was out checking on some fence work my darkies were supposed to finish yesterday. You can never trust them to do what you say— they're such a lazy lot. I was near the old Brown land and I rode over and found myself retracing some of our favorite trails. I suppose I lost track of the time. It's still hard not to think of it as the Brown tract."

"I know what you mean," rejoined Richmond. "I find my thoughts straying in such veins as well, even though it has been part of Greenwood since long before my father's death."

"Those were great years we had together."

"Sometimes I think it's too bad one has to grow up, though everyone does. There was nothing we enjoyed so much," said Davidson, turning toward his wife, "as being out romping the woods. Denton and I and my brother used to ride every inch of these hills for miles."

"What adventures we had!" added Beaumont. "We knew every tree and hill and ravine on both sides of the ridge."

"We called ourselves the three musketeers," laughed Richmond.

"There were a few who called us rascals."

"And rogues! But most of our escapades were harmless enough."

Another peculiar smile passed over Beaumont's face.

"It sounds wonderful," laughed Carolyn. "I wish I could have known you both then."

"Don't be so sure, Carolyn. You might not have liked the result."

"I doubt that."

"Adventures notwithstanding," said her husband, "we were afraid of Mr. Brown, although my father thought a great deal of him. And there was no denying that his odd methods produced the best crops in the region."

"Where is he now?" asked Carolyn. "What happened to him?"

"No one knows," answered Beaumont. "He disappeared and was never heard from again."

It grew silent a moment.

"Speaking of old Mr. Brown," said Beaumont at length, "is there still no chance you would sell me part of his land?"

"I continue to think about it," replied Richmond. "But I am reluctant to part with it for my father's sake—he had such a tender spot in his heart for Brown. I always regretted never seeing him again after I returned from England. My father always seemed to think that he would return someday to reclaim the land."

"There seems little chance of that now, after all these years."

"No, I suppose not. Yet I feel bound to be faithful to my father's wishes. He never really considered the Brown land ours, though legally I suppose it is by virtue of the fact that we hold the deed. In my father's mind, we were merely keeping it for Mr. Brown until his return. But as you say, that is certainly unlikely now. Perhaps my desire to retain the land is sentimental. However, I will continue to pray about it."

"I will make you a generous offer."

"I'm sure you would!" laughed Davidson. "It may turn out that my cousins will force my hand," he added more seriously. "Until then, I will have to give you the same answer as before—we shall see, and I shall continue to pray."

"Well then, I shall let the two of you continue on to town, and I will be on my own way—Good day, Carolyn."

"Good-bye, Denton. It was good to see you again. Greet your wife and daughter for me."

"I will, thank you, Carolyn."

"How is Veronica?"

"She will be fifteen in a couple of months and precocious enough to pass for several years older."

"I am not surprised! She always seemed older than she was. And your sons?"

"Chips off the old block!" laughed Beaumont as he began to swing his mount around.

"Let's get together again!" Richmond called after him. "Next time you go riding, come by Greenwood on your way and I will join you!"

"And race again to the top of Harper's Peak?"

"You're on!"

The two men laughed, then Beaumont rode off. Within seconds, however, for vastly different reasons, the smiles faded from both their faces. Davidson was aware that he had not been altogether forthright with his friend, and the realization stung his conscience. On Beaumont's part, his thoughts turned to the real reason he had strayed across the former boundary between Brown's land and his own. After leaving Richmond and Carolyn, he continued to ride about the old Brown tract for another hour, as he often did when he had the time. The broken fence at the edge of his plantation's holdings had in truth been but a thinly disguised ruse. His actual business did not lay on his land at all. He had come out specifically to snoop about on that portion of the Davidson acreage they had been discussing, which he would have given almost anything to purchase.

"I feel bad that I didn't tell him where I was going," said Richmond as he and Carolyn continued on their way. "I suppose all along I had been hoping he would be in attendance too. Obviously, though, if he is out riding at this hour, he won't be. I should have said something, but I didn't know how to bring it up. I have the feeling, though it is nothing I can put my finger on, that he was not invited for a reason."

"Were you and your brother as close as you and Denton seem to have been?" asked Carolyn.

"Not really," replied Richmond. "It was actually the two of them who were close. I was the youngest and I suppose I looked up to the other two. I thought they could do no wrong. I was more like the tagalong younger brother. No doubt they led me into a few scrapes I would have been better to avoid. I've never quite forgiven myself for being overseas when my brother died."

"Surely you don't think you could have prevented it?"

"How can you not wonder such things?" rejoined Richmond seriously. "The possibility of it haunts me. If I had been there, Clifford might not have been out riding, or perhaps he and Denton and I would have been together. In any event, I cannot help but think the accident might have been prevented had he not been riding alone."

"You cannot blame yourself."

"I know. But my father was so devastated by Clifford's death, he was never the same afterward. I just wish I had not been so far away."

"You were obviously embroiled in difficulties enough of your own at the time. You came as soon as you heard."

Richmond nodded reflectively, then flicked the reins and urged the horse on. He had been over this same ground in his mind too many countless times already, and always with the same inconclusive result. It was time to think of the future, not the past.

Four

The gathering at the North Carolina plantation of Congressman Jeeves Hargrove proved smaller and more intimate than Richmond Davidson had anticipated. He arrived in Burlington on the 1:17, where a buggy and two silent and formally attired Negro attendants were waiting to transport him the three miles to Cedar Grove. There he would spend the afternoon and evening, before returning home the next morning.

As they emerged from the winding, tree-lined drive, Davidson saw Frederick Trowbridge standing in front of the white-columned home of the congressman.

"Richmond!" he exclaimed, walking forward with outstretched hand as Davidson stepped to the ground. "I am so glad to see you. Come, come . . . most of the others are enjoying drinks on the back lawn. All but one or two have already arrived."

They walked through the house chatting freely. As he emerged into the enclosed garden behind it, Davidson was surprised to see only eight or ten others spread about the grassy expanse, all men.

"I am anxious to introduce you," said Trowbridge as they went. "There is one very special guest I know you will want to meet—Gentlemen," he said loudly as they approached the group, "our guest of honor is here! May I present Richmond Davidson."

Not having an idea what the appellation could possibly mean, the newcomer quickly found himself swallowed in smiles, introductions, well-wishes, and handshakes.

"And if you have not recognized him already," said Trowbridge, beaming with pride as they made their way around the small coterie of influential politicians, "I would like you to meet your fellow Virginian, John Tyler."

"Mr. President," said Davidson respectfully, shaking the elderly former president's hand, "this is indeed unexpected. I am honored to make your acquaintance."

"And I am pleased to make yours," rejoined the nation's tenth president. "Frederick has told me a great deal about you."

"And," Trowbridge continued, "Secretary of War Jefferson Davis."

"Mr. Davis," said Davidson, "again . . . this is an honor."

An hour later, though the conversation had been pleasant and the food and drink, set out on two tables in their midst, superb, Richmond Davidson still knew no more the purpose of the gathering than he had when the invitation had arrived, nor why he, a humble Virginia plantation owner, had been accorded such a show of respect by men far more well-known in national circles than himself. Gradually they began to take chairs about the lawn and, as cigars were produced for most of those present, their host at last began to steer the discussion in the direction of the day's business.

"It is no secret," said Congressman Hargrove, "that, notwithstanding last year's Kansas-Nebraska Bill, things in Washington are not, viewed in the long term, moving in our favor."

It was Watson McNeil, a prominent North Carolina plantation owner, who next spoke up. "With most of the South already in the Union," he went on, "and all the new territories coming from the North and West, the situation can only grow worse as time passes."

As he listened, Davidson could not avoid the sensation that many of the remarks had been scripted for his benefit, and that this was not so much a discussion of where events stood, but a series of preliminaries leading to some as yet unforeseen conclusion.

"It is still possible," now added Upton Byford, a federal circuit judge in the District of Columbia, who, though presumably impartial on the bench, was a Southerner through and through, "that Kansas and Nebraska could come in under the terms of the compromise, and vote for slavery. That would return the majority to us."

"Or they could vote *against* it," countered McNeil.

"Watson's point is well taken," put in their host. "Even if we do manage in the near future to regain a one-state majority with Kansas and Nebraska, Oregon and Minnesota are waiting in the wings to wrest it from us . . . with other new states beyond them in areas completely opposed to slavery."

"And we have to admit," nodded Trowbridge, "that Nebraska is as far north as Pennsylvania. The North would not cede to our interests there without a bitter public fight. I think it highly unlikely that we could win Nebraska with a public vote."

"The point is," said Hargrove, "we are all in agreement that something must be done, that measures must be taken. That is why we are here, to discuss alternate strategies."

It was silent a moment. A few glances strayed in the direction of Richmond Davidson.

"What, if I may ask," said former president Tyler, the elder statesman of the group, "is *your* perception of the future, Mr. Davidson?"

Davidson glanced around. Every eye was on him.

"In what regard, Mr. President?" he replied. "With regard specifically to the balance of power between free states and slave states . . . or with regard to the prospects of the South in particular?"

"Both," answered Tyler. "Or either question you may choose to address. I am simply curious how you see the nation's future, and the future of the South, in a general way."

Davidson nodded. "A sweeping question," he said, then added with a slight smile, "and one which might easily entrap an unwary man in unguarded words."

A ripple of good-natured laughter filtered around the group. As it grew silent again, however, it was clear from the expressions on the rest of the faces that they expected an answer.

"I suppose I would say, then," Davidson began, "that it seems to me that we can regard neither time nor circumstances as static. Times change and circumstances change. My feeling is that we must be prepared to meet the challenge of change on both fronts, and have the courage to face it. . . . "

He paused thoughtfully, reflecting on his choice of words. His tone made it clear that he had stopped in midsentence, and had more to say. The silence about him was palpable. The others waited patiently.

"I would add," he went on after a moment, "that we must pray for the courage to face change with dignity, honor, and character."

A few nods went around the circle. Frederick Trowbridge glanced about at each of his friends and colleagues, eyes aglow as if to say, *Did I not tell you!*

At length Trowbridge smiled. "I assured you, did I not," he said, raising his glass as if in triumphant toast, "that he was our man!"

Prominent Maryland landowner Abraham Seehorn wore a more cautious expression.

"You mentioned prayer, Mr. Davidson," he said. "Tell me, are you a religious man?"

"I try not to be," answered Davidson.

"I'm sorry . . . I don't think I understand you. You mentioned that you pray."

"I do."

"But you are not religious?"

"I hope I am a praying man, but not a religious one."

"And what would be the distinction?"

"There are too many to go into now," replied Davidson. "I would not bore you with my ideas on the matter. I would only say, in brief, that it is the distinction between obedience and dogma."

Even as he said it, Davidson sensed that his answer was lost on most of those present. But he did not exacerbate the problem, as is the normal custom when discussing matters of faith, by trying to explain further. Rather he let his words stand.

"Be all that as it may," said McNeil, bringing the discussion back to the point at hand, which was the future of the South, "how would you put your words into practice if change does come to our region, unexpected change that could hurt you economically?"

"I suppose, like everyone else, I would do my best to adapt."

"You own slaves, of course," asked Seehorn, "as do most of the rest of us here?"

"I do," replied Davidson.

"They are vital to the prosperity of your plantation?"

"Absolutely. I could not get by without them."

"You are concerned about the economy of the South?"

"Of course. I am a businessman."

Seehorn took a long puff from his cigar and seemed satisfied.

There was a momentary lull as two black slaves came from the house with trays. A few of the men stood to replenish their drinks or relight their cigars.

As her husband was engaged in the eventful discussion concerning his own outlook and the future of the nation, that same afternoon Carolyn Davidson walked from their plantation house the three-quarters of a mile to the slave village where their thirty-four black slaves lived in a collection of eight small one- and two-bedroom cabins. She was carrying a large basket of vegetables.

At forty-three, Carolyn Davidson's face and other features revealed the dignity of age along with sufficient lingering reminders of youth to make her a stately and beautiful woman able to command attention from anyone able to see her for who she was. The maturity in her gaze and the peace that shone from her countenance had, like her husband's, not come without pain. Her hair was lighter than his, though not fully blonde, and thus showed no hint of gray. Eyes of emerald green looked out above a small, well-shaped nose, and wide and pronounced cheekbones that accented a rounded though strong chin below. Her mouth was not large, but contained well-formed teeth that revealed themselves readily in laugh or smile, and was framed by lips capable of much expression.

She reached the village, where a half dozen or so small children were playing and running about. Several black women hanging laundry on their lines greeted her as she approached. Singing could be heard from one or two of the cabins. Though plain, the wood dwellings were in better repair and generally larger and more comfortable than the slave hovels that passed for homes throughout much of the South.

She entered one of the buildings without knocking.

"Hello, Nancy," she said. "I brought you some vegetables."

"Dat's right kind ob you, Miz Dab'son," said a black woman of some thirty-five or forty years as she took a handful of greens and carrots from the basket. "Dese'll cook up right fine in da stew I's be makin'."

She set the carrots on the wood table in the middle of the room, picked up a knife, and began trimming off the tops. But within a few seconds her hand stopped and she turned back to her mistress with an expression of anxiety.

"Does you min' if I talks to you, Miz Dab'son . . . 'bout sumfin ob a personal natshur."

"Of course not, Nancy. Let me just take some of these around to the other women, then I'll come back."

"Thank you, Miz Dab'son."

⟳

"It is no secret," said Congressman Hargrove, addressing Davidson after a momentary lull in the conversation, "that I am an outspoken states' rights advocate. Such could be said for most of the rest of us. We have spent our careers articulating the interests of the South. We are attempting, however, to be realists. We see the handwriting on the wall. Changing times are coming, and, as you point out, we have to face them shrewdly. We are asking ourselves what can be done to preserve the Southern way of life, and especially the right of the Southern states to slavery. That is why we have asked you here, Richmond," he went on, "to share with you a plan that some of us have come up with that we feel may, if successful, prove of great benefit to the South."

He took a sip from his glass, drew in a breath, then continued. "Our plan is simply this—to win new loyalties in Washington by putting up Southern candidates who will speak with a voice of moderation. The problem is that many in the North view men like us with suspicion because our views are so well-known and because the debate has become so contentious. We need new faces and new voices who will be able to bridge the gap with Northern voters. Otherwise the South will have no voice at all in a few years."

"The old 'catching more flies with honey than with vinegar' ploy!" laughed Trowbridge. "We're trying to be wise as serpents, as it were, while coming across innocent as doves."

"Precisely," rejoined Seehorn.

"I do not see what all this has to do with me," said Davidson.

"There are those who think that you could become such a voice, and could gain widespread support, even in the North."

"Are you talking about *me* . . . in politics?" said Davidson, glancing around at the group with a smile of incredulity. "You men are the politicians. I am only a farmer!"

"But one with a spotless reputation and known to be a man of reason," said Trowbridge, "respected throughout the state. Your father was a well-respected moderate with strong ties to Pennsylvania. In short, you are exactly the kind of man we are looking for, and why I have lobbied so strenuously on your behalf."

"But what could I possibly do?"

"It is very simple, really," said Hargrove. "We want you to run for the Senate next year."

"But I am a complete unknown!" laughed Davidson.

"The Davidson name is hardly unknown in Virginia politics," said the former president.

"Perhaps. But my father's involvement was years ago."

"True enough. So perhaps it is time for the Davidson legacy to resurface. I assure you," Tyler went on, "with our backing, the seat will be yours if you want it."

"Senator Smith is stepping down," Trowbridge went on. "The state committee will select the candidate and we are confident you can win."

"And I would, as you say, present a more widely acceptable public image," said Richmond, "—innocent as a dove, as you say, than a known and more strident figure?"

Laughter again circulated.

"Your man is a shrewd one, Frederick," chuckled McNeil. "He catches on quickly. I predict we will make a politician of him in no time."

The comment was not lost on Davidson, nor was he sure he altogether liked its implication.

"But what about my neighbor Denton Beaumont?" he asked. "Surely he is far more qualified than I?"

A few significant glances were exchanged.

"To be truthful, Richmond," said Trowbridge, lowering his voice in a confidential tone, "there are those in Washington whom he has already offended. He is far too outspoken for our purposes."

"Let me say, for the sake of argument, that I agreed," said Davidson thoughtfully, "and even that I were successful, what is your objective in the proposal? I suppose what I am asking is, what could I do that would benefit . . . you . . . the South . . . the nation?"

"You are a new face," replied Hargrove. "We would hope that you would gain new support among Northerners as well as Southerners. By speaking with a voice of moderation, you would earn the trust of those even of different political persuasions and in time help give a new face to the interests of the South."

"Toward what end?"

"We are looking to the future, to potential national candidates."

The secretary of war, who had remained mostly silent throughout the latter portion of the discussion, now spoke up.

"To put all our cards on the table," said Davis, "I intend to run for the Senate again myself next year, preparatory to a presidential bid in 1860. To win the nomination I will likely have to defeat Douglas or Breckinridge. I know it is five years away, but our strategy is a long-range one. What interested me in Frederick's plan when Hargrove told me of it was this, that I will need a vice-presidential candidate on the ticket with me who has earned respect and loyalty throughout the North. In short, Davidson," he said, "we think you could be that man. That is why we want to place you in the Senate next year, and then begin advancing you slowly into the national lime-light."

It was silent for a moment as Davis waited for the weight of his potential offer to sink in.

"My name, of course, may be controversial," Davis went on. "But with the right man on the ticket with me, speaking as we have noted, with moderation, a man with ties to the North as well as the South, we believe that we could win two or three of the Northern border states and carry the election. I need hardly tell you what having a Southerner in the White House would mean. And after my own term," he added, raising an eyebrow, "who is to say how high you might eventually rise."

Ten or fifteen minutes later, when Carolyn Davidson returned from visiting every one of the small homes in the village, her large basket now empty, she poked her head again into the cabin where Nancy and Malachi Shaw lived with their three children. A girl of about fifteen turned to face her.

"Hello, Phoebe," said Mrs. Davidson. "I was looking for your mother. Where has she gone?"

"Yonder . . . tards da big house," answered the girl with a nod.

From the porch, Carolyn glanced in the direction of her home and saw Nancy walking slowly in the distance. She left the village and made her way back up the slight incline she had come down earlier, and quickly overtook Phoebe's mother. They walked along together in the direction of the plantation house.

"It's 'bout my Phoebe, Miz Dab'son," said the black woman after a minute. "She's gettin' ter be a fine-lookin' girl an' she's at dat age, you know. . . ."

"I understand, Nancy. She is a very lovely young lady."

"Thank you, Miz Dab'son. An' she's worried 'bout what Massa's gwine ter do wif her."

"Worried . . . about my husband, about Mr. Davidson?"

"Yes'm. She's already older'n da time w'en mos' girls is dun sumfin wif. She's feared dat he's gwine ter bed her down an' make her git married, or maybe eben sell her."

"He would never do that without talking to you and Malachi. . . . and to her too, of course. Surely you know Mr. Davidson better than that."

"Yes'm. Master Dab'son, he's a kind man, but Elias, he say—"

"Elias," interrupted Carolyn. "Is that what all this is about?"

"Yes'm," replied the black woman, glancing down at the ground. "It's jes' dat he's been on other plantashuns, an he's seen more'n da res' ob us. He knows—"

"What are you listening to him for?" said Carolyn, more than a little perturbed. "You should know better, Nancy. You can trust us. And so can Phoebe. Mr. Davidson will do nothing but what he thinks is best for you all."

"Elias, he say massas always jes' do what's bes' fo dem."

"Well that's not the way we run this plantation, Nancy. We're a family, and you are part of it."

"I knows dat, Miz Dab'son. You an' da massa, you's 'bout as kind as kin be."

"Then you oughtn't to listen to what Elias says."

"Yes'm. I's try, Miz Dab'son. You be comin' down ter read us from da Good Book ternight?"

"Of course, Nancy. I'll be down right after supper."

Five

*E*lias Slade was a big hulking black man, with rippling shoulders and biceps and a look of danger on his face. He was only twenty-three but had been bought and sold so many times before and after the several years he had spent on the McClellan plantation, that there was no one place over another that he considered home. Whether the word *home* would ever be used in connection with someone of his temperament was doubtful. Whatever family he had was lost to the distant memory of his infancy.

The scars that crisscrossed his back, as well as his rippling shoulders and biceps, were all the evidence needed that the white man's whip had been used to greater effect to curb his insolence than under-standing or deprivation. That he was finally learning to hold his tongue did not lessen the silent rage fermenting beneath the surface that had been responsible for the whippings. In truth, Slade hated more deeply in his silence. Though his present master had recognized him on an auction block in Richmond, had bought him and brought him back to the area and attempted to befriend him, Slade only despised him the more for his kindness.

Slade kept to himself, slept in a cabin with several other single men, but never entered into the singing or other social activities that bound the Davidson slaves together in a familial bond tighter than most. By this time most of the slave men on the Davidson plantation had learned to leave him to himself. At the same time, however, his talk about the wider world, and what he had seen and heard on other plantations fascinated them strangely. Most of them had grown up on the Davidson plantation and they could not help listening to him with eager curiosity.

Slade was on his way back from the creek where he had been cooling himself from the hot day in the sun. Bare chested and dripping, he heard the sound of a woman's voice ahead of him. It was a white voice.

He stopped and listened, then crept slowly toward the clearing where the women gathered with the master's wife. He knew of the meetings but ignored the invitations. Even some of the men occasionally joined their wives. As he looked through the trees he saw a few of them sitting there. They were women too, thought Slade spitefully, listening to such fool talk.

"'Heed that ye do not your alms before men, to be seen of them,'" came Carolyn Davidson's soothing voice as she read. "'Otherwise ye have no reward of your Father which is in heaven. Therefore when thou doest thine alms, do not sound a trumpet before thee, as the hypocrites do in the synagogues and in the streets, that they may have glory of men. Verily I say unto you, They have their reward. But when thou doest alms, let not thy left hand know what thy right hand doeth: That thine alms may be in secret: and thy Father which seeth in secret himself shall reward thee openly.'"

She paused briefly. Before she could continue, one of the black women spoke up.

"I knows well enuf what a hipokrit is, Miz Dab'son," she said. "But what's dat *alms* dey's always talking 'bout?"

Carolyn smiled. "That is money given to the poor," she said. "The Lord is telling us to do good deeds, and to help the poor, but secretly, without letting everyone else know about it."

"What 'bout us, Miz Dab'son? We's da poor folks ourse'ves. We don't got none ob dem alms ter gib nobody no how. I neber had no money in my life. What's we surpozed ter do?"

Chuckles and laughter spread through the group of slaves.

"The Lord understands that well enough," she replied. "Alms can be anything you do for someone, any good deed. It doesn't have to be only money."

"Like what?"

"Well, for instance, Mary—what if you were to help Nancy with her washing tomorrow when you had plenty of your own to do? That might be a form of alms—a good deed, an act of kindness. And to obey what the Scripture teaches, you would want to help her without telling everybody else about it and bragging about how good you had been."

"I's neber do dat, Miz Dab'son!" laughed Mary.

"Of course you wouldn't. I know that. Jesus teaches us to do good secretly so that we won't become proud and puffed up about it."

She looked around at the fifteen or twenty black faces, all listening intently. "Do any of the rest of you have questions?" she said. "The Scriptures can sometimes be very puzzling, and the only way to under-stand how God wants us to live is to ask questions."

She glanced about the group and waited for a few seconds.

"All right, then," she said, "I will continue reading. 'And when thou prayest, thou shalt not be as the hypocrites are: for they love to pray standing in the synagogues and in the corners of the streets, that they may be seen of men. Verily I say unto you, They have their reward. But thou, when thou prayest, enter into thy closet, and when thou hast shut the door, pray to thy Father which is in secret; and thy Father which seeth in secret shall reward thee openly.'"

She paused again. "Do you understand what the Lord is saying?" she asked, glancing about the group.

"Dat we's supposed ter pray in secret too?" said one of the men.

"That's right, Moses. Jesus says in many different ways that we are not to make a show of religion, but to live it. And one of the best ways not to make a show of it is not to try to impress other people with our good deeds or our prayers, but just do them quietly. That's what this whole Sermon on the Mount emphasizes—practical faith rather than showy religion. Jesus was a very practical and down-to-earth man."

"Is dat why you's always talkin' 'bout jes' doin' what he says, Miz Dab'son?" asked another of the women.

"Exactly. People who make it into a complicated religion don't understand what Christianity is. It's a way of life. Jesus taught us how to live, how to treat one another, how to think. It's something a rich man can practice, or a poor man, a beggar or a banker, a white man or a black man, a plantation owner or a slave. That makes it a beautiful thing, don't you think? Christianity is for everyone."

"You make it soun' simple all right, Miz Dab'son, but I wonder effen you's makin' it a mite too simple."

"It is simple, Wilma. It's not always *easy*. Following Jesus and doing what he says is hard . . . but simple. It's not complicated, though it's hard to lay down your own wishes in order to obey what he wants you to do. But you and I all read the same words and can do them. Anyone can obey Jesus. That's why in him we are all brothers and sisters. I am your sister and you are my brothers and sisters. None of us is any better than anyone else. You are my equal in Christ, and I am yours."

Elias Slade had heard enough. He had not paused because he cared for the Word of God or the words of a rich white woman. Something else was on his mind. Where he stood among a clump of trees at the edge of the clearing beside the stream where the Scripture readings took place twice weekly when the weather permitted it, the big man's eyes scanned the gathering.

Sensing eyes upon her where she was seated on the ground beside her mother, Phoebe Shaw turned and saw Elias staring at her. Their eyes met. He gestured with his hand. Imperceptibly she shook her head and turned away. She did her best to listen but was too distracted by her awareness of Elias.

A minute or two went by. Phoebe turned and again caught his eye. This time Slade gestured urgently, motioning for her to come. Again Phoebe shook her head. When this time she turned again to face the mistress, she kept her face forward and did not glance back again.

Annoyed, the big man turned and tramped away through the trees.

⸻

Later that evening, as dusk gave way to night, Nancy Shaw left her cabin in search of her daughter. When inquiry at most of the other

slave homes resulted in the same answer, that no one had seen her, she
began to grow genuinely worried.

Half an hour later, Phoebe walked into the small house. Her
mother glanced up, relieved. Almost instantly, however, the look on
her daughter's face filled her with suspicion.

"Where you bin?" she asked.

"Nowhere," answered Phoebe. "Jes' out."

"Where?"

"Nowhere. Jes' out fo' a walk."

"Wif who?"

"Jes' Elias, Mama."

"Why him?"

"He ax'ed me ter go fo' a walk wif him."

"I wan'chu ter keep away from him, Phoebe."

"Why, Mama?"

"Because I don' like him, dat's why. He ain' up ter no good no
how."

Further talk was cut short by the entry of Nancy's husband. She did
not want to involve Malachi for fear of what he might do. He may
still have been a strong man for his age, but Malachi Shaw was no
match for Elias Slade. And Nancy considered it best to keep this incident between herself and her daughter.

Six

*R*ichmond Davidson sat in the northbound train gazing out at the passing countryside reflecting on yesterday's discussions, which had lasted long into the evening.

A journey away from Greenwood, whatever the occasion, inevitably sent him into a flurry of wide-ranging emotions. And now the return to his plantation and country estate, especially given what had transpired the day before, could not help but turn him pensive.

It was not just his absence from home. The inner conflict came from the dissonant chord he felt in his soul between the many divergent paths of life and the one he personally had chosen. He had been the obvious center of attention at the gathering just past. Yet in some ways he had felt like a stranger in their midst. It was clear none of the others present knew him at all. They were just looking for someone to act as a stand-in for their plans. The question boiled down to a simple one: Given the life choices he had made, could he ever really fit in with their world?

Finding himself in settings like yesterday's always deepened his reflective bent. The result of such soulful wanderings was usually the same—a great sigh of relief as he neared home, and a continued thankfulness for the life and family God had given him.

Davidson gazed outside at the passing North Carolina countryside. They would cross into Virginia any mile now. His would probably

not be called the most scenic state in the American union. There was
no romance of gold in Virginia as in California, no flowing of milk
and honey as were the claims about Oregon. But it was the birthplace
of nationhood. The soil was as rich as Virginia's heritage and the
climate temperate. It was a good place to live, to grow things, to raise
a family . . . and to seek to be God's man.

"Ticket, please."

Davidson pulled his gaze back from the window. There stood the
conductor in the aisle.

"Oh, yes . . . sorry," he said, digging into his pocket. He handed his
ticket to the man, who then moved on down the center of the coach.
Davidson again turned toward the window.

If Virginia represented the cradle of America's democratic origins,
that history was in danger of being forgotten and swept aside. The
nation of thirteen colonies was no longer in its infancy, but had grown
rapidly. The whole world was watching what happened in America.
And forces within it were threatening the very fabric of the freedom
that had been born here.

He was a Virginian, from a respected family in America's history.
What role did destiny have for him to play at this critical hour of crisis
and decision? Was that role to be a political one? As much as he
recoiled from city life, did the nation's Capitol beckon him?

In his heart lay not only questions about his own future, but anxieties for his beloved nation. It was changing rapidly. Too rapidly, he
sometimes thought. With westward expansion that had begun with a
few handfuls of wagons now becoming a tidal wave, new states were
bound to keep entering the Union. The powerful men of the South
were not about to let their way of life fade into the past without a
fight.

He prayed the result would be peaceable. Yet he could not still the
tremors in his breast. With those anxieties came the question, Might
he be able to do something to prevent a conflict which seemed to him
almost inevitable? If so, was Washington, D.C. the place in which to
do it?

"Hey, mister . . . like to buy a newspaper?"

Davidson turned. There stood a boy looking at him, carrying a satchel of newspapers and a few sandwiches.

"What paper, son?" he asked.

"Raleigh *Gazette*, sir."

"Any good news today?"

"I don't know, sir. I can't read."

"Well, I will take one and see," said Davidson with a smile. "What else do you have there?"

"Sandwiches, sir."

"How much?"

"Two bits."

"Well then, young man, why don't you give me a newspaper and a sandwich . . . and here is an extra two bits for you to keep for yourself."

"Gee, thanks, mister!"

With an inward smile the traveler watched the boy go, then gradually resumed his reflections.

Richmond Davidson's predecessors had fought in the War of Independence, as well as the War of 1812 only two years after his own birth. They had helped tame the land and had occupied it since. His father had been involved in state politics, and had been grooming Richmond's older brother Clifford toward yet more lofty objectives. But neither politics nor plantation life had been among his own goals. He was a student, and had traveled to England to study law and had begun to make a life for himself there. But his own personal crisis, and the near simultaneous unexpected death of his brother back home had changed all that. Suddenly he found himself on a ship bound for the States, divorced, devastated, and alone, with his plans for the future shattered and his aging father depending on him to step in and take over in his brother's stead.

He had resisted at first. But then he met Carolyn, found new purpose in the Lord, and everything changed. The new life they discovered together was not what either had anticipated or planned. Yet out of such unexpected beginnings they had built a good life. Twenty years later this life that had at once seemed foreign to him was

so natural that he could envision nothing else. Notwithstanding the
estate pressures being brought to bear by certain grumbling relatives
since his mother's death, all he needed to find satisfaction was here, in
the hundred and ninety acres of the family plantation known as
Greenwood.

He had traveled widely in his youth, and had been enamored of
Europe and its culture and history. He was well read and spoke tolera-
ble French and German. His knowledge of history was far reaching and
had law not drawn him to Oxford as a young man, he would surely
have become a distinguished professor of history. But in recent years he
had been content to work the land. That he was well off was clear
enough. But until his mother's death two years before he had rarely
given finances a second thought. Though his own knowledge of law
was vast, since his formal education had been cut short and he had
never passed the bar himself, he used his uncle's son in Richmond to
handle the family's occasional legal matters, such as had become necessary in view of the fact that his mother had died without leaving a will.
Like this lawyer-cousin, there were several other relatives who viewed
him as an irritating anomaly in the Davidson lineage, and would have
done anything to worm their way into the Greenwood bank accounts.
Indeed, they had already set a plan in motion to do just that.

None of them would have dared call Richmond Davidson a simpleton, for, though soft-spoken and unambitious according to their
worldly standards, five minutes' conversation with him revealed a
wise, knowledgeable, and refined man of undisputed character, intelligence, and integrity. Neither did his relatives consider their cousin a
fool, only an enigma whom they both envied and despised. They
would have been shocked had they known what had driven him away
from England in addition to his brother's death. It is doubtful they
would have used such knowledge to move against him in other ways
than they were attempting. Still, it might have been a lever to bring
against his otherwise spotless reputation, which, if shrewdly wielded
could be used to undermine if not outright blackmail him, and thus
wrest from him control of the family estate.

Had they known what gnawed away at his soul, not only would his cousins have been stunned, his political associates would almost certainly never have asked him to represent Virginia in the Senate.

But for now his secret was safe. No one but Carolyn knew of it.

When he reached home, the weariness was immediately evident on his face. His wife recognized the look, and that it had not been caused by mere travel fatigue.

"Your mind is heavy," she said as they walked from the station to the buggy she had brought to pick him up. "It is written all over your face and sagging shoulders."

"You know me well," he laughed wearily as they climbed up and began the three-mile ride back to Greenwood.

"What is it?" she asked.

"Oh, nothing much . . . only that President Tyler, Jefferson Davis, and Frederick Trowbridge and a few others asked me to run for the Senate next year, with the hope of a vice-presidential bid in five years when Davis makes a run for the White House."

"What!"

"I told you it was nothing much." He laughed and shook his head, reaching his arm around her to pull her next to him. "The implication was even around the edges," he added, "that I might one day occupy the White House myself." As he spoke, he sounded as if he himself did not believe what he had just told her any more than she did.

"But, Richmond . . . that's an enormous opportunity!"

"Which is precisely why my thoughts are weighed down."

"What are you going to do?"

"I don't know. Obviously we need to pray. It came so unexpectedly, I don't know what to make of it."

"Was Denton there? I would have thought him a more likely choice."

"Exactly what I said to them. But he wasn't in attendance. As I suspected, Denton knows nothing about it."

"He's liable to be jealous, Richmond. He is far more ambitious than you. For them to offer such a thing to you, while ignoring him—I cannot imagine he will be pleased."

Davidson nodded, an expression of concern passing over his face.

"I will have to talk to him," he said, "though I admit I am not looking forward to it. He has to be told . . . whatever we decide."

"*We?*"

"This is an important decision, Carolyn. It is one we must make together."

As their conversation continued, she explained what Nancy had told her about Elias.

"He is spreading rumors and gossip," she said, "and creating division. I fear his words will sow distrust."

"I am afraid he is a troublemaker. It was a mistake to buy him. But Malachi and Moses and the other men needed help with the heavier chores and machinery. I thought we could make him content here."

"It's always useless to try to reform people who don't want to change."

"It's a lesson my father tried to teach me when I came back from England to take over the plantation," sighed Richmond. "The first lesson in buying slaves, he always said, was to look for signs of trouble and not to involve yourself with one who has the signs—a man with too many whip scars, a flirtatious girl, an angry or lazy or contentious spirit. It's a lesson I never learned very well. I always think we can help them. But there are some people you just cannot help."

"You have too kind a heart."

"As do you, you must admit. But why should kindness be a problem, Carolyn? I don't understand it."

"Because people do not always respond to it. There are those who despise it as a sign of weakness. It is obvious that as hard as we have tried to treat him with kindness, Elias does not respect us."

"What can we do? Should we sell him?"

"So that he can cause some other plantation owner even more trouble than he has caused us, and then be beaten within an inch of his life?"

"You're right. I would sooner sell an ill-tempered horse than an ill-tempered slave. Of course, we can do neither. But we cannot have him creating dissension among our people."

"Denton would probably take him off your hands. He seems to like such types."

"Whatever our differences, I could not do that to him."

Davidson paused and a strange light came into his eyes, followed by a curious smile.

"Perhaps," he said, "the best solution would be to set him free."

His wife stared back at him, wondering if she had heard right.

"Are you serious, Richmond?" she said.

"I don't know," he laughed. "I said it half in jest. We would lose the money we paid for him. But at least we would know that we had not passed along our troubles to someone else."

"Would you come so close to defying the law?"

"What about your teaching our slaves? You could be in just as much trouble as me."

"Then we will both go to jail together! But I justify what I do by saying that I *read* to them from the Scriptures, I don't actually teach them."

"There would be some who would call that splitting legal hairs."

"Well, no one has bothered me about it yet," laughed Carolyn. "And even if it is against the law to teach slaves, it's a bad law and ought to be changed. So I will continue to read to them and answer their questions, and let the law take care of itself."

Seven

*R*ichmond Davidson awoke. It was dark and quiet. He had no idea of the hour.

His mind had been plaguing him most of the night with thoughts about his conversation with Carolyn on the way back from the station.

His own words haunted him. *Perhaps the best solution would be to set him free.*

He had said it without thinking. Yet might it in fact be the best thing to do, the perfect solution to a difficult problem? On the other hand, what kind of precedent would it set? How would their other slaves respond? And what of the legal ambiguities? Virginia's laws regarding freeing slaves may have been more lenient than those of some states in the Deep South. But they were not without their complexities.*

It would be a relief to be rid of Elias, that could not be denied. The investment would seem a small price now to be free from the grief the big black man was causing. If he seriously intended to pursue the offer that had been made two days ago, Davidson had to know things could run smoothly at Greenwood during the inevitable absences a Senate

---

*"It was legal in Virginia to emancipate one's slaves, though if the freed slave was over twenty-one years of age, he or she had to leave the state within one year, or risk being re-enslaved. And the widow of a deceased slave-holder who had freed a slave, could claim a 'third' ownership of that slave to which a widow is entitled. . . .

". . . slaveholding Quakers in North Carolina . . . empancipated 134 slaves in 1776, only to see them re-enslaved."—William Goodell, *The American Slave Code.* New York: The American and Foreign Anti-Slavery Society, 1853, reprinted by Arno Press, New York, 1969, pp. 342–43, 375.

seat would necessitate. Why should he not simply give Elias a document releasing him and put him on a train anywhere he wanted to go? As far as reaction among the other slaves, he could simply send him away without telling the rest of them anything. On the political side of it, might such a move instantly ruin his political stand . . . or, if a national reputation of moderation was what they wanted, perhaps freeing Elias would *enhance* his standing rather than damage it.

The wide range of potential implications was confusing!

God, what do you want me to do? he sighed inaudibly.

His mind full of the many decisions facing him, as well as those that might be forced upon him, Davidson drifted into an uneasy sleep. The rest of the night passed fitfully.

Later that morning as he sat with coffee in hand perusing the newspaper, a caption caught his eye. He began reading the article beneath it with interest.

"Listen to this, Carolyn," he said after several minutes. "A symposium is being held in Boston on the spiritual pros and cons of slavery. Martin Wingate will be one of the featured speakers."

"The theologian from England?"

"The very same."

"Haven't I heard you mention him more than once?"

"I met him as a young man when I was overseas. I would dearly love to see him again. There will also be representatives from both Northern and Southern states and several different church groups, all offering their perspectives on the basis of the pros and cons from Scripture. That should be quite a meeting."

"It sounds fascinating. Why don't you attend?"

Davidson laughed. "I told you . . . it's in Boston."

"You could go."

"All that way?"

"Why not? Maybe the break would be good for you. You always say that getting away once in a while helps clear your brain."

"Not always," laughed Davidson. "The trip down to North Carolina sent me into a turmoil of reflection I have not been able to get out of."

"You know what I mean—when you go away alone, to think and pray and be with God. With this decision before you about the Senate, I think such a trip might be the perfect thing."

"I wonder what the weather is like in New England in April. Hmm . . . well I shall think about it," chuckled her husband. "I must say, a trip to Boston is the last thing I anticipated when I awoke this morning!"

Eight

A knock sounded on the front door of a fashionable Boston home located in the exclusive district of Constitution Hill. The man who answered it was dressed in a business suit and appeared to be approaching fifty. His black hair had given way to about an equal proportion of gray, and the mingling of the two as it spilled down over the tops of his ears gave him the distinguished look of a diplomat, though his chosen profession was actually on the opposite side of the fence. He *wrote* about events rather than *participated* in them. In the South, today's visitors might have been greeted by a tall, stately Negro butler. But though he could have afforded several servants, the man's progressive views prohibited such a luxury. He would not have made a good Southerner, for equality lay as the foundation stone of his informal life's outlook. A paid cook and part-time housekeeper had, out of necessity, helped him manage since the loss of his wife. But that was as far as he was prepared to go in bringing domestics into his home.

Three women stood on the porch. He recognized them, though they would hardly have been termed acquaintances, much less friends. Their expressions were serious.

"Good morning, Mr. Waters," said one a little stiffly.

"Hello, Mrs. . . . Foxe, isn't it?"

"Yes . . . and this is Mrs. Bledsoe . . . and you remember Mrs. Filtore?"

"Of course—hello to you all," he said, nodding to each of the others. "It has been a long time. It is good to see you ladies again. Won't you come in?"

He led them into a spacious and well-appointed parlor where they sat down.

"Would you care for tea?" asked the impromptu host.

"No, thank you, Mr. Waters," replied Mrs. Foxe, the unofficial spokesperson of the committee. "We won't be long. The purpose of our visit is not social," she added as she glanced about the room as if unconsciously checking for dust.

"Ah . . . I see," said Waters. "Then what would be its purpose?"

"We are concerned about your daughter, Mr. Waters."

"Cherity?"

"Yes. We saw her in the city two days ago . . . in trousers."

"Was she in some sort of trouble?"

"She was in trousers, Mr. Waters. She was wearing *men's* trousers."

"I understand, but I confess myself at a loss to see—"

"We are concerned, Mr. Waters," now interposed Mrs. Filtore, "that you are allowing your daughter to run wild. She is displaying habits that are anything but becoming to a lady."

"I'm not sure I follow you," said Waters incredulously, beginning at length to get a sense of the conversation's drift. "Is it because she was not wearing a dress that you have come to see me after all these years?"

"Such things are indications of deeper matters, Mr. Waters. What is her standing with God?"

"To tell you the truth, I have not asked her."

Almost in unison, the noses of the three women tilted imperceptibly into the air, as if the reply confirmed their worst fears and revealed all there was to say on the matter. They continued in another vein.

"We never see either of you in church, Mr. Waters," commented Mrs. Bledsoe.

"That is true. We do not attend."

"Do you not care for your daughter's salvation, Mr. Waters?"

"It is not something I think about."

"Your dear wife certainly would have cared about it."

"And what good did it do her?"

"She was saved, Mr. Waters, and is now with the Lord."

"Perhaps. But to me she is dead. And Cherity has had to grow up without a mother. So perhaps I should ask what good my wife's religion did her daughter? I considered it my religion for many years too, and I could equally ask what good it did me. My prayers were answered with my wife's death. From where I stand, he must be a heartless God who would leave an infant without a mother."

A barely audible gasp sounded from one of the women at the statement.

"God's ways are higher than man's ways, Mr. Waters," said Mrs. Foxe. "He cannot be understood by mortal souls."

"I agree with you completely. Therefore I have determined no longer to attempt to understand him."

"But what about your daughter, Mr. Waters? Do you not care about her eternal soul? Your dear wife was our friend. We feel it our duty, for the sake of her memory, to urge you to—"

"I am sorry if I seem rude," interrupted Waters, beginning to lose patience, "but where have you been all these years? You did not care enough to help me when Cherity's mother died. Those were difficult years. But I heard virtually nothing from anyone in the church where my wife gave so much. And now you come here, all this time later, to accuse me of being a negligent father because you saw my daughter wearing trousers. It is people like you that made me leave the church."

"It is not only the men's clothes, Mr. Waters," said Mrs. Foxe, ignoring his words. "She has been seen by others as well as ourselves. It is said she rides a horse about Boston . . . unsupervised."

"She loves horses. What is wrong with that?"

"She has far too much freedom for her age."

"I do not happen to see that as such a bad thing. In fact—"

A sound on the stairs behind them interrupted him. Their heads turned as a girl of fourteen came bounding down two steps at a time, clad in trousers with her auburn hair tucked under a wide-brimmed cowboy hat, and breezed toward the parlor in a rush.

"Cherity, my dear," said Waters, "come in! I would like you to meet some old friends of your mother's."

"Hi, Daddy!" she said, then walked to each of the women in turn and extended her hand as her father introduced them. Mr. Waters, on his part, could not help enjoying the discomfiture of his guests at both her appearance and boisterous nature.

"Are you, uh . . . attending a costume party?" asked Mrs. Filtore.

"No," said Cherity with a merry laugh. "I always wear a cowboy hat. I'm going to be a cowgirl someday."

"A cowgirl . . . good heavens!" exclaimed Mrs. Filtore.

"That's not very ladylike, my dear," said Mrs. Foxe in a condescending tone.

"But I don't want to be a lady. I'm going to go back to the West when I am old enough and work and live on a ranch and be a cowgirl."

"Well," said Mrs. Bledsoe, rising. "I think it is time for us to be going. I hope you will consider what we have said, Mr. Waters."

He did not reply.

"Good-bye, Cherity," said Mrs. Foxe as he led them to the door.

"Good day, ladies," said Waters.

"Who were they, Daddy?" asked Cherity as soon as the door had closed behind them. "What did they want?"

"Your mother knew them from the church we used to attend. They do not feel I am raising you properly."

"Why, Daddy?"

"Because you dress in cowboy getup and ride a horse, I suppose," he laughed. "I think they are mainly concerned because we don't go to church."

"Why don't we, Daddy?"

Waters did not answer immediately. When he did, his voice was reflective.

"I used to be so active in church that you wouldn't have recognized me," he said at length. "I was what they call converted when a traveling evangelist came to speak at the boarding school where I lived. That was long before I met your mother. I threw myself into it with everything I had. I was as devout a young man as you could ask for. But when your mother died . . ."

He did not complete the thought. "Let's just say," he went on, "that when I lost a wife I also lost my faith in whatever I had thought I had faith in up to that point. I lost all interest in church. Anne and Mary wanted to take you once you were old enough, but I did not want them to until you were old enough to make your own mind up about such things. That in a nutshell is why we do not go to church. And another reason is that Sunday is the only whole day every week that you and I get to spend together. I don't want to give that up."

"Neither do I! I love Sunday. I will always think of it as the day I spend with my father."

"But your mother was very faithful to church," her father went on. "You are free to go anytime you like. It's just that I'm not interested myself."

He looked her over with admiration. "You know," he said, "it wouldn't hurt for you to have a little training in how to be a lady. You are growing up fast, Cherity, my dear. Perhaps I should send you to a finishing school."

"Ugh . . . Daddy, you can't mean it! I would hate it."

"It couldn't hurt you."

"But I don't want to be a lady. I want to live in the West. I don't need a finishing school for that."

"Maybe it was a mistake for me to take you out to Kansas," he laughed.

"Don't say that, Daddy! I love the West."

"I know! That is obvious. You are reading those dime novels about cowboys and Indians and the gold rush from morning till night!"

He glanced at the clock on the wall.

"Oh, oh," he said, "it's getting late. It's almost five. I've got to finish getting ready."

"You're not going away again, Daddy?"

"Just into the city. There's a meeting in Boston tonight, at the Lyceum. I have to cover it for the paper."

"Can I go with you?"

"I'm afraid not, dear. The evening will be late and you would be bored to death. It's only going to be some religious men discussing slavery. I think I will be bored to death too!"

"I'm so tired of hearing about slavery, Daddy. I wish everybody could be like they are out West."

"It is a very complicated issue. And it's not so peaceful out West anymore either. Kansas is almost in the middle of a war over it."

"I still don't see what's so complicated about it."

"As much as I detest the idea, the plantation owners in the South depend on their slaves to work their cotton and tobacco crops. They are afraid the entire economy of the South would collapse without slavery. Maybe they are right, but that still doesn't justify it in my mind."

"Well it seems simple to me. People are people. What more is there to it than that?"

Waters laughed. "Perhaps they should have you address the meeting!"

"I would, Daddy, if they'd let me!"

"I am sure you would! But I have to get ready to go. I'll grab some supper in the city. Will you be alright alone?"

"Of course, silly Daddy! I'm reading about Sarah Sacks. I will not be lonely even for a second."

Waters smiled, then reached over and tousled his daughter's hair. "I wonder what those three busybody ladies would think of that," he said. "They would probably be upset that you are not reading the Bible."

"But it's boring, isn't it, Daddy?"

"Not all of it. Some of it is really quite interesting. But who can tell what is true and what isn't?"

"Do we have a Bible, Daddy?"

"Your mother and I each had one."

"Where are they?"

"I put your mother's away with her other things."

"Oh well . . . I think I'll keep reading my *Sarah Sacks, Cowgirl of the West.*"

Nine

*O*n his way into the center of the city, Cherity's father could not help reflecting on the recent discussion from that afternoon. Though reminders of the visit by the three ladies irritated him, he found himself wondering if he had in fact done altogether right by his daughter. The state of her spiritual soul was not on his mind, however, but whether he had properly prepared her for adulthood. In allowing her so much freedom, had he perhaps erred on the other side?

She's a wild one all right, he mused. He could not help smiling at the thought. Yet what could he do? He had not intentionally made her into a tomboy. Now she was so thoroughly enamored of the West that he could not so much as even imagine her in a dress. His older daughters had admonished him, too. They suggested that Cherity might come live with them for a while. He could not bear the thought of parting with her, though he had reluctantly begun investigating a few boarding schools that might provide her what he could not.

He reached the Lyceum and sought the balcony. At such functions, he usually sat as far back as possible. He was less interested in what was said by the various speakers as the reaction of the crowd. That he could best gauge from its midst, with as many people as possible in front of his range of vision. As the auditorium filled and the hour of eight o'clock approached, he pulled out his notebook and pen.

Some thirty minutes into the debate and discussion, a slight

commotion to his right drew his attention. A latecomer with a traveling bag was standing beside him in the aisle.

"I am sorry to disturb you," the man whispered as he leaned down.
"Might I just trouble you to squeeze into that vacant seat next to
you?"

"Of course," replied Waters, wondering what kind of person
brought luggage to such an event. The man set down a suitcase next
to Waters in the walkway, then inched past him and sat down. Both
men turned their gaze forward and Waters tried to refocus his attention on the speaker at the lectern.

Another thirty minutes or so passed. A break between two of the
speakers gave rise to shuffling and murmuring among the crowd. The
newcomer had noticed the busy activity of Waters' pen taking notes.

"Are you transcribing the talks?" he asked when Waters paused
momentarily and glanced up.

"Oh . . . this—no," replied Waters. "I'm a journalist. I'm covering
the event for my paper and I like to make certain I get my quotes
accurate. So I make every effort to write them down word for word
rather than trust my memory."

"How interesting. And a sound policy, I must say, for a journalist."

"What about you? I detect from your voice that you are not a
Bostonian."

"It is that noticeable?" smiled the latecomer.

"To a Bostonian," rejoined Waters. "Our speech is said to be the
thickest in New England! Our tongue sounds equally foreign to some
as any drawl from the Deep South of Mississippi," he added with a
laugh.

"My own Southern roots are not quite so deep as that. I am a
Virginian."

"Ah," nodded Waters. "That accounts for the polish of your Southern tongue. Though if I am not mistaken, I hear a hint of something
else I cannot quite put my finger on."

"Would it perhaps be British in nature?" smiled the Southerner.

"Yes, of course—that is it!"

"I spent several years in England in my twenties."

"What were you doing there?" asked the Northerner.

"I studied at Oxford. I intended to make a life for myself there. But circumstances forced me back to the States." A pained expression passed briefly across his face. "I have been in Virginia ever since," he added.

"What are you doing so far north?"

"I came to attend this evening's symposium, though snow delayed my train and I arrived far later than I expected. Spring is already in bloom at home. I never dreamed I would encounter inclement weather conditions. I'm afraid I am ill-prepared for them, without so much as an overcoat, and arriving too late to secure lodgings. I came straight here from the station."

"Ah . . . so that would explain the luggage. I must admit, I was baffled at first."

"It was more than a little embarrassing to walk in late like that, carrying a bag and scouring the auditorium for a vacant seat. But I had traveled such a long way to hear Dr. Wingate. My name, by the way, is Richmond Davidson," he added, extending his hand.

"I am pleased to meet you," said the reporter. "I am James Waters."

They shook hands as the next speaker rose and stepped to the podium.

An hour later, as the meeting broke up, the two new acquaintances stood and moved into the aisle. Davidson retrieved his suitcase and they began slowly inching in the midst of the crowd toward the exit.

"I want to make my way down front and try to speak to Dr. Wingate," said Davidson as they went. "It was very enjoyable visiting with you. Before we part, I wonder if you could direct me to some-place I might spend the night? Is there a reputable hotel or boarding house nearby that would take in a traveler at this late hour?"

Waters took in the question with a thoughtful nod. His reply was not what Richmond Davidson expected.

"I have a better idea," he said. "I cannot pass up such an opportunity to show a Southerner what Northern hospitality can be like. I would be pleased if you would come home with me."

Davidson stared at him a moment, then smiled in astonishment.

"That is more kind of you than I can say," he replied. "I don't know how to reply."

"Just say that you will accept. We would love to have you."

"But your wife . . . will she—"

"It is just my daughter and myself, Mr. Davidson," said Waters. "She is fourteen and full of energy. Believe me, she will love to have you."

"Then . . . I will accept your kind offer. Thank you very much!"

"Good! Well then, why don't you go down and visit Dr. Wingate while I secure my buggy from the stables? I shall wait for you outside the front entrance."

Forty minutes later, the two were seated in the small carriage, somewhat cramped for two men, in which Waters had made the twenty minute excursion from Constitution Hill into the center of the city. It was about ten-thirty and the evening was chilly and crisp. As they moved out from the center of Boston, other traffic thinned until they were virtually alone, the only sounds accompanying their conversation the rhythmic *clip-clopping* of Waters' single horse trotting briskly along the hard-packed dirt street, punctuated by a few creaks and groans of the wood, springs, and leather beneath them.

"Was it merely to see Dr. Wingate that you came all this way?" asked Waters, giving the reins a brief flick with his wrists.

"No, although I do respect the man highly," replied Davidson. "But the subject matter of the symposium interested me highly as well."

"How so?"

"Slavery, Mr. Waters . . . isn't that the issue on everyone's mind these days—in the North and in the South? I was curious to find the matter discussed from a spiritual perspective."

"Ah, yes . . . I see."

"I look forward to tomorrow's follow-up discussion at the Presbyterian church," Davidson went on. "All one gets in the South are the economic considerations and states' rights arguments. Inevitably the balance of power in the Senate looms large as the most prominent factor of all. The Southern states are very worried if present trends continue. That anxiety tends to dominate everyone's outlook. But such things are not of paramount concern to me."

"What is?"

"As I say—the spiritual considerations."

"Why is that?" asked Waters.

"Because that is how I make my decisions—by considering the spiritual implications. My only concern is what God wants me to do."

A cloud passed over Waters' brow, though unseen in the darkness by his Southern guest.

"Some might consider that quite an eccentric, even a backward thing to say," observed Waters wryly, but with a hint of bite in his tone.

Davidson laughed good-naturedly. "You are right!" he said. "Believe me, many do consider me eccentric . . . and worse! Most people have no idea what to make of a man who tries to order his affairs by the New Testament."

"Is that what you do?"

"It is what I *try* to do. It is the only thing I believe we have been put on this earth for. But as to the charge of being backward—stop and think about it. In what age or former time, with the possible exception of thirty or forty years following his death, have those who call themselves Christians actually tried to live their lives on the basis of wholehearted obedience to Jesus Christ? I would certainly not say that such is the case in our time. Nor can I think of any such era in the history of the world outside the first century, where daily obedience was the primary driving force of the thing called Christianity. Therefore, it seems to me that *backward* is the last description accurately to apply to one making such a commitment, but rather progressive, even revolutionary."

"Do you consider yourself a revolutionary, then, Mr. Davidson?" asked Waters, beginning to seriously question the sanity of this man he had invited home, yet unaccountably intrigued by the lucidity of his expression.

"No, not a revolutionary, Mr. Waters, only a disciple, and a weak one at that. Revolutionaries tend to want to change the world. Jesus himself would certainly be considered one on that basis—a spiritual revolutionary. My wife and I, however, are simply two ordinary people attempting to come to grips with an accurate understanding of who God is, and then live our lives on the basis of that deepening process of daily discovery. The world is not ours to change, only our own hearts. We have our hands full with that."

"Why do you say that?"

"Because we're all rebels deep down, Mr. Waters. Subduing that tendency, and bringing one's actions and attitudes into obedience to the lordship of Christ—that is an extremely difficult process. That's why I say we have our hands full. It is *hard* to be a true Christian."

The night was silent as they rode along, the buggy's wheels occasionally crunching over snow though most of the day's fall had already been worn and melted away.

After a minute or two Waters spoke again. "You mentioned a moment ago decisions you were facing?" he queried.

"There are a few important things on my mind," replied Davidson. "Actually . . . two—decisions I must make that may affect my life for many years to come. One is of a political nature—an opportunity that has arisen that I am not quite sure what to do about. The other is a decision my wife and I must make that will effect our plantation—how to handle some trouble we are having with one of our slaves."

"One of your slaves!" said Waters in astonishment, glancing to his side. "You actually . . . own *slaves?*"

"Yes. Did I not tell you—we own a sizeable plantation in northern Virginia. We have thirty-four slaves. Most are good and well behaved, but there is one troublemaker in the lot."

Waters hardly heard the rest of the explanation. He was still reeling from the shock of realizing that he had invited a slave owner into his home.

They rode most of the rest of the way in silence. Davidson was aware that a cloud had suddenly come between them. It was with relief to both that at last they pulled up in front of the Waters home.

Fifteen minutes later, after they had put away the buggy and fed and watered the horse, the two men sat down inside together. Though Waters' daughter was already in bed with her book, the sound of a strange voice mingled with her father's brought her downstairs moments later, without the boots and hat this time, only trousers hastily pulled on over her nightgown. Her lively energy soon dominated what remained of the evening's light conversation. Soon the temporary awkwardness between the two men had disappeared and they were laughing and chatting freely.

The matter of slaves did not come up again.

The following morning, when breakfast was over the two men enjoyed a final cup of coffee together as they discussed the day.

"When do you return to Virginia?" asked Waters.

"Tomorrow," replied Davidson. "Which reminds me . . . I appreciate your hospitality more than I can tell you. But I am perfectly able to find a hotel for tonight. If you could direct me—"

"Think no more of it, Mr. Davidson. You are here, and here you shall stay. My daughter loves having you. You are welcome as long as you like. I may not agree with your views on slavery, or on religion either for that matter. But I am a tolerant man. We liberals can take the rough with the smooth."

"You are very kind."

"But you still haven't told me exactly why you hoped last evening's symposium would help you with the decisions you have to make."

"I don't know exactly either," replied Davidson, taking a sip from his cup. "I suppose I was just curious what the wider world was saying about slavery. I hoped it would help me more clearly discern God's will in a general way on the subject."

"And has it?" asked Waters, a hint of sarcasm in his voice.

"I think it may," said Davidson. "Such things take time. God's voice can be faint, even when clear. Perhaps it is the philosopher and historian in me coming out," he smiled. "God's perspective on things intrigues me, let me put it that way—his large general will for the world and mankind and eternity, and his specific will in my own life. Of course the two must dovetail or one is not discerning them correctly. But occasionally one is the primary focus, occasionally the other."

"Well, don't talk to me about God's will," laughed Waters, though it was not a laugh of humor. "When my wife was lying on her death-bed, she said something about it being God's will for her to die. I don't think I have ever heard anything so absurd. As much as I loved her, I could not go along with such an outlook. Since then, if that was her God, I haven't wanted anything to do with either him or his so-called will."

Davidson took in the comments thoughtfully. "I am sure it must have been very difficult," he said. "I am very sorry. But I intend to pray for you, Mr. Waters, and pray that the time will come when you will see the goodness of God's Father heart, even in the midst of death and heartache and much in life that we cannot understand."

"Save your prayers, Davidson. They will be wasted on me. I'm not your typical skeptic or agnostic. I was deeply involved in matters of faith for years. I've prayed all the prayers myself. And I've seen far more prayers go unanswered than are answered. Any belief system which fails in its efforts more often than it succeeds doesn't seem to me that it has much to offer."

"So you once considered yourself a Christian, but do not now?"

Waters nodded. "I suppose that is a fair description."

"I see. Well, I am glad to know that. But prayers are never wasted, Mr. Waters, even in the face of what *seems* to be the case with regard to their answers."

"Suit yourself. But I have heard it all before. Just tell me one thing—if your God is so full of love, why did he take my wife? God knows, I prayed as hard as I knew how."

"For one thing, he is not *my* God, as you say. He is everyone's God. His being and purpose is unaffected by who happens to believe in him and who does not. Even should the whole world turn against him and profess unbelief, down to the last man and woman on earth, he would still be our creator, our God, our Father, and our friend. But as to your question—I do not know. Perhaps because he wanted you to discover how good a Father he is."

"You must be joking!"

"I never joke about the goodness of God."

"That is as nonsensical a statement as my wife's saying that her dying was God's will. How could such a thing possibly be? I ask about my wife's death, and you counter by talking about God being a good Father. It's self-contradictory."

"I absolutely disagree, Mr. Waters. Puzzling . . . yes. Occasionally frustrating and painful . . . yes. But contradictory—no. The dichotomy between human suffering, even death, and God's goodness only seems contradictory because we are capable of seeing so little into it. But when we are able to see all the way inside it, we will at last see clearly that the goodness of a perfect Fatherhood lies as the creating and loving foundation for the entire human experiment."

"An interesting expression to use for life," smiled Waters. "But I am curious why you do not see the goodness you speak of as in conflict with life's pain."

"Because heartbreak, grief, and pain have all been included in the grand and wonderful scheme of life as means for our betterment," replied Davidson. "God does not necessarily *originate* them, but he *uses* them as instruments to help us grow, though how exactly he wields them is often a mystery to our sight. I suppose to answer your question—I do not see pain as evil but as an agent for good, providing opportunity to allow God's goodness into our lives in fuller measure than would otherwise be possible."

"All I know is that I have had a rough time being a father without a wife."

"Cherity . . . it is an unusual name—did your wife give it to your daughter?"

"Actually, no. It was my idea. I thought it a good way to remember the old—"

He stopped and smiled. "It is unimportant," he added. "But it is a name that suits her well."

"I take it, Cherity is your only child?" said Davidson.

"No, she has two sisters, eleven and thirteen years older, both now married. Kathleen and I were both well into our thirties when Cherity was born. Kathleen died shortly after giving birth. Maybe it is my age, I don't know—I am a little old to be raising a daughter alone. And Cherity is a bit of a renegade, I'm afraid."

"I have found her nothing but charming," said his guest. "I hope you will one day allow me to return your hospitality and come for a visit. We raise a few horses, too, which should be—"

A shriek interrupted them as Cherity bounded into the room.

"Do you really, Mr. Davidson!" she cried. "I couldn't help hearing what you just said. Do you really have horses on your plantation!"

"Yes, we do," laughed their guest. "Only eight or ten, but there are several I am certain you would enjoy riding."

"Oh! Daddy, can we go for a visit? Can we please!"

"We will see, my dear," laughed Waters. "Virginia is quite a long way."

"We are famous for making ladies of young women."

"My Cherity . . . a Southern belle!" laughed Waters.

"Oh, no . . . please, Mr. Davidson, don't say that!"

"Why not?"

"My daughter does not want to be made into a lady, I'm afraid," said Waters. "Her intention is to become the next Sarah Sacks and tame what remains of the wild West."

During the day's meeting at the Presbyterian church, Richmond Davidson found it difficult to keep his concentration from wandering. His thoughts continued to stray in the direction of his two new acquaintances. He wondered what purpose God might have in sending him to a man who, on the surface of it, was so completely different from him in outlook.

"The matter is not one of slavery per se," the present speaker was saying, "but of the constitutional right of the states of this nation to determine their own laws in this and other such matters. The national government was not established to legislate morality but to govern by law. The right of the states to determine their own law must be preserved at all costs or the foundation of the constitution will ultimately crumble."

"Surely," countered another, "you cannot use such an argument to justify something so odious as the vile slave trade that makes of human beings mere chattel to be bought and sold as animals? There are times when governments simply must step in to regulate human behavior, and now is such a time."

"I grant you that such times exist," rejoined the first speaker. "But if now is indeed such a time, it must be the government of the *states* that does so, not that of Washington. We must keep in mind that the Savior never condemned slavery in and of itself, nor spoke out on political issues. If one is to make the Word of God the basis for one's position, one simply cannot find a condemnation of slavery anywhere within its pages. . . . "

Davidson found the arguments on both sides persuasive, yet to some degree also tedious. He had heard them all many times already. That both sides remained intractable, each seemingly as incapable of listening with an open mind as the other, did not fill him with much hope that the issue would be resolved amiably. If Christians could not arrive at a harmonious meeting of the minds, how could politicians be expected to?

As he made his way back to the Waters' home by horse-drawn cab, reflecting on all he had heard, Davidson realized that the decision before him concerning the Senate must in the end be a personal one.

What did God want *him* to do?

If it was to serve in Congress, could he hope to influence events and accomplish significant eternal good for the cause of Christ? If he could not hope to do so, what would be the objective in his making the attempt? If argument and persuasion were of so little effect among Christians, as seemed obvious from the day's meeting, what could he hope to achieve as a Christian in the political arena? Was not example perhaps a more powerful influence than persuasion? If so, how could he most effectively influence by example?

With much on his mind, when he arrived, Davidson found Cherity Waters home alone engrossed in her novel about the West.

"Hello, Mr. Davidson," she said, answering the door. "Come in. My father said to tell you he will be home about five o'clock," she added as she led her guest inside. "Mrs. Porterfield will be here soon to help me with the supper. You *are* staying, aren't you, Mr. Davidson?"

"I would not forgive myself if I declined your hospitality," he replied.

"Oh, good—I'm so glad. How long will you be in Boston?"

"My train leaves tomorrow morning."

"Was your meeting interesting?"

"I suppose so," he replied as he sat down, "although I sometimes think that so much talk actually accomplishes very little."

"Was it all about slavery, Mr. Davidson?"

"Yes, that was the subject of the discussion."

"I don't like slavery, although my daddy says the South depends on it. Do you depend on slaves, Mr. Davidson?"

"Yes . . . yes, we do. We have a great deal of land and it takes many people to work it."

"I think there must be a better way. I don't know how you can stand to own slaves."

"We try to treat them fairly."

"But they are still slaves."

"I suppose you are right. But since Jesus never said that owning slaves is wrong, I have simply always tried to treat our slaves as he would want me to."

"What does Jesus have to do with it?" asked Cherity, with an innocent matter-of-factness.

"He has everything to do with it. Though he lived many years ago, he was much more than a mere man. He was a very unique man, unlike anyone who had ever lived before, or that has ever lived since."

"But he's dead now, so what can he have to do with you and your slaves?"

"I don't believe he is dead, Miss Waters. That's why I say he has everything to do with it. I believe with all my heart that he is still alive and that he is my Lord. In other words, I am *his* slave, although I don't really think of it like that. What I mean by that is that I try to do what he says—everything he says. Obeying him is what my life is all about."

"I've never heard anything like that. My older sisters are religious, and so was my mother, and I guess so was Daddy when he was younger. But I have never heard he or my sisters say anything like that. How can you possibly know what he wants you to do?"

"Because four men who knew him wrote down what he said and taught. So we can still read his words and try to obey them."

"I still don't see how that can have anything to do with life today when he lived so long ago. How can someone still be alive after so long? You make it sound like a riddle, Mr. Davidson."

He laughed. "Well, perhaps one day I will have the opportunity to explain it to you. But I am curious—how did you become so interested in the West, Miss Waters?"

"That sounds funny for you to call me that. Nobody calls me *Miss Waters*."

"I was trying to be polite," smiled Davidson.

"Is that how people talk in the South?"

"I suppose so."

"Well I would rather you just called me by my name. Friends ought to call each other by name, don't you think, although I have to call you *Mister* Davidson because I am just a girl. But I don't like the sound of Miss Waters."

"All right then, Cherity," laughed Davidson, "is that better?"

"Much better."

"So tell me why you love the West?"

"I went to Kansas with Daddy three years ago when he was writing a story that had to do with the Kansas territory and something about some compromise or other and slavery. I don't know—I don't understand any of that. But he took me on the train with him, then we rode horses all around and we visited ranches and forts and saw buffalo and Indians and everything."

"It sounds like you had a good time. But there are hostile Indian tribes there too."

"Yes, the Kiowa. But we didn't see them. I really wanted to see the Cherokee. They're one of the civilized tribes, did you know that? I've read all about them. Do you have any children, Mr. Davidson?"

"I have a daughter too, although she is a few years older than you."

"What's her name?"

"Cynthia."

"I have two older sisters too, but they're both married and they were already practically grown up when I was a little girl, so I didn't really have anyone to play with. Does Cynthia have people her own age to play with?"

"Well, she is eighteen now, so she doesn't play like she used to. But her two younger brothers were playmates when she was young. And a girl named Veronica at the neighboring plantation."

"How old are Cynthia's brothers?"

"Seth is fifteen and Thomas is thirteen."

"I am right in between them! I wish I could meet Cynthia. She is probably pretty if she is from the South."

"I think she is," laughed Davidson. "But then I am her father."

"What is Cynthia's mother like, Mr. Davidson?" asked Cherity.

"She is my wife, so of course I think she is the most wonderful woman in the world. Her name is Carolyn."

"Do she and Cynthia talk a lot?"

"Yes, they do."

"I can't imagine what it must be like to have a mother," said Cherity, an uncharacteristic note of melancholy entering her voice.

"You have a mother, Cherity."

"But she's dead. I never knew her."

"You will know her one day."

"How can that be if she's dead?"

"You and she will meet in heaven."

"Maybe," said Cherity almost disinterestedly, "but it won't be of much use there. I won't be a girl who hasn't had a mother then. So what difference will it make?"

"All the difference in the world," replied Davidson. "God knows you have had to grow up without a mother. He's the one who loved your mother so much he wanted her to be with him. He will make the love between you and your mother so special when you and she finally meet that this whole life you have had to live without her will seem like just a few seconds. You will altogether forget that you haven't had a mother here because of how wonderful that love there will be."

"You make it sound too good to be true, Mr. Davidson."

"God is so good that such things *must* be true, Cherity."

The sound of the door opening put an end to their conversation. Both turned to see the cook walk in. Davidson stood as Cherity introduced him to Mrs. Porterfield. Cherity's father returned within the hour and neither the subject of slaves nor the Bible came up between them again.

Ten

*R*ichmond Davidson made use of the opportunity of being away from Greenwood to stop by his cousin's office in Richmond, where a few pending legal matters required his signature.

The law offices of Harland Davidson were located on the third floor of a modern office building in the heart of the Richmond business district. The Davidson cousin, son of the brother of Richmond's father, was seven years younger than Richmond himself, though at just thirty-eight years of age was already recognized as one of the city's shrewdest and most skilled attorneys. All his wily expertise, however, had proved powerless to help his own sister and two other cousins, not to mention himself, in gaining the larger share of the Davidson family inheritance to which they felt entitled. That he had had to draw up the papers for the final settlement of his deceased aunt's estate, even act as Richmond's agent in its disposition, only deepened his sense of injury and injustice in the affair.

The son of his uncle Grantham had always baffled and irritated Harland Davidson. Richmond was an intelligent and educated man. As Harland understood it, he had nearly had as much schooling in law as he himself. There was, however, a naïveté in his manner and mode of expression that grated on him. The man could carry himself with a certain degree of sophistication, it was true, yet at the same time he held such odd beliefs. Religion was one thing, but to interpret the

Bible so personally, trying to apply its ancient texts in literal fashion in today's modern world—the thing was absurd. He was a churchman himself, a deacon in the city's most prestigious Baptist church. But he knew where to draw the lines with one's religion, and professed himself unable to make heads or tails of most of his cousin's spiritual hogwash. Yet what choice did he have but to put up with it, as one puts up with a doddering uncle who yet held the power over the family purse strings?

Of more concern to Harland were his cousin Richmond's and his wife Carolyn's notions of magnanimity toward those of darker skin. Comments had been made in his hearing that worried him. The younger Davidson wracked his brain to remember a time in Richmond's younger days when he had espoused such beliefs. But he had gone off to England to study, then come back and turned into a religious fanatic. Maybe something had happened to him there. Harland could overlook his cousin's eccentricities. But if such habits persisted, who could tell what might happen to the Davidson estate? That's why he had been keeping a close eye on things even before Aunt Ruth had passed on. Now it was more important than ever that his cousin not be allowed to go off any deep ends.

New times were on the horizon. The standing of decades-old names of repute in the South must be guarded by cautious behavior. These were not times when it was prudent to show too much benevolence toward those of African descent. One's loyalties might be called into question. That could prove untoward for anyone associated with such a man as Richmond Davidson. Especially a close relative such as himself. He had his own reputation to consider.

"Ah . . . Cousin Richmond," said the attorney, glancing up from his desk as his secretary entered with the source of his reflections.

"Hello, Harland," said Davidson. "I was up North for a few days and decided to stop by on my way home. You had written that you had some papers for me to look at?"

Richmond sat down in a chair opposite the desk as the secretary left the room and closed the door behind her.

"Yes," said the lawyer. "Stuart has decided to formally contest your mother's estate." He opened a cabinet to his right.

"Do you honestly feel that is the right course, Harland?" said Richmond as his cousin produced the file and set it on his desk. "Surely it was not my mother's intent that money would come between us all—"

"It was your own mother's fault," said the lawyer a little coldly. "If her intentions were otherwise, she should have left a will. But to leave nothing more than a handwritten note to you, with such an unclear phrase as, 'see that all other relatives are treated equitably and fairly,' is bound to create sticky legal ambiguities."

"Of course I realize it was ambiguous. That is why I directed that you, Stuart, Margaret, and Pamela each be paid two thousand dollars immediately."

"A mere pittance considering Greenwood's value."

"Hardly a pittance, Harland. There was six thousand dollars in the bank at the time, which to my knowledge is probably more than there had ever been. It is not as if the account has had tens of thousands sitting in it. We had to borrow the additional two thousand, which was a heavy burden to lay on the plantation. And after doing so, for Stuart to contest the estate and expect more . . . I don't know, Harland. As both Mother's attorney and Stuart's, it seems that you would understand the unreasonable grounds of such a claim."

"According to my evaluations, Greenwood is worth a great deal of money."

"Not nearly so much as Stuart seems to think. Not to mention that my mother and father, and Carolyn and I, have worked the land most of our lives. You and Stuart have other careers, other sources of income. Margaret and Pamela are married to husbands with careers of their own. Greenwood is our only source of income. Each of you has already received two thousand dollars from the estate, which is a sizeable sum given Greenwood's limited resources. And the simple fact is—I was the only direct heir left to my father and mother. There was no other decision the court could have made."

"None of that changes the fact that when Grandfather Albert died, my father, who should have inherited a third of his estate, was left with nothing."

"Not exactly nothing, Harland. You seem to forget the four thousand dollars he and Aunt Sarah were both given, which was considered to be two-thirds of the estate's value and a good deal of money at the time. Uncle Oscar then spent his portion traveling in Europe and South America and never worked another day in his life. If you and Pamela were left with nothing, it is to your own father you should look rather than to mine."

A flash of anger appeared in the attorney's eyes, but for the present he kept his composure.

"I apologize,." said Richmond almost immediately. "I had no right to say that. But the fact remains that Aunt Sarah left Stuart and Margaret plenty from her share to see them through. You are well acquainted with the family finances, Harland—you know of Stuart's investments, and that he is worth more than the two of us together by a good deal."

"And you should know that to be as red a herring as ever swam in the North Sea!" snapped the attorney, his temper momentarily getting the better of him. "Need has no bearing on legalities in estate disposition."

"Of course not. I was not suggesting any legal precedent arising out of Aunt Sarah's and Stuart's very successful investments. But if *need* has no bearing, neither does mere *want*, which is all Stuart's claim is—"

"Look, Richmond," interrupted Harland curtly, "granted, the estate has been passed down intact to the eldest for three successive generations. But these are new times. This is not feudal England. This is nineteenth-century America. The point of Stuart's claim is that it is time to redress that inequity. That the younger heirs in each case were given some token settlements to insure their silence—"

"Good heavens, Harland . . . that is a completely erroneous construction to place on it!"

"They were paid off, Richmond. It is as simple as that."

"They were given sizeable legal settlements as their portion of the inheritance. There is a big difference."

"They were given a mere portion of the estate's value."

"An equitable portion."

"As you see it, perhaps."

"I grant you that. Certainly there are judgment calls that must be made in such situations. Grandfather Albert, as well as my father and my mother, and I would have to include myself along with them—we all had to make judgments of what we considered fair. Grandmother Zena was already dead when Grandfather Albert died. So he made financial provision for your father and Aunt Sarah. My mother was still living when my father knew he was dying, so he left Greenwood to her, and she in turn assumed that it was the right and fair thing that it be left to me since I was the only direct heir."

"She would have been better to have trusted in the law, and allowed me as her attorney to make those determinations."

"So that you could split up Greenwood, or sell off portions, and make it impossible for it to continue as a viable plantation?"

"If such became necessary."

"That is exactly why she did not, and why Grandfather Albert and my father assured that the plantation was kept in one piece as well. A family farm, or business of any kind, requires substantial assets to be able to produce a sustainable income. You know that, Harland. You have studied business as well as law. You are well enough aware of the economics of land use and production. One hundred and ninety acres is not a large plantation. Greenwood is a very modest-sized operation—"

"You are omitting the sixty acres of the Brown tract."

"A good deal of that is forested and hilly. Only about twenty or so is arable, that portion Mr. Brown cultivated himself."

"Some of the choicest land in Virginia. It would fetch a tidy price."

"Perhaps. But I doubt it is any different than most of the land surrounding it. Mr. Brown was simply a genius in making crops grow. He understood things most farmers have no inkling of. He had instincts of what to grow, and when, and on which parcels, and what the weather patterns would be ahead of time."

"There are some who say that his powers were supernatural, and not of the heavenly variety. They say his ghost haunts the land."

"You can't believe that. He had his peculiarities, I will admit. But he knew the land—that's why he was able to make it produce. Neither my father nor I have had any more success with crops there than anywhere else throughout Greenwood. The larger issue involved is that my father did not consider the Brown land ours. He always hoped Brown would return."

"All of which is beside the point . . . which is that all of those two hundred forty acres might not rightfully belong to you—and I am not referring to Mr. Brown—and that it may be necessary to sell some of it to meet your family obligations."

"It is easy for you to recommend such drastic measures—you have another career. But as I said earlier, Harland, Greenwood is the only livelihood Carolyn and I possess. We have nothing else."

The attorney shrugged. He was unmoved by the argument.

"To survive," Richmond went on, "a working plantation needs a certain amount of acreage . . . a hundred twenty, a hundred fifty acres minimum. Split it into pieces and none of the smaller parcels could sustain themselves. Cattle and other animals need land. Crops need to be rotated, and there needs be sufficient leeway that if one crop fails in a given year, the harvest of another will make up the difference. And before you say that I am being unfair, remember that I was not the eldest. I never planned to inherit Greenwood. All five of us knew when we were growing up—you and I and Pam and Peggy and Stuart—that one day Clifford would be its owner. The fact that Grandfather Albert made provision for Aunt Sarah and Uncle Oscar too, as I have attempted to do myself toward the rest of you—I think that speaks of equitability in the arrangement, while recognizing the necessity to keep the land intact, as well as recognizing how much work is involved in the operation of such a plantation."

Harland listened dispassionately, obviously bored and unpersuaded by his cousin's arguments, and only waiting for him to conclude his speech so that he could get on with it.

"You know as well as the rest of us, Richmond," Harland went on, "that Greenwood was a family estate back then. It should have been split between Grandfather Albert, my father, and Aunt Sarah, years ago. Stuart's suit attempts to address that imbalance now. Since you possess the land, and as your mother did not see fit to split it between us all at her death, that obligation naturally falls to you."

"Is that the gist of it—that you want the estate actually *split* between all five of us?" said Richmond, unable to conceal his astonishment. "I had no idea."

His cousin did not reply.

"To split up the land would doom Greenwood," Richmond said in a soft voice, sitting as one stunned. He knew that his four cousins expected more from his mother's estate. They had discussed the matter any number of times over the course of the past two years. But he had not dreamed Stuart's lawsuit would go so far.

"I will have to talk the matter over with Carolyn," he sighed at length.

"I need hardly remind you, Richmond," rejoined his cousin, "that she has nothing to do with it. This is strictly a matter between direct Davidson heirs."

For an instant it was now the elder Davidson's eyes that flashed. "Carolyn has everything to do with it," he said. "Not only does Greenwood belong equally to her as it does me, she is also the one who will help me decide how to respond to this . . . this news of what Stuart expects."

"There is really no decision to be made. If you do not agree, Stuart insists that he is prepared to continue with formal proceedings against Greenwood."

"He could not hope to be successful. Surely as his attorney, you realize that."

"He has sought other legal counsel as well. He has been assured that a formidable case will be mounted against you."

When Richmond Davidson boarded the train an hour later to

continue on to Greenwood, the documents of the lawsuit folded inside his coat pocket, his brain was numb. He could think nothing but that his peaceful world had suddenly crumbled around him.

Carolyn was furious at the news.

"They have no right to make such demands!" she said angrily, her emerald eyes flashing. "And after you already gave them each two thousand dollars—you didn't *have* to do that. I thought you were being overly generous back then . . . but this!"

"Harland does have a legitimate point," said Richmond quietly. His spirit had calmed and collected itself as he had attempted to pray and gain a higher perspective during the final portion of his train ride home. "You and I do hold title to the entirety of the land."

"Which is exactly as your father and mother wanted it," rejoined Carolyn. "After Clifford's death you were their only son. Who else should their property go to?"

"But perhaps Harland is right, and Grandfather Albert should have—"

"Oh, Richmond!" interrupted Carolyn. "You can be so infuriatingly understanding and generous at times. You've told me yourself that your uncle Oscar was a wastrel. The fact that he squandered Harland's and Pamela's inheritance gives Harland no right to come to you for a handout. Besides, I'm sure he's financially better off than we are. We know Stuart is! Why do you always insist on seeing things from the other person's point of view . . . and placing it above your own?"

"Isn't that what we're supposed to do?" he said, glancing at his wife with a gentle smile.

"I suppose. But this upsets me. They're only threatening to contest the will because they know you won't fight back."

"I can fight well enough if I am sure of the cause, and know it is right and just. But I am very reluctant to fight for myself."

"Sometimes I wish you would. I hate it when people take advantage of you."

"I confess I do not care much for it myself. It is never pleasant. But we are called to walk the low road, Carolyn, not to defend ourselves or fight for our rights."

"I know, I know . . . why do you always have to be right?"

She leaned over and kissed him affectionately. "It makes me angry, but that's why I love you, because of the man you are. Still, you must know that you *could* fight this in court, and win."

"Of course," he sighed. "Stuart's claim has no legal leg to stand on as I see it. I am surprised he has the gall to try it. If there was ever going to be a split such as Harland proposes, it should have come from Grandfather Albert. Once Greenwood passed into my father's hands, it seems that the dissolution was permanent. For several cousins to come back now, a generation later . . . it does seem a little presumptuous."

"Which is why I say again—they would have no case in court."

"I am sure you are right. In any event, we shall have to ask God what he wants us to do. If he wants me to fight and tell them that their request is not of the truth and that they need to repent of greedy motives, I will. But I find that is rarely God's way. We are rarely called upon to say such things when we are personally involved ourselves."

"But it's so unfair!" said Carolyn, her hackles rising again.

"Finances in families of means can be complex and subject to many a heated quarrel," rejoined Richmond. "This is certainly not the first time money has come between family members. You and I simply have to keep ourselves from being drawn into the fray, keep our own motives pure, and then find a way to walk through this quagmire as God's man and woman."

Carolyn gradually calmed. "How much *is* Greenwood worth?" she asked at length.

"Hmm, I don't know . . . that's a good question," replied her husband. "It might be worth thirty or forty thousand. Let's see . . . the house is probably worth five, the land fifteen or twenty thousand, possibly more, and the Brown tract ten. I don't know. The value of our slaves, if we were to sell them all at the slave market in Richmond, might bring six or eight thousand, maybe ten. We would never do that and I don't consider them in financial terms at all, but I'm sure Harland is thinking of our assets in such a way. To tell you the truth, Carolyn, I have no idea what Greenwood is worth. You don't just sell a plantation like this. You have to have a buyer. Without a buyer, it's worth nothing."

"You're *not* thinking of selling . . . are you?"

"Of course not. That wouldn't be fair to Cynthia and Seth and Thomas. It wouldn't be fair to my father either . . . or to you. Nor would it be right. I'm not prepared to go that far. There are principles involved beyond financial considerations."

"Good!" she said with a sigh of relief. "For a moment you had me worried."

She leaned her head against his shoulder where they sat on the divan. Richmond stretched his arm around her and they sat for a long time in silence.

The money was not really such a paramount concern. They would get by. God would take care of them. Greenwood was his, not theirs. Most importantly, they had each other. That was worth any ten estates twice the size of Greenwood.

"I don't want to talk about cousin Harland or any of the rest of them anymore," said Carolyn at length. "Tell me about your trip to Boston. What was the symposium like? And did you have the chance to talk to Dr. Wingate?"

"I did," replied her husband. "But first let me tell you about some interesting people I met."

Eleven

*T*wo months passed, during which most of Richmond Davidson's waking thoughts dwelt in some fashion on the political decision before him.

Though he had never before considered becoming politically active as his father and grandfather had been, now that such a potentiality—and at such a high level—had suddenly crossed his path, he found himself drawn toward it in ways he would never have expected. He could not deny that it would offer him an opportunity granted to very few—to make a difference in the world.

How could he not seriously consider it? He had been offered something many men covet but can never hope to achieve. Such a chance would probably never come again. The part of his inward being that reasoned thus wanted to cast caution to the wind, answer the summons with an enthusiastic, "Yes!" and begin making plans immediately for what he might accomplish.

Another side of him, however, confronted an entirely different set of questions:

Was it the *right* thing . . . right for him? Was he temperamentally and spiritually suited for it? Was the political world one in which he could feel comfortable? Did he really want to leave the peaceful surroundings of Greenwood? How would it affect his family? Most importantly, was it what God wanted him to do?

So it went—the two sides within himself each posing difficult questions to the other . . . with no indication on the horizon which of the two would win out in the end.

Carolyn's response surprised him as much as did his own. He had expected her to be against it, yet found her pushing him forward with enthusiasm.

"There are enormous issues on the horizon," she had said. "The country may need you. . . . Virginia may need you."

Richmond nodded. "I realize that is a possibility," he said. "It sounds exciting. Just imagine—running for national office, possibly even the vice presidency. What man wouldn't jump at such an opportunity? If you had asked me six months ago about running for office, I would have laughed. Yet now the idea excites me. It is the thrill of a great challenge."

"It sounds like you are leaning toward accepting their offer."

"I wouldn't say that exactly. It is only that I see that it *may* be something God wants me to do. On the other side of it, I have always felt that the Christian's true calling is *not* to change the world through politics, but in more personal ways. It is the distinction of being *in* the world but not *of* it. Politics, it seems to me, represents the ultimate in being of the world."

"But you say you feel drawn to accept their offer?"

Richmond nodded. "It is a dichotomy, I admit. Is it merely the pride of manhood desiring to be looked upon as someone of importance, or is it truly something I am supposed to do?"

"You are surely not being influenced by pride," said Carolyn, as if the idea was ridiculous, "or by wanting to be important."

"No man is immune from pride, Carolyn. It can rear its head in a thousand ways. There are certain things all men feel. I am no exception. To hold power over other men is one of the great snares of history. I must walk very carefully."

"Of course. But that argues in favor of your acceptance all the more."

"How so?"

"Because men like you, who are aware of its pitfalls, are needed in politics far more than those who do not see the dangers of pride."

"Ah, yes . . . I see your point. Perhaps you are right. But I have never felt that politics was God's preferred method for effecting change and good in the world. Jesus was not interested in politics, why should I be? Obedience can only be lived personally, not nationally."

"There are Christian men in politics."

"Of course. But I would say that they are involved in politics as honorable citizens, not as Christians. If I choose to say yes to this offer, I would agree as a citizen trying to do good, not as a Christian trying to carry out Christ's commission through what is essentially a worldly institution. The former, in my opinion, is a legitimate role for a Christian to occupy, while the latter I feel is an impossibility."

"I had not thought of that distinction before," said Carolyn.

"The Lord's commission is to make disciples. That cannot be accomplished through worldly means, politics included. Though many nations have tried, like the Romans in the fourth century and the Russians in the tenth, spirituality cannot be legislated. As both the emperor and the tsar discovered, there is no such thing as a so-called *Christian nation.* What I have to decide is whether to run for office as a *citizen* who happens to be a Christian."

"In that case, then," said Carolyn, "I think you should say yes. I see no conflict at all. Your wisdom and compassion would be so valuable for our state in what are bound to be difficult times ahead. Your presence in the Senate could mean nothing but good for the whole country."

Richmond laughed. "I am surprised to hear you talk so! I thought you would be apprehensive about the change my running for the Senate would bring to us, to our family, to the life we have here."

"Of course I am concerned," said Carolyn. "But you could do so much good. It would hardly be fair for me to keep you all to myself if the country beckons."

"Have you considered the implications to *you* if I accept? Do you want to move to Washington and find yourself in the thick of the social vortex as a senator's wife?"

"Ugh . . . no!" laughed Carolyn. "Couldn't you just go by yourself?"

"And be away from you six or nine months of the year—not a chance!"

"If God is truly calling you to this, we will both have to make whatever sacrifices are necessary. I am certainly not eager to leave Greenwood. But we can adjust. Times change. Maybe we have to change too."

"Don't start packing yet," laughed Richmond. "I am far from convinced that God *is* calling me to it. As much as the *citizen* half of me wants to jump at it, my *Christian* self carries the tie-breaking vote."

"When do you have to give them an answer?"

"They didn't set a deadline. The election is over a year away. There is no hurry. I just have to do the right thing. I have to choose between the good that I can do here in my own small sphere of influence, and the good that I might be able to do in Washington. Does God want me to widen my sphere? Or are the urgings I feel in that direction merely the urgings of men?"

"Why do you say that?"

"It was obvious from the meeting that they hadn't selected me because of my wisdom and compassion, as you say, but rather for political reasons—to advance their own political agenda."

"What agenda specifically?"

"That of the South—making sure that slavery survives and that the interests of the South are not swallowed up by Northern antislavery interests."

"*Could* you promote the interests of the South?"

"To an extent, of course. I am a loyal Virginian. But how far I could do so . . . who can answer such questions in advance? I could tell that they were doing their best to appeal to my pride. So another question I ask myself is whether it would be dishonest of me to pursue it, knowing that my motives would be different from theirs. No doubt they would expect me to be a mere puppet for their aims, and yet I would have to follow my conscience."

"Once in Washington, you would *have* to follow your conscience. I cannot see how they could expect otherwise."

"I don't know," said Richmond. "If I were to go against the expectations of the very men who put me in the Senate, they would not be pleased. I would be assured of being ousted after a single term."

"What is wrong with that?"

"Maybe nothing, but why not just avoid such a conflict altogether and say no from the outset? How honest am I being with them if I consider their political aims against my conscience?"

"Are their pro-Southern interests in conflict with your conscience?"

"I don't know. Probably not yet. But what if that situation arose in the future?"

"You don't know that it would."

"You're right. But I do know that they don't care about me as a man, and about what I believe and stand for. They are only looking to advance the pro-slavery interests of the South. I am fairly certain that they would expect to dictate my every move."

"Could you be comfortable with that?"

"I am not sure. In routine matters, of course. In larger matters that might come up . . . there again is the matter of my conscience, as well as what role Senator Hoyt, as Virginia's senior senator, would occupy in the whole thing."

It fell silent for a few moments.

"It is a complex decision," said Carolyn at length. "I think my inclination is still that you should do it. The world needs more voices like yours to be heard."

"I agree," nodded Richmond. "But does politics represent the best means to be heard? It is certainly the most visible podium from which to speak. But might God have another and better—less visible perhaps—means for me to convey his truth? I don't have the answer. But that seems to be the pivotal question before me."

Twelve

*H*igh summer came to Virginia. The sun beat down, humid heat rose from the fields, and sweat dripped from the bare chests, backs, and foreheads of slaves throughout the South as they dug and tilled and hoed and reaped and gathered in endless fields of tobacco and cotton that made the largest of landowners wealthy. Whether their taskmasters were kind or cruel, the fields were hot. The work was long. The life was tedious. And none could envision an end to such a system where men of one color considered it honorable before God to own men and women of another race, and to do with them as they wished.

But there were men in the midst of this evil whose consciences had begun to stir. Times were changing, though all such change must advance one individual at a time.

Whenever truth begins to emerge onto a higher plane, there are those who close their eyes to the wonder of its possibilities. Strange to tell, many prefer a dead conscience to a live obedience. They will fight to the death to preserve an old order with self-will at the helm, or to prop up a stale theology where narrow dogma provides the ruling dictum. All God's highest principles are wide-embracing truths, however, not constricting ones, as all hearts that love Fatherhood above the traditions of their elders must recognize before the light of eternity breaks at last upon them.

When the consciences of enough men and women come awake, the history of nations groans and trembles toward higher realms of decency and freedom. Yet it does not do so without conflict. The conflict of such an awakening of decency was even now on the horizon for this, one of the world's youngest nations—a clash that would test whether its foundational pillars of freedom would endure . . . or crumble.

Richmond Davidson knew that it was finally time to tell his neighbor, Denton Beaumont, about the meeting in North Carolina at the estate of Congressman Hargrove. He had waited far too long. He had not wanted to cloud his own decision with his friend's potential reaction. Now that his mind was made up, he was ready to face Denton. But he was not looking forward to the exchange.

Midway through one hot day in late June, he mounted his favorite mare, a white four-year-old Shagya Arabian of fifteen hands whom he called Moonwhite, for she had been born in the middle of the night of a full moon. He was in no hurry. He rode first northward from the stables, across the ridge toward that portion of his land that had once belonged to Mr. Brown, then circled back south, climbing the ridge again from a northerly direction, circling around below Harper's Peak, then moving eastward toward Oakbriar.

His mood on this day suited itself to a long ride. He knew Denton would not be pleased with what he had to tell him. That, along with reminders of the offer that had been made and what he had decided to do about it, made him thoughtful about many things.

As he went, he reflected on these byways he and his brother and neighbor had explored together. He had not consciously thought of it before, yet as he rode, many memories returned to him of the year or two prior to his leaving to study at Oxford. For the first time he saw that he had already begun to drift apart from the other two. Perhaps he and Denton had never really had as much in common as he once thought. It was not just the fact that he was younger. If anything, the slight differences in their years should have vanished as they grew older. That it did not revealed deeper divisions between them than mere age. The realization made the memories bittersweet and increased all the more today's reluctance to tell his friend what had transpired.

Richmond Davidson rarely set aside specific seasons for prayer. His communion with his Father was unstructured and did not often form itself into specifically worded petitions. But that did not mean he was not a man of prayer. Quite the contrary. He brought God *into* every-thing, made the unspoken *What do you think about this, Lord?* the guid-ing principle to lead his mind wherever it went. Beneath the surface of active conscious thought, the continual prayer, *God, infuse me with your perspective, your outlook, your purpose, and your desire for me,* informed his every waking moment. His was an outlook that sought not its own will in the affairs of his life, but the will of Another.

Deep spiritual and mental activity had churned below the surface of the preceding months as Richmond wrestled with his decision on many levels. It only complicated matters that he and Carolyn had taken different points of view. They did not disagree often, and they never did so with vehemence. Yet his respect for his wife's perspectives made going against them all the more difficult. At long last he had finally made up his mind just the night before.

By the time he descended the northeast slope of the ridge and began to clear the trees and move down into cultivated fields and pastureland, the roofs of Oakbriar at last materializing in the distance, he was calm, at peace both with his decision and what lay ahead, and looking forward to the discovery of what God might have for him in new directions of life's adventure.

⟨⟩

As he rode into the precincts of the Beaumont plantation, yells and shouts coming from somewhere jarred harshly against the quietness within Richmond Davidson's spirit. Voices were raised in anger. He heard the crack of a whip followed by a cry of pain.

He dug his heels into his mare's sides and galloped toward the fray.

As he came into sight of the stables, he saw several of Beaumont's men standing in a semicircle watching some commotion in their midst. The plantation owner himself was in front of them, horsewhip in hand. The shouts Davidson heard came from the mouth of his friend.

"Get on your feet, you good for nothing—," Beaumont cried.

A violent sting from the leather whip came crashing down, and another terrified howl of pain burst out. At Beaumont's feet, a Negro knelt in the dirt, hands covering his face in desperation to keep the leather tongs from his eyes, bare back riddled with open, bloody wounds.

"Please, massa," he whimpered, "I's say nuffin no mo effen—"

Again the whip split the skin of the man's shoulders with all the force his owner could summon. This time the man's body shuddered, but he did not cry out, then at last slumped into the dirt, apparently unconscious.

Beaumont continued to whip fiercely at the lump of half-clothed humanity.

"Get up!" he cried. "Stand and face your punishment like a man! Get up, I tell you!"

Again and yet again the hard leather cracked down on the prostrate body. Even Beaumont's men, who had all made free enough use of the whip themselves, were finding their stomachs growing queasy at the sight, though none dared utter a word in protest. Beaumont's fury had risen to such a frenzy that he did not hear the horse ride up, nor see its rider swiftly dismount in a cloud of trailing dust and rush toward the scene.

He raised the whip again above his head to deliver another punishing blow. Suddenly he felt his arm arrested in midair. A strong grip took hold of his wrist and held it fast.

"For the love of God, Denton, stop!" cried a voice behind him. "The poor man is senseless!"

Beaumont spun around, yanking his wrist free. In the same motion he raised the leather against whatever interfering fool dared come between him and one of his slaves. He was about to strike when his flaming eyes came to rest on the face of his friend standing less than two feet from him.

He paused, eyes flashing, whip poised, breathing heavily.

"Denton . . . please," said Davidson in a calm voice and with expression—though worlds different at root—equal to Beaumont's in intensity. "You don't need to do this. There are other ways. Whatever he has done, surely you have punished him enough."

Having spoken, he now walked slowly around Beaumont, whose arm was still upraised, and knelt beside the slave who lay crumpled on the ground. The man had not moved a muscle throughout the last several blows.

Recovering himself, mortified to appear weak in front of his men, Beaumont's anger quickly boiled over again.

"With their kind, there are no other ways!" he yelled. "Now get out of my way, Richmond—this is none of your affair. If you don't have the stomach for it, go inside until I am done." He grabbed at Davidson's shoulder to restrain him.

Davidson stood and faced him but did not move aside. "Denton, please," he repeated in a yet quieter tone than before, "this man is unconscious. If you continue to whip him, he will die. Surely you don't want murder on your conscience."

"My conscience is my own affair!" shouted Beaumont. "As are my slaves! Now get out of the way, Richmond."

"I'm sorry, Denton . . . I will not let your whip touch that man again. I cannot let you kill him, as much for your sake as his."

"How dare you—," began Beaumont, raising his hand to strike his neighbor. But the cool gaze staring back at him somehow prevented it. The two men stood facing one another for several long, tense seconds.

The look in his friend's eye caused Beaumont to think twice about the advisability of bringing the leather down on him. His judgment was doubtless influenced by the fact that Richmond Davidson, though the youngest, had been the strongest of the three musketeers by the time they were teenagers, a fact Beaumont had just been reminded of by the pain in his wrist. Richmond, a year younger, stood four inches taller than Beaumont himself. Whatever chagrin he felt at being thus challenged and made to look the fool in the very sight of his own house, it would be far worse to be thrashed in an ill-advised dual of fists.

Slowly Beaumont lowered his arm and turned away in a wrath of impotence. The next instant Davidson was on the ground beside the unconscious man.

A few of the other slaves gathered around, while Beaumont's men stood aside. "Get me some cool water and a towel," ordered Davidson, glancing up at several of the black faces staring down at him. "Hurry!"

Within minutes, the man had begun to revive, though his injuries were severe. Some of the other slaves lifted him from the ground and carried him back to the shack that was his home.

Richmond rose. He glanced about but saw no sign of his neighbor, then walked toward the house.

Thirty minutes later, Denton Beaumont walked into the kitchen of his home where his wife and eldest son were seated with their guest, each sipping at glasses of cool tea. Beaumont's temper had moderated but he still wore a gloomy countenance as he sat down.

"Would you like something to drink, dear?" asked Lady Daphne.

"Get me a julep," he replied without expression.

"Wyatt here has just been telling me," said Richmond, trying to sound as upbeat as possible under the circumstances, "that you and he and Cameron shot a nine-pointer up near the peak last week."

"That's right," said Beaumont coldly.

"That must have been quite an adventure for little Cameron—how old is he now?"

"I'm twelve!" shouted a high-pitched voice, bounding into the room. "But I didn't get to shoot the buck," he went on enthusiastically. "Papa wouldn't let me hold the gun."

"There will be plenty of time for that when you get to be your brother's age," laughed Davidson. "And you, Wyatt—you've put on at least three inches since last time I saw you."

"Yes, sir," said the oldest of the three Beaumont children.

"And how is Cynthia?" asked Mrs. Beaumont as she set the mint julep down in front of her husband.

"Well, Lady Daphne," replied Richmond.

"Is she still sweet on that naval man I heard about?"

"Indeed she is. There has even been talk of marriage, though she just turned nineteen. Carolyn and I don't quite know what to make of it, though he is a very pleasant young man. Seth and Thomas hardly realize girls exist, while their sister is talking about being married. Girls do seem to mature sooner than boys, don't they? And your Veronica—I imagine she is growing fast as well?"

"She talks of nothing but having a beau," replied Lady Daphne. "You really must tell Carolyn and Cynthia to come for a visit before it is too late and they are all grown up and gone from us."

"I shall do so, indeed. What about you, Wyatt? Any young lady friends on the horizon of your life?"

"Not yet, Mr. Davidson," replied the sixteen year old.

"Well as I told Cameron about guns, there will be plenty of time later. Am I right, Lady Daphne?" he added with a smile to Beaumont's wife. "Girls and guns—both dangerous for young men if handled unwisely."

"I don't know if I care for your characterization of the fairer sex as dangerous, Richmond!"

Davidson laughed good-naturedly. "Perhaps I should reserve my cautions for my own sons!"

All the time they had been talking, Beaumont had been sipping moodily at his julep, not once glancing up nor showing the slightest interest in the conversation. A lull now fell around the table. Cameron scampered off and Davidson looked across at his friend.

"I came to talk to you about something, Denton," he said. "Perhaps this might be that opportunity for us to take a ride together."

"May I come with you?" asked Wyatt eagerly.

"I'm sorry, Wyatt," replied Davidson. "There are some important things I need to discuss with your father . . . political matters that would probably bore you anyway. But tell you what—I'll come back with Seth and Thomas one day this summer and we'll ride up to Harper's Peak together. I'll show you the stretch your father and I used to race."

Without speaking and obviously unmoved by the reminder of
happier times, Beaumont drained what remained in his glass, stood
up, and walked toward the door. Davidson rose also, and, after final
words of appreciation to Lady Daphne for her hospitality, followed
him outside.

The two Virginia landowners rode away from the white plantation
house of Oakbriar a few minutes later with considerably less verve
than had characterized their discussion of the joys of riding together as
they had envisioned them to Carolyn two and a half months earlier.
No words had been spoken since leaving the kitchen.

When they were well away from the last of the outbuildings, at last
Davidson ventured to bring up the topic he had come to discuss.

"There is something I need to talk with you about, Denton," he
began. "I'm sorry to have waited so long, but I wanted to have my
own mind made up before I—"

At last out of earshot of wife and children, his neighbor's
suppressed fury could hold itself back no longer.

"Don't you *ever* do something like that again, Richmond!" interrupted Beaumont, seething. "*My* slaves on *my* property are *my* business. If you forget it, by God next time I *will* take the whip to you!"

"I am very sorry, Denton," said Davidson. "I enjoyed that no more
than you did. But it was clear you had lost control. I believe the time
will come when you will thank me for what I did."

Beaumont did not reply, except to mutter an expletive or two under
his breath about how soon his neighbor might expect said word of
thanks, and under what conditions.

"All right, then," said Beaumont curtly, "get on with it. What do
you have to tell me?"

The sounds of their horses' hooves were for several seconds the only
reply that came to his question. As long as he had deliberated about
what to say, now that the moment had arrived, Richmond found
himself at a loss for words.

"As I said," he began at length, "I am sorry to have waited so long to tell you this, Denton. It has been especially difficult knowing of your own interest in politics. But there are some men who spoke to me a while back about the possibility of my running for Congress."

The unexpected words at last succeeded in helping Beaumont forget, for the moment, what had occurred back at his house. He turned and gaped at Davidson with a look of incredulity.

"You?" he said in a tone of disbelief. "I had no idea you had political aspirations."

"I don't. But as I say, there are certain men who approached me and expressed their desire to support my candidacy."

Beaumont's initial surprise quickly gave way to annoyance. "What men?" he asked.

Richmond had debated whether or not to divulge the men's names. But since all would likely come out in the end, he judged it best to hold nothing back.

"Frederick Trowbridge was the chief mover in the affair," he replied.

"What about Smith?" queried his neighbor.

"The senator is apparently stepping down. He plans to retire and is not seeking reelection." ·

Beaumont nodded, doing his best to hide his mortification at this humiliating news. He prided himself on knowing all there was to know about Virginia politics. To discover that his apolitical neighbor was privy to such an important development, while it had been kept from him by those in the know, added all the more insult to his sense of injury.

"I must say I am more than a little astonished," he said, trying not to divulge his chagrin. "Frederick and I are old friends. I can hardly imagine that he would stab me in the back like this. I am surprised at you too, Richmond. How could you betray me like this, after all we have been through together?"

"I am sorry, Denton. I certainly did not intend to betray you. That is why I have come to you now, so that you and I could talk about it like old friends."

"Friendship would not appear to count for much in politics," said Beaumont acridly.

"What do you mean?"

"Don't be a fool, Richmond—you know well enough what I mean."

"I . . . I'm sorry, Denton, but I don't."

"I have been laying the groundwork for a run of my own for years. Had I been apprised of Senator Smith's retirement, this would give me an ideal opportunity. Yet now I find you sneaking in and undermining all I have worked for."

"Denton, how can you say such a thing? I told you how it came about, that they—"

"You could have come to me sooner," interrupted Beaumont in rising vexation. "You could have declined their offer. You could have thrown your support behind me instead."

"That is exactly what I did, Denton. I brought your name up immediately and told them you were far more qualified than I. In all sincerity I still believe that."

Wondering if he had heard correctly, Beaumont sent a questioning glance toward his neighbor.

"And?" he said slowly.

"They continued to try to convince me to run myself."

"I take it they were successful."

"I felt I had a duty at least to pray the matter through in order to find out what God wanted me to do."

"Did you?" said Beaumont cynically.

"I think so."

"I thought as much. Your prayers hardly disguise your ambitions. I would respect you more, Richmond, if you simply told me you had decided to run for the seat you knew I had been eying myself."

Davidson smiled thinly. It was not for the relinquishment of worldly prestige that the words saddened him, but that after all these years his neighbor knew him so little.

"The result of my prayers, Denton," he said, "is that I have decided *not* to run."

Beaumont eyed Davidson for a moment, one eyebrow cocked upward.

"Do the others know?" he asked.

"I plan to write to Frederick this afternoon. I wanted to tell you before doing anything."

"Hmm . . . I see . . . well, I appreciate your consideration."

"So it would seem that the field is wide open for you to—," Davidson began.

He was interrupted by a bitter laugh. "You don't think after all this," said Beaumont, "that I would go crawling, cap in hand, to ask them to support me in *your* stead!"

He spat out the words with derision. There could be no mistaking his meaning.

"Believe me, Richmond," he went on, "when I go to Washington it will not be as second fiddle to the party's first selection."

"I only meant that if you do run, you can count on my support in any way I might be of assistance."

"I can manage just fine without any *more* of your assistance! In the future, I will thank you to keep out of my affairs and keep your so-called help to yourself."

Beaumont spun his horse around, lashed him viciously, and galloped back down the hill in the direction of Oakbriar.

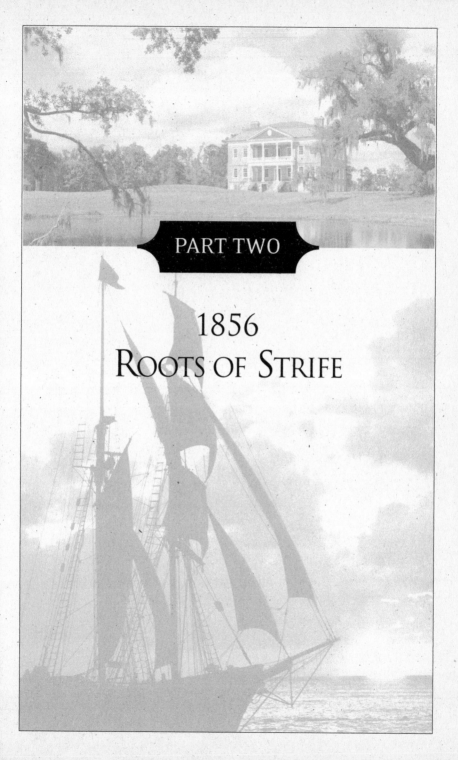

PART TWO

1856
ROOTS OF STRIFE

Thirteen

A thick, heavy mist from the nearby swamp had risen to meet the South Carolina December dusk as a large-framed black woman left the big house. The lantern bobbing in her hand sent uneven light bouncing along the path as she made her way toward the slave cabins about half a mile away.

The woman called Amaritta did not tend every birth on the plantation. But poor Lucindy had been so despondent ever since the loss of her husband that Mistress Crawford was afraid the birthing might kill her. So she sent the housekeeper along to make sure nothing went wrong. Lucindy was too young and too valuable to lose that way. Nine months before the master had insisted that Amaritta check on Lucindy almost daily, anxious to know the instant "the business was done" as he called it, so he could get Caleb Eaton on the block and gone. Now that the time had run its course, he would take out his wrath on every woman of the place if she died in childbirth.

The black midwife from the slave village had already been inside Lucindy's little shack for an hour when the housekeeper arrived. Even as Amaritta walked up the steps, another old black woman, one of the matriarchs of the slave community who helped hold together its family bonds, walked outside to meet her. The expression on her face did not bode well.

"Ah be too late . . . hit already come?" asked Amaritta.

"Dat it did," answered the woman, "'bout ten minutes ago—but hit ain't no man-chil'."

Amaritta shook her head. "Dat ain't good," she said. "Massa'll be parful upset by dat turn ob events."

"'Deed he will," assented the other. "He still got it out fo' Lucindy on account er Caleb."

"He's likely only leab her alone fo' two seasons at da mos' fo' he'll be wantin' ter put sum other man wif her ter git her wif chil' agin."

"Ah sure be glad dem days is dun gone fo' me," said the older woman, shaking her head.

"What we gwine do fo' po' Lucindy?" said the housekeeper. "We's got ter do sumfin."

"She ain't strong enuf fo' anuder baby dat soon, no how."

"We gots ter do what we can t' protec' her."

"Ah'm thinkin' dat she's be likely ter be gittin' real sick long 'bout six months from now," mused the matriarch.

Illuminated by the lantern, a knowing look passed between the two women in the night. A few silent nods followed.

"You know how it gits sumtime long 'bout den, wif nursin' da baby takin' all yo' strenf, an' how a woman gits weak an' sick, an' ain't much good fo' nuthin no how."

"Da massa, he'll be makin' me come down an' check when she's ready," said Amaritta.

"You kin check all right, an you's boun'ter fin' her in a bad way, I'm thinkin'. Yes, sir . . . I'm thinkin' dat it jus' might be a sickness dat'll keep her outta any man's bed fo' a good long spell."

Fourteen

*J*ames Waters had been looking forward to seeing his daughter for weeks.

He had enrolled her in boarding school the previous fall, thinking she needed more socialization with other girls. She was a young fifteen, and not as physically developed as many her age. She seemed to enjoy school at first. Recently, however, her letters had contained hints that made him wonder if things were going as well as before. That was one of the reasons for his visit in early February of 1856. He had not seen her since Christmas.

When he arrived at the Cambridge Boarding School for Young Ladies, he saw a troop of girls walking back from chapel toward the dining hall.

He was reminded of his own early years after his uncle brought him north and planted him in a boarding school not very different from this one. As hard as he had tried to separate himself from his roots, a stab of ethnic nostalgia suddenly swept over him. For the first time he wondered if he ought to tell Cherity. Not even Kathleen had known. But with his daughter's fascination with Indians and the West, it seemed only right that she know eventually.

He shook the thought from his brain. Whether he decided to tell her or not, he would not do so today. He returned his focus to the present and scanned the group of girls looking for his daughter. She was not among them.

He watched them go, then continued to the main building, where he found the headmistress in her office.

"Hello, Mr. Waters," she said as he entered.

"Miss Baird," he nodded with a smile, thinking to himself that her manner seemed a little cool. "I came to visit Cherity. I hope it is a convenient time for me to take her for a couple of hours—I did not see her with the other girls as they were coming across the yard a moment ago."

"No," replied the headmistress, "she was not among them."

"There's nothing wrong?" he asked in concern. "Is she ill?"

"No, Mr. Waters, she is not ill," replied Miss Baird. "But I am afraid there is something wrong."

"What is it?"

"I am afraid she is in detention, Mr. Waters. We have found it necessary to discipline her."

"*Discipline* her!" repeated the journalist in disbelief. "My Cherity . . . for what? She doesn't have a rebellious bone in her body."

"We find parents are often the last to know," said the woman with a hint of self-importance.

"Know what?" he asked, his perplexity mounting.

"Of the misbehavior of their children."

"Misbehavior? I can hardly believe it. Tell me please . . . what happened?"

"We found *this* in her room, Mr. Waters," she said in a tone to indicate that the damning evidence was all the justification needed for strict disciplinary action.

From a drawer in her desk, she removed a small book and handed it across to the concerned father. He took it, then broke out in a relieved smile.

"Ah . . . Sarah Sacks!" he said. "I'm glad to see it is nothing serious."

"I take it you find your daughter's infraction amusing?" said the headmistress, drawing herself up slightly in her chair.

"Surely you don't mean . . . she's not being disciplined for *this*?"

"It is a dime novel."

"I certainly see nothing sinister in it. Don't you find it humorous?"

"I do not."

"It is just a book," chuckled Waters.

"And one that is not on our approved book list."

"Is she not keeping up with the rest of her reading?"

"No, she has done all her assignments."

"Then what is wrong with reading about the West in her free time?"

"We do not encourage such fancies of imagination."

"What do you encourage instead?"

"That our young ladies learn sophistication," replied the woman. "Your daughter is extremely unladylike and this is the evidence of it. I thought that was your reason for sending her here, so that she could learn to be a lady."

"Of course, but not necessarily all at once, and not at the expense of reading and pursuing her own interests, for heaven's sake."

"If she continually fills her mind with . . . with such trash as that, her attention will be distracted from the sort of behavior we try to instill here."

"She is only fifteen. There is plenty of time. I surely don't see how reading such as this will prevent her from maturing."

"Perhaps you do not understand young women as I do, Mr. Waters."

"In any event, I presume you will have no objection to my visiting with her. You can carry out the remainder of her incarceration," he added with a smile, though one that revealed a hint of annoyance, "later."

Waters found his daughter in her room.

"Daddy!" she exclaimed after opening the door to his knock. "I thought you would never get here!"

"Yes, I just came from Miss Baird," he said laughing. "She told me of your many sins!"

"She's so stuffy! They're all so stuffy. They want us to act all grown-up. You should see some of the girls—trying to pretend they're in their twenties. I hate it."

"So what do you do?"

"I do my schoolwork, but act however I want to act, without trying to pretend to be something I'm not."

"Good girl! Why don't we get out of here and go for a ride and have a talk?"

"Will Miss Baird let me?"

"I told her you could complete your punishment for your unlady-like behavior after we get back," said her father with a smile.

"To be honest, Daddy, I don't really mind so much. It gives me more time to read."

"But she took your book."

"Oh, Daddy, I have at least ten more I brought with me. Look!"

She pulled a box out from under her bed, revealing a stack of biographies and adventure stories.

"You are a naughty one!" laughed Waters. "Maybe you are more a rebel than I realized—let's go!"

A few minutes later they were out together in the spring air.

"Do you dislike it here, Cherity?" asked Waters in a more serious tone as they climbed into his rented buggy and rode away from the school. "It doesn't sound like . . ." He let his sentence go uncompleted.

"I like some of the girls. I have a few friends. It's not really so bad."

"They don't think you're ladylike enough."

"Who cares what they think!" she giggled.

"You can come home any time you want."

"I want to finish the year out at least."

"And next year?"

"I don't know. Maybe I'll have to think about that. We can talk about it when summer comes."

"What would you think of us taking a trip as soon as the term is done?" asked Waters.

"Where—to Kansas!" exclaimed Cherity excitedly.

"I'm afraid not," replied her father. "Things are heating up there so much over the slavery issue that it's becoming downright dangerous. I wouldn't think of taking you out West now."

"Where, then?"

"I thought we might go down to see Mary and her new baby. You are an aunt now, you know . . . Aunt Cherity."

"Oh, Daddy, that makes me sound so old. I'm just a girl."

"You'd better get used to it. That's what Mary's little boy will call you someday."

Fifteen

$\mathcal{N}$early a year had passed since Richmond Davidson's visit to Boston. The fields of Greenwood again lay fallow for the winter to do its invisible work in making them ready for the approaching year's ploughing and sowing, growing and reaping.

Yet the brain of the Virginian had been anything but fallow. The seeds that had been planted, both in North Carolina and in Boston, had germinated in the fertile soil of his heart. Now the shoots sent out from those seeds were growing in many directions he could no longer ignore.

Shortly after his tense ride and discussion with Denton Beaumont, he had written to Frederick Trowbridge and, with kind regards and sincere thanks for their consideration, said that it was his decision to decline their offer to make him a candidate for a seat in the U.S. Senate. The matters of his plantation, his family, and his personal life, he said, required a more complete level of his attention than would be possible should a Senate bid prove successful. Again he recommended his friend and neighbor Denton Beaumont for their consideration.

He heard nothing in reply, nor was he aware of the level of annoyance his declining the offer aroused. There were those who had gone to considerable trouble to gather so select and impressive a roster with which to welcome Richmond Davidson into the upper echelons of Virginia's political elite. It never entered their considerations that he might actually decline. They took his doing so as a personal affront upon all those who had been present at the meeting where the offer was presented. Did the man not realize how things stood: They were not merely *asking* him if he was interested . . . they were *telling* him that he had been chosen. It was his duty to accept, for the sake of Virginia and the South.

Frederick Trowbridge tried to take the news as calmly as possible, for he had always considered Richmond a friend. Jefferson Davis, however, was furious. The secretary of war vented his wrath on whoever would listen, especially on Trowbridge, since it had been his idea in the first place, declaring that if he had anything to do with it, Richmond Davidson would never find himself with an opportunity to hold public office again.

All this, however, took place beyond the ken of Davidson himself, who remained content with his decision. He did not receive a reply to his letter from Trowbridge or from any of the others. Nor had he again seen his neighbor after their chilly parting.

In the early months of 1856, news reached him that an aging former congressman from Virginia by the name of Everett had been named as the senatorial candidate put forward and favored by the political hierarchy. Why his friend had been passed over, Richmond Davidson had no idea.

But his mind dwelt little on such matters. Once his own decision was made, he put politics behind him as much as was possible. His thoughts, rather, continued to focus more and more on the events of his two days in Boston the previous spring. Most of the speakers, on both sides of the issue, had recited the same arguments that were now familiar to most serious, thinking persons in the country. It seemed to Richmond that both sides sought more to justify existing positions than discover overspreading truth that would lead the nation out of the quagmire of increasing conflict. What had lodged most deeply in Richmond's mind, however, was the statement made by his onetime acquaintance Wingate.

"This matter, as is true of all matters of an ethical nature," the English theologian had said, "concerns far higher truths than what might be allowed technically by the letter of the law. Certainly, the *letter* of imperfect law gives rise to the justifications of many actions and positions that do not reflect God's deepest intent. Jesus himself spoke of divorce in such a way, indicating that while it may in fact be *allowed* by the law's letter, it was yet an abomination in God's sight and had not been intended by God from the beginning.

"We observe precisely this dichotomy between God's original intent and the lesser 'allowances' that human sin and human law have made inevitable, even sometimes necessary, in a multitude of institutions and human ethical dilemmas," Wingate had continued. "Whenever justification is one's objective, it is not difficult to find ample basis for such no matter what one's position. The politics of your nation, and the fundamental principle of what you call the right of states, may well validate the institution of slavery according to your Constitution and the law of your land. That is not for me to say one way or another, especially as I am a mere observer to your unique constitutional system. In like manner, the Bible itself would seem to justify and validate opposing sides of many issues, divorce and slavery certainly among them. However, I would ask in all seriousness and sincerity, are there *higher* considerations to be weighed? And what, I would ask further, is the highest such consideration of all?

"So then," he had concluded, "for the true Christian individual—seeking not his own will but God's will, seeking not mere justification for a position according to human reasoning or constitutional analysis, but seeking God's highest original intent, seeking not what a law may *allow* but what it may *intend* at its foundation—the question becomes, not a matter of what may be justified, even allowed in Scripture or allowed by your Constitution or by law . . . but what is *right*?

"What did God purpose from the beginning? Ignoring the many arguments with which we are familiar and which we have heard again this evening, I believe the question reduces to a far simpler equation of truth: *What is right?* What did God *intend* when he created man in his image?

"Any moral or ethical dilemma can be resolved, in my view, by examining it prayerfully and personally through just this lens—the lens of God's eternal and perfect *intent*. When decisions are called for, though they may involve thorny conundrums of great division and debate, inquiring what is God's intent will clarify the most fundamental issues of any matter. Then every man and every woman must live out their own answers to those questions as God gives them the strength and courage to do so."

Wingate's talk had so lodged in his mind that he had written to his new acquaintance James Waters to obtain as much of it in writing as the journalist had been able to transcribe. As he read and pondered the quotations Waters had sent, Richmond Davidson found himself more and more unsettled. He was not so much convicted of wrongdoing in the matter of ownership of slaves, but disturbed that he had not brought the question of God's eternal purpose into his considerations. Why had he found it so comfortable to accept the status quo simply because he was a Southerner and because slaves had been part of Greenwood as long as he had been alive—and for years before that? Why had he accepted it without question? Why had God's design and intent not risen to prod him toward a more prayerful reflection of his own position?

Suddenly such questions began to loom large in his consciousness.

He had always been a compassionate man to his slaves. He had grown up in the system. After inheriting the plantation, he had thought of nothing more than continuing his father's practices while being as kind as possible to those under his charge. He and Carolyn had gradually tried to improve the living conditions and skills of their slaves. He had installed a water pump for their cabins. He made sure their food and clothing allotment was more than adequate. He did not work them harder than he was willing to work himself alongside them, which he often did. He had no overseer, but saw to everything himself. As his sons grew into teenagers, he planned to add more and more supervisory duties to their shoulders as well. Seth had recently turned sixteen and Richmond had begun bringing him into more specific positions of oversight. The blacks all thought the world of Seth for he treated them with equality and respect. In spite of laws prohibiting the teaching of slaves, he and Carolyn provided a few simple books and what other small luxuries lay in their power to give them. Carolyn taught the women about childcare and hygiene. She not only read aloud from the Bible and taught them how to apply its teachings, she met privately with those who desired it and gave reading lessons in hopes that one day they could read the Bible for themselves. Richmond knew her doing so was against Virginia law, and that presumably she could have been arrested for it.*But they had discussed it, and concluded that they must obey God's law of love and justice above man's law, which was clearly unjust. If they were punished by man, then so be it.†

Their blacks may technically have been *slaves*, yet in a very real sense, Richmond and Carolyn Davidson considered them part of their extended family.

All these measures, however, did not address the fundamental question precipitated by his trip to Boston—the question of freedom.

Wingate's talk was not the worst of it. Nothing at the symposium had jolted him so deeply as the stunned expression of shock and disbelief in James Waters' voice when he exclaimed, as they rode through the chilly night together, *"You own slaves!"*

Waters' reaction had returned to him many times since, forcing him to reconsider the implications of his position in a completely new way.

How could a Northerner, Richmond thought, *who did not even*

---

*"The South never got over Nat Turner. He made very clear what the form of slave revolt would be—wholesale murder of white people. . . . Slave owners and the legislatures of slave states took elaborate precautions to avoid another Nat Turner. The whole system making the Negroes inferior . . . while rooted in racism, also served to forestall a revolt by diminishing the slave's will to resist. The law forbidding the teaching and reading and writing of slaves was intended both to prevent slaves from reading abolitionist literature or the Bible, which might inflame a desire for liberty, and to make communication between slaves difficult. The restrictions on slave assemblies and travel were intended to make a large-scale conspiracy impossible. The harshness and injustice of punishment inflicted on slave wrongdoing was calculated to break the spirit of any would-be leader and provide an example to possible followers. Planters made an effort to spot potential leaders and either watch them carefully or sell them into hard labor. An informal system was organized. Owners courted pet or privileged salves who would inform on activites in the slave quarters.

"The South sought to discourage insurrection by making freedom as undesirable as possible. There were 250,000 free Negroes in the South in 1860, but . . . 'the distinction between slaves and free Negroes had diminished to a point that in some instances it was hardly discernible. . . .'

"Every effort was made to keep the slave from being freed or from keeping freedom after winning it. The free Negro lived in constant fear of being kidnapped back into slavery. . . . The free Negro was restricted at every turn."—Robert Liston, *Slavery in America.* New York: McGraw-Hill, 1970, pp. 108–09.

†An 1848 Virginia statue made teaching salves to read or write illegal. In 1853, Mrs. Douglass of Norfolk began teaching black children to read and write. She was arrested and sentenced to a month in jail.

acknowledge God, view slavery as an abomination, while he himself, a professing Christian, had never examined its deeper implications, or even inquired of God what might be his mind on the matter?

Something was wrong. Wingate's words would not leave him: *What is right? What did God intend from the beginning?*

Did God intend for one human being to own another? That was the question on which everything hinged.

Sixteen

*P*hoebe Shaw was not able to turn away the attentions of Elias Slade forever, nor did she want to. She was at that age where vulnerability and stupidity combine, causing the attentions of a man older than herself to outweigh consideration of a man's character obvious to everyone else. It was not long before Phoebe no longer sat at the Bible readings beside her mother but instead disappeared when the day's work was done, often not to be seen again until after dark.

Everyone in the slave village knew she was with Elias Slade. But none dared say a word. By now every man, woman, and child among the Davidson's slaves had more than good reason to fear Slade. Some said he hid a knife under his bed. No one doubted he would use it if provoked. If Phoebe couldn't see what kind of man he was, then she deserved whatever trouble he brought her.

And it came soon enough. By the middle of March it was clear enough that Phoebe Shaw was in a family way. She was growing plumper by the week and no one doubted that Elias Slade was the cause of it. Now that the deed was done, he showed less interest in her. Phoebe became sullen and downcast, as much from guilt as from the shame of giving herself to such a man. Though none of the other slaves could be said to shun her, neither did they go out of their way to show her kindness. The friends of her childhood avoided her.

Nancy was beside herself with grief and anger, toward both her

daughter and toward the father of the child growing inside her. Thus
far she had been able to prevent Malachi from confronting Elias, but
how long she could do so was questionable. With the righteous anger
of a protective father, he seethed with silent fury that would have
exacted its revenge on Slade at first opportunity. The other men
would gladly have helped him. Together they might have overpowered
the big man and slit his throat. But every man of them knew that the
master abhorred violence. No matter what Slade had done, they loved
their master too much to incur his wrath by bringing the cloud of
murder over Greenwood.

So they continued to avoid him, and Slade kept silent, while
Phoebe and Nancy took to crying themselves to sleep.

Because of Phoebe's absence from the readings and Nancy's reluctance to tell her the cause, it was not until after it was no longer possible to keep it a secret, that Carolyn learned of the girl's condition. She
went straight to the Shaws' cabin, where she found Nancy alone.

"Nancy," said Carolyn, "I just heard. Is it true?"

The black mother's eyes filled with tears that were all the answer
Carolyn needed. She walked across the floor and took Nancy in her
arms.

"Oh, Miz Dab'son, I knowed I shud tell you," sobbed Nancy. "But
I jes' din't hab da heart. I's feard ob what you an' massa'd think."

"Don't say another word, Nancy," said Carolyn gently. "We will
think nothing ill of you, I promise."

"I's afeard massa'd sen' my Phoebe away."

"Don't worry about a thing, Nancy. I told you, there is nothing to
worry about from the master or me. But I have to know who it was,
Nancy. You know how my husband and I feel about these things?"

"Yes'm."

"Who was it, Nancy?"

Nancy turned away and stared down at the ground.

"Was it Elias Slade?"

"Yes'm," said Nancy, nodding slowly. "I don' know what ter
do—how's my Phoebe gwine tell her young'un ob da ribers an' da

legends er dose ol' books when her mind's filled wif a bad'n like Elias Slade?"

"What's that?" asked Carolyn with a confused expression.

"Oh, nuffin, Miz Dab'son. My heart's jes' sore 'bout what's ter become ob poor Phoebe, an' I wuz jes' thinkin' back on sumfin' Malachi's mama used ter tell me afore she died, dat's all. But I jes' don' know effen I can keep from hatin' dat awful man, Miz Dab'son. He's a right bad'n."

Anger filled Carolyn's heart. She did her best not to let Nancy see it, then turned and left her. She had to tell Richmond.

Whatever was to be done about Slade, it was obvious they had waited too long.

Carrying an extra shirt and pair of trousers, Elias Slade walked into what was known as the big house a few steps behind Moses, who ran the master's errands and had summoned him and said the master wanted him and for him to bring whatever belongings he possessed. Moses knocked on the back door. They were shown inside by Mrs. Davidson, who led the way to her husband's study. There Moses left them.

Richmond Davidson was seated behind a large oak desk. Carolyn closed the door behind her as she left the office, leaving the big black man and his owner alone.

Slade was not surprised at being called before the master. He had been expecting it for weeks. He knew the consequences for the kind of things he did. But he saw no reason to change. The anger burning inside him was stronger than the desire to avoid punishment. This was not the first time he had gotten a girl pregnant, nor would it likely be the last. Whippings were part of it. He knew it. But he had reason to think that the whipping he would receive today would not be as bad as most. Master Davidson was one of those white men a slave encountered once in a while, a white man with scruples. The fact didn't make Slade hate him any less, he just found it curious.

"I have tried to be a good master to you, Elias," Richmond began.

Slade stood looking down at the floor, unrepentant and unfeeling, and said nothing.

"Have either I or your mistress been unkind to you, that you would betray our trust such as you have with Phoebe?"

Still he did not answer.

"All right, then," Richmond went on. "I waited before bringing you to see me until we had a chance to question Phoebe. My wife has spoken with her. Phoebe has admitted that you did not force her and that she is as much to blame as you are. So I see no grounds for any unusual punishment other than to tell you that you should have known better than to take advantage of a girl so much younger than yourself. Every man has a conscience, Elias, though I have not seen that you have made a habit of paying much heed to yours. It is my hope and prayer that the day comes when you will learn to do so. In any event, it appears that I should have listened to mine sooner, otherwise this might have been avoided. Carolyn also questioned Phoebe concerning her feelings. Phoebe says that it is not her wish to be your wife. So now I must ask you, what were your intentions when you sought her out and became involved with her? Was it with the thought of marrying her?"

Slade stood silent.

"Answer me, Elias."

"No, suh," Slade finally said sullenly.

"And is such your intent now?"

"No, suh."

"I see," nodded Davidson. "I thought such to be the case, but I had to be certain."

He paused, drew in a breath, then picked up a paper that was lying on top of the desk.

"Can you read, Elias?" he asked.

"No, suh."

"Then you will just have to trust me and take my word for what I am about to tell you. This paper I have here is a legal document which

I have signed. It states that I am, as of today's date, releasing you from my ownership and am giving you your freedom."

He handed the paper to Slade, who took it and looked at it, though without comprehension.

Davidson opened one of the desk drawers and removed several bills.

"Along with that document," he said, "I will give you eight dollars. You are free to use it however you like and to go wherever you wish."

He rose and handed the money to him. "Now if you will come with me, my buggy is hitched outside. I will take you into town and from there you will be free to go wherever you wish. Only do not return to Greenwood. As you are a free man now, I will have grounds for having you arrested for trespassing if I see you on our property again. In addition, the law reads that you must leave the state of Virginia within one year. If you do not, you may be reenslaved."

He led the way out of the office and outside. Slade followed without expression. He uttered not a word during the entire drive to Dove's Landing.

When the two parted, gratitude was the furthest thing from Elias Slade's heart. His parting glance toward the man who had just given him what every Negro throughout the South dreamed of was filled only with contempt.

Seventeen

$\mathcal{U}$pon leaving the house Carolyn Davidson could not see far among the trees. She knew, however, that she would find her husband somewhere in the midst of the two-acre cultivated plot on the slope behind the plantation house where they developed their love for growing things. They called it simply the arbor, though the enclosed area represented far more than a mere garden retreat and arboretum. Many might have considered their effort and expense over shrubs, ornamentals, dwarf trees as well as peach and magnolia and other flowering species, ponds, paths, flower beds, tree-lined pathways, and roses, a waste of energy that could have been devoted toward more productive uses. Indeed, such would say, the two acres could have been planted with a lucrative money-making crop and to use it otherwise was foolish. But for Richmond and Carolyn Davidson, the hours spent in their beloved arbor were essential to happiness in the midst of the rigors of plantation life.

Ten minutes later she found him, as she thought she would, seated on a bench beneath the boughs of a huge overspreading magnolia. To his right a small stream burbled its way over rocks down the incline where it met a larger stream some fifty yards away. He was staring into the trickling water as if mesmerized by its flow, though in truth his thoughts were miles away.

He heard Carolyn coming up behind him and turned. He smiled as she sat down on the bench beside him.

"You have hardly said a word since taking Elias into town yesterday," she said.

"It was a large step," he said, smiling again. "I suppose it took something out of me emotionally."

"Why—was it so difficult?"

"Difficult . . . no, not difficult at all. It is a relief knowing that Elias is gone. Though I may live forever with that final look he cast me before he walked off—as if he hated me more for having given him his freedom than he would have if I had whipped him mercilessly. That is hard, Carolyn, to know you are hated for no reason but trying to do good."

She put her hand on his shoulder. "Shall a servant be greater than his master?"

He nodded. "You are right. It is still hard."

"And always will be for those who are his followers. But you did the right thing." She paused, then added, "Is it only the look Elias gave you that has turned you melancholy?"

Richmond sighed deeply. "I feel change coming, Carolyn," he said. "Yesterday may be only the beginning. Where it will lead, I cannot say. Yet I have the sense that our former way of life may be gone forever."

"What do you mean, Richmond?"

"That the door we opened by setting Elias free may have consequences that extend much further, and may lead—"

He paused and turned to face her. His expression was serious.

"I have been doing a great deal of soul searching," he went on after a moment, "and praying. You know that."

"Of course. I can tell."

"It is not just Elias. It began when I went to Boston. I told you how shocked the man Waters was when he learned we had slaves."

Carolyn nodded.

"I think I began to feel the Lord nudging me toward it even then. But I wanted to be certain. It was such a big step, I did not want to make a hasty decision if it was not truly the Lord speaking. I would always rather move too slow than too fast, to make sure I do not outrun the Lord in my own eagerness for something. Yet I cannot but regret moving perhaps too slow for poor Phoebe's sake. Now she must pay for my indecision."

"I will tell you the same thing now that I said concerning your brother's death, Richmond—you cannot blame yourself."

"Perhaps. Yet if we had acted sooner, when I first mentioned setting Elias free, we may have spared Phoebe all this."

"She made her own choice in the matter too," said Carolyn. "One thing I know about you, Richmond, once God shows you his will, you will do it. If in this case it took some time for that will to become plain to you, it only showed wisdom to wait."

"I will take what you say as from the Lord," he replied. "But having opened this door, as I say, I do feel he has made the next step plain. Therefore, in this case I do not want to hesitate but to act promptly."

"The next step?"

"When I tell you, you will see why I say that life for us may never be the same again. Everything will change. We cannot predict the consequences. Because, Carolyn . . . I think it is time not just to free one troublesome slave, but *all* our slaves."

Tears filled Carolyn's eyes. "Oh, Richmond, I am so glad!"

"You are not shocked?"

"Not at all. It is the right thing to do—I am sure of it. I have actually been thinking of it myself for some time."

"Why didn't you tell me?" he asked.

"Because it had to come from you. It is your plantation and was your father's and grandfather's before you. I knew that if it was the right thing to do, God would show you."

"I will have to go see Harland again and have him draw up papers for all of them, just as he did for Elias. We have to make sure everything is legal so none of them find themselves in trouble later because of it. The one-year clause could prove troublesome."

"Will Harland do it?"

"I don't know. He resisted even in the case of Elias. He said it was a bad precedent to set. He will be furious at the thought of us freeing the rest of our slaves. He will see it as throwing away thousands of dollars that he feels ought to belong to him and the others. I'm sure it will also complicate Stuart's claim and make it all the more acrimonious. But if he will not draw up the necessary papers, we will find an attorney who will."

It was silent as they both reflected on what they were about to do.

"You are right about what you said earlier," said Carolyn at length. "There are certain to be consequences. Word of it will get out. It is likely to make some people angry."

"Perhaps many. But if it is what God wants us to do, that cannot deter us. I have not forgotten something Wingate said in Boston. He spoke about having the strength and courage to live out the implication of God's plan and intent. I think such a time has come for us now."

The next evening, as soon as the five Davidsons were seated around the dining table for dinner, Richmond brought the conversation around to what he and Carolyn had discussed in the arbor.

"I gave Maribel and Moses the night off," he began. "I told them we wanted to be alone with just our family. There is something your mother and I want to talk with the three of you about." As he spoke, he looked into the eyes of each of his children, one at a time—twenty-year-old Cynthia, then sixteen-year-old Seth, and finally to Thomas, who was fourteen. The young people could tell from the tone of his voice that their father was serious.

"Is something wrong, Daddy?" asked Cynthia.

"No, dear, nothing is wrong," replied Richmond. "Well," he added, chuckling lightly, "there might be some who would say there is definitely something wrong—namely, that your mother and I have taken leave of our senses! Would you agree, Carolyn?"

"I am sure such things will be said!"

"What are you talking about, Daddy?" said Cynthia, glancing back and forth between father and mother in bewilderment.

"In a nutshell, just this—your mother and I have been praying about and discussing the possibility of giving all of our slaves their freedom, just as we did Elias Slade."

The statement fell like a bombshell around the table. The three young people sat in stunned silence, wondering if they had heard their father correctly.

"Can you do that, Father?" asked Seth after a few seconds.

"Legally . . . yes," laughed Richmond. "Virginia's laws have tended to be much more liberally interpreted than in the Deep South. What consequences it may have, that we don't know, though there should not be legal repercussions. But we think it is the right thing to do."

"Jeffrey will be so pleased," said Cynthia. "I can't wait to write and tell him! He never could understand how we could own slaves."

"What about you, Seth?" asked Carolyn. "What do you think?"

"I don't know, Mother. . . . I guess it sounds fine. But how will we get all the work done without the slaves?"

"We hope they will want to stay at Greenwood," answered Carolyn.

"I thought you said you were going to free them."

"Yes, but we will let as many stay as want to."

"I don't get what you mean."

"We will pay them wages," said Richmond, "just like we would a free white man who came to work for us."

"Oh . . . yeah, well then I guess it sounds fine by me."

"What made you think of doing this, Daddy?" asked Cynthia, who was old enough to recognize more of the implications of what it might mean than her two younger brothers.

"It has been a slow process," replied her father. "You remember when I went to Boston last year?"

Cynthia nodded.

"I was very challenged by much that was said by one of the speakers at the symposium there. He talked about what is *right* being more important than what is *allowed*. He said that we should look to what God *intends* rather than what the laws of men might allow. When I saw that distinction, I realized that slavery wasn't right because it could not possibly represent what God intends. Once those ideas began to work on me, it was only a matter of time before I realized that we had no choice but to free our slaves."

Again it was quiet. Thomas was the only one who had said nothing throughout the meal. The look on his face made it plain what he was thinking. Now at last he spoke up.

"Do you really agree with all this?" he said, turning toward Carolyn. His words sounded more like an accusation than a question.

"Oh, yes, Thomas," she replied. "More than just agree with it, I think it's exciting!"

"I don't. I think it sounds crazy."

"Why?"

"What will people think? My friends are sure to make fun of me if they find out. Nobody sets their slaves free. I think it sounds idiotic."

"I don't think it will be as bad as all that."

"And I suppose now I'll have to obey some nigger and do what he says just because he's older than me."

"Thomas!" said Richmond sharply. "Every human being is made in God's image no matter what the color of his skin. There will be no more remarks like that."

Thomas gloomily returned to his food and said no more.

"Returning to what you said a moment ago, Seth," Richmond continued, "my hope is that we will get *more* work done even though perhaps we will have fewer hands than we do now. I think they will work harder knowing they are being paid for their work."

"But what if they do all leave?"

"Then we will hire new workers. But they won't. Most of them have no place else to go. A few may leave, but I'm sure most will choose to stay. It will surely mean change, for all of us. But I hope it will be good change."

Eighteen

The next visit to the law offices of Harland Davidson by the attorney's cousin did nothing to enhance the bonds of filial relationship between the two men.

"Have you reached a decision in the matter of the disposition of your mother's estate?"

"Carolyn and I are still praying," replied Richmond.

"I had hoped that your visit might indicate your decision to settle the suit out of court," rejoined the lawyer, doing his best to hide his annoyance at what he considered his cousin's idiotic reply. "Time is moving swiftly, Richmond. To forestall a court case, I suggest you consider selling off some portions of the land. One of your neighbors, in fact, contacted me a while back. Knowing that I handle your legal affairs, he inquired about the purchase of the Brown tract."

"Denton has been in touch with you?" said Richmond in surprise.

"I assume you are referring to Mr. Beaumont . . . yes. I told him I would talk to you about it. As I understand it from him, that plot alone would provide sufficient means to clear up this whole business."

Disturbed that his neighbor would attempt to go behind his back, Richmond tried to reply calmly. "Yes, Denton and I have discussed the matter," he said. "I told him I was not interested in selling at this time."

"Suit yourself. But as I say . . . time is passing."

"I understand. But I came today about another matter. You recall the slave we had difficulties with for whom we drew up a document giving him his freedom?"

"Of course I recall it—a mistake in my view, but what's done is done."

Richmond went on to explain the reason for his visit.

"You want me to what!" exclaimed the lawyer.

"It is very simple, really, Harland," replied Richmond. "I want you to draw up the same kind of documentation you did before, this time for all our slaves. I have the list of names right here."

"You can't do it, Richmond. It would be the ruin of Greenwood. Don't forget, the rest of us have a stake in this too."

"You may have a claim to put forward because my mother did not leave a will," said Richmond firmly. "But that is strictly a financial matter, and a flimsy one legally at that. However, you can have no possible interest in the ownership of the slaves themselves."

"There are certain states where such action is illegal. You could find yourself in difficulties with the law."

"But Virginia is not one of those states. In any case, I am willing to risk it."

"This whole thing is preposterous! Don't expect me to do your dirty work for you!"

"If you do not draw up the papers, I will go to someone else. I think you know the law well enough to realize that it would be pointless to try to block the thing in court."

His cousin fumed awhile longer but eventually consented. Given the way things stood with his sister and two cousins and the thin legal grounds they had for pressing their claim further than Richmond was willing to allow, he did not want to run the risk of involving another attorney in Richmond Davidson's affairs.

"Give me two weeks," he said at length. "You can pick up the papers after that time."

There were two occasions every year when all the Davidson slaves were invited to celebrate at the big house, Christmas and Easter. The invitation to come again on a Saturday afternoon in April of 1856, only three weeks after the latter, set the entire Negro village buzzing. None could imagine the reason for such an invitation. They knew that Elias had not been seen since being summoned by the master. Most speculation in that regard concluded that he had been sold, and good riddance they all said. Probably the master wanted to talk to them about it. None suspected the true cause of the invitation.

White-haired Uncle Moses led the way inside, followed by Maribel, then Nancy and Malachi Shaw with Phoebe, Isaiah, and Aaron, who were followed in turn by the other families and single men and women. They walked in gingerly with careful step, silent as if entering a cathedral, glancing about as they went. When they had crowded into the largest room in the house, which had in former times been used as a ballroom but had not seen such use in Richmond and Carolyn's time, the women sat in what chairs were available. The men stood stoically waiting, hats in hand.

Carolyn, Seth, and Thomas passed among them with trays filled with glasses of lemonade. The youngsters took them eagerly, the women gratefully, the men cautiously. They were not used to being waited on by their owners. Nevertheless, the glasses were all empty within a minute or two, when the trays came through again to collect them. Cynthia and Seth had by this time become so thoroughly enthusiastic about their parents' scheme that they enjoyed the role of host and hostess and entered into them gaily. One look on Thomas's face, however, showed that he was anything but pleased. He wore a scowl that said he would have rather been anywhere else on the planet than here.

After he had greeted each individually with a shake of the hand, Richmond Davidson stood in front and addressed them.

"Some of you may be aware," he began, "that a great debate is underway in our country about the issue of slavery. Obviously, this discussion concerns all of you as it does us. On our parts, I will just tell you that I have been praying earnestly about what God wants us to do. You know that Carolyn and I do not base our decisions on what others may do, or on what others may think we should do. We try to base our lives on what God wants us to do. It is not always easy to know, but one must nevertheless make the attempt.

"We have recently come to a decision about the future of Greenwood. It will change life for all of us from this day on—every one of you, as well as all of us. It is an experiment. Perhaps it will fail, though I cannot imagine it. I pray that it will prove wonderful for each of you, and that this will be a happy day for you.

"Our decision is this: As of today, you are all slaves no longer, but are free men and women."

He paused to allow his words to sink in. Around the room a few eyes widened, first wondering if they had heard him aright and what it meant. None seemed to grasp the full import of what their master had said.

"We are giving you your freedom," Richmond went on. "It will cost you nothing. You will owe us nothing. I have had papers drawn up and have signed them, which makes your freedom legal and binding."

Gradually a few of them began to understand that they were indeed being set free. A few murmurs of disbelief began to accompany the wide eyes and expressions of astonishment. That this signaled a change they were slowly beginning to realize, but they had yet to recognize it as joyful news.

"But what's gwine happen ter us, massa?" asked Moses, speaking the question that was on all their minds. "Is you gwine make us leab Greenwood? Where's we ter go, what's we ter do?"

"I think perhaps you misunderstand me, Moses," replied the master. "None of you will *have* to leave. You are welcome to stay and continue to live here and work for us. But you will be your own masters. You do not *have* to stay. You may go or stay, but the decision is yours. You are free men and women. If you decide to stay, then I will hire you and pay you wages as I would any white man I hired to work for me. Those of you who want to continue living and working at Greenwood and want to work for us, the men we will pay thirty cents a day and the women who have no children and who work all day twenty cents. Women with children will be paid according to the time worked. You will be *hired* men and women rather than slaves.

"Now from the wages you earn, you will have to pay us rent for your houses and for the land you use for your gardens. You will begin to support yourselves, paying for your own food and clothes and whatever else you might need. The economics of capitalism will govern our finances in a new relationship between employer and employees, not master and slaves."

"But, massa," said Malachi Shaw, who, along with Moses, had been longest at Greenwood, "we don't know nuffin' 'bout all dat. How's we gwine know what ter do?"

"Don't worry, Malachi. Carolyn and I and Cynthia and the boys will help you. We want this to be an exciting time for you, and we will help you learn to use money. We will teach you to go into town to buy what you need. Please, have no anxiety—those of you who stay will be taken care of. We will make sure that all your needs are met and we will help you with everything. We want to help you begin learning to live on your own, as free men and women, just like white people and blacks in the North do. We will help you with everything. We will no longer be your owners, but your employers. We hope that you will consider us your friends as well. In the end, it is our sincere hope that this change will prove profitable for us all, that we as landowners will continue to make money from our crops, and that you will be able to save money from your wages after your expenditures as well. But there is one legal technicality you must know. The law says that any freed slave must leave Virginia within one year. Those of you who choose to remain here will not find that a problem. If anyone contests your freedom, you can voluntarily become our slaves again until the threat is past. But any of you who do leave should plan to leave Virginia, and I would suggest you go to the North."

Gradually as it began to sink in that they had nothing to fear, a few smiles and murmurs of pleasure began to filter around the room.

"To begin with," Davidson went on, "we will pay you each twenty dollars per family, or eight dollars to each single adult. That will be your very own money to keep or spend. You might want to buy new clothes with it, or save it. For those of you who do decide to leave and start new lives for yourselves elsewhere, this will, we hope, be enough to get you situated."

Nineteen

The troop of former Davidson slaves filed out of the plantation house with words of thanks and nods of appreciation to the master and his wife, clutching almost in bewilderment the documents and money that had been distributed among them.

They made their way to their own homes in complete silence, each lost in his or her own thoughts, still not quite sure what had happened and whether to believe it or not. The instant they were back to the slave quarters, however, their tongues were loosed. A few whoops and shouts of delight echoed back toward the big house. Within minutes several clusters formed in several of the houses, and the feverish discussion and intense examination of the papers by those who could read did not cease for the rest of the day nor long into the night.

Most of the Davidson slaves, including every one of the two-thirds or so who had been at Greenwood all their lives and recognized how good conditions for them had always been, declared themselves content to stay and work for the master and mistress.

"Ain't no amount er money gwine make me leab da mistress no how," said Nancy Shaw emphatically, her husband Malachi standing by nodding his head in agreement. "She's learnin' us outta da Good Book, an' she says I's kin read it myse'f sumday, an' I figure dis be 'bout as good a place ter work as any fo' a slave or a free colored. Where else we gwine fin' whites who'd pay us an' help us an' treat us wif respeck. My mama an' papa raised me here. Dey loved massa's papa and mama. Dis be where I's raised my Phoebe an' Isaiah an' Aaron, an' dis be where I stay."

"Ain't you a mite curious ter see more ob da worl'?" asked Jarvis Nance.

"No I ain't," replied Nancy. "I may not know much. But I knows enuf ter know dat da worl' ain't none too kind ter free blacks wanderin' 'roun' about. No suh, we's be stayin' right here."

Once the full implications of the change began to dawn on the collective Greenwood Negro community, however, there were several who began making preparations to pack their belongings and seek their fortunes elsewhere.

One young single man in his late twenties known only as Willie shared the sentiment of several. "Da massa an' da missus, dey's been good enuf ter me," he said, "an' ah's grateful dey ain't whupped me eben once. But ah's got me a bruder up norf who's been after me ter run away an' cum work wif him. He dun run away years ago, an' he hid out an' kep' outta sight an' he made it all da way norf till he wuz safe an' cud git himse'f sum work. He's a blacksmif, an' he say a colored man kin make good money in da norf effen he's willin' ter work, an' ah's gotter take dis chance ter make sumfin' ob myse'f afore massa be changin' his min'."

With his eight dollars and the clothes on his back and what food he could carry, he was gone three days later, talking about nothing else all the way to the Pennsylvania border one hundred miles away, proudly displaying what he called his "paper ob freedom" to any and all who cared to listen to his story.

An event so momentous as for one of Virginia's well-known plantation owners to free every one of his slaves lock, stock, and barrel—not to mention actually handing them a handful of cash to boot—was not something to be kept quiet. How the news spread so rapidly, neither Richmond nor Carolyn ever knew. Everyone recognized that invisible communications networks existed among the slaves throughout the South that extended to the Negro populations in the North and West as well, though how exactly news made its way from plantation to plantation remained a mystery to whites. Most slaves were not mobile and traveled little. Yet somehow word among them always seemed to move with uncanny speed.

Doubtless Willie's tales did much to ignite the initial spark which soon fanned into flame and led within weeks to accounts, some accurate and some greatly exaggerated, of the story in most major newspapers up and down the eastern coast of the nation.

It was doubtful that the expanding revelation of the affair was in any way helped along by the firm *Harland Davidson, Attorney at Law, Richmond, Virginia,* in that the proprietor of said firm was anything but anxious to circulate knowledge of his own involvement. Indeed, he would have done almost anything to keep his name out of it. Yet the documents he had drawn up were of public record, and once that fact was known, inquisitive newsmen from half a dozen states began appearing at his door. The younger Davidson vigorously maintained that he had not been influential in the affair, indeed that he had vehemently opposed and had counseled against it. Yet as his cousin's attorney, he had had no alternative but to comply with his wishes. Complicit or not, however, through a series of such interviews, not always willingly nor graciously granted, the details of the case were not long in coming out, and along with them a more thorough sketch—cast in what could hardly be denied was a generally unfavorable light—of the man at the center of the tempest of sudden curiosity, Richmond Davidson.

Approximately one week after the distribution of the freedom papers, a strange sight was witnessed in Dove's Landing that if they had not seen it with their own eyes, those who spread the story about the community on the authority of their own eyewitness account would not have believed it themselves.

Carolyn and Cynthia walked into Baker's Mercantile with three Negro women who were dressed up in their finest. One look at the strange assembly told the story—the three black women were not waiting on mother and daughter. If anything, just the opposite appeared to be the case. There had already been a few scattered rumors of some strange shake-up at Greenwood. This sight seemed to confirm the worst.

Slowly they made their way about the store, Carolyn showing the black ladies where things were, explaining about fabric and how much things cost and about different denominations of money.

At last Mrs. Baker approached.

"Hello, Mrs. Davidson," she said tentatively, unconsciously glancing at Nancy Shaw, "is there anything I can help you with?"

"These ladies are thinking of buying material for new dresses, Mrs. Baker," replied Carolyn. "They will be your customers from now on, so you should know their names—this is Nancy Shaw, and this is Mary Nance, and this is Wilma Brady. Ladies, I would like you to meet the shopkeeper, Mrs. Baker."

All three of the black women smiled a little nervously, and extended their hands. Reluctantly, the storekeeper, taken aback by the turn of events and temporarily without words, shook each in turn as if it were an eel rather than a hand. The moment the ordeal was over, she turned again to Carolyn.

"But . . . but, Mrs. Davidson," she said, lowering her voice, "how will they *pay*?"

"Just the way any customer pays, Mrs. Baker—with money."

"They have money . . . of their *own*?"

"Indeed they do, and I am helping them learn how to manage it. We are going to the bank next, where each of them will open an account in their very own names."

Just then the door opened and the bell above it tinkled to announce the entry of two more ladies, giving the relieved Mrs. Baker the excuse she needed to absent herself. The hushed tones and glances from the opposite side of the store indicated clearly enough that she lost no time in giving the newcomers an earful, as she proceeded to give everyone who came into her shop for the next several days. By then most of the townspeople had seen similar occurrences for themselves, either Carolyn with her black women, or Richmond doing the same with some of the black men at the feed and hardware store.

Twenty

*I*n Boston, though news was his business, James Waters did not hear of what his acquaintance from a year earlier had done until perusing a copy of his own newspaper one morning and chancing upon a piece that had been picked up from one of the Philadelphia papers.

The caption above the small article caught his eye immediately: *Virginia Plantation Owner Releases Slaves, Issues Documents of Freedom.*

"In a move that not only stunned the thirty-four Negro men, women, and children listening to the announcement," Waters went on to read, "but has had repercussions throughout the South, Virginia landowner Richmond Davidson recently gave all his slaves their freedom in addition to a small cash settlement reportedly amounting to approximately $10 for each adult. According to several former slaves who have since left the Davidson plantation, after informing them of his decision, Davidson went on to offer any who chose to remain work at a fair wage and housing at a fair price, hoping, he said, to establish the finances of the plantation for the first time on a foundation of market capitalism between employer and employees rather than upon the institution of slavery. All but a handful reportedly decided to remain. These are now employed as hired workers—receiving a wage thought to be thirty cents per day for men working ten hours a day—and are responsible for their own food, housing, and other expenses.

"While abolitionists signal the 'Davidson experiment' as the wave of the future, pro-slavery sentiment through the South dubs it instead the 'Davidson folly,' insisting that it is doomed to fail even before it begins. Virginia senatorial candidate Winston Everett, when reached for comment, had nothing but derision for both Davidson and his experiment.

"'This is the one thing the North consistently fails to grasp,' the former congressman was quoted as saying, '—the economics of the South are vastly different than elsewhere. To upset the delicate balance between many complex economic factors could have serious repercussions in the North as well as in the South. Mr. Davidson's experiment is one that cannot but fail. When bankruptcy results and creditors are forced to move in, what good will the freedom of his slaves do either them or him? It is not merely a folly, it is a dangerous precedent that will accomplish nothing but raise false hopes and expectations, and may exacerbate far more than ameliorate the tensions between pro-slavery and antislavery constituencies. In the end this experiment will reveal Richmond Davidson as no hero, but as the laughingstock of Virginia.'

"Davidson himself has remained persistently unavailable for comment, answering all inquiries only with the cryptic statement: 'We have done what we felt was right to do. Let each judge truth for himself, and let the eternal results in lives and in hearts speak for themselves.'"

Waters set down the paper and smiled.

That is Davidson, all right, he said to himself. *Still speaking about eternity and truth!*

But he had to hand it to the man—he backed up his talk with deeds and action. That was not something he was prepared to say about most church people he had been acquainted with. Or *any* that he was acquainted with for that matter! And apparently Davidson didn't care what anyone thought of him—another admirable quality.

Perhaps he had misjudged the man. In spite of an annoying propensity to turn every discussion toward God and religion and truth, the man was certainly no hypocrite. That was no small praise for James Waters—who as a newsman, it might be said, was paid to be cynical—to extend to any man.

"What are you smiling at, Daddy?" said a spirited girl of fifteen as she bounded into the room. She had been home from boarding school for a week since the end of the spring term.

"Ah, Cherity," replied James, glancing up, "I was just reading a small article in the paper that struck me as humorous, I suppose, in an ironic sort of way. Do you remember Mr. Davidson?"

"Oh, yes! The man with the horses who visited last year!"

"Well, it seems he has made the news. You might even say he is famous."

"Really! Why, Daddy—what did he do?"

"It seems he set all his slaves free."

"That's wonderful! I'm so glad."

"He has created quite a stir, from the sound of it."

"Then we must go see him, Daddy. When can we go for a visit? He invited us . . . remember? He said I could ride his horses."

"I don't know!" laughed Waters. "Virginia is a long way, Cherity."

"Daddy . . . please!"

"You are not an easy young lady to refuse!" laughed Waters. "But I doubt the doctor would allow me to take such a long trip."

"He can't tell you what to do."

"Perhaps not . . . but still I need to heed his advice. That's what doctors are for—to keep old men like me alive long enough to see their daughters grow into women."

"Daddy, you're not old!"

"I am older than most fathers of fifteen year olds. In any event, we shall see what the doctor says."

"It's not as far as Kansas."

"You're right about that," he laughed.

"And besides, isn't Virginia where Mary lives?"

"You're right—of course! Why hadn't I thought of that? We were going to see Mary anyway before long. What do you say we stop by the Davidsons', then, for a visit on our way to Norfolk?"

"Oh, yes! Do you think I will be able to ride Mr. Davidson's horses?"

"I don't know, Cherity," laughed her father. "We shall have to wait and see."

"But what did the doctor say about us taking the train to Norfolk?"

"Actually . . . I didn't ask him. I want to see my new grandson, and I wasn't about to let him say no!"

He handed her the paper.

"Here is the article about Mr. Davidson. I think you will find it interesting. The front-page news is all about the violence in Kansas, by the way. Things are not good there these days. I do not imagine us returning to see our friend Ellis anytime soon."

"What's the fighting all about?"

"Since Congress decided that the people of Kansas and Nebraska will each decide for themselves whether to be free states or slave states when they enter the Union—if and when they become states, that is—both pro-slavery and antislavery forces are trying to send as many of their own people as they can to settle there. At the same time, they are trying to drive out people of the opposing view. So there is bloodshed all over the state."

"That's terrible!"

"That's how far both sides are willing to go to get their way. I doubt if Kansas will be the end of the fighting."

Reaction among Southern politicians, landowners, and pro-slavery advocates was swift in its denunciation of the Davidson move. Economic chaos, social upheaval, and a disruption of the natural order of creation were just a few of the calamities predicted to follow if such trends were allowed to continue. Though hailed in the North as a progressive display of courage, a move was set in motion in the Virginia state legislature to block the action in the courts on the basis of certain obscure legal technicalities stemming from the fact that Davidson was keeping his former slaves in his own employ, thus rendering them, after a year, free to be enslaved by another. The bill was not expected to gather much support but was indicative of the stir the move had caused.

Why the Davidson news should cause a virulent reaction among such men as Denton Beaumont, Jefferson Davis, Abraham Seehorn, Watson McNeil, Congressman Jeeves Hargrove, and other leaders and landowners throughout the South would have made an interesting inquiry. That men of power feel threatened when the status quo of their creation is disrupted by free-thinking men and women of individualism and courage, has been a plague against progress in all ages.

Suffice it to say that throughout the North there were those who championed Richmond Davidson as a hero, while throughout the South there were yet more who branded him the worst traitor since Benedict Arnold. If the man's bold actions were allowed to gain a widespread foothold in the public consciousness, they said, they could have catastrophic repercussions and lead to a groundswell of favorable sentiment in certain quarters. That this was the very man they had offered to raise to the highest levels of national leadership only added to their sense of injury and anger. That he had become a fool in their eyes did little to moderate the stupidity they felt at having nearly been taken in by him, and coming so close to making such a disastrous blunder as installing him as their representative in the United States Senate.

They could not allow Davidson to become a hero or spokesman for the abolitionist cause, nor a hero-savior figure to blacks. But neither could they crucify him publicly and allow him to become a martyr. Such publicity was not good. The matter had to be handled carefully.

Accordingly, word began to spread throughout the Southern corridors of power that the Davidson affair must be put to rest and further news of it silenced, except where the facts could be twisted and Davidson made to appear a misguided simpleton. Influential newspapers and editors were contacted, certain pressures applied, and within weeks little more was heard of it in any of the pro-slavery newspapers. At the same time, a discreet campaign was subtly set in motion to discredit Davidson and render his actions those of a fringe figure, even a lunatic, rather than a man of conviction. Word was cleverly leaked to certain sources that he was not all he appeared, that he held radical religious views, and that his wife conducted strange observances with their former slaves and held them in the grip of cultish teachings ostensibly based on the Bible. How many of these rumors originated with Davidson's neighbor and longtime friend, and how many were based on conversations with the few slaves who had left, was impossible to ascertain. Though all the slave reports were favorable, they were also capable of being distorted to yield almost any impression desired.

Within a few months, the hubbub over the affair had died down. As nothing more came of it and little more was heard of it, most people gradually forgot about it. The only memories that lingered had little to do with slaves, but rather Davidson himself and the odd things they had heard about him.

Twenty-one

*R*ichmond Davidson walked slowly through the garden and arbor in deep reflection. It was finally time to come to terms with and reach a decision concerning his cousin's demand.

The question before him was a simple one: To fight or give in?

That dilemma came to him not in terms of right and wrong. He knew well enough that any man can persuade himself that he is *right* about anything, and yet base a string of faulty choices on that mistaken view. So he did not come to the decision before him from that vantage point. He knew his own fallibility too well. Rather, the only answer he sought was: *What did God want him to do?*

He could pray anywhere. But he preferred the garden to anyplace else on the property, with the possible exception of Harper's Peak, although that was not so much a place to gain solitude with God as to relish in his majesty.

He and Carolyn had planned and developed, cultivated and refined the walkways and hedges and small theme gardens within the arbor all to provide a place of prayerful retreat that would, in its very essence, remind them that they had a good Father watching over them. Just as they could enter the arbor at any time, so they could enter the Father's care and seek his loving and perfect counsel at a moment's notice.

Now was such a time. He never wanted to rush his Father, and always chose, even when he had a sense in which direction the divine

will was likely pointing, to give God time. He was all too well
acquainted with the human tendency to rush. He thus tried to counter that tendency within himself whenever large decisions were at
hand, knowing that, if he were indeed hearing truly, time would only
confirm the still small Abba-Voice yet the more distinctly.

His petitions on this occasion were neither specific nor audible. He
had been here before, to this throne—or was it an altar?—of personal
relinquishment. Though it was a familiar place to which his heart
often returned, nonetheless it hurt to walk the well-trod, invisible
pathway each time he felt the divine prompting to revisit his inner
Gethsemane.

In truth, the stones of that invisible seat of worship comprised both
a throne *and* an altar. For in relinquishment of the will is worship
perfected, and out of the ashes of sacrifice is born the childlike nature
that can approach the King.

At no other moment did Richmond Davidson feel so weak. Yet at no
such moment did he approach so closely the true character of his name.

The heaving of his soul as he walked on this day reflected no resis-
tance, merely the anguish of difficult obedience as it battled the final
death throes of self. That he would not do other than put his very self
to death in whatever ways he was able did not make his old Adam any
less vigorous an adversary. It was a sacrifice given willingly—even
eagerly, to the extent that mortal man is capable of desiring to become
the executioner of its own flesh—yet agonizingly rendered.

"God . . . oh, God!" he sighed as the dam of months-long prayer
burst from his lips. Then he slipped to his knees beside the first
magnolia he and Carolyn had planted shortly after their marriage, and
a few quiet tears began to fall from his eyes.

When Carolyn found him seated on the stone-wall edge of the bridge
over the small creek an hour later, she knew from the look on his face
that the final battle within himself had been waged and the decision
made.

She sat down beside him. He glanced up with a sad but peaceful smile.

"I don't know why it is difficult to lay down what your flesh fights so hard to preserve," he said softly. "I don't *want* what my flesh cries out for. The selfishness of my old man is abhorrent to me. Yet there is a stubborn part of my being that doesn't want to have to give in. It is such a dichotomy. One would think the battle could be fought once and be done with."

"That is not the walk of faith," said Carolyn softly.

"Of course . . . I know. But it is frustrating. It seems my progress is so slow."

"But if I know you . . . you prayed the prayer. You always do."

He smiled and nodded.

"You always come back to *not my will* in the end," Carolyn added. "It is the path you walk. I know that whatever you face, that is where your steps will lead."

They sat for several minutes in reflective silence.

"What course of action do you feel we are to follow in the matter of Stuart's claim?" asked Carolyn at length.

"Only to wait," replied her husband. "Wait, pray for my cousins, and pray for God's will to be done."

"You have always said that in God's economy, to wait is one of the foundational pillars of wisdom."

"I suppose the Lord is giving me a chance to practice what I preach," laughed Richmond lightly. "If Stuart's claim is truly unfair, God will see to it. That is no doubt one of the reasons he would have us relinquish our grip on such matters, so that we might give him opportunity to work in ways that are not possible so long as we try to control our own affairs. Our responsibility is to relinquish our hold and then to wait, with a willing and self-denying heart, for God to work."

"And if Stuart presses the suit?"

"Then we trust God to be our advocate."

"Then I trust you," smiled Carolyn. "I am not quite as willing to see you taken advantage of. If I had my way, I would fight your cousins tooth and nail. Not because of what they would take from *me*, but that they have accused you, and your mother and father, of being unfair. It makes my blood boil if I let it. But I trust you. As I said before, that you can lay it down only makes me love you more."

They rose and hand in hand left the arbor and walked back toward the house.

Twenty-two

A knock sounded on the front door at Greenwood. A gray-haired Negro man ambled toward it. Too old to do much good in the fields, with rheumatism in his knees, he had been brought to the big house, provided a room of his own on the ground floor, and given a few duties about the place. He also ran errands for the master.

"Mo'nin', Moses," said the visitor as the old man answered the door.

"Mo'nin' t' you, Rev'rund," said Moses respectfully.

"Yo' mistress be 'roun' 'bout an' hab a minute er two t' speak wif me?"

"I reckon, Rev'rund," said Moses. "She's out back t' da garden wif Mistress Cynthia. Come in an' sit yo'se'f down in da parlor an' I'll fin' out direckly."

He turned and led the second black man, who was as old as he, into the house. Neither of the two hesitated or commented on the peculiarity or presumption of thus making themselves at home in a white man's plantation house. Though every black man, woman, and child at Greenwood had been trained from the day of birth to show what amounted to groveling deference to any white person, the changes at Greenwood had quickly and thoroughly taken root within its black community. That these former slaves could so quickly learn to walk with their heads high was daily testimony to how well they knew their beloved master and mistress, as they still thought of them, and trusted in the goodwill of their hearts.

Carolyn and Cynthia returned to the house three or four minutes later a good way ahead of Moses.

"Hello, Reverend Jones," said Carolyn warmly. As he rose, she shook the hand of the minister of a small, unofficial, and clandestine congregation of slaves from around the area, a free black man from Ohio who had come to the area about three years before. He lived in Dove's Landing and did odd jobs around town without arousing too much suspicion or drawing undo attention to himself. *

"Good day, t' you, Missus Dab'son . . . Miss Cynthia," he said.

"How nice to see you," said Carolyn as they all took seats. "Would you like something to drink . . . lemonade, tea?"

"Lemonade soun's right nice, thank you, Missus Dab'son. But I's wonderin' if it's so good fer you ter be callin' me da Rev'rund. Dere's a heap er folks wouldn't take kindly t' know dere's a black man what used ter be a preacher roun' dese parts."

"I only do so out of respect for your position with our people," said Carolyn as she started to rise. "We will make sure the *Reverend* stays here with us."

"I'll get it, Mother," said Cynthia. "You sit and visit with Mr. Jones. What can I get for you?"

"Thank you, Cynthia . . . I'll have a glass of tea."

"I hope you'll forgive da impertinence ob my call like dis—," the former minister began as the young lady walked into the kitchen.

"That is the last thing I would ever call a visit from you, Reverend Jones," said Carolyn.

"That's right kind ob you ter say," chuckled the minister. "To be truthful wif you, Missus Dab'son," he went on more seriously, "I been a mite concerned lately 'bout our Sunday meetin's in da woods. We'se been safe enuf up till now, but sumethin's givin' me an uncanny

---

*A Virginia law of 1832 provided that "no slave, free Negro, or mulatto, whether he shall have been ordained or licensed, or otherwise, shall hereafter undertake to preach, exhort or conduct, or hold any assembly or meeting for religious or other purposes, either in day time, or at night." The minimum penalty was 39 lashes. Whites could take Negroes to their churches, and white preachers could preach to Negroes, but they were forbidden to teach blacks anything that might be construed as seditious.

feelin' 'bout hit. I can't rightly say what it be, but hit's almost like sumeone's listenin' or watchin' like. It ain't dat I's concerned fo' mysel'. Gracious no, hit ain't dat—"

"We need to be concerned for you," interrupted Carolyn. "If certain people, as you say, were to find out that you are preaching to the slaves, they would have you arrested. We can't have that."

"I appreciate yo kindness, Missus Dab'son. But da good Lord's given me a long an' good life, an' if I get throwed in jail fo preaching da Word ter dese precious brothers an' sisters roun' here, dat be a small price ter pay fo' spreadin' da Lord's gospel. I's worried fo' dem, you see. An' you's so good wif yo' people, readin' to 'em from da Good Book like you does, I knows you's as concerned fo' dere spiritual welfare as I is."

"Of course we are. And the people think a great deal of you as well."

"Dat's kind er you t' say, Missus Dab'son."

"So what can my husband and I do for you?"

"I ain't altogether sure, Missus Dab'son, I jest reckoned as hit's on your land where we's meetin', an' as you'd likely get in some kind er trouble too if we's foun' out, dat I ought ter speak wif you 'bout hit."

Cynthia returned with a tray and three glasses and handed one to the minister and one to her mother, then took one herself and sat down.

"Cynthia, do you know where Father is?" asked Carolyn.

"Last time I saw him, he and Malachi were hitching two horses."

"Where were they going?"

"I think over to one of Mr. Brown's old fields."

"He's been talking about whether some of that fallow land might be reclaimed," nodded Carolyn, "and brought again under cultivation. They will probably be gone several hours. I shall talk to him about it this evening, Reverend Jones," she said, turning again to the minister. "We shall see if we can think—"

Carolyn stopped. Slowly a smile spread over her face.

"Reverend Jones," she said, nodding her head thoughtfully. "Being reminded of Mr. Brown's land has put an idea in my head. I will most definitely talk to Richmond about it. We have wondered for a long time how to put his little house to use rather than continue to let it sit empty. This just may be the idea we have been looking for."

"Dat's good er you, Missus Dab'son."

"What I'm thinking, if my husband agrees and we think you will be safe, will at least keep your people from having to worry about getting rained on during your sermons!"

Harland Davidson had been giving the matter a great deal of thought since his imbecile of a cousin had caused such a ruckus by setting his slaves free. He had originally been furious at having been drawn into the thing and made to look like he was part of it. Whether his own reputation had suffered he had no way of knowing. If so it didn't seem to have affected his business. Upon reflection, however, he had begun to wonder if perhaps this gave them a far greater opportunity.

It was time he sat down behind closed doors and had a serious talk with the others.

It took three weeks to get his sister and two cousins to Richmond.

"What is all this about?" said his cousin Stuart once they were seated in his office with drinks in hand. "Your letter said there had been important developments. All I want to know is whether Richmond is inclined to settle out of court."

"I have heard nothing from him."

"Then let us proceed to—"

"Wait a moment, Stuart," interrupted Harland. "Just hear me out."

Stuart eyed him skeptically but allowed his cousin to continue.

"You all know that he freed his slaves?" said Harland.

"The whole world knows," said Stuart. "The fool—I can't imagine what he was thinking."

"Exactly. It is a fool's dream. Everyone knows it cannot but fail. Several of his slaves have already left. The others he is paying nearly a white man's wage. I see nothing in our dear cousin's future but increasing financial difficulties."

"Which is why we have to act now, if you ask me," said Stuart.

"Not necessarily, Stuart," rejoined Harland. "Just hear me out."

"What do he and his slaves have to do with us?" interjected Stuart's sister Margaret.

"Just this," replied Harland. "If we press the claim now, I have to say I consider our chances of winning a large settlement in court to be thin. However, if we wait until he has a failing plantation on his hands, we can then move in with a much better chance of success. My recommendation, therefore, is that we bide our time and see what events bring us in the way of opportunity."

"Bide our time for what?" said Harland's sister Pamela with a confused look. "I don't understand any of this. I thought we were just going to sue him."

Stuart, however, was beginning to catch on to his cousin's thinking. Slowly a smile crept across his lips.

"Of course!" he said. "Harland, your scheme is brilliant! We wait for him to go bankrupt *on his own,* without us pushing him over the brink or risk losing in court. *Then* we move in with the lawsuit against Aunt Ruth's estate, claiming that four-fifths ownership of the place should have been ours all along. We are not put in the position of *causing* his failure, but of coming in to *rescue* our misguided cousin from his own hopeless actions. If we play our cards right, we will wind up owning *all* of Greenwood and squeezing him out altogether!"

"Precisely," smiled Harland with a cunning grin. "You have articulated the nub of the thing to perfection. After all these delays, we may thank Cousin Richmond for dragging his feet after all."

"You see, Margaret," said Stuart, turning to his sister, "when Richmond freed his slaves, he cut his own throat. There is no way he can make a go of it under such conditions. Every Southern economist and plantation owner knows it. For us to settle now . . . we would only wind up going down with him. His creditors, or possibly the three children, would be given whatever shambles Greenwood was left in."

"I would still rather just get what we could out of him," said Pamela.

"But you *won't* get it. He has let go of his primary asset. He has

given away the only thing that makes a plantation function—his workforce. Without his slaves, he has no hope of keeping the thing going
indefinitely. The coloreds are lazy and greedy and, mark my words,
will all leave him in time. The day he freed his slaves, he undercut our
strategy. Harland is right to have rethought the thing along different
tactical lines. What do you calculate Greenwood is worth, Harland?"
he asked, turning again to his cousin.

"At present, functioning profitably—I should say six months ago
and functioning profitably—I would say forty or fifty thousand,
perhaps more. The monetary value of his slaves is gone. We could
never hope to get that back. They are now, for good or ill, free. Richmond made sure the documents I drew up contained not the slightest
potential loophole in that regard. But even if they all leave and the
fields go to seed, the house and land has to be worth thirty thousand.
When we come in, of course, we will have to make a modest investment to get it up and running again—an overseer who knows how to
use the whip and a new stable of slaves—but then we will have a
profit-making enterprise that should pay us all handsome dividends
every year thereafter."

"You see, Margaret," Stuart went on, "all we have to do is wait him
out, and then advance our claim to Greenwood after Richmond has
nailed his own coffin shut. It's brilliant, Harland. All we have to do is
wait!" he said.

He raised his glass of Scotch to the others.

"To Cousin Richmond!" said Stuart. "May he receive everything he
deserves!"

"Here, here!" laughed Harland. "Well spoken indeed, Stuart."

All four now lifted their glasses toward one another in toast of
bright hopes for their future.

"To Cousin Richmond!" they said in unison.

Twenty-three

Richmond Davidson was the first to see their unexpected visitors coming up the drive in a buggy and horse rented from the livery stable in town.

He approached with a great laugh of disbelief.

"James Waters . . . I don't believe my eyes!" he exclaimed, running toward them from the direction of the barn. "Is it really you . . . not only in Virginia, but in Dove's Landing . . . and on the very threshold of Greenwood!"

Hearing both the buggy and her husband's voice from the kitchen, Carolyn hurried outside almost before Waters had explained the purpose of their visit.

"Carolyn, can you believe it!" exclaimed Richmond as Waters and his daughter climbed to the ground. "Look who's here!—James," he added to their guest, "please meet my wife, Carolyn—Carolyn . . . James Waters."

"I am happy to meet you, Mrs. Davidson," said Waters, offering his hand.

"Thank you," replied Carolyn. "And I you."

"And this is my daughter."

"Hello, Mrs. Davidson," said the girl who was nearly a foot shorter than her father, walking toward Carolyn with a bright smile and extending her hand. "I am Cherity Waters."

Their eyes met. For an instant, the world stood still. Each gazed into depths of silent recognition that was yet but a glimmer, a germ, a mustard seed that faith and further knowing would have to nurture into life. Yet in that moment, the seed also became for both a reality only time would bring to fruition.

Carolyn took the offered hand and found its grip strong in spite of the girl's diminutive size.

"I am so happy to meet you, my dear," said Carolyn. Though she smiled, her voice choked on the words. Her throat had suddenly gone very dry at hearing the girl's name.

"Carolyn," said Richmond exuberantly, "Mr. Waters is the renowned journalist from Boston who took in a wayward stranger from Virginia last year."

"Not renowned," laughed Waters. "But I enjoy what I do."

"That James Waters—how wonderful!" said Carolyn as she turned again toward the men and regained her equanimity. "I could tell from your voices that you were from the North. Richmond spoke of you after his trip to New England. He was full of praise, I should add. I am so happy to finally meet you."

"Your wife is as charming as you said, Davidson!" laughed Waters.

"Now I see why my husband is so astonished," added Carolyn. "You are indeed a long way from home."

"We are on our way to Norfolk where my daughter, one of Cherity's sisters, had a baby about six months ago."

"Oh, I see—the new grandchild! A boy or a girl?"

"A little boy."

"Congratulations."

As her father began moving toward the house with the two Davidsons, already Cherity Waters was gazing about and wandering off.

"You are something of a celebrity in the North," said Waters as they went.

"I'm afraid I don't . . . what do you mean?" said Richmond.

"What you did with your slaves."

"Ah . . . you heard!"

"Your grand experiment made the papers even up in Boston," replied Waters. "You are quite a hero in some circles there."

"And a traitor in most down here," rejoined Richmond with a humorless smile.

"That is one of the reasons I wanted to stop by on our way to Norfolk, to offer my personal congratulations, if that is the right word. I could not help reading the account with pride. I am eager to hear more about your decision." He glanced about as they reached the house. "I wonder where Cherity went," he added.

"She'll be fine," said Richmond. "As I recall, she was fond of horses."

"The understatement of the year!" laughed Waters.

"Well then, she should find plenty to interest her about the place!"

Not wanting to impose unannounced, and intending that he and Cherity would catch another train later that same day to Richmond where they would spend the night, James Waters had planned merely a brief visit to the Davidsons. But neither his acquaintance from Boston, nor his wife, would hear of it. Within an hour of their arrival, the hospitable Virginians had insisted they spend the night, and were doing their best to convince the New Englander to extend the visit even longer than that.

"My husband tells me you have three daughters," said Carolyn, as she and her husband and their guest sat down on the back porch with tall glasses of cold tea.

"Yes. Actually, my wife and I had four children in all. First we had two daughters, now married, then a son who died at birth, and then some years later, our delightful surprise. Unfortunately," he added as his tone grew melancholy, "it was her birth that cost me my wife. Kathleen died after Cherity's birth."

"I am so sorry," said Carolyn.

Waters acknowledged her sympathy with an appreciative nod.

"It was . . . let me just say, a difficult time for me. She was a good woman, a faithful churchgoer, and I still do not understand why God would—"

He stopped himself and smiled mordantly. "Well . . . old wounds, deep scars," he said. "No sense in spoiling the day by dredging up all that," he added, glancing momentarily toward Carolyn's husband.

Meanwhile, Cherity had discovered the corral and pasture where most of the horses were kept. She stood looking out over the fence at the dozen or so horses grazing in the distance.

When sixteen-year-old Seth Davidson came around the barn and saw the strange figure with its back turned standing beside the pasture, from the trousers, boots, and cowboy hat he assumed it a boy, and from the fact that whoever it was stood barely tall enough to see over the top rail, he judged it to be a boy of ten or eleven, several years younger even than his brother, Thomas. A glance toward the house, where the horse and buggy still stood, told him half the truth, that his parents must have visitors. He continued forward.

"Hi," he said as he walked up. "They're beautiful, aren't they?"

"Oh, yes!" said Cherity, turning to face him, her expression alive with pleasure at her surroundings. "Who are you?" she asked, with more candor than abruptness.

"I'm Seth Davidson," replied Seth, trying to recover from his shock at finding the face of a girl beneath the wide brim of the cowboy hat. Why he hadn't noticed the long hair spilling out below it, he did not stop to ask himself. He was not overly sophisticated for a sixteen year old. Yet his was nevertheless an age at which younger years, in his perception, fell back exponentially into memory. Whether she was ten or twelve, maybe even thirteen, made little difference. She was obviously several years younger than he was, and for a sixteen year old that meant she was a child.

"Hi," she said. "I'm Cherity Waters. My father and I are visiting. You must be Mr. and Mrs. Davidson's son."

"Yeah," nodded Seth. "So can I ask you the same thing," he said with a smile. "Who are *you*?"

Cherity giggled. "Mr. Davidson visited my father and me in Boston last year."

"Oh . . . now I recall the name. Sorry—I didn't remember at first."

"That's all right. How could you possibly know who I was?"

"And walking up from behind, when I saw your hat I didn't expect a girl."

Cherity laughed again. "Nobody does!" she said gaily. "Are these all your horses?"

"If you mean my father's—yes."

"Wow—there are so many!"

"I never thought of that before. I guess you're right."

Seeing his brother talking to someone he didn't know, fourteen-year-old Thomas now walked up behind them. Cherity turned.

"Hi," she said.

"Hi," returned Thomas, glancing at Seth with a look of question.

"This is my brother, Thomas," said Seth. "Thomas, this is—Sorry, I forgot your name."

"Cherity."

"Oh, right . . . Cherity Waters."

Cherity extended her hand to the newcomer. "Hi, Thomas," she said. "My father is visiting your parents."

"I wondered where you three were!" said a voice from the direction of the house. They looked up to see the elder Davidson walking toward them.

"I got distracted looking at your horses, Mr. Davidson," said Cherity. "I hope you don't mind."

"Of course not. I see you've met my sons. How would the three of you like to come up to the house for something to eat?"

The two young men did not have to be asked twice when it came to food. As they began following them back toward the large brick house, Davidson fell in step with their guest. "My wife has just about got your father talked into bringing your bags in from the buggy," he said, "and staying on an extra day with us."

"Oh good!" exclaimed Cherity. "I can hardly wait to see everything there is to see!"

Thomas glanced back briefly, concluding, like his brother, from her

high voice and girlish enthusiasm that the daughter of his parents'
guest was only eleven or twelve.

⌒

A couple of hours later that afternoon, as Richmond and his guest
were discussing a walk down to the former slave quarters, which
Waters was eager to see, the sound of horses riding up to the house
interrupted them. Thomas leaped from his chair and ran from the
room.

He reappeared a minute later.

"Wyatt and Cameron are here," he said to his father. "They want to
know if Seth and I can go riding. They're going up on the ridge."

"Sure," replied Richmond. "Bring them in so they can meet our
guests."

Thomas disappeared again. When he returned, two other boys
followed him into the room, one taller and older than Seth, the
second a year younger than Thomas.

"Hello, Wyatt . . . Cameron!" said Richmond pleasantly, rising and
shaking hands with both boys. "Out for a ride?"

"Yes, sir," said the older of the two in a deep, manly voice.

"It's a fine day for it. I would like you to meet our guests from
Boston. This is Mr. Waters —James, these are our neighbors, Wyatt
Beaumont and his brother Cameron."

"Pleased to meet you, sir," said Wyatt, shaking his hand.

"Hello, Mr. Waters," said Cameron politely in a high boy's voice.

"And this is his daughter, Cherity."

"Miss Waters," said Wyatt with a nod, allowing his eyes to glance
over her face briefly.

"Hi, Wyatt . . . Hi, Cameron," said Cherity. "I am happy to meet
you."

"Well, I guess we'll be going, then," said Seth, rising from the table
to join the three boys.

"Maybe Miss Waters would like to join us," suggested Wyatt.

The words seemed to fall like cold water on the countenances of the other three boys. They hesitated and glanced at each other with looks that conveyed anything but enthusiasm at the thought of having a girl along to slow them down.

"I think that's an excellent idea," said the elder Davidson.

"Uh, I don't know, Dad," said Seth. "Some of the footing up there's not the best."

But Wyatt glanced toward Cherity, whose eyes had widened considerably more than usual at his suggestion.

"Do you ride?" he asked.

"A little," she replied, trying not to sound too eager, glancing toward her father, who could not help smiling at her answer.

"Let her come, then," Wyatt said to the others. "We'll take it easy—if you want to, that is," he added, again turning to Cherity.

"Uh . . . sure—it sounds fun!"

"Then let's go," said Wyatt.

Cherity rose and followed the four out of the house. As they walked toward the barn, Wyatt fell into step beside her.

"I'll saddle up a horse for you," he said down to her, for her head barely came to his chest. "Which horses are you going to take, Seth?" he asked, turning toward Seth.

"I don't know. I guess I'll ride Dusty. What about you, Tom?"

"Paintbrush."

"What about for Miss Waters?" asked Wyatt.

"I guess we'll put her on old Diamond," said Seth.

"He sounds slow," said Cherity with disappointment. "And old."

"But he's reliable," said Seth. "I don't want you getting thrown off."

"I won't get thrown off," she rejoined confidently. "And I don't want to just plod along—I want a horse that's fast enough to keep up."

Seth and Thomas glanced at each other, Thomas's expression saying *Girls always think they can keep up . . . but they never can.*

"My sister never rides," said Cameron, now coming up on the other side of Cherity with boyish eagerness as they continued to the barn.

He was still young enough to be excited at the prospect of having someone new along.

"How old is she?" asked Cherity.

"Sixteen," replied Cameron.

"Why doesn't she ride?"

"I don't know. I don't think she likes horses."

"What's her name?"

"Veronica. She's sweet on Seth."

"She is not, Cam!" said Seth, though the color rising in his cheeks showed that he took the words more seriously than he let on.

"She is, too. Everyone knows it—don't they, Wyatt?" said Cameron, appealing to the wisdom of his older brother.

"I don't know, Cam," he said. "Since Veronica isn't here, let's leave her out of it and stick to horses."

"Oh, all right . . . but it's still true."

No more comments followed in that direction. They reached the barn, Seth and Thomas called three horses from the pasture to be saddled, and ten minutes later the five set off up a gentle slope toward a wooded hillside in the distance.

"What's this one's name?" asked Cherity as they went. "It's not old Diamond, is it?"

"No," laughed Seth. "I thought maybe you would like Silverfoot better—she's reliable *and* reasonably fast. But I wouldn't gallop her if I were you."

"Why not?"

"Like I said before, some of the terrain is uneven and steep. I don't want you getting hurt."

"I will make sure nothing happens to her," said Wyatt.

They reached the woods and continued through it. The conversation was subdued except for Wyatt at Cherity's side who kept up what he could of a conversation. Before long Cherity realized that she was the reason that the other three seemed bored with the slow pace.

Gradually they emerged into a clearing about two-thirds of the way up the ridge. There the path widened and eventually gave way to a flat

expanse of lush grassy pasture where the Davidson horses were sometimes taken to graze and roam and run.

"Oh, it's beautiful!" exclaimed Cherity as they came out of the
shadow of the trees behind them. "I had no idea we would find such a
place up here after we'd climbed like we had."

"It's like a hideaway of meadow with hills all around," said Seth.

"We bring the horses here to graze," added Thomas. "Sometimes
we train them here."

"But there are no fences."

"We don't need any."

"Won't the horses wander off?"

"There are enough natural barriers to keep them here," replied
Seth. "The only way up to this meadow is through woodland, some of
it steep. It's surrounded on two sides by the slope of the ridge up to
the summit, and on the third by a small river that runs over there
behind us. The horses could leave the meadow, I suppose, but they are
content to remain here, or to wander back down by the trail we just
came up, which takes them straight back to their pasture by the barn."

"What's that up there?" said Cherity, pointing to the highest point
rising beyond the meadow.

"That's Harper's Peak," said Cameron.

"It's the highest mountain around here," added Thomas.

"It's not a mountain," said Wyatt, riding alongside Cherity again,
"but it's all we've got for one."

"Can we ride up there?" asked Cherity.

"That's where we're going," said Wyatt.

"Now that we are on the flat . . . did you say this horse can run?"
said Cherity, a gleam in her eye.

"Yeah," began Seth, "but—"

Before he could reply further, the girl they thought they had been
pampering since leaving Greenwood shouted and lashed her horse's
rump and tore off across the grassy expanse.

The two older boys looked at each other in astonishment, then one
by one the four took off after her. Catching her, however, proved
easier said than done. Whatever the other qualities of the steed they

had selected, with a light girl in the saddle, the mare called Silverfoot was capable of moving with greater speed across the meadow than any of them could have predicted. Fifteen seconds later, the four boys, galloping as fast as they were able and yelling at their mounts at the top of their lungs, all still trailed her.

She glanced back, saw them desperately trying to catch her and could not help laughing with delight. When the faint sound of her laughter reached them over the wind, it made her pursuers—in two groups now, the sixteen and seventeen year old side by side, followed a few lengths back by the thirteen and fourteen year old—dig in their heels all the more, but without effect.

As Cherity turned to look behind her, the brim of her hat caught in the breeze and flew from her head. She gave a little cry as she watched it sail back, only missing by inches being trampled under the four sets of hooves behind her. But she turned forward again and continued on, flying across the grass, her auburn hair flowing out behind her, a great smile of exhilaration on her face.

At length, some two hundred yards farther on, suddenly Cherity reined to the side and peeled off in a great arc which gradually took her back the way she had come. The boys' horses thundered past as she galloped back in the direction of her hat. Glancing back, she saw one rider, light hair blowing wildly, following her, while the other three disappeared in the distance. By the time she reined in, her lone pursuer had nearly drawn even. The sides of both horses were heaving and great puffs of air burst from their distended nostrils.

"That was wonderful!" exclaimed Cherity.

"What happened?" laughed Seth as he cantered up behind her.

"My hat flew off—didn't you see it! I thought it was time I came back for it or I might never find it."

She hopped down to the ground, ran a little way, picked up the hat and replaced it on her head, and was quickly back in the saddle.

"Oh, that was so fun!" she said. "I'm not used to being able to gallop at full speed. In Boston where I ride at the outskirts of the city, you have to be careful since there are so many people about. But here . . ."

She could think of no words to express her delight, though the expression on her face said more than even the most perfectly chosen words could have conveyed.

"You fooled us all!" said Seth. "You didn't tell us you could ride like that!"

Cherity threw her head back and laughed with glee, almost losing her hat again.

"You didn't ask!" she said. "You just assumed, because I'm a girl, that I couldn't ride as well as you. Then you were going to stick me on some old plough horse!"

"Diamond isn't a plough horse!" laughed Seth. "He's just—"

"Old and slow . . . and *reliable!*" added Cherity with mock annoyance. "How insulting!"

"I'm sorry. I didn't mean . . ."

"I'm only joking!" she laughed. "And it doesn't matter. That was a great ride. But where are the others?" she asked, glancing about.

For the first time Seth realized they were alone. "There," he said, pointing, "there's the dust from their horses, see . . . where it disappears into the trees at the end of the pasture."

"Do you know where they're going?"

"Up to the top of the ridge, like we were talking about before. They'll wait for us there. Come on, we'll take another way."

"Will we be able to catch them?"

"Not if I know Wyatt," laughed Seth. "He's competitive enough, once the race is on, he won't look back."

"Where does he live?" asked Cherity as Seth led the way and they began cantering gently across the grass toward the opposite side of the high meadow.

"On the other side of the ridge."

"Is it true what his brother, the little boy . . . what was his name?"

"Cameron?"

"Oh, yes—is it true what Cameron said about his sister?"

Seth laughed a little uncomfortably. "We all sort of grew up together," he replied. "Wyatt and Veronica and Cameron, and Cynthia and Thomas and me. Veronica's at that age where she's sweet on every boy she sees. But that was really something back there," he added, anxious to change the subject, "I've never seen Silverfoot move so fast! She must like your touch."

"I did nothing except let her run," said Cherity.

"Maybe. But some people possess a knack for letting them run faster than others. Horses know when they can trust whoever's on their back."

"She's a beautiful animal."

"Do you have a horse of your own in Boston?" asked Seth, leading diagonally across the pasture-meadow toward the narrow trail that would lead them to Harper's Peak.

"Just buggy horses. But my father takes me to some stables where they rent horses for saddle riding."

Seth led them off the level and soon they were climbing slowly over rocky ground, moving steadily higher up the ridge to the plateau that ran along its crest. As once more they pulled even with one another, Seth spoke again.

"Horses are such noble creatures, don't you think?" he said.

"Oh, yes!" rejoined Cherity enthusiastically. "I know they call the lion king of beasts, but I've always thought horses far more regal and kingly."

"And they seem to have such a special bond with men . . . like dogs do too."

"I don't know about dogs," laughed Cherity. "I've never had a special dog."

"I'm not quite sure about dogs either," said Seth. "But I think there will be horses in heaven—because of their stateliness and nobility."

"Heaven!" laughed Cherity. "You make it sound like a real place."

"It is."

"What do you mean?" said Cherity. "It's just a fairy tale place, isn't it? I mean people don't *really* live in the sky after they die and go around doing things like riding horses!"

"Maybe not in the sky—but they go to heaven . . . someplace," rejoined Seth. "Don't you think heaven's real?"

"I've never thought about it."

"What about the church you go to—don't they talk about heaven?"

"We don't go to church."

"Oh . . . why not?"

"I don't know. My father's not very interested. He used to be, I guess, and my mother was. Why, are you religious? Do you go to church all the time?"

"Not *all* the time, but often enough I guess," replied Seth. "It's not that I think we are religious or anything like that. But God is a part of our lives."

"What does that mean, exactly?"

"That God lives inside us and is our friend, that he is involved in what we do and think, and that we try to live the kind of lives he wants us to."

"That sounds a lot like something your father said to me last year. But why would you want to have God be part of your life? It sounds stuffy and boring to me."

"If God made us and loves us and wants the best for us, shouldn't he be part of our lives?"

"I don't know—I guess that's another thing I've never thought about. Do you really think God is everywhere, I mean that he's around . . . *right here?*"

"Sure!" laughed Seth. "If he created the universe, and made you and me . . . where else would he be but everywhere?"

"So you think he's even listening to what we're saying?"

"I suppose so."

"That's spooky!"

Again Seth laughed. "I don't see why. I think it's kind of nice that he's so close. But then I suppose it depends on what kind of person you think God is."

Cherity did not reply. The brief conversation had already succeeded in turning her thoughts into channels where they had never ventured before. She wasn't quite sure what to make of it.

"Come on!" said Seth. "Let's have another gallop—we're almost to the top!"

He led out, not so fast as they had below for the footing was not

quite so secure, but at a good easy gallop, until at last they crested the
top of the ridge, then continued on to the summit known as Harper's
Peak.

He reined in and they sat gazing all about them at the low lying
hills and valleys and the river winding its way in the distance. The
only sound for several minutes came from the breathing and fidgety
movements of the two horses beneath them.

"I thought you said Wyatt and the two younger boys would be
waiting for us up here," said Cherity.

"I thought they would be," replied Seth, glancing about and listening for any sound of horses. He thought her comment a little strange
since, in his eyes, their guest for the day was easily a year or two younger than Thomas.

"Where is Greenwood?" she asked after she had gazed in nearly
every direction.

Seth pointed to a collection of red roofs in the distance. Then he
turned in the opposite direction and pointed down the northeasterly
slope of the ridge. "That's the Beaumont plantation down there," he
said, "where Wyatt and Veronica and Cameron live. Over there," he
added, swinging around southward, "you can see the town of Dove's
Landing."

"Are your family and Wyatt's good friends?" asked Cherity.

"My father and Mr. Beaumont grew up together and rode all over
these hills."

"Do you and Veronica and Wyatt—"

"Oh, look—there they are!" said Seth. He pointed down the slope
about halfway between Oakbriar and Dove's Landing.

"Where are they going?"

"I don't know. But I know which trail they took . . . come on!"

They turned and began the ride down the opposite side of the
ridge. It was quiet as they went, a more subdued mood settling upon
them.

Suddenly Cherity cried out.

"Look . . . what's that!"

"A cave," laughed Seth. "There are all kinds of them around here."

"Can we explore it?"

Without awaiting an answer, Cherity was off. By the time Seth had pulled up behind Silverfoot, she had dismounted and was running inside the cave's mouth.

"How far does it go!" she asked, her voice echoing into the black void in the side of the hill.

"I don't know," replied Seth. "I've only gone a little way inside this one. You need a lantern to go past where you can see . . . and they say they're haunted."

"Phooey! You don't believe any of that, do you?"

"This used to be Cherokee land . . . so you never know. Besides, caves are dangerous."

At the words "Cherokee land," a strange sensation suddenly swept through Cherity's frame, a tingling feeling that gave her goose bumps all up and down her back. What had caused it? Why did she almost feel like she had been here before? That she somehow knew this place . . . or ought to?

By now they had turned slightly so that the cave's mouth was no longer visible, and were standing in near total darkness. As Cherity continued to creep forward, she stretched out her hands to make sure she didn't bump into anything.

"Why do you say caves are dangerous?" she asked at length.

"I don't know—legends, ancient burial sites, hexes and curses and witch doctors . . . you know."

"Phooey!" said Cherity again. "The Cherokees are civilized just like us. Did there used to be a Cherokee tribe around here? I've always been very interested in them and have read about them. I thought they were farther south."

"I don't know about a tribe . . . I don't think so. Mr. Brown was a Cherokee, that's all, and we're on what used to be his land."

The words "Mr. Brown was a Cherokee" again caused the uncanny feeling to flood her, a sense that said she ought to know more about the enigmatic Mr. Brown than she did . . . or perhaps it was the feeling that one day she would.

Finally Cherity stopped. "Well, you're right . . . it is starting to get a little spooky," she said. "I'm ready to get out of here and get back to where we can see where we're going."

She turned, but as she tried to make her way back, she bumped straight into Seth.

"Oops!" she exclaimed.

"You see," Seth laughed. "You've got to go slow when you're in a cave—you never know what you might run into."

A minute later, they were walking back out into the bright sunlight.

They remounted and rode on. Again Cherity saw something in the distance that attracted her notice. "There's a house down there," she said, pointing through some trees to a clearing behind. "That's not the big plantation you showed me where your neighbors live?"

"No, that's Mr. Brown's house. No one lives there now."

"Why not?"

"I don't know. You'll have to ask my father. Mr. Brown gave the house and his land to my grandfather, and no one's lived in it since Mr. Brown left. We use the land and occasionally some of his barns and stables for storage or for some of the animals. But mostly it's not used except the land."

"It seems too bad."

"I suppose. But there's not much my father can do with it—it's too far from our house to be of much use."

"How far is it?"

"Two or three miles."

"Doesn't it get used for anything?"

But Seth pretended not to hear as he rode a few paces away. He had promised his parents to tell no one that Reverend Jones' secret congregation of slaves from the area was now using the old Brown house as a makeshift church. It was easier not to answer at all than try to make something up without crossing the line into actually telling an untruth.

By the time the two riders reached the valley west of Dove's Landing, there was no sign of the others and they had no alternative but to make their way back to Greenwood by the most direct route. Seth did not want to go to Oakbriar looking for them and run into Veronica just now. And he thought he ought to get the girl home before her father began to worry about her. He didn't know how long their guests planned to stay.

As they skirted along a seldom-used road about a mile west of town, they rode up to a walker coming toward them. As they reached him, Seth reined in.

"Hi, Scully," he said to a sloppily dressed young man a year or two older than himself.

"Hey, Davidson," said the other, glancing up toward the girl on the other horse, then back at Seth, without smiling at either.

"Have you seen my brother or Wyatt Beaumont riding along here?" asked Seth.

"No, I ain't seen nobody. But me and Wyatt's good friends."

"Yeah . . . but they haven't been around here, huh?"

"I said I seen nobody."

"All right . . . see you later, Scully."

"Why didn't you introduce me to him?" asked Cherity after they continued on and were out of sight.

"I don't know," replied Seth. "I guess I didn't think of it. He's from . . . you know, the wrong side of town, if you know what I mean."

"I don't think I know what you mean."

"Let's just say that Scully Riggs isn't the kind of person you need to know. I mean, he's all right, I guess—I've known him all my life, just like Wyatt. But he's just . . . I don't know, different."

"He seems to like Wyatt."

"He looks up to him. A lot of the boys around Dove's Landing do. Wyatt's the kind of guy other kids want to be around."

They rode into the precincts of Greenwood a couple of hours after setting out. They saw Thomas just emerging from the barn after unsaddling his horse.

"Hey, Thomas, how long have you been back?" called Seth.

"Ten or fifteen minutes," answered his brother.

"Where'd you go? We tried to catch up with you."

"Wyatt just kept galloping," said Thomas. "He didn't say anything even after we got to the top, but just kept going."

"Yeah, we saw you down the ridge."

"Then when we got to the bottom, he headed back to Oakbriar, so I just came home."

"Did you run into Scully?"

"Riggs . . . no."

"And Wyatt didn't say anything?"

"Nope."

Just then the two men came walking toward them from the direction of the slave village.

"Cherity!" called Waters. "You were gone a long time—did you have a good ride?"

"Oh, Daddy . . . it was spectacular! What about the train? When do we have to go?"

"I finally convinced your father that you two ought to stay and spend the night with us," said Richmond.

"Oh, good—then maybe I can have another ride!"

Twenty-four

The uniformed rider who appeared on horseback one afternoon in the fall of 1856 had not been seen at Greenwood for several years. He was, however, instantly recognized for he was an old family friend.

"Colonel Lee!" said Carolyn, walking from the house to meet him as he dismounted. "How good to see you again!"

"Carolyn . . . it has indeed been too long, for which I apologize."

"You are a busy man, Colonel. Your duties take you far from home. We certainly understand that."

"Not so far that I should neglect old friendships."

"But I thought you were commanding a regiment in Texas after leaving West Point. How do you come to be here?"

"A brief trip home for family business. Unfortunately I must be back in Texas next month."

"How is Mary Anne?"

"Well, thank you, and Richmond?"

"Well also," replied Carolyn. "I am sure you have heard about the changes around here?"

"All of Virginia has heard of them!" laughed Lee. "Indeed, if not all the nation, certainly all of the South. The news did not actually reach Texas, but as a fellow Virginian, I keep up on these things! That is why I have come. I had to see you and tell you personally how proud I am of your decision."

"That will mean a great deal to Richmond, as it does to me . . . especially coming from you. There has been much criticism."

"I can imagine."

"Come in!" said Carolyn, leading him toward the house. "Would you like a julep or cold tea while I ride out to tell Richmond you are here?"

"Where is he?"

"Out with the slaves. We're in the middle of harvesting a field of cotton—but what am I saying? You see, the change is even difficult for us to get used to! He is out in the fields with *our hired workers*."

Lee laughed. "A julep sounds wonderful," he said. "Perhaps Richmond can take a break and join me. I will go find him myself. Just point me in the right direction."

"Let me get Moses started on the juleps, then I will ride down with you."

An hour later Richmond Davidson and Robert Lee were seated in the midst of the Davidson arbor sipping mint juleps and reminiscing about old times, when their fathers had visited one another at their respective plantations.

The two had not been bosom friends as children and youths, only occasional acquaintances. Their fathers, who encountered one another through Virginia politics, had developed a mutual respect and an abiding bond of friendship, which they passed on to the sons. Circumstances and geography, however, prevented them seeing one another oftener than every two or three years. The sons were always included in such meetings and thus kept in touch as they grew—first as playful boys, then as rambunctious teens, then as thoughtful young men, and during the last ten or fifteen years as representing Virginia's rising new generation of leaders. The Davidsons had followed the rise of their friend's military career with pride. Though they saw less of one another than both might have wished, Lee perceived a deepening spiritual wisdom in the countenance of his friend. In recent years he had come to consider it a relational touchstone in his own life that kept him oriented through the troubles that were steadily encroaching upon their beloved Virginia's former peaceful existence.

"Times are changing, my friend," mused Lee after a reflective silence had settled on the conversation. "One senses it among the troops—an imperceptible tension between the young men from the North and those from the South. We all wear the same uniforms, but there is a difference. It was especially pronounced at West Point, but you even see it as far away as Texas."

"Where will it lead, Robert?" asked Davidson.

"Ah, Richmond, that is the question," replied Lee. "If one only knew! It seems, however, that you have not waited for events to over-take you. You have stolen a march on them by setting history in motion yourself!"

Davidson roared with laughter.

"You make it sound rather more noble than many of our Southern colleagues and fellow plantation owners consider it—my neighbor being a notable example."

"Beaumont?"

Davidson nodded. "He has not spoken to me in more than a year."

"One cannot judge matters of conscience by the standards of men like Beaumont," rejoined Lee. "I have had a run-in or two with him myself over the years."

"Still . . . it is difficult to lose a friend."

"Certainly. But would you not agree that such is occasionally the price of following one's conscience?"

"Of course."

"Well, I assure you that whatever comes, you will not lose this friend. I cannot tell you how much I admire what you have done in the matter of your slaves."

"Your words mean a great deal, Robert."

They each took sips from their glasses, then glanced up to see a young man of sixteen approaching. He was nearly as tall as his father, filling out nicely in chest and shoulders, with blond hair waving in the afternoon's breeze. He wore dirt-stained dungarees and a blue cotton shirt, equally work worn, rolled up to the elbows.

"Hello, Colonel Lee!" he said, extending his hand to his father's visitor. "My mother told me you were here."

"Would this be Seth!" exclaimed Lee as he stood to shake the boy's hand. He glanced toward Davidson with a wink and smile.

"Indeed it is, Robert."

"Seth, my boy—you have become a man since I saw you last!"

"Yes, sir," said Seth with a smile.

"And a strong, hardworking one at that, judging from the look of it."

"Seth is my right-hand man," said Davidson. "I could not run this place without him. How goes the cotton, Seth?"

"The second wagon is nearly full," replied the lad. "Malachi and the others are finishing it now. Do you mind if I quit a little early today? Wyatt and Veronica asked me to come for a visit."

"Sure, Seth. I see no reason why not."

"Thanks. Good-bye, Colonel Lee . . . it was good to see you again."

"A pleasant young man," said Lee as Seth left the garden in the direction of the house. "You and Carolyn must be proud."

"We are. Seth is a good boy and I believe he will be God's man one day."

"And little Thomas?"

"He is not so little anymore."

"How old is he?"

"Fourteen. And sad to say, he is listening to contrary voices. He has not been supportive of what we have done and is gradually voicing his opposition in more strident ways. It is early to tell, but I fear it may come between us."

"And Seth?"

"He endorses our action wholeheartedly. I think he is proud of the stand we have taken."

"As well he should be."

"But it is a puzzle how you can raise two sons in exactly the same manner alongside one another, and yet they react so differently to the training you instill in them."

"Indeed, it is surely one of the great puzzles of life. These people Seth is going to visit . . . do I recognize—"

"Yes," nodded Richmond, "they are Denton's two oldest children. Hardly children any longer. Wyatt is a year older than Seth."

"And the daughter?"

"She is sixteen, although you would never know it. She easily looks eighteen already and I think may be fascinated with Seth."

"It is not hard to see why. He is strikingly good-looking and well developed for a boy of sixteen."

"You're right," laughed Richmond. "He is naive for one who looks so mature. Though he and Veronica are the same age, I fear that she is decades ahead of him when it comes to the games of romance with which her kind are so skilled. I hope he keeps his wits about him."

"As long as he depends on you for counsel, he will learn from the experience. And speaking of young women, how is your Cynthia? I haven't seen her."

"I think she is at the colored houses helping the women. Today is wash day. She is twenty and we expect her engagement to be announced almost any time. It is younger than we would have wished, but these things happen."

"Who is the lucky young man?"

"A military man like yourself—a naval cadet by the name of Jeffrey Verdon."

"I am glad to hear it. I think I may recognize the name. Is his father also a military man?"

Davidson nodded.

"Where is the young Verdon stationed?"

"Annapolis. He has another year before his first assignment."

"Has he spoken to you?" asked Lee.

"He has," smiled Davidson.

"And?"

"I gave my consent. He is all I could hope for in a son-in-law. Both Carolyn and I are very pleased."

Another thoughtful silence was broken only by the sound of the trickle of water past them in the brook a few yards away.

"Would that I had your courage, Richmond," said Lee at length. "If I owned four million slaves, I would cheerfully sacrifice them for the preservation of the Union. I loathe the thought of owning another human being created in God's image. Going into the military saved me from having to make that decision. Still, I am uncertain whether slavery is a strictly personal issue, as you have chosen to define it in your case, or whether states' rights as a national issue should take precedence when it comes time for me to face similar decisions. In any event, I am not pleased with the course of the 'Cotton States,' as they term themselves. I am opposed to any form of slave trade on every ground." *

"These are not simple matters to resolve, it is true," said Davidson. "I am sure you have prayed and will continue to pray about your own course of action."

Lee nodded. "I have indeed sought God's will, but as yet the way before me remains unclear."

"We must each walk out the path he shows us," rejoined Richmond. "And he does not give all men the same course of action to follow."

"How true! Yet ever since I heard what you and Carolyn had done, I found myself wishing I could take some equally public stand against the evil system."

"Perhaps such a time will come. When it does, I have no doubt you will follow your conscience no less than I have mine."

"Perhaps you are right. One never knows. Yet I find myself constricted by my position. Not that I am so well known in the army. Yet after being in charge at West Point for the last three years before being transferred to Texas, my name is sufficiently known in military circles that any action I take could have widespread ramifications. Although I don't know what I am worried about," he added, chuckling. "You are certainly now as well known as I!"

---

*The first two sentences of this paragraph, and the last two, as well as certain other statements in this section not specifically related to this fictionalized conversation with Richmond Davidson, are direct historical quotes made by Lee himself. Lee was given a number of slaves in the will of his father-in-law. When his wife's father died and the slaves became Lee's property, he granted them their freedom.

"Not by choice, I assure you," laughed Davidson. "Still," he added, growing serious again, "I understand completely what you mean and the caution you feel. A man in your position must walk with measured step. Much is at stake. Many will follow your example. You are a prominent figure. The same cannot be said for me."

"Don't be too sure, Richmond. It may be your example that will show the light through the darkness for us all."

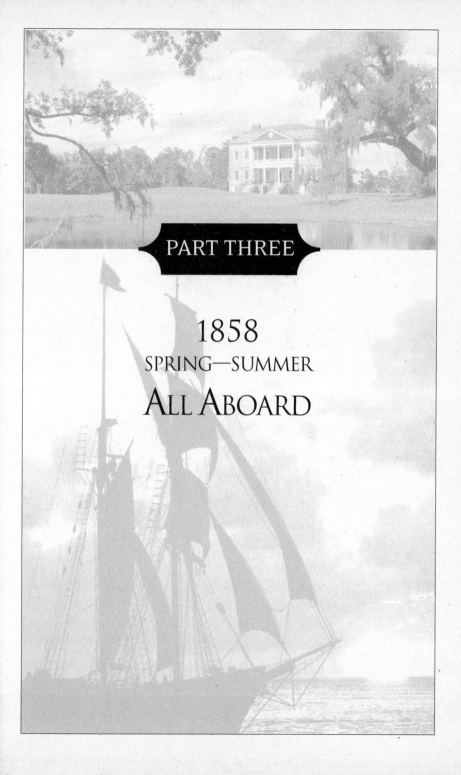

PART THREE

1858
SPRING—SUMMER
ALL ABOARD

Twenty-five

~⌒

A huge jet-black thoroughbred was rearing, bucking, plunging, and doing everything in its power to unseat the teenage rider on its back. That the magnificent beast had been ridden before, many times in fact, would not have been immediately apparent to any but one knowledgeable in the breaking of horses, as was the black man standing calmly watching the display.

"Whoa . . . easy!" cried the youth, nearly losing his balance. "What did you put in Demon's oats this morning, Alexander!"

"Ain't da oats, massa Seth!" laughed the onlooker. "He jes' knows da meanin' ob his name, dat's all!"

The animal's name, in fact, had been perfectly chosen, given by Seth's father, who, from the moment they had begun trying to tame the energetic foal, recognized a greater than usual amount of self-will in the animal's makeup. And though a strong will is a valuable asset for the development of personality in either man or beast, unless it is well directed it will usually come to ruin in the end. It was just because their efforts had been so unsuccessful in taming Demon's tendency toward devilry that Seth had lately been trying his hand at stronger measures.

"Open the gate, Alexander!" he called, holding on to the reins for dear life, "I'm going to let him go!"

The black man quickly hurried to the opposite side of the enclo-

sure, unlatched a wooden gate, and swung it wide. Even as Demon
reared high on his back hooves, Seth yanked his head around, coming
dangerously close to pulling him over on his back, then leaned as far
forward as he could, laying his own body lengthwise against the
maned neck, and, the instant Demon's forelegs touched the ground,
gave him both heels and whip in good measure. Demon was through
the gate in less than a second and galloping away from the barn at
what would have been frightening speed had any but Seth Davidson
occupied the saddle. Sending clumps of earth and grass up behind
them, the two thundered away in a wild display of raw animal energy.
Alexander watched them go with mingled reverence, awe, and fear, for
he loved horses as much as Seth, until horse and rider had together
become a mere speck in the distance, then muttered something to
himself with a smile—which words may have included a brief prayer
that the next time he saw Seth he was alive—then turned back toward
the barn.

Seth's plan was to run Demon until he tired and then run him
more. And a great deal of space was required to do it, for never had he
encountered an animal with such a reservoir of strength. Halfway
toward town by the back road, Seth wheeled Demon off onto a dirt
path leading toward the river. Another three-quarters of a mile farther,
Demon's speed showing no sign of flagging, Seth turned off toward a
point where the riverbank gently sloped down to meet the water. Still
digging in his heels and once more lashing his hindquarters, he drove
Demon straight into the gentle flow, pushing him forward until the
water reached a depth where he must swim. Rather than hold on for
the other side, however, he now turned his head upstream straight
into the current, and there let him struggle against it for two or three
more minutes.

Finally Seth jumped from his back, bringing the reins over
Demon's head, and swam himself until his feet found the bottom,
then pulled the horse back toward shore.

Emerging from the water with great splashing and a frenetic
display, he led him up onto the sandy riverbank, the huge dripping

black sides heaving and the breath coming from Demon's nostrils in great bursts.

"Had enough yet, Demon?" Seth shouted. For his only answer the beast reared again, plunging and kicking with his forehooves even as Seth danced about and struggled to maintain his grip on the reins and stay out of the way of danger. He would have kicked Seth's brains in, which was surely his intent, had not Seth's own feet been nearly as quick as his.

"I see you haven't!" cried Seth. He sprinted to one side, and before Demon could kick at him or maneuver to prevent it, leapt into the saddle and tore off with Demon again, this time up the rising incline of the ridge along whose base the river ran.

Another two miles was consumed by the huge four-footed strides in less than five minutes. Any normal horse would by this time have been exhausted enough to give up the contest of wills. But Demon was no normal horse.

Suddenly Seth reined in sharply and pulled back on the bit until Demon reared. Seth held on, allowing him to rear and kick and try to unseat him, until he reared a little too far, coming nearly straight to vertical on his hind legs. With one swift motion, Seth let himself fall rearward out of the saddle, slid to the ground straight down his back bringing the reins with him, pulling Demon's head further behind him as he came.

The moment his own feet landed, Seth pulled Demon's head hard sideways, only barely avoiding the flurry of legs and hooves.

Surprised and off balance, Demon fell backward with a screaming whinny.

Demon thudded to the ground on his left flank, writhing and kicking. Before Demon could regain his feet, Seth jumped forward and pressed the horse's head to the ground by sitting on Demon's left ear, the other ear flat on the ground as Seth's rump pinned the huge skull immobile to the earth. Unable to move his head, Demon was thus rendered helpless and soon gave up the struggle. He lay quietly panting for air through mouth and nostrils beneath the weight of Seth's body.

There Seth remained contentedly for ten minutes, then fifteen, then twenty. An occasional upward glance of Demon's one visible angry eye was the only indication of the animal fury left within him.

Fifty minutes later, Alexander saw them again coming toward the barn, Demon walking quietly, the fire of his rebellious nature temporarily spent, with Seth seated calmly in the saddle.

"I see you managed ter run some ob dat anger out er him," he said as Seth dismounted.

"Only for the moment," rejoined Seth. "I had to try his patience severely."

"What you do, massa Seth?"

"I pulled him over and sat on his head."

"You what!" laughed Alexander.

"It didn't hurt him. I hope the lesson will pay off in the development of his character, once he understands that it is only because I am his friend that I discipline him to my rule."

"You think he be capable er understandin' all dat?" asked Alexander.

"Not in the way *we* are meant to understand the same principle at work in us toward God," laughed Seth. "But surely Demon has *some* inkling of the fact that it is his duty to obey me. At least I hope so. Otherwise, my treatment of him would be sheer cruelty."

Seth continued on into the barn, where he unsaddled the great black, then attached a nose bag of oats to his head and proceeded to brush down his glistening coat. The huge ribs still moved in and out with a little more rapidity of rhythm than normal.

Though his own personality and character were still in the process of formation, to one extent, no less than Demon's, Seth was farther along in the recognition of where that process was leading and who was its Author. Yet he had this in common with the beast he would tame—neither could he see its end result.

At eighteen, Seth Davidson was both boy and man. He intermixed humor, innocence, and pluck in rare combination. He could at one moment enter into childish sport with his brother as if he were still ten, at another make comments that displayed insight beyond his years, at another tell of some incident with wit and wry grins of humor that kept his parents in stitches, and at yet another walk up to a rattlesnake with only a stick in his hand without the least fear of being bitten. His father occasionally worried that he was *too* confident in himself, yet saw also that Seth's courage was born more of sincerity and meekness than bravado.

Seth's was a trusting nature. Because he trusted he neither feared nor cared what people thought. In the bedrock of such a nature, with such a father and mother as he had, it was only natural that the spiritual regions in Seth's consciousness would send down roots, invisible at first, but deepening as he progressed from youth into manhood. The plant from those roots would eventually rise to become a faith-tree of his own, whose trunk circumstance and trial would toughen and make strong. Seth had begun to turn the budding leaves and branches of his growing being to the light, which is the greatest step toward manhood it is possible to take.

And yet, for one more season of his youth, the very trusting innocence, and boyish naïveté that was his strength would also be the very thing that would land him into water a little hotter than was comfortable.

"You are beautiful, Demon," said Seth, speaking softly as he usually did when he was alone with any horse. "Your coat would look almost as good if I didn't brush it. But you let me brush it, don't you? You let me because you are learning to trust me. If you can learn to trust me just as much when I am in the saddle, you will be glad. I am sorry I had to do what I did today, though I don't think it hurt you too much. But you have to learn to control your temper, otherwise someday you may kill someone who doesn't know how to handle you like I do. It is for your own protection, and theirs, that I must do what I do."

He continued to brush at the black coat, then smiled. "Your hair and mane remind me of Veronica's hair," he said. "Hers is just as black, and when the sun catches it just right, it glistens like yours.

She is like you and yet not like you. Beautiful as your coat is, though, I do not think Veronica would take kindly to being compared with a horse!" he added with a laugh.

Thought of Veronica turned Seth's reflections toward the future. From force of habit he continued to speak aloud, as if Demon were his equine confidante.

"What do you think, Demon," he said, "what will become of Veronica and me? We have known each other all our lives. Will we marry one day? It almost seems inevitable, yet I can hardly imagine Veronica content forever as a farmer's wife. She would always be wanting to throw parties!"

He let out a long sigh as he stooped now to brush the underside of Demon's great oxygen-furnace.

"She is beautiful," he continued, still talking to himself, "as beautiful for a girl as you are for a horse. I like how I feel when I am with her. Is that what they call love, Demon? I wonder what she would think if she had seen you and me out there today. Would she think me cruel and heartless? Would it make her hate me to see me treat you so . . . or would she even care?"

Again Seth began to laugh. "Actually, Demon, sometimes I think that Veronica is trying to tame *me*!"

Suddenly something splashed from above into the bucket of water at his feet. Startled, Seth jumped, and then saw that a brush had fallen into the water. At the same moment he heard giggling. He spun around and looked above him through the hole into the loft.

"Thomas, you rascal!" he cried. "How long have you been up there?"

"Long enough to hear everything you said about Veronica!" laughed his brother.

"What! Why you—"

Seth dropped the brush in his hand and dashed for the stairs. A squeal of terrified laughter sounded above him as Thomas ran frantically to hide. Seth took the narrow stairs three at a time, and hit the loft running.

The expansive space was only about a third full of straw and hay bales at this time of year. Cobwebs hung from every beam above and but a few shafts of light pierced diagonally through from one or two small windows.

All Seth could see was Thomas's back racing for the far side of the huge room.

"Thomas!" he yelled, sprinting forward. But by the time he reached him, Thomas had scampered up a precariously balanced stack of bales.

Suddenly Seth saw a bale flying toward him from above. It was too late to escape it. It struck him on the shoulder and he tumbled to the soft floor. Almost the same instant, a cry sounded from up near the rafters. Thomas had failed to account for Newton's third law of motion, and the equal and opposite reaction force to his footwork now became all too obvious.

"Oh!" he cried as the whole stack gave way. The bales tumbled and rolled and crashed down, Thomas in their midst, in an avalanche of straw and hay, burying Seth somewhere beneath it.

"Hey, what's this all about!" Seth called in a muffled voice from beneath the rubble. "What are you trying to do, get us both killed!"

Then came a great earthquake from below as Seth struggled to stand, knocking bales about every which way. Laughing again, Thomas picked himself up and fled. But his lead this time was not enough. Seconds later, Seth tackled him from behind. The two went sprawling onto the straw and hay in an ecstasy of boyish pleasure.

"Hey, what's going on up there!" called a voice from below. But the two boys, enjoying the increasing rarity of playing together as if they were eight and ten instead of sixteen and eighteen, scarcely heard it.

A few seconds later, their father's face appeared at the top of the narrow stairway, smiling broadly. It did not take much to bring the boy out of Richmond Davidson at any time, for a playful spirit of fun always lurked just beneath the surface. And his own boyishness was all the more likely to erupt when his sons were involved.

Laughing with the relish of anticipation, he ran forward to join the fray.

"I can still take you both with one hand behind my back!" he called. He found Thomas half buried where Seth had tackled him, pulled him to his feet, then picked him up and tossed him into the middle of a tall pile of loose straw.

"Eeee . . . !" cried Thomas.

Seth was not quite so easy to outmaneuver. He stood to face his father, grinning from ear to ear, made a quick swipe at his legs, which failed, then suddenly found himself rammed in the stomach by his father's head. The two fell headlong over each other atop several of the bales that Thomas had just avalanched.

"Come on, Thomas!" Seth called to his brother. "We've got him now—grab his legs!"

But Richmond was too strong for Seth to keep down. He leapt back to his feet, more wary now that he had to face counteroffensives on two fronts. Thomas made two or three quick dashes at him, both times ending up on his face in the straw, while Seth tried to detect some weak spot in his father's defenses.

Thomas flew forward again. As Richmond warded off the attack, Seth dove headfirst for his father's legs and yanked them out from under him.

A great *Oof!* sounded. Seconds later all three were rolling on the floor in a melee of laughter, flying straw, tickles and scrambles and attempts by the two young men to secure their father's hands and feet. But the quarry was too big and strong to be easily subdued, and the battle proved a standoff. Before long exhaustion caused the efforts of all three to flag, until finally they lay in a panting and dusty heap all over each other.

"Whew! You guys are tougher than you used to be!" laughed Richmond, slowly climbing to his feet.

"And you are just as tough as you always were!" rejoined Seth.

"Well, not for long. Age is on your side—you two are getting too strong for me!"

He walked toward the stairs as Thomas and Seth picked themselves out of the straw and followed. They walked squinting out of the barn and into the sunlight a minute later. Thomas drew close to his brother.

"Are you really going to marry Veronica?" he asked in a soft voice.

"I don't know, Thomas!" laughed Seth. "I was just thinking aloud. But one thing I do know," he added, grabbing him and tickling him once more in the ribs, "you had better not say anything about what you overheard!"

Twenty-six

A tall wagon rumbled toward a large, white, well-to-do plantation house in May of the year 1858, clattering and banging with pans and pots and brooms and mops and paraphernalia of every diverse kind. On its sides were painted in bold letters the words, *Professor Weldon Southcote, A Woman's Best Friend: Housewares, Utensils, Tools, and Supplies.* The man seated gaily atop the bench seat guiding his team of two aging but serviceable horses toward the South Carolina home was nearly as colorful as the lettering on the sides of his traveling emporium. Pudgy, with girth to stature running in approximately equal proportions, he was slightly balding—though at present that fact was hidden by a rumpled and dirt-splotched top hat that appeared as a castoff from some fancy dress ball that he had retrieved from the refuse heap and taken a fancy to. His suit likewise could have been appropriated from the same pile, and was comprised of a faded purple jacket of some silkish substance and bright red trousers. He wore the perpetual smile of a natural-born salesman. The gift of gab accompanied his odd but colorful appearance. Any woman (or man, too, for that matter—money was money and he wasn't particular from whom his sales came) to whom he could make himself heard was subject to his familiar, "Ho, young lady . . . might Professor Southcote have a word with you concerning your welfare and quality of life?"

All he needed was a glance in his direction. From there, his winning smile, persistent manner, and a variety of sales pitches to suit every occasion and personality—guaranteed to make every one of the one-thousand-and-one useful items in his wagon sound absolutely essential—was sufficient to turn 90 percent of such glances into cash sales. He had been conducting business along the back roads between New York and Georgia for so many years, and recognized the meaning of every expression so well, that he knew just what items to feature and what tack to use before the unwitting lady had taken two or three reluctant steps toward him. He knew from the expressions on their faces what each was going to say before she even knew herself. He was therefore at the ready to meet every reservation with confidence and the optimism of a man who knew how to close. He knew how to address every possible objection the reluctant might advance as adroitly as any street evangelist who stood ready with his scriptural proof texts to ward off the "common objections of unbelievers."

As Southcote clinked and clanked to a stop in front of the large white-columned house on this particular day, his visage might have been seen to peer out from under the thin brim of his top hat with a slight gathering of his bushy eyebrows, as if he was looking for something, or someone, but was not anxious to be noted doing so. His travels had not brought him to this place before and he must watch himself. He had an errand to attend to that did not concern his merchandise. He must shrewdly assess the best means of carrying it out without inviting suspicion.

Mistress Crawford was the first on the premises to hear the jingling of his wagon pulling to a stop in front of her home. She walked outside and immediately found herself the recipient of tipped top hat, toothy smile, and Southcote's patented, "Ho, good lady . . . a minute of your time?" She had encountered his kind before, however, and was already doing her best to get rid of him when her housekeeper appeared on the porch behind her. In her increasing annoyance, an imperceptible glance in the direction of the large black woman from under the floppy rim of the peddler's hat went unnoticed by the white mistress to whom he was addressing his verbal spiel.

"And you, ma'am!" he said after a moment, turning his attentions toward the approaching black woman. "I am certain that you will find yourself interested—"

"She's no *ma'am*," interrupted Mistress Crawford pointedly. "She's just a slave."

"Unless I miss my guess, good lady, she carries out a great deal of the work of the place."

Amaritta continued toward the wagon and began looking at the pans, dish towels, and other kitchen items.

"Suit yourself," said Mrs. Crawford, "she's got no money anyway."

Glad to have an easy way to excuse herself, she turned and made her way back to the house. "But be quick about it," she added over her shoulder. "It's precious little work I get out of her and I don't want her frittering away the day on useless gawking at things we don't need!"

The moment they were alone, Southcote's salesman's demeanor vanished and his expression immediately became serious. He drew close to the black woman.

"You the one they call the ticket mistress in these parts?" he asked under his breath.

"Dat's me, mister," said Amaritta, "but keep yo' fool voice down."

"I'm the telegraph man," he whispered. "And I've got a special on soap just now."

"We makes our own soap 'roun' here, mister."

"Then how about these bright copper cooking utensils?" he said loudly. "They are the latest in cookware, straight from New York."

He took down a pan from where it hung on the display wall of his wagon and proceeded to show it to her, again drawing close. "Mine is a very special kind of soap, good ticket mistress," he said in a voice barely above a whisper. "I'm certain you will find it most enlightening."

"You heard my mistress—I ain't got a cent to my name."

"Then, good lady, I will make you a gift of a cake of my special hand soap—it comes all the way from Pennsylvania," he added, glancing into her eye with a significant look, "and the manufacturer of this soap is hopeful that the generosity of my gift will be returned one day to its rightful place.

"—And," he went on, again speaking loudly in case anyone was listening, "if cookware isn't your interest, I have every kind of cleaning brush known to man."

They continued to walk about the wagon slowly. At length Southcote paused at the soap. He picked up a bar wrapped in brown paper and handed it to her.

"This is the soap I was telling you about," he said, now making no effort to keep his voice down. "I'm sure you will find its cleaning properties beneficial. Take it please, good lady, with my compliments. But—" and again he lowered his voice until it was barely audible— "study it carefully before using it. Remember . . . it comes all the way from Pennsylvania, and the train is waiting for return passengers."

He climbed back up onto his seat, tipped his hat without expression, and with a flick of his reins bounded into motion and was soon clattering away in the direction he had come.

Amaritta reentered the house a few moments later.

"It took you long enough," snapped her mistress. "What have you got there in your hand?"

"A cake er soap, missus," replied the housekeeper. "He gib it ter me."

"What for?"

"Don' know, missus. He say we might like ter hab it."

"Give it to me."

Amaritta handed the bar to her mistress, who looked it over quickly, sniffed it, then handed it back.

"Well I've got no use for it—it's not even scented," she said. "He just gave it to you?"

"Yes'm."

"The man's a bigger fool than he looks if he thinks he can give away his merchandise to penniless coloreds."

"Yes'm."

Amaritta dropped the mysterious gift into one of several pockets hidden beneath the apron in the folds of her large dress, then proceeded to continue with the chores with which she had been occupied before the appearance of the strange Professor Southcote.

It was not until she was alone in her own room later that evening that she had the chance to look at the day's gift more closely. She removed it from her pocket, then carefully unwrapped the paper around it. The cake was plain white, of the most common type of hand soap. She turned it over in her hands and there saw the reason it had been delivered along the telegraph to her. Etched in the surface was a message, cryptic and employing as many symbols as actual words so as to avoid decoding should unfriendly eyes chance upon it, the meaning of which after three or four minutes gradually became clear—as clear to the ticket mistress as an electromagnetic telegraph message to any above-ground railroad station master in the land.

Slowly a smile spread over her lips as the full meaning presented itself.

Why, Caleb, you ol' cagey nigger! she said to herself. *You dun it—an' now we got's ter git da res' ob yo' family aboard dat train too!*

She went outside to the pump and washed her hands vigorously with the professor's gift until all hint of its purpose had vanished in the bubbles and suds soaking into the dirt at her feet. The instructions were in her head now—the repository where all messages that came to this ticket office disappeared in the end.

Twenty-seven

Cherity Waters sat in her room at the Cambridge Boarding School for Young Ladies.

She sat quietly in her chair gazing at a tiny tintype of her mother which rested on top of one of her mother's most prized possessions. Why she had brought the book to school with her she could not exactly have said. She had not taken it out of her chest until this day.

Her third year here would be over in a few weeks. She would return to Boston and not come back. She and her father had decided that she would remain at home next term and that she would continue her education by means of private tutors. She was seventeen and beyond the age when most girls were studying to great extent anyway. But she was interested in history and literature and did not want to stop learning just because most girls did so at her age. She and her father were both alone and there was no reason for them to spend any more time apart than they already had. Even more importantly, her father's health was not as robust as it had once been. She wanted to be home for him. Why should they have a housekeeper to clean and cook for them when she was capable of doing both? The fact was, she had missed her father sorely during these years at the boarding school and would be glad to get back to Boston for good.

Not that the years here hadn't been good in their own way. She had learned a great deal. She had made friends she would cherish for years.

She had even managed to win over stern old Miss Baird, she thought with a smile, something she never thought would happen. The dear old spinster would probably cry when Cherity said good-bye for the last time. She might cry herself, she thought. She would miss this place. But it was time to return to her father.

She had changed in these three years. She had finally begun to grow and had added several inches in height. She had become more resigned to the dress that was required of her here, though she kept her boots and hat in her trunk for special occasions. Occasionally she even passed muster in Miss Baird's eyes as a "presentable young lady."

But she had never given up on her dream of returning to the West, nor relinquished her love affair with horses. With regard to the former, the terrible bloodshed in Kansas during the past two years over the slavery issue prevented her from harboring any thoughts about an actual trip West again until things cooled down. With regard to the latter, however, she and her father had picked out a horse during her most recent visit home. They planned to purchase it the moment she returned and board it at one of the stables not far from Constitution Hill. The prospect of having her own horse was almost too exciting for words . . . not to mention being able to wear trousers and boots every day if she wanted!

But Cherity's reflections on this day were not only about horses and the future.

The girl who shared her room had left a few minutes earlier.

"Who's that?" she had asked, glancing at the small photograph in Cherity's hand.

"It's my mother," replied Cherity.

"Really . . . you actually have a *picture* of her!"

"My father had it taken at one of Boston's first photographic studios."

"I . . . uh, thought your mother was dead," said the girl.

"She is," replied Cherity. "She died when I was born."

"Oh . . . uh, well I'm going to lunch—want to come?"

"Go on ahead," said Cherity. "I'll be along in a few minutes."

She stared down again at the faint brown image of the woman, so familiar to her eyes and yet so filled with vague mystery in her girl's heart. Eventually she set it aside and reverently opened the black leather-bound book beneath it. Why had this Bible been so special to her mother? she wondered as she absently turned through its pages. What had her mother found in it that was so full of meaning?

From the very feel of the pages beneath her fingers, from the occasional smudges and creased corners and many underlinings and handwritten notes, it was obvious that her mother had read every page of it. What were the mysteries Kathleen Waters had discovered here?

Mother, mother, whispered Cherity silently, *how I wish you were here! I have so many questions to ask you. Just imagine all the things we could talk about and everything you could tell me. What were you like? How did your voice sound? What did your face look like when you smiled? If only this picture could move and come to life! What did you think when you held me in your arms before you died?*

As she continued to flip through the pages, several words caught her eye. They were underlined. She paused to read them. "'The wages of sin is death; but the gift of God is eternal life through Jesus Christ our Lord.'"

She continued slowly to turn the pages, reading more underlined passages and an occasional note in the margin. Some of the words she read sounded like another language. It was so old-fashioned and contained so many odd words she didn't understand that she could make little sense of its meaning. It was just like the readings in chapel at school—so hard to understand.

She reached the end of the book. Before she closed it, her eyes fell on several blank pages which were full of handwritten notes that her mother had added. She began to read some of them.

"Christ is coming . . . behold, he cometh!"

"Deepen my faith, dear Lord, that I might understand thy ways."

"Bless thy church, Lord, where thy saints worship in order that they be kept spotless from the sins of the world. Convict the world of sin and judgment."

Even her mother's own handwritten words were written in the same old-fashioned language the Bible used.

Then unexpectedly Cherity's eyes fell upon words that plunged straight to her heart: "A prayer for my daughters."

Thank you, dear Lord, she read, *for my wonderful daughters. I love them so much. They are truly a gift from you. May they grow in wisdom and in stature and in favor with God and man. Most of all, may they come to know you as their Savior and Lord, and may you reveal yourself ever more fully to them all the days of their lives.*

Cherity knew that the words had been written for her older sisters. But had her mother felt the same thing, and perhaps uttered a similar prayer for her before she fell asleep for the last time? It felt so warm and full of love.

The poignant words of a mother's prayer, in a language of the spirit she hardly understood, reached out as from the grave, stretching across that invisible barrier of death and linking the present with eternity, and touched the heart of the motherless girl. She was reminded of Seth Davidson's confident assertion about heaven. If only she could know for sure that her mother was still alive and in heaven right now.

She felt a tremble in her heart, and unbidden, a tear rose in one eye. Unconsciously she brushed at it, but found more following in an increasing flow.

Cherity sat for several minutes quietly weeping, though she knew not why.

A seed of determination began to sprout, invisible yet, for its growth would be slow, to understand this strange thing her mother called faith, and to know what her mother had discovered in this Bible, seemingly so unintelligible, and in the church her father said he and she had attended every week without fail.

Cherity Waters seldom cried. Hers was too upbeat a personality to remain thoughtfully melancholy for long. After a few minutes she brushed back the tears that remained in her eyes and rose to her feet with a deep breath and a smile.

She could go out to meet the rest of the day now. But she would not forget her resolve to find out more about what had given her mother's life such meaning in the pages of the big black book. When the right time came, she would try to learn more.

Twenty-eight

$\mathcal{A}$ good ticket mistress for the U.G.R.R. had to resort to subterfuge. Amaritta Beecham had been part of the invisible slave network so long she knew just about every trick in the book.

Her mysterious errands through the years, cleverly disguised under a cloak of affected mental density, had only confirmed to Amaritta's mistress that her housekeeper was ignorant and slow of mind. Mrs. Crawford never had a suspicion that Amaritta could read as well as her own children, or that the woman she so looked down on as her racial inferior was contributing a vital chapter to the history of her people, and that it was being written right under her own unseeing eyes.

That the ticket on this occasion had come for one of Master Crawford's own slaves made the housekeeper's job easier. It was not difficult to manufacture a pretense to walk to the slave quarters the day following the arrival of the soap letter. Without drawing suspicion to herself, for the activities of her ticket office must remain concealed even from their own slaves, she gradually drew Lucindy Eaton aside. Confused by the furtive manner of the mistress's house slave, Lucindy followed with her two year old. When they were out of earshot, even from Lucindy's two older children, Amaritta put her lips close to Lucindy's ear.

"Dere's a message come ter me yesterday, Lucindy dear," she whispered. "Hit's a message sent here jes' fo' you."

266 Dream of Freedom

"Wha'chu mean . . . fo' me?" said Lucindy, confused. "What kind er message?"

"I gets messages, Lucindy dear. Dey come ter me from all 'roun'. But afore I tell you 'bout it, you gots ter promise not ter say a word, no how."

Lucindy eyed her with a little remaining suspicion, but saw how serious Amaritta was.

"I's promise," she said slowly.

"Den hit's dis," whispered Amaritta, "—dere's a black man by da name er Eaton who's dun excaped to da Norf."

Lucindy's eyes shot open and she stared at the housekeeper with sudden curiosity.

"Excaped!"

"Shush—keep yo' voice down."

"He ain't at dat place no mo'," whispered Lucindy excitedly, "where massa dun sol' him to?"

Amaritta shook her head. "He dun take dat railroad all da way ter Zion. An' he sez dat he's jes' like one er dose twelve spies like his name say. He been spyin' out dat lan' er milk an' honey, an' he's ready fo' you ter join him cross dat ol' Jordan. So he dun sent fo' you an' da chilluns."

"Sent fo' us—how kin dat be!"

"Dat was da message dat I got."

"But how's we gwine git ter him . . . how we know where he is?"

"You leab dat ter me. But you gots ter leab in da middle ob da night."

"Why?"

"Cuz nobody kin know—not whites, not coloreds. Ain't nobody kin know but me."

"When I gotter go?"

"I's tell you what's ter do. You jes' gotter be ready wif yo' chilluns, ready da minute I come fo' you. An' you can't blab a word ter nobody."

"How I know where's ter go?"

"Da railroad'll take you. You jes' go from station to station. Dey'll tell you what ter do."

"What effen we's caught?"

"Den you's likely git whupped bad. But effen you don' go, ain't long afore da master's gwine bed you down wif sumbody. You don' want dat?'"

Lucindy shook her head vigorously.

"An' you wants ter see Caleb agin?"

"Yes'm. I's been waitin' fo' dis chance long enuf," said Lucindy. "I's ready ter run ter freedom effen I kin. I dun tol' myself dat I'd git dese chilluns er mine ter dat ol' riber Jordan effen I cud. So I's ready. I's go."

"Den you be ready w'en dat train ter Zion cum. W'en I cum fo' you—you an' da chilluns gots ter go right den. Dat train ter da promised lan' don't wait fo' nobody. An' when you gits ter dat las' station, you jes' 'member dese words from da message, *Look fo da win' in da horse's head.*"

"I don' know what it means."

"Neither duz I, chil'. But you will when da time cums."*

---

*"The Southerner's perpetually reiterated defense of slavery was that the slaves themselves accepted their status and were, in the main, carefree, happy creatures, devoted to their kindly masters and mistresses. Every black man or woman who escaped gave the lie to the story of the contented slave, and gave it in a peculiarly striking fashion by enduring great hardship and danger, including cruel punishment and even mutilation if caught and returned to his/her master. The so-called Underground Railroad, one of the most remarkable clandestine operations in all history, grew up gradually to assist fugitive slaves to reach freedom. Each year, as the moral outrage over slavery grew in the North, new recruits were added until the Railroad had thousands of conductors and hundreds of escape routes that reached from the Pennsylvania and the Ohio borders to Canada."—Page Smith, *The Nations Comes of Age,* New York: McGraw-Hill, 1981, p. 625.

Twenty-nine

How an important man like Senator Hoyt heard of him, Cecil Hirsch didn't know. But he wasn't asking too many questions. This was the opportunity he had been waiting for. If he could just make good on it, there was no telling where it might lead . . . Washington, London, Paris, Rome!

He had never thought of himself as particularly ambitious, just a guy trying to make two bits however he could, or a buck if his luck was on a hot streak. He had started in the information game as a kid hustling tourists in New York City, passing himself off as an expert on local history and gossip and architecture. This he supplemented by hanging around hotels and grabbing bags from outside in hopes that he'd get thrown a nickel or two by carrying them in for somebody. If he had a few newspapers to sell, so much the better.

As he got better at it, he moved toward nicer hotels, learning to spot the most likely marks by studying their faces for a few minutes, or listening in on conversations between husband and wife. All he had to do was hear a chance comment about wanting to see the city, or wondering about something they had noticed, and then walk up as the pleasant, polite, and cute little local tour guide.

By the time he was twelve, he could hop in the carriage of a visiting family or businessman and guide them all over the city and keep them entertained for hours, leaving them thinking themselves experts in most of what anyone needed to know about the great American metropolis. That much of what he fed gullible Midwesterners and Europeans, while perhaps based here and there on pieces of truth, was mostly fictitious was a fact that never bothered him and that most of his clientele would never know. They were happy, and he learned that it was a lot nicer to hear the jingle of coins in his pocket than feel the pangs of hunger in his stomach. It wasn't a bad living for a kid who had grown up on the streets.

As he had grown older, and learned to take on more mature mannerisms of sophistication, adding nicer clothes and more polished speech to his act, he had discovered that truth paid even better than fiction. Why bother making up stories when he could pass himself off as a legitimate expert and command yet higher prices?

So he boned up on local facts, adding truth to his tales a little at a time. The next discovery proved the most important of all, a discovery that would set him on course toward his future—that the sort of truth that tourists found most interesting of all was truth about people. *Gossip*, to be plain about it. He could tell stories about what buildings were built when and about the city's growth and how much the Dutchman Peter Minuit had paid the Indians in beads and furs for Manhattan in 1626, and they would be yawning in the aisles. But let him dish the dirt on this socialite or that wife of an important figure, or in low confidential tones disclose a rumor about such-and-such politician and his mistress, and they came awake and hung on his every word.

At first it had almost been a lark to see what he could discover and then watch how tourists responded to the information. But gradually, young Cecil realized he was onto something big. People would *pay* for information. The juicier the information, the more they would fork over.

By the time he was twenty-three, Cecil Hirsch had taken to wintering in the cities of the South—Charlotte, New Orleans, Birmingham. He brought a Southern air of refinement to the tour guide motif, frequenting now only the finest hotels where people could afford to pay greater amounts and where he cut a dashing enough figure to fit in just about anywhere.

In Dixie, being a broker of local gossip made him all the more sought after, for the South loved its dirty little secrets. For one like him, who had been watching, observing, and listening to people all his life, and who had made a practice of moving in and out of character like a chameleon as circumstances dictated, to perfect the dialect of Alabama, Louisiana, or Georgia was the work of a mere week or two. Within no time he could affect with equal ease the drawl of the Deep South, or speak in flawless New York or Boston twang, as it happened to suit his purposes.

Senator Hoyt's message had been brief but tantalizing: *Understand you have information about various people of importance, or know how to get it. Would like to discuss proposition.*

Now here he was on a train heading south to see what would become of said proposition. Hoyt had hired him to get the goods on a political opponent. If he succeeded, it could open his way further into the world of politics—the most dangerous, but lucrative, world of all.

He still wasn't quite sure whether to don his Northern or his Southern persona, thought Hirsch. He would dress appropriately for either, then wait until he arrived at the event and see how the thing felt. He liked making spontaneous decisions of character.

It kept him on his toes.

Thirty

The morning was well advanced. Carolyn Davidson wondered where her men were.

She walked from the house and glanced about just in time to see the back of her husband disappearing in the distance. She smiled, thinking to herself that if he found the slightest legitimate excuse, he would probably not keep the afternoon's appointment at all.

Closer by she saw Seth in the pasture with a pure black horse, the two walking slowly side by side almost as friends having a chat together. She sometimes almost wondered if the animals *could* understand him, as Alexander claimed. To all appearance, an earnest conversation was in progress. She walked down the porch and across the entryway.

Seth was so engrossed with Demon that he did not see his mother in the distance. He had just extended his hand toward the long nose of his companion. A gentle snort of pleasure sounded as the horse took a piece of apple and chunk of sugar in the same motion of his fleshy lips.

"You see, Demon," said Seth, "you are happier now that you know that I am not only your master but your friend. I want to be to you just what God wants to be to us—master and friend."

He glanced up and saw Carolyn at the fence watching him. "Hi, Mother!" he said. "Where are you going?"

"Nowhere. I'm just making sure everyone is ready for this afternoon," she said.

"I'm all dressed."

"I can see that," she laughed. "But why did you get dressed before going out into the pasture? You'll get soiled. What will Veronica's friends think?"

"I'll be careful."

"You sound just like your father!"

"Besides, who cares what her friends think?"

"What about Veronica herself?"

Seth laughed. "I've given up trying to predict that! When do we need to leave?"

"In about an hour."

"I'll be ready . . . and don't worry, I won't have manure on my shoes!"

As Carolyn walked back to the house, her thoughts turned toward her youngest son. She wondered where Thomas was. A momentary cloud passed over her brow. She knew he was changing. Too fast, it seemed. It had only been a couple of months since Richmond and the two boys had laughed and roughhoused in the hay loft. She had not been able to keep from laughing herself as Richmond told her about it.

But Thomas rarely laughed now. She could not imagine him laughing and having fun with his father in his present mood. Would such times ever come again when they would hear him laugh like a boy? What had come over him? Why was he drifting from them?

If she was honest with herself, she realized that the change wasn't as sudden as it seemed. There had been subtle signs of discontent for years. She had hoped he would grow out of them and learn to trust them more the older he became.

But it was becoming all too obvious now . . . that didn't seem likely to happen.

❧

Richmond Davidson smiled as the sounds of two dozen singing Negro voices raised in rich harmony over the cultivated fields faded behind him.

They had always sung, he thought. Music was tonic to their soul. But the sound here at Greenwood was so much happier than before. The songs were not so melancholy. They truly seemed to *enjoy* their work these days.

"We'll be away most of the day, Malachi," he had said a few minutes ago, after taking aside the great muscular black man who was now called his foreman. "I would like you to get as far with the western ten acres as you can. But don't go past about six o'clock. I want you and your men to leave yourselves time to work on your houses. Do you have the lumber you need?"

"Yes, massa, we's—"

Davidson held up an interrupting finger. The black man stopped abruptly.

"I've told you, Malachi—it is no longer *Master,*" said the plantation owner, sternly but with obvious love in his tone. "You may call me *Sir*, or *Mr. Davidson.*"

"Yes, sir . . . Mister Dab'son," nodded Malachi. "Ah's tryin' ter mind, but it's sum par'ful hard fer me ter 'member."

"I understand, Malachi," smiled Richmond. "That's why I will continue to remind you. And I want you to take care that your people do not refer to me as master in your hearing. They have to learn to think differently about many things, themselves most of all."

"Much oblige, Mister Dab'son . . . sir," replied Malachi, showing a smile that revealed sparkling white teeth.

"Do you hear anything from Joseph?"

"Not fer a mumf er two, sir, but his mama sez he's gwine ter make out jes fine up dere in da Norf."

"Well, I am glad to hear it. Don't work your people too hard today, Malachi—it feels like it will be hot."

"At's mighty kind er you, sir. You en da missus hab a fine time, Mister Dab'son, sir."

"Thank you, Malachi."

Richmond continued on to the pleasant sound of the singing behind him, reached the house about five minutes later, and paused

on the porch and glanced back and took in the scene spreading out
before his eyes.

The plantation was doing well under the changes they had instituted, better even than before. Whether it was because of God's blessing or the simple effects of democracy and free capitalism at work,
who could say. Nevertheless, the results could not be denied. For the
half dozen or so who had left, Joseph among them, there had been an
equal number of free coloreds, hearing about Greenwood, who had
come asking for work, far more than they needed or could possibly
hire. After the first year, they had instituted a moderate bonus system
whereby the workers shared in the profits if the harvest was bountiful.
And to encourage their women to spend as much time as possible with
the children, they had begun paying the married men more, on the
basis of how many mouths they had to feed, than the single men. The
fact was, he required *fewer* workers now, even though they had cleared
and begun to plant even more land than they had been able to culti-
vate before, simply because the men were working so much harder
now that they had a personal investment in the plantation's success. In
two years neither he nor Carolyn had heard so much as a word of
complaint from anyone, male or female, married or single. Morale had
never been higher, as evidenced by the happy sounds resonating
behind him.

If only the rest of the South could see the benefits of the experiment
they had put into practice here at Greenwood. But apparently eyes
were too blinded by self-interest to see the plain fact that this happy
experiment had proved a wonderful success.

Indeed, the situation throughout the rest of the South, if anything,
had grown worse. Whatever trend the Davidsons might have hoped to
set in motion by their action had seemingly been invalidated, if not
reversed, by last year's Dred Scott decision by the Supreme Court. No
black man, declared the highest justices in the land, who had ever been
a slave or who had descended from slaves, even if living in a free state,
could ever be a citizen of the United States. Suddenly pro-slavery sentiment had been given a monstrous victory, and the contempt of those
who had laughed in their sleeve at Richmond Davidson's idiocy now

appeared to be well justified. News of the financial success of his enter-prise did not so readily find its way onto the pages of the Southern papers as had the scandal caused by the emancipation of his slaves. By now, relishing in what appeared to be a new tide moving in their favor, most prominent Southerners had forgotten about him altogether, or, if reminded, his name only brought a snicker to the lips.

In certain regions, however, Dred Scott only intensified the debate, and the conflict between pro-slavery and abolitionist forces was approaching the boiling point. In border states like Virginia, where abolitionist sentiment was strong in the north and west, tension mounted monthly with uncertainty over where the great birthplace of freedom would ultimately place its loyalty.

News of the Dred Scott decision demoralized Richmond and Caro-lyn Davidson for a time, though it did not lessen their resolve to continue on the path they had chosen. It seemed to undo the very thing they had tried to accomplish. They might have freed their slaves, but if they could not be citizens, what good would that freedom do them anywhere but Greenwood?

In the backlash of cruelty toward blacks that resulted from the high court's stand, Richmond and Carolyn worried about those who had left and were now struggling to make a new life for themselves as freedmen.

The fact that things were going well at Greenwood did not hide mounting tensions elsewhere. Both whites and blacks were becoming emboldened. More and more runaways fled to the North every month, and more and more cruel became the white reaction to the increasing cries for freedom. Joseph had made it successfully to the North. But poor Rufus hadn't been so fortunate. He too had left Greenwood with his eight dollars and high hopes, only to crawl back two days later, beaten to within an inch of his life and his money stolen. When ques-tioned, the Davidsons were shocked to learn that his assailants had been mostly black themselves, though the name Wyatt Beaumont was also mentioned. It seemed that, rather than being happy for their freed brethren, the Oakbriar slaves resented them just as much as their owner resented the man who had freed them. Looks and glances and threats

even became part of the Sunday ritual at the secret black gathering in
the Brown house, where those who remained slaves on the surrounding
plantations looked down on the Greenwood blacks as traitors, refusing
to greet them or shake their hands. Even then, however, they would
not betray the fellowship of black believers.

Thus, with freedom came new fears. Though Carolyn had taught
the black ladies how to buy things for themselves in the shops in
Dove's Landing, most of them were afraid to venture into town. As
time went on, several of the men, and one family who had left,
returned and asked to be rehired by "Master Dab'son." They all told
the same tale. "Hit be bad out dere," they said. "Things be diff'ert at
Greenwood. Ain't like dat nowhere else. Whites an blacks alike—dey
all hates free coloreds."

In their more pensive moments alone, Richmond and Carolyn
occasionally questioned whether they had really done their people
good or ill. But there was no going back. And in the depths of their
hearts they held no regrets.

Senator Everett, who had been victorious two years before, despite
his advancing age, in the race which Richmond Davidson might
instead have entered, was one of slavery's most vocal advocates.

Even when he read Everett's strident oratory, Richmond did not
regret his decision to bow out of potential political involvement, or
wish himself in the senator's place. He was where he wanted to be,
where he knew God wanted him, content not to change the world but
to do his best to live out his convictions, and thus influence others by
example rather than rhetoric.

In truth, despite the puzzling ongoing uncertainty of his cousin
Stuart's legal claim—about which he had not heard a whisper in two
years, for reasons he could not understand—he had never been
happier.

Events were about to come into the lives of Richmond and Carolyn
Davidson, however, that would take them both in many directions
they could not foresee, and involve them in events and lives that
would reach far beyond the security and peacefulness of their beloved
Greenwood.

A few minutes later Richmond Davidson walked toward the house. Seeing his approach, his wife came out onto the porch.

"Richmond," said Carolyn, "you haven't forgotten?"

"No, I am aware of the time," sighed her husband, "merely postponing the inevitable. What about the boys?"

"They're getting ready."

"Then I shall go upstairs and change . . . in a minute or two," he added, sitting down on the porch seat. His wife eased onto the bench beside him.

A peaceful silence descended. "If there was any way to avoid this—," Davidson began after a moment, then broke off what he had been about to say with another sigh.

"I know you detest socializing," said Carolyn. "Notwithstanding the coolness between you and Denton, we must be good neighbors. Especially now. Eyes will be watching."

"I doubt that," he laughed. "Most have forgotten us . . . which is fine with me. Actually, I am a little surprised we were invited at all."

"Do you have any idea who will be there?"

"None. The cover of Veronica's birthday and coming out celebration, I don't doubt, is but an excuse for Denton to lubricate the political machinery to whatever advantage he can. I imagine most of the principle players in Virginia politics will be there, as well as a number of national figures. That is another reason I would rather stay home. I do not look forward to seeing some of those men again."

"I thought there was bad blood between Denton and the men who wanted you to run."

"Everything is temporary in politics. There are smiles and handshakes and subtle games brought out at such times to mask deeper motives and differences. I'm sure all that's been soothed over now that his hat is in the ring. In social circles, everyone is everyone else's friend. Probably he has made sure the press is in attendance too, which insures that everyone will be on their best behavior.

"All the more reason for you to be there to affirm your convictions."

"You are right, my wise wife!" said Richmond with a smile. "It is only that I feel more and more distance between myself and other men of my position. The border is not really so far north, only a hundred miles. Why could I not have been born a Pennsylvanian?"

"These days a hundred miles is a great distance. It might as well be a thousand."

"Sometimes I think we ought to sell the plantation, give our workers enough to get them started somewhere else, give Cynthia and the boys their inheritance and my cousins their coveted windfall . . . and move to Oregon!"

"A radical suggestion!"

"But don't you sometimes want to leave it all behind and . . . you know, go somewhere far away?"

"I love Greenwood, Richmond. And as appealing as that may sound, you cannot run away from your destiny."

"As you like to remind me."

Davidson smiled and kissed his wife.

"What would I do without you to knock sense into this brain of mine when it gets tired of the fight?" he added.

"It makes it doubly difficult knowing that we were probably only invited because of the young Miss Beaumont's interest in our son."

"An interest I would happily see directed elsewhere."

"I know what you mean. But with Denton having announced his candidacy against Senator Hoyt for Virginia's second Senate seat this November, don't you think he may have wanted you present simply to appear magnanimous? He might have thought that for you to be missing might be a conspicuous political omission."

"You are a shrewd political analyst, my dear!" laughed Richmond. "That is quite a series of deductions! In truth, I have to say that I doubt your conclusion. On the few occasions when we have seen one another recently, his coolness has been marked. He did not invite me to the announcement of his candidacy, and I am certain he wants to place as much distance between us as possible. Virginia is still a reasonably solid slave state. I imagine Denton views any connection with me as a political, not to mention a personal, annoyance and liability. As far as Veronica is concerned, I cannot imagine why she is so interested in Seth."

"He is as handsome as you, Richmond. And being six months younger, she has been captivated with him since they were children."

"It still baffles me. She could have any young man in the county swooning on her doorstep with the snap of her fingers. I'm certain her father would prefer anyone else too."

"But you know Veronica—she is as wily as they come, and head-strong. She wants anything she can't have. Daphne has never been able to control her, and I doubt, now that she is eighteen, that Denton is any more successful. She bends all to her will eventually. I hope Seth is not quite so easily swayed."

"She is not really such a bad girl, Carolyn."

"I do not trust any girl with a flirtatious spirit. It is a character flaw and a sign of selfishness, immodesty, and mischief deep inside. I don't like it."

"You fascinate me strangely, wife, with your strong words!"

"I feel strongly, husband, about the wiles of young women!"

"Well, we shall just have to keep an eye on how things develop—Come, let's go upstairs and get ready . . . as you say, for our destiny!"

He rose, offered his hand, and pulled his wife to her feet.

"We must do something about your hair!" she teased.

"I'm afraid it's hopeless," he laughed. "It has refused to lie flat for forty-eight years. It is not going to start now!"

Thirty-one

*A*t first glance it might have been difficult to determine whether the occasion was primarily social or political. Young belles in expensive dresses of every color bustled in groups about the lawn, giggling and making eyes at young men who greeted each one with a chivalry that seemed beyond their years. That the invitation had specified dancing at the top of the list of entertainments, and that a small orchestra was already warming up, kept the young women at a pitch of anticipation. Their friend, however, had not yet come out of the house. She was waiting for just the right moment.

At the same time, a glance about the grounds revealed an equal number of men, clustered in small groups with drinks in hand, the looks on whose faces indicated that the latest fashions from Paris or the latest beaux of their daughters were the last things on their minds. In a half dozen small discussions about the place, the future of the Union was the topic at hand.

Even for a slave state, Virginia was a little far north for such a distinctively Southern gala. These sorts of things were usually reserved for the plantations of Charleston or Atlanta. But the hosts for this afternoon's long-anticipated lawn party had spared no expense to put on a lavish affair that would not soon be forgotten.

Much of the social elite for several hundred miles was on hand, coming from as far as Richmond, Washington, and Raleigh. The guest list included some of the capital's most distinguished senators, congressmen, as well as several foreign ambassadors. It had been rumored that President Buchanan might make the trip, though nothing had been confirmed.

There was no way other than the sound of one's tongue to distinguish those of Southern roots from their Northern counterparts. And in border states like Virginia, loyalties and accents carried many subtleties and shades of contrast, and were thus sometimes difficult to determine.

Among the guests was one who appeared alone in the midst of a crowd comprised chiefly of couples and small groups of young people. He moved about almost unnoticed, silently observing everything and everyone around him. His light gray suit had been chosen to blend in, to call no attention to its owner, a young man of perhaps twenty-five or twenty-six years, medium build, handsome in spite of thin-set eyes that took in more of his surroundings, especially people, than most observers realized. He was young but had already begun to rise high in certain circles because of his shrewd insight into character, along with a keen memory that never forgot a face or personal detail. In Georgia he often wore a wide-brimmed white straw hat, less to shade his eyes than to fit in with the genteel society in which he mingled and among whose wealthy he sought whatever opportunity his knowledge might afford him. In New York or Boston he might sport a silk top hat. But this was neither the Deep South nor the Yankee North. And noting that many men's heads in today's warmth were bare, he had eschewed covering a head over which was tightly combed a crop of thin but longish brown-black hair.

Cecil Hirsch had been sent here to gather information. Though he was wandering about, drink in hand, apparently aimlessly, he was already at work . . . watching, eavesdropping on bits of conversation. Anything might prove useful in ways one could never anticipate. He had done his homework on most of the people here. So many of the tidbits of conversation had meaning for him. There were people for whom information was power, and who would pay to obtain it. Information was his stock in trade. And Cecil Hirsch never forgot a detail.

Oakbriar, the Beaumont plantation, one of the largest and wealthiest in all Virginia—with more than fifty slaves and everything necessary for self-sufficiency—provided a distinctively old-world ambiance for an event that was as pro-slavery in tone as it was Southern in style. A few known abolitionists from the western part of the state, as well as a handful of Northerners, had been strategically invited as well.

Indeed, both politics and high society had prompted today's gathering. Veronica Beaumont, the lovely daughter of Denton and Lady Daphne Beaumont, had turned eighteen two weeks before and had been planning this birthday celebration for a year. In addition to marking her coming of age, the day provided a convenient backdrop to further her father's political aspirations. He had recently announced a bid for the Senate in November's midterm national elections, and today offered an ideal opportunity to wine and dine the nation's powerful leaders whom he hoped would be his governmental colleagues by this time next year. Denton Beaumont's Senate run as a staunch state's-rights advocate and slave owner could not help but land him in the middle of a congressional debate that would decide the course of the nation's future. He saw no reason not to start making his influence felt at the earliest possible opportunity. That his neighbor would be here was an irritating thorn in the side of his ambitions, it was true, but his daughter had insisted. And Richmond would probably keep his mouth shut and would not prove troublesome.

In an upstairs room of the house, mother and daughter had just made the final adjustments to the expensive dress purchased in New York three months before.

"You look lovely, dear," said Lady Daphne, as she fussed with the bow in her daughter's silky and glistening black hair. Veronica squirmed away and ran to the window to look out over the throng at the carriages arriving in a continual stream.

"Where is Seth?" she said, glancing about. "It is—what time is it?"

"A little after one-thirty."

"Why isn't he here yet!"

"I am certain he will be soon," replied her mother.

"If only I can get him away from his parents. That mother of his is so . . . I just don't know why they won't let him grow up."

"Perhaps you can help," said Lady Daphne with a smile.

"That is exactly what I intend to do, Mother," rejoined the daughter. "After one or two dances with me, I will make him forget everything!—Oh, there he is!" she added, spinning away from the window. "I am going now, Mother!"

She ran toward the door.

"Just be cautious around your father, dear," said Lady Daphne as she followed her toward the stairs.

"Why doesn't he like Seth?"

"Because of Seth's father, you know that. But I am sure they will be friends again one day very soon, just like when they were young."

"It doesn't matter anyway," said Veronica playfully. "I don't intend to marry Seth's father!"

"You know what they say," added her mother, "—like father like son."

"I will make sure Seth turns out nothing like his father. I just have to get him away from his parents long enough, that's all!"

She reached the bottom of the stairs, slowed and tried to calm herself, pinched both cheeks two or three times to make sure they were pink and flushed, then left the mansion with a flourish through the tall front doors. Immediately, several of her friends scurried to meet her.

"Veronica, have you seen Seth?" asked one.

"I just saw him from the window! He's over there."

"Do you think he'll ask you to dance?"

"I intend to make sure of it, Julia. If he doesn't . . . this is my party, so I shall ask him!"

She continued through the gathering crowd spread out on the expansive lawns to the side of the house, with an entourage of four or five young ladies at her side, joined by others as they went, every one as beautiful as she, turning heads and gathering looks and greetings as they went.

Veronica slowed briefly. Her gaze was arrested by a man in a light gray suit standing by himself as she swept by. He was staring straight at her, as if he knew her, though she could not imagine ever seeing him before. It was a face almost as good-looking as Seth's—she would surely remember it had she seen it before. He was older than she, in his late twenties probably.

His head nodded ever so slightly, as if he too had noticed the invisible affiliation between them. A quick involuntary smile flashed from her lips, the nature of which it would have been difficult to define with certainty. A coquettish playfulness was the natural mode of her existence where the opposite sex was concerned, though at first glance she had little interest in this man. Perhaps it had been drawn out by the nervous uncertainty of realizing that his eyes were boring into hers.

Whatever the cause, the locking of their gaze onto one another lasted but an instant. None of her friends even noticed. Quickly she continued on. She loved the attention. But no matter how many eyes might be drawn to her this day, Veronica Beaumont reminded herself that *she* had eyes for only one of the invited guests.

With wide-skirted orange dress rustling, and well aware of the heady aroma of perfume she had liberally sprinkled on wrists, neck, and behind her ears, she drew up to a small group that had pulled into the estate only moments before. As Richmond handed the reins of the horses to the black groom standing beside him, she bore straight ahead to the older of the two young men who had just arrived.

"Hello, Seth," she said, dropping her eyes for just the right effect.

"Hello, Veronica," replied the handsome young Davidson with a smile. "Happy birthday."

"Thank you. I'm so glad you could come."

As she spoke she gradually eased him away from the others. Unconsciously Seth followed and soon they were alone.

"The orchestra is about to begin," she said, slipping her hand through his arm and leading him across the grass. "I hope you brought your dancing shoes."

A figure crept through the woods at the edge of a brown ploughed field. He had skillfully avoided a few working slaves and dogs after leaving his horse tied to a tree about a mile away near the back road he had taken from town. Now he had managed to get within sight of the plantation where his own father worked as assistant overseer, but where neither of them would ever be welcome on a social occasion such as today's.

He stopped as he crested a slight incline, then looked out from amid the cover of trees and undergrowth.

He was close enough to hear the music, voices, and laughter drifting toward him from the birthday celebration.

He had never attended such a gala in his life. Creeping closer, he could see the partygoers. Watching them filled him with many conflicting emotions he himself would have been the last person capable of fully identifying. This was a culture where class was everything. No one expected it to be otherwise. It was the way things had always been. Some were born to wealth and prestige. Some came from the other side of the tracks.

He was the latter. He knew men like Denton Beaumont thought he was poor white trash. Let him think what he wanted. He didn't care. He would make something of himself. Then they would see that white suits and mint juleps weren't everything.

Besides, right now he wasn't looking for Denton Beaumont, but for another member of that prestigious family.

The eyes of twenty-year-old Scully Riggs flitted back and forth trying to find Veronica in the crowd. He had been possessed by her beauty for years. Had his father been able to get him on at the plantation it would have been a dream come true, but this job at the train station was better than nothing. Soon he would have money of his own. He could buy her things, and maybe save up enough to buy himself a suit of clothes that would make her take notice, and show that father of hers that he could be a gentleman, too.

The sound of a barking dog startled him.

He spun around, pulse suddenly racing. The noise came from at least a quarter mile away. No one had seen him. But the sound trig-

gered the memories and as usual, he was powerless to stop them. A
sweat broke over his face.

He slumped against a tree, trying to shake off the terrible phan-
tasm.

Suddenly he was running . . . running . . . glancing back . . . still
running . . . stumbling . . . the sound of barking, growling dogs
behind him and gaining rapidly.

He could never hope to outrun them. There were too many, and
they were bigger and faster than he was. He was only eight then . . .
some of the boys chasing him had been ten, even twelve.

He remembered glancing back again. They were closer yet, sprinting after him, big grins on their ugly black faces.

"Hey, little w'ite boy!" he heard a voice he knew well enough call
out behind him. "Who's gwine ter save you now, you little w'ite
trash!"

He wanted to be brave. He should turn around and face them . . .
put up his fists and fight them as best he could. But he was too afraid.
He knew that tears were streaming down his face and he couldn't stop
them. He was a coward and they knew it.

He heard the footsteps now—they were getting close—laughter and
taunts and the sound of vicious dogs.

He felt a hand on his back. He cried out in terror.

The next instant a great shove sent him sprawling onto the ground
face down in the dirt.

For a few seconds he lay in terror. All he heard was the deep breathing of his five or six pursuers. Slowly he tried to raise himself. He saw
their shadows surrounding him.

"We gwine beat you up so bad!" said one. A swift kick in his ribs
followed.

He screamed out. "Please . . . please, Elias, don't . . . help . . . somebody—please help me!"

But the only answer to his screams was more laughter from the
group of young Negro teens.

"He's callin' fer help, Elias," said one of Slade's friends. "Well, I'll
help!"

He felt himself dragged to his feet by a fist clutching his shirt. An evil-looking black face pulling him up to within two or three inches, spit into his eyes two or three times, then threw him toward one of his friends, who doubled up his fist and delivered a powerful blow into the middle of his stomach.

He doubled over and collapsed, frantic and unable to breathe. Now what seemed a dozen hands and feet at once attacked him, pulling his hair, kicking, delivering blows all over his body, to his face and private parts and stomach and back. All he could do was crumple into a ball and try to keep his face protected from their feet.

How long the torment lasted, he didn't know. It seemed an hour. In truth it was probably less than five minutes.

Eventually he became aware that he was alone again, whimpering on the ground in agony.

Slowly Scully Riggs came to himself. He was still leaning against the thick pine trunk, and slowly the sounds of music and laughter drifted again into his hearing. He was breathing heavily in a cold sweat. The day was warm, but his shirt was drenched in an icy chill.

It was his secret. His terrifying secret. The day he realized that he was too much a coward to stand up and fight. He hated the memory of it. He hated what it did to him.

He could still see the little boy of his imagination, limping home crying, bloody and splattered with dirt, clothes torn, face and chest bruised, one rib broken, blood from his nose smeared all over his mouth and chin.

He had not even told his mother what had happened. Somehow he knew that even if his father went to the McClellan plantation over the river and registered a complaint, nothing would be done. They didn't care about men like Leon Riggs and what happened to his little brat of a kid. So a few colored boys got rowdy. If the same thing had happened to one of McClellan's own sons, there would have been whippings, possibly even a hanging. But not for the son of poor white trash. The fact that Slade was a troublemaker and that McClellan had gotten rid of him less than a year after the incident had nothing to do with his having thrashed Scully Riggs.

So he said he didn't know who the boys were, and the incident was dropped. Whether his silence made the culprits respect him any more, he didn't know. It didn't really matter to Scully what they thought. He had vowed that same night, lying in bed aching and crying himself to sleep, that he would get even in his own time and in his own way.

It was a vow he had not forgotten.

As the years went by, Scully occasionally saw one or another of the colored boys around town or, more recently, when he made his deliveries. He looked at them, and they looked at him. Eyes met, but there were no smiles. Neither had forgotten. It had just been a relief that Slade was gone. And when he learned two or three years ago that he was back at Greenwood, meaner and stronger than before, Scully couldn't help trembling at the thought of running into him alone.

If he hated Elias Slade worse than all the rest, it was not by much, for by the time he was fifteen he had learned to hate all coloreds. If he hated anything more, it was whites who gave their coloreds too much freedom.

Thirty-two

Out of the line of sight of the watchful son of his overseer's assistant, and having no idea of the role his daughter occupied in the young man's stratagems, on the other side of the grounds the day's host was involved in a discussion with several prominent Virginia plantation owners and state legislators.

"So, Denton," the Irishman McClellan, whose plantation house as the crow flew lay but three miles north and across the river, was saying, "how does your Senate race appear to be shaping up?"

"It is early yet, William," replied Beaumont. "I only announced last month. But things look good thus far. I am confident that by summer I will have Democrats throughout the state backing my candidacy."

"And Republicans?"

"I look for no support from the abolitionists. In today's climate, no abolitionist candidate has a chance in Virginia."

"The West is almost entirely abolitionist," commented one Ford Hayden, a congressman from Lynchburg.

"Perhaps," rejoined Beaumont, "but without the population or votes of the East. The Democratic tide will carry Virginia, and I intend to ride it all the way to Washington."

"Hear, hear!" said William McClellan.

Light laughter and a few toasts followed.

"What will you do about your role as commissioner?" asked Hayden.

"I shall have to resign the post when I move to Washington," replied Beaumont. "We have had so few runaways in Spotsylvania County, there's not much to the job."

"Fugitives are on the increase everywhere," said McClellan, "and we are in a direct line to the North."

"Then perhaps you shall have the job, William—that is, unless my son Wyatt seeks it! Then I shall have to cast my weight of influence behind him! But seriously, I do not see this region becoming a conduit for runaways. In all my years as commissioner, I have only had one fugitive bounty hunter come through looking for slaves. I sometimes wonder if the position is more honorary than legitimate!" *

"I say, Beaumont," now put in a relative newcomer to the region, a certain Nugent Bayhurst who had come from Louisiana but was wealthy enough to be considered one of Virginia's most vital political contacts, "I was just talking to Frederick Trowbridge a few minutes ago. What's this he tells me about your neighbor?"

"You mean about his slaves?"

"Yes, is it true?"

The candidate nodded. "You didn't read about it two years ago? It was in all the papers in the East."

"Now that you mention it, I think I do recall something about it," mused the Louisianan. "But I didn't know it was him. I couldn't believe it when I heard. I know you Virginians have more Northern blood in your veins than we of the *Deep* South. But I didn't think your radicalism had gone quite that far!"

"Believe me, it hasn't!" rejoined Beaumont, shaking his head. "The

---

* "On September 18, 1850, Congress passed the Fugitive Slave Law. This law allowed a former slave owner to recapture a runaway slave even in a free state . . . Because of the Fugitive Slave Law, a runaway could not truly be free in America. Canada did not allow slavery and wouldn't return escaped slaves to their masters. Hundreds of runaways made the long, hard journey to freedom in Canada."—Angela Medearis, *Come This Far to Freedom.* New York: Atheneum, 1993, p. 32.

"In 1850, Congress passed a new Fugitive Slave Law [Following original Fugitive Slave Law of 1793] that imposed severe penalties for aiding runaways, denied the accused any right to testify, and required citizens to help catch runaways. Slavery's violence spilled into Northern streets. Whites who had believed that slavery would not touch them now faced jail and fines if they refused to follow the commands of slave-hunters.

"Black communities prepared for battle. Former slave Reverend Jarmain Loguen announced, 'I don't respect this law—I don't fear it—I won't obey it! It outlaws me and I outlaw it!' Fugitive Lewis Hayden, who hid runaways in his Boston home, announced that he had placed two kegs of explosives in his basement and would blow up his house rather than surrender to anyone. . . .

"Slave-hunters rode into the North and civilian forces were deployed and ready."—William Katz, *Breaking the Chains.* New York: Atheneum, 1990, pp. 130–31.

man is not representative of Virginia. This is a slave state and will always be a slave state."

"Then why did he do it?"

"He maintains it is the principle of the thing."

"Is he mad?"

"No, just a fool."

"Strong words for one's neighbor."

"His action two years ago in my view qualifies him for the label."

"I understood you and he were friends?" put in Hayden.

"I have known him all my life. We grew up together. I used to ride with him and his brother when we were boys. Had his father known what his son would do with the plantation he worked for all his life, he would never have turned it over to him after the, uh . . ."

He hesitated. "—After the accident with his brother," he added.

"But why . . . *why* is what I want to know?" persisted Bayhurst.

"Who can say with such fanatic types," commented McClellan.

"Who can possibly benefit from such a scheme, surely not the darkies?" asked Bayhurst. "They will be lost. They haven't the capacity to take care of themselves. And how will he keep his plantation afloat?"

"He has many old-fashioned notions," replied Beaumont. "He has odd views about any number of things. He doesn't seem to mind the consequences of his actions either to himself, his family, or his state and country. But he should be here today, why don't you ask him for yourself?"

"You invited him?"

"Had to!" said Beaumont, continuing to laugh lightly. "My daughter fancies his son, you know! If you do find out more about the state of his mind," he added, "please let me know. I would be most interested!"

"He's not actually . . . pro-North, outright abolitionist in his views?"

"I doubt it extends so far as that. He cares nothing for politics. He says his decision was merely a private matter."

"Such things always have consequences," noted Bayhurst.

"You may be right. In all honesty, most of Virginia has forgotten him. It is an experiment doomed to fail."

A few more men sauntered toward the small group. One of them was considerably younger than the rest. Wearing a gray suit, he blended in as if he were one of them, though in truth not a single man present actually knew him. He smiled and laughed at all the right moments, carrying himself as if he were completely in the know about everything they were talking about. In fact, he was listening, observing, staring into eyes, noting body language, and making a hundred little mental notes of what he heard and saw. All the while he himself said nothing.

"I just heard the most unbelievable rumor," said one Harrison Roberts, a lawyer from Alabama as he approached the group, "—you must know, Denton. Some people were talking over there, and said that Richmond Davidson freed his slaves two years ago."

"We were just talking about it," nodded Beaumont. "I am afraid you heard correctly. You didn't get news of it down in Alabama either? I thought you Louisianans and Alabamans kept up on events. It created quite a stir here."

"No, I've heard nothing about it."

"It is actually true!" added Abraham Seehorn, walking up puffing on a large cigar.

"I can hardly believe it!"

"Believe it, Harrison," said one of the more distinguished of today's guests, newly appointed Supreme Court justice Upton Byford. "He had legal documentation drawn up, did he not, Beaumont?"

"Not only that, he gave every adult eight dollars in cash, as I understand it, including the women. Those who wanted to remain, he offered jobs as wage-earning workers like any white man."

"You seem remarkably well informed on the matter."

"Word gets around. Besides, for good or ill, he is my neighbor."

"But he didn't get his odd notions from association with you, eh?" said Hayden with a grin.

"Please—don't even suggest such a thing! I will admit that Richmond

Davidson has indeed had a profound effect on the development of my
political outlook . . . pushing me yet farther in the opposite direction!"

Laughter followed as they paused to take sips from the glasses in
their hands.

"The thing's preposterous!" huffed Seehorn, who had not joined in
the laughter. He did not particularly like Denton Beaumont and was
here only out of loyalty to the party. However, he despised Richmond
Davidson. He had detected an oddity about the man at their first
meeting three years ago, and reading about what Davidson had done
had angered him to the depths of his Southern sensibilities.

"How will they live?" now put in Hayden. "What will they do
without him taking care of them?"

"He is giving them wages," replied Beaumont, "and they are paying
him what he considers a fair rent for their living quarters. Whatever
they have left after paying living expenses is theirs to keep."

"I take it, then, that they opted to stay on?" asked Roberts.

"Mostly. Though there were some who went North. Isn't that what
you've heard, William?"

McClellan nodded. "Our two sons and his are friends, but the
information I receive is limited. I don't think he's lost more than half
a dozen."

"Nevertheless, he will be bankrupt in no time!" laughed Hayden.

"What is he doing, hoeing his own cotton, sowing his own seed?"
asked Bayhurst.

"Apparently it hasn't come to that yet," said McClellan. "I've
wanted to pay him a visit just to see, but to be honest, I haven't
wanted to be seen fraternizing with the man. Have you been to
Greenwood lately, Denton? What's it like over there now?"

"Me . . . no!" laughed Beaumont. "I wouldn't darken the door of
the place. But my Wyatt is over there, like your Brad, from time to
time and tells me that he takes to the fields regularly."

Beaumont paused, chuckling, then went on. "Actually, I did call on
him once—I've forgotten why," he said, "about a year ago. I found
him in work clothes out in a field with four or five of his slaves talking
with them as if they were his friends."

More laughter circulated around the group.

"Some say he is turning a profit," McClellan added, "even with his Negroes as hired laborers. That's the local scuttlebutt at least—whether it is true or not, I cannot say. They insist the plantation has never been healthier."

"I don't believe it for a minute," growled Seehorn.

"Nor do I," agreed Beaumont.

"Only time will tell, I suppose," remarked Roberts.

"He sounds like a madman, if you ask me," Seehorn continued to grumble. "The only time I ever met the man he was carrying on with incomprehensible religious nonsense. This is no doubt the result. Whenever men take religion too far, fanaticism invariably results."

"You may not be so far wrong in your assessment," Beaumont laughed. "A wolf in sheep's clothing is how I would phrase it. Richmond Davidson will be the ruin of us all. Once you let the darkies start thinking of themselves as free, the whole economy of the South will unravel. What the man has done is dangerous. I am taking steps to have it looked into, discreetly of course," he added quietly, "to see what might be done."

"Possibly a shrewd campaign move."

Beaumont nodded but did not reply to the comment directly. "After the Dred Scott decision last year," he went on, "for which we have your brothers of the Supreme Court to thank, Upton, we may perhaps have some legal recourse against him."

"Hmm . . . a good point," nodded the Alabama lawyer. "I will look into the legal precedent and see what I can uncover."

"Keep me informed, Harrison," said Beaumont.

"You say he is here?" asked Bayhurst, glancing about the lawn.

"Unfortunately," Beaumont answered, "I had no choice. My wife and daughter sent out the invitations. Who can refuse Veronica now that she is eighteen?"

"And a very eye-catching eighteen at that!" added McClellan. "My own sons talk of nothing else. Your daughter is considered the prize catch of northern Virginia, Denton."

McClellan sent two or three knowing winks around the small group.

"Would that she had the good sense to pay a little more attention to your boys, William!" lamented Beaumont. "For some reason that I cannot comprehend and have not been able to get·to the bottom of, she has an absurd fancy for the Davidson boy. But . . . ," he added, lowering his voice and glancing around the group, "it would seem that here comes Davidson now. Be on your guard, gentlemen."

The man who had been the object of both discussion and derision now walked toward them from across the lawn. Broad shoulders and muscular arms, as well as in the rugged tan of his face even this early in the season, attested to the fact that he had worked hard most of his life in spite of being a landowner. Despite an early leaning toward books and law rather than tools and fields, his strong shape displayed none of the signs of sagging and widening that distinguished many of his contemporaries. Most of his personal features, however, escaped one's notice at first meeting. It was the energetic pale blue eyes and bright smile that gave Richmond Davidson's face its character and personality, and that drew one toward him. The smile, usually present, was subdued rather than radiant—a smile of peace if not always joy, an expression of contentment if not always exuberance.

It was his confident gait, however, and the peaceful calm radiating from the face of his forty-eight-year-old neighbor that annoyed his boyhood friend most of all as he observed his approach. That a man could be an idiot, and at the same time so thoroughly satisfied with himself, Denton Beaumont found inexcusable, and irritating almost to distraction.

The newcomer smiled and extended his hand as those surrounding their host parted slightly.

"Hello, Denton," said Richmond Davidson.

"Richmond," nodded Beaumont without expression. "I believe you know Ford Hayden—"

"Yes . . . hello, Ford."

"Davidson."

"—and Abraham Seehorn."

"Of course. How are you, Abraham? It has been several years—you're looking well."

"Thank you, Davidson," said Seehorn stiffly. "So are you."

"And this is Harrison Roberts from Montgomery . . . and Judge Byford from the capital."

"Yes . . . Mr. Byford and I have met," said Davidson. "Congratulations on your appointment to the bench."

"Thank you, Davidson."

"How are you, Richmond?" said William McClellan, turning to his near-neighbor.

"I am well, thank you, Bill. It's been too long. You must stop by."

"That reminds me—my son and your youngest have been badgering me to take them hunting . . . any objections?"

"None at all."

More handshakes followed and several more introductions around the group, accompanied by a few awkward coughs and glances at finding the man they had just been ridiculing suddenly in their midst and treating them so affably.

"I want to wish you the best on your Senate run, Denton," said Richmond, turning to their host. "I haven't seen you since I read the announcement in the *Register*."

"Do you really mean that?" rejoined Beaumont, an imperceptible edge creeping into his tone.

"Of course."

"Surely you would be more supportive of, shall we say, a more antislavery candidate, would you not, Davidson?" suggested Roberts significantly.

"Not necessarily. My view on the matter is entirely apolitical."

"Ah . . . I see. I must say," said Justice Byford, "after your recent . . . ah, your controversial actions, I find that surprising."

"What my wife and I did in the decision regarding our slaves," Davidson went on, "was a matter of conscience, not politics."

"Your wife was part of the decision?" asked Bayhurst with raised eyebrow.

"We make all decisions together. In any event, the politics of such disputes are not paramount in our considerations."

"What is, then?" asked Roberts.

"Living as we have been told to live."

"An interesting point of view," observed Hayden. "So you did not support John Fremont two years ago, or this upstart Midwesterner Lincoln in their antislavery positions?"

"Let me say that I am in sympathy with certain of their views, though I still believe strongly in the right of states to determine their own courses. But I do not support such men politically. As I said, for us the politics are secondary to the deeper morality."

"Do you intend to support your friend here in his bid against Senator Hoyt?" asked Bayhurst, nodding his head in the direction of their host. "The conventional wisdom has it that Hoyt is in low repute right now and that our kind host is a shoe in. Where will your support lay, Mr. Davidson—with your friend and neighbor?"

The question brought immediate silence to the lips of everyone within earshot. Only a few chinks of ice in their glasses could be heard as they waited, along with distant laughter and music in the background.

"Certainly," replied Davidson, "as far as my conscience will allow. He has not asked me to actually campaign for him, and if he did I would probably have to say no. But neither would I campaign for Senator Hoyt or any man. I do not believe politics to be the primary arena in which I am to be actively involved, and to that conviction I must be faithful. But of course Denton has my support and best wishes."

The words sunk in to varying levels. Most of those listening seemed satisfied with the statement, however vague.

"Getting back to what you said a moment ago," said Byford in a puzzled tone, "what do you mean, how we are told to live? Told by whom?"

"He who has a claim upon us," replied Davidson.

"Speaking for myself," said Seehorn, "I will always be a Virginian first and a citizen of the country second. No president in Washington will ever be worthy of the level of loyalty you speak of. Well," he added, glancing around the group knowingly, "unless we should succeed in placing our own Jeff Davis in the White House, of course! That would be different!"

Nods of agreement indicated well enough that the others were of like mind.

"My point is that I do not consider any Northerner to have a claim on me at all, as you say."

"So where *are* your primary loyalties, Davidson," asked Bayhurst, "—with Virginia or Washington?"

"Neither, I am afraid," he replied with hint of a smile. "I always try to be loyal to our nation *and* to Virginia. But my highest allegiance belongs elsewhere."

Before Seehorn or Bayhurst could say anything further, the lawyer spoke up.

"You mentioned morality a moment ago, Davidson," said Roberts. "Do you consider slavery a moral issue or a political and economic one?"

"A good question, Mr. Roberts," smiled Davidson. "In answer I would say, all three."

"And is ownership of slaves, in your view, immoral then?"

Again, Davidson smiled.

"That is not a judgment for me to make," he said. "The Bible neither condemns nor condones slavery—a fact I find intriguing. I would really not care to comment further, gentlemen. I must simply heed my own conscience, and walk in the light I have been given. If you will excuse me, I deserted my wife a moment ago. Again, Denton, best wishes with your candidacy."

He moved off and disappeared through the crowd.

The gray-suited observer, who had been listening carefully to every word, watched him go. He weighed his options, whether to follow the man who held such obvious interest or whether to remain with the Beaumont group and see what might come of it.

He thought about it but a moment or two. From the little he had seen and heard, especially from gazing unseen into the man's pale blue eyes, he could tell that the Davidson fellow was an honest man without an ounce of guile in his bones. What he needed to learn from him he could get anytime, simply by walking up and asking him. The comments made by the others in his absence, however, would not be so easily recaptured—a chance remark, a stray observation, a glance, a flash of the eyes. . . .

He would remain where he was.

By now the dancing was in full swing. Veronica Beaumont was enjoying a second waltz with the young man, as she supposed, of her dreams, unaware that they were being watched from behind the trees in the distance by Scully Riggs. A few of the other girls, following her example, had succeeded in enticing a handful of brave young men in the direction of the music. Gradually the dance area filled with couples of all ages, though most still preferred to watch from the safety of little cliques spread about the lawn.

"A waltz, my dear," said Richmond as he returned to his wife, extending his hand and giving a slight bow.

"Thank you," replied Carolyn, taking his hand. "I wondered what happened to you."

"Merely paying my respects to our host," he replied, leading her toward the orchestra.

"And . . . ?" said Carolyn as they fell into step with the music.

"From the looks around the group," replied her husband, laughing, "I suspect I interrupted a discussion in which I had myself been playing a key role. Those poor men," he added, "they don't know what to do with me! Have you spoken with Lady Daphne?"

"I haven't seen her yet. Someone said she was still inside."

As dancing and discussions continued, black waiters moved silently among the guests carrying trays laden with tall glasses of lemonade, iced tea, brandy, Irish coffee, mint julep, and, for the most special of guests, samples from Beaumont's private reserve of thirty-year-old whiskey imported from the Scottish highlands.

Around the grounds, most of the men in their light-colored suits stood sipping drinks in small clusters, speaking earnestly about politics and crops and the status of slavery throughout the Union. It was the chief topic of interest whenever and wherever Southerners gathered.

Their wives of all ages from eighteen to fifty were likewise bunched about the lawn, some standing, some seated in circles of benches and chairs. Fanning themselves and shading their white faces with lacy parasols of diverse colors, they chatted about husbands and children and everything else wives and mothers talk about. These included several newly married young ladies not yet twenty years of age, suddenly transformed from belles to matrons and thus the recipients of constant advice from their experienced elders concerning everything from childbirth and sickness to the canning of peaches. One or two of these cast about an occasional distracted glance, accompanied by an inward twinge of envy, to think that they had married too young, and would never more know the gaiety and freedom that Veronica Beaumont and other of their former friends still enjoyed.

Inside the drawing room of the mansion, through open French doors, the grandmothers and great-grandmothers in long dark silks and satins flapped their palmetto fans yet more diligently in the heat. They sat on soft sofas and chairs and talked even more earnestly about the things that old women in black dresses had talked about from time immemorial.

Children ran excitedly about everywhere, rambunctious and frolicsome.

But the sentient vortex of such gatherings in the South was always reserved for the unmarried belles and beaux who had been fortunate enough to receive invitations. Among them stirred budding affections to pluck a thousand invisible heartstrings, passions that would result in a hundred individual dramas of hope and heartbreak, triumph and disappointment, being played out before day's end.

Swirling and twirling and moving with flourish in their wide-hooped crinolines of pink and orange and blue and yellow and every other color imaginable, topped with wide bright hats and encircled with ribbons and sashes and bows, a dozen and a half young women between fifteen and eighteen were engaged in the not-so-subtle art practiced since time began, of attracting the eye of every young man on the premises between sixteen and twenty-five. Some of their flirtations were modest, others bold, others outright brazen, but all had the same end in view—to be *noticed* . . . then to draw a second, and perhaps even a third glance. To draw a *fourth* such diversion of the eyes, and with it a lingering shy smile, from some handsome and eligible boy—to be followed, whether in ten minutes or two hours, it mattered not just so long as the moment came eventually, by the bashful invitation to the dance floor—was the most sought after prize the day could bring.

The most eligible of the young men, on their parts, carried out to perfection their own vital function in the timeless ritual, which was to pretend *not* to notice. All the while they spoke of hunting and horses and guns and sundry boasts of manhood and strength, seemingly oblivious to the bashful looks and giggles and fluttering eyelashes directed toward them.

Yet the older and more handsome among them knew well enough that every smile and laugh and gesture was capable of causing one or another of the girls to swoon. Thus they chose exactly when to allow a grin, and how much of the teeth to reveal, occasionally accompanying one or the other with a brief dart of the eye in the direction of some vulnerable heart. The young men knew how to flirt, too, after their fashion, and the launching of such subtle arrows were the prized rewards the young ladies sought from the day's outing. This was the Southern variation of the timeless English "coming out" rite, practiced on the yearly foundation of London's social "season."

It was precisely this undercurrent of coquetry on the part of the young ladies, and roguery on the part of the young men, that kept Richmond and Carolyn Davidson away from such gatherings as often as it could be avoided. It made their skin crawl to watch the shallow and self-preoccupied interplay among a youthful generation that had been pampered all its life in wealth.

Both knew that many of today's charms on the part of the one who swirled at the center of the activity had been specifically designed in this case to lure, fascinate, and attract one of their own sons, and it broke their hearts. It was part of youth, they tried—without success—to tell themselves. The fact that their own romance had begun in a church, and that they had prayed together long before they had so much as touched one another, was a fact they tried not to add as an invisible expectation upon their own sons. Seth and Thomas were growing up in different circumstances and a different era. They knew they must allow their sons to find God and to find love, each in his own way. They were also well enough aware that to some degree, God had to "find" them. They mustn't interfere—by their own orchestration or with burdensome expectations—with that process.

Seth was now eighteen. His own faith was developing rapidly. They had every confidence in him. Yet they knew that he must grow in character and move toward his own future, in gradually increasing ways, on his own.

It was a painful process to watch, seeing him involved with such young people as Veronica and her crowd. They only hoped that the roots of his own spiritual fiber would prove deep enough to enable him to discern with clarity the character of those around him.

Meanwhile, Thomas's time to fly was approaching more rapidly than either realized, and in ways neither was aware of. Even the most sensitive and thoughtful of parents can remain oblivious to undercurrents of dissatisfaction brewing beneath the surface. For the direction in which roots grow has as much to do with the soil of individuality in which they are planted as the nourishment those tender roots receive in their early years. Already Seth and Thomas, in ways neither the parents saw nor the young men realized, were directing their roots and wings toward vastly different life-courses.

At present, Seth's sixteen-year-old brother was off with Jeremy McClellan and some of their friends, followed like a puppy dog by fifteen-year-old Cameron Beaumont, with other things on their minds than girls.

Why the guest of honor was so enamored with Seth was still a puzzle to Richmond and Carolyn. His dashing good looks could hardly be denied. Perhaps the fact that he was polite and intelligent and did *not* try to make himself noticed set him apart from other young men in the region with whom he seemed to have fewer and fewer close friendships the older he got. Strange to say, mischief is a more magnetic bond between the young than is virtue, which perhaps explains why the former is in such ample supply, while the latter is so scarce. A corollary of this principle may also have explained why Richmond and Carolyn Davidson did not find themselves blessed with many close friendships or an active social life. In any event, despite his looks, intelligence, respectfulness, and, in his parents' eyes, winsome personality, Seth Davidson was no longer as close to Wyatt Beaumont and Brad McClellan as he once had been, and was even viewed by some as a loner. At the same time, as Thomas advanced through his teen years, his comrades and acquaintances from around Dove's Landing seemed to multiply.

The Davidsons had known Veronica Beaumont from the day she was born, as her family had Seth. Though the mothers had never been close, and the fathers had grown apart in recent years, Seth and Veronica's older brother Wyatt had been good friends in their younger years. In the last two years, however, Wyatt had begun moving in different circles, and now seemed increasingly to regard his childhood playmate as something of a bumpkin.

The elder Davidsons finished their dance and walked toward the tables where a lavish assortment of meats and cakes, fruits and drinks, was being spread in preparation for later in the afternoon. This had not been promoted as a full barbeque in the Southern tradition. The invitations had specified "an afternoon of light fare and dancing." It was already clear, however, that anyone would easily be able to eat his fill. The aroma of mutton and pork drifted toward them on an occasional gust of smoke from the nearby cooking pit.

"Would you and da missus care fo' some refreshment, Massa Dav'son?" asked a tall black butler as they approached.

"Hello, Jarvis," said Davidson. "Two mint juleps, please, and *plain*, if you don't mind, without the bourbon."

"Yes, suh, Massa Dav'son. I'll jus' fix up two speshul ones myself."

They were just taking the two tall, icy glasses from him several minutes later when a greeting sounded behind them.

"Richmond Davidson . . . is that you!" The voice that had spoken was clearly that of a New Englander.

Both Davidsons turned.

"James," Richmond exclaimed exuberantly, his face spreading into a wide grin as he extended his hand, "what in the world are you doing here!"

"I'm here to interview the Senate candidate Beaumont," laughed Waters. "I had no idea you two would be here—hello again, Carolyn."

"Hello, James!" said Carolyn. "What a delightful surprise!"

"You came to Dove's Landing . . . and did not even let us know!" said Richmond, still grinning.

"My apologies," nodded Waters. "Actually, I was planning to try to see you when this was over, but in truth I had no idea how close or far away you would be."

"Our plantation is just on the other side of that ridge there," said Richmond, pointing westward, where, from their vantage point on the lawn, a green tree-covered ridge of hills, with one high peak at approximately its midpoint, was clearly visible.

"Once I arrived and saw how short a ride it was from town, I realized I was near Greenwood. If the assignment had been planned ahead of time, I could have come down a day or two earlier. As it was, it was very last minute—I barely had time to jump on a train. There was no time to contact you. As I said, I hoped to stop by later. From your different positions on slavery, I never imagined that you would be in attendance. But this is wonderful—you are here! I had no idea you and Beaumont were friends."

"How are things up in Massachusetts?" asked Richmond.

"Well enough," replied Waters.

"How did a Northerner like you manage an invitation from our staunchly antiabolitionist neighbor?"

"The *Globe* sent me down, not only to get a feel for sentiment in Virginia, Maryland, and Delaware, but most importantly to find out how the congressional election could be affected by the last month's admission of Minnesota to the Union. The senatorial contest between Hoyt and this fellow Denton Beaumont is beginning to attract some notice up North. The balance of power in the Senate is delicate. This is one of those races everyone is watching. As it stands right now, it appears Beaumont is likely to knock off Hoyt, who is a moderate, and give the Senate a bold new pro-slavery voice. So there is a keen interest in the outcome."

"Well, we are delighted to see you!" said Carolyn. "But we would have loved to put you up."

"I would like to have accepted. As I say, it was a very last minute thing. Actually, I haven't traveled much in the last couple of years. My doctor says my heart isn't what it once was and says I need to scale back."

"And in this case?"

"I didn't consult him!" laughed Waters. "I just packed a bag and dashed to the station."

"And your editor wrangled you an invitation!" laughed Richmond.

"That he did. He told me to get an inside story on the Beaumont fellow. Perhaps *you* would grant me a confidential interview about freeing your slaves."

Davidson laughed. "Not on your life!" he said. "I keep well out of politics."

"In any event, I am hoping for an introduction to Denton Beaumont. I would like to interview him."

"An introduction will be easy to arrange," rejoined Richmond, glancing across the lawn and gesturing toward their host. "Denton and I are old friends."

Waters followed his gaze. An odd expression of question came over his face.

"What is it?" asked Davidson.

"Oh . . . uh, nothing," replied Waters, turning back. "I just saw a face I thought I had seen last week in Boston. But that could hardly be."

"Someone you know?"

"No, only a face in a crowd. But to return to what you said a moment ago, surely you and Beaumont are not political allies?" said Waters.

"No," smiled Richmond. "Our friendship does not extend to politics. We are neighbors and our plantation borders Oakbriar in a number of places. And we rode together as boys."

"Tell me about Beaumont, then?"

"I will say no more than that he is rather put out with me these days," replied Richmond. "That is why I will make no official comment on the record."

"Is there any chance Cherity came with you?" asked Carolyn, glancing about.

"I'm afraid not, though I would have loved to bring her."

"How is she?"

"Well, growing fast, rambunctious as ever, and still talking about going west to be a cowgirl," replied Waters. "We have decided for her to remain home next year rather than return to boarding school. I fear I am getting too old to be alone for such long periods of time."

"Hardly that!" laughed Richmond.

"I am over fifty now, my friend," said Waters.

"You don't look a day over forty," said Carolyn.

"You are still a charmer!" laughed Waters. "Nevertheless, reality compels me to admit that it is all too true. I was born when Thomas Jefferson was president. That dates me to the era of the founding fathers, and occasionally reminds me how young our republic still is. In any event, I realize that I do not have many more years left with my youngest daughter, and I want her with me for as much of that time as we do have. I am very much enjoying having her with me again. How about your three?"

"Cynthia was married only last year," replied Carolyn, "and now lives up in Connecticut."

"We're practically neighbors!"

"Both our boys are here," Carolyn added. "Seth is now eighteen and was dancing with Mr. Beaumont's daughter the last time I saw him. Thomas is sixteen and is off with a few friends. Some of the younger girls are trying to get their attention, but for all I can tell without success. But would it be possible for you to return to Greenwood and spend the evening with us?"

"I would love to. I had planned to try to squeeze in a visit. But now that I have seen you, my schedule is so tight that it would really be best for me to catch the late train north. I've got to be in New York in two days where my boss wants me to interview the mayor."

"Will you stay over there?" asked Richmond.

"Just for a night. My editor has me booked in at the Fairmont. But I should be back in Boston the following afternoon, just about the time Cherity gets home from a short visit to her older sister."

"You are not even going to see your other daughter and grandson in Norfolk?"

"I'm afraid not."

"Well then," said Carolyn, "if and when your travels bring you to Virginia again, I hope you will definitely spend a few days with us—you and Cherity!"

"We would be honored. Thank you very much."

"Please . . . I mean it sincerely," added Carolyn.

"I add my own to Carolyn's invitation," nodded Richmond. "You are welcome anytime, with or without notice."

"We will consider our invitation open ended," persisted Carolyn.

"Seriously, James," added Richmond. "We have a great deal more room than we need. A serenity seems to have settled upon our grounds of late. It has made me wonder if it might have something to do with having freed our slaves and given them a share in the profits of the place. In any event, I think you would find it both invigorating and peaceful. The arboretum, especially, we find always restores our spirits. It would be our privilege to have you and your daughter share it with us."

"Thank you very much. We shall definitely consider it among our possibilities."

Thirty-three

The ride back to Greenwood in the warm dusk was quiet. The distance between the houses of the two plantations, whose properties adjoined along several miles of common boundary, was less than six miles. Yet it lately seemed to Richmond and Carolyn Davidson like the distance between two different worlds.

The drive back helped return their spirits to a calm and common center, though both were also uneasy, knowing that their sons had had to endure a certain unpleasantness with their peers as a result of their stand with their slaves.

On Richmond's part, visiting his childhood friend in such a gala, social, and political setting, accentuated the contrast between the two different paths in life they had chosen. Indeed, to all appearances, Denton Beaumont was easily outdistancing his neighbor in all the ways by which the world would judge success.

Carolyn felt such things too. She was perhaps even more set apart from women such as Lady Daphne Beaumont than her husband was from his peers. She had never fit in here. Richmond had grown up in the area. He knew these people intimately. He had ridden and hunted and got into youthful mischief with his brother, Denton, and William McClellan from time to time, and had many other boyhood acquaintances whom he still considered friends.

But she had come from the far west of the state. She had always been looked at as an outsider. As a minister's daughter, she had never been familiar with this upper-class plantation lifestyle and was more than a little uncomfortable with it. She had never been a belle, and now was no more a wealthy Southern matron than Richmond himself was. Therefore, while he could mix, she could not, and the ladies of the region always treated her with that vague hauteur especially reserved for outsiders.

She didn't mind. She was happy. And Carolyn knew that having grown up here actually made it more difficult in some ways for her husband. The looks and condescending comments occasionally bit deep.

"You and Veronica certainly stole the show with your dancing," commented Carolyn as they rode.

"Yeah . . . Veronica makes sure people are looking at her, doesn't she?" laughed Seth.

"What do you think of that, my boy?" asked the elder Davidson.

"I don't know," replied Seth. "I guess I'm not too comfortable with it. It puts me more in the limelight than I would like."

"Get used to it!" said Carolyn. "I have the feeling that wherever Veronica goes, especially as she gets older, she will be the center of attention. I'm not sure she would know what to do with herself unless she was."

"What I meant," Richmond went on, trying, as was his invariable practice, to guide the conversation toward its most significant point, "is what do you think of it with respect to Veronica herself?"

"What do you mean?" asked Seth.

"What do you think that tendency to draw attention reveals about her . . . as a person?"

"I don't know," replied Seth. "Any one of those girls at the party today would have gladly traded places with Veronica. Aren't all girls that way?"

"Your mother certainly wasn't!" laughed Richmond, but with seri-ousness. "She never put herself in the limelight. I saw a humility and gracefulness of character in her face almost the moment I laid eyes on her. It drew me, and eventually I fell in love with her—not because she was the radiant star of the show, but because of what I saw inside her . . . her character . . . the real person."

As he listened beside Seth in the backseat, Thomas inwardly sneered to hear his father talk so. It was just like him to use everything that came up as a chance to preach at them. He had grown sick of his father's lectures all those years the three of them were growing up. He was sick of hearing how it was when *they* were young, and about how great *they* had been, how spiritually superior *they* were to everyone else, and what idiots the whole rest of the world contained. If he and Cynthia and Seth didn't agree with every word that proceeded from his mouth, he would tongue-lash them for their immaturity. What did he think he was, anyway, some kind of encyclopedia on virtue and knowledge? Did he think that anyone *cared*? Did he have to lecture about everything!

But his mother's voice interrupted his sullen reflections.

"And what about you, Thomas," Carolyn asked, "did you have fun?"

"I don't know," he answered. "It was okay."

In actual fact, Seth's brother had been derided by some of his friends about the status of his father's former slaves, and he had found the experience humiliating.

Both sons were feeling the pressure of the stand their mother and father had taken. But they were reacting in far different ways. Seth was proud of his parents for their convictions. Thomas was coming to resent them for what he judged the absurdity of their beliefs. His resentments were directed equally toward their religion, their methods and practices as parents, and their social standards of equality between the races.

When derisive comments were made to Seth about his father's treatment of blacks, the indignation of sonly pride rose up within him in defense of his father. If ever there was a time when Seth Davidson was tempted toward, indeed, came close to physical violence, it was at such times. He would have taken on anyone to defend his father's honor. Thus, he was teased less about it because his friends knew it would do no good. Their words would not sting him, but might, if they pushed him too far, turn the tables against them. For Seth was no weakling. Though his preference was not to fight, he was strong enough and quick enough that anyone considering taking him on would have been well advised to weigh their options prudently.

Thomas, on the other hand, cringed in humiliation at the taunts and teases. Thus they were aimed more frequently in his direction. The embarrassed silence told his so-called friends that their arrows had hit their marks and encouraged them all the more. Reacting wrongly within himself, he turned blame toward his father rather than taking refuge from the criticism in the character of his father.

Thomas saw his father as neither a refuge nor a comfort against the pains of his life, but as the cause of them. Thus, he could not see that his father had in truth taken the high ground. It was the low and mean-spirited ignorance of his friends that deserved his derision. But wrong response bred wrong response, and Thomas sunk more and more deeply into a peevish and moody irritability that had by now grown critical toward everything his parents said or did.

Neither father nor mother had any idea the extent or depth of his resentment against the upbringing they had given him, or that, without consciously realizing it, Thomas was already mulling over various schemes that would enable him to get away from the Greenwood prison as soon as he was old enough.

The party continued traveling east on the road between Fredericksburg and Charlottesville that passed near the Beaumont estate of Oakbriar and then through Dove's Landing. As they jostled along, Carolyn's thoughts, like her younger son's, turned reflective, though in much different directions.

Remembering the kind of person she had been when she and Richmond met filled her with many emotions, even now. Her overriding feeling, however, was always one of quiet thankfulness for sending Richmond to love her in the midst of her desolation. Returning to her father's home after the tragedy that had changed her life forever, she had never expected to know love again. Whatever was left of her faith at the time hung by the slenderest of threads. In her hopelessness, she did not even care whether she believed. What did it matter? What difference did it make? What difference *could* it make?

Then Richmond had walked into her life.

Not that he was in much better shape. He was more despondent than she was! Moreover, he had no belief in God to sustain him at all, only a heart hungry for truth.

Yet somehow, in their common heartache, they had together discovered the reality of life with God . . . and in the process fallen in love.

A quiet smile of melancholy on her face, Carolyn's thoughts drifted back to the years leading up to that day. . . .

Randolph was a visionary before he and Carolyn met.

Her father called him an impractical dreamer. But his enthusiasm for the Lord's work swept young Carolyn Peters off her feet. Having grown up in the church, she had known no other kind of life. Randolph offered adventure . . . spiritual adventure!

She had always vaguely wanted to serve the Lord, especially to work with children and teach them to read. She had even thought about joining the mission field. With Randolph it seemed she might have the chance to do just that.

But when he began talking about the untamed and frightening West of this continent, a host of misgivings rose within her. It was not at all the mission field she had envisioned.

"But just think, Carolyn," he had insisted, "there are people out West—settlers and trappers and explorers—who need the gospel. And Indians! There are dozens of tribes that have never so much as heard a word about Jesus."

"Yes," she said, "Indians who kill white people."

"But think of the opportunity! We'll start a church . . . maybe several churches. Doesn't the thought of being the first missionaries to enter a

region and establish communication with the people of another race and tongue . . . doesn't the thought of it thrill you!"

What could she say without sounding like she didn't want to further the gospel? But it was not her vision to do it in that way.

"Just think, you can be the first woman to cross the Rockies into the Oregon Territory. You will be famous, known as the first woman missionary to the west of the American continent."

The prospect did not sound particularly appealing. "I care nothing about being famous," said Carolyn. "I would rather stay alive."

Her father's objections were stronger yet.

"I am not convinced it is right," he said. "There are many dangers."

"I know," said young Randolph, "but we can meet them."

"I am not sure that the two of you are old enough or experienced enough for it yet. Why not wait a few years? Give God time to make his will clear to us all. You do not need to be the first."

"That is the thrilling part, to be the first, to go where no one has gone before and do what no one has done before. If we wait, we will be treading over ground that others have trod before us. It takes away the sense of adventure."

In the end Randolph's vision and enthusiasm and assurances that God was leading carried the day. They were married, and within six months the former Carolyn Peters was on her way to join a handful of other intrepid pioneers and several wagons leaving Independence, Missouri, and striking out across the vast western prairie of North America.

She had forebodings almost from the day they set out. It was hot and dry, their progress slow. No Indian attacks hampered them, but several storms did, as well as one flash flood, one broken axle, and a missed landmark that cost them a week in the wrong direction. Midway across the great plains, two wagons turned back, then in sight of the Platte River, another two. With only four wagons left, by then she was the only woman. If they were harassed by Indians now, there were too few of them to fight back. They would be massacred.

It was not Indians that ended her husband's adventure in tragedy, but a six-foot-long rattler snoozing in the shade beside a large rock next to the stream where they had paused to water the oxen and fill their containers.

As Randolph jumped over the rock with the last of their canteens in hand, the startled snake struck with lightning speed, its fangs sinking deep into Randolph's leg.

His cry brought Carolyn running. She stared aghast to see him struggling to run toward her, dragging the hideous thing, still attached by its wicked teeth, behind him across the ground. Her screams brought the other men. They quickly drew pistols and blasted the rattler into half a dozen bloody pieces.

Two carried her husband to the stream to cool the leg while another ran for a knife. Within minutes, they had cut a deep gash, sucked out what they could of the yellow venom, and applied a tourniquet at the knee. But it was not enough. The wound was deep, and his brief attempt to run for help had pumped the poison rapidly up the leg, past his knee and into his bloodstream. They carried him back to the wagon, where Carolyn attempted to make him comfortable.

By evening, he was unconscious, his skin on fire.

By morning she was a widow.

The other men offered to help, but Carolyn buried her husband of a mere few months alone . . . then turned back. As she saw the last of the wagons, with their six men, disappearing west toward the Rockies, she stood a few minutes longer beside the lump in the ground where her husband lay. The cross made of two sticks bound together by a strand of leather hardly seemed a fitting tribute to a human life. She stared at it a moment, unseeing. Then she climbed back up onto the wagon, took the reins, slapped them and called to the two oxen, and set out at a painfully slow pace back toward the east.

In truth, she never expected to survive the return journey. How could she find her way, find water, keep the oxen fed and healthy? All she needed to do was encounter one other human being, of any race—because out here what could it be but a man?—and she was sure to be raped or killed. Not only that, she might starve or die of thirst. She was only twenty-one . . . how could she possibly survive out here alone?

But God had been with her more than she realized or acknowledged at the time, watching out for her, guiding her, protecting her, and making her path straight. She met a couple of groups going west. They refilled her

*water barrels and gave her fresh game. After a month of the loneliest days
she had known before or since, and feeling the twinge of autumn in the
air, she began recognizing signs that said she was approaching civilization
again. Carolyn had often wished she could look back and know that in the
spiritual desert of her despondency she and the Lord deepened the bonds
between them. At the time she could not discern it. All she felt was heartache, grief, aloneness . . . and no sign of God anywhere.*

*She reached Independence, with the kindly help of a number of people
along the way, sold the team and wagon and everything else she possessed
for whatever she could get for them, bought a one-way ticket back to
Charleston, and by winter of the year when she and Randolph had
expected to be in Oregon, she was passing out hymnals at her father's
church, a widow at the age of twenty-two.*

"Here we are!" said her husband's voice, bringing Carolyn's thoughts
back to the present.

She wiped a solitary tear from one eye and drew in a deep breath as
they entered the long drive up a tree-lined incline to their home.

Richmond led the horses along a winding drive through a sparsely
clustered wood of beech, oak, and ash. The trees were far enough
apart—indeed, the natural wood in whose midst the original plantation house had been set a century earlier had been expertly thinned,
leaving only the stateliest of its specimens—such that it could not
properly be called a forest in either size or density. Yet the trees which
remained, surrounding the house on almost three sides, were huge,
wide spreading, and magnificent. When walking in its midst, the
enveloping canopy overhead, and the massive thick trunks below, sent
one's thoughts toward fairy tale woods of the black forest of Germany
rather than a plantation of northern Virginia.

It was this three acres of magnificently clustered giants which they
simply called "the wood" and which offered a visitor his first impression of the grounds, from which Greenwood Acres derived its name.
It had also been the inspiration for Richmond's and Carolyn's smaller

and more ornamental arbor which stretched down the slope on the opposite side of the house. The two "woods"—the one natural, tall, and ancient, the other new and thus smaller of height and more planned and cultivated—bordered one another in such a way that one might easily walk between the two without being able to identify the exact point of transition between old and new, between *arbor* and *wood*.

Not only were the gardens and arboretum of Greenwood of some renown, so were its stables. Everyone in the family was accomplished in the saddle. Besides having had a slave, formerly, now a hired black, to act as gardener to the estate, they also employed one of their former slaves, a man of about fifty-five, graying but sinewy, strong, and keen of mind, as full-time trainer, groom, and tack man all in one. Where this Alexander had come by his uncanny way with horses was a mystery. But no one harbored the slightest doubt that he possessed a sixth sense with the stately monarchs of the animal kingdom. A look of the eyes, a snap of the finger, a word, a gesture, was all he needed to communicate his will to any horse of any age, color, temperament, or breed. To see him whisper gently in an animal's ear, one hand holding the long nosey head firm with leather halter, the other open to fleshly lips with a chunk of sugar or slice of apple, was to observe a genius at work. Much to the delight of the elder Davidson, Alexander seemed, whether consciously or unconsciously, to be passing on a portion of his gift to Seth.

Richmond Davidson's father and grandfather had made use of horses only as the utilitarian tools of their trade, to pull their wagons and carriages and ploughs. The recent development of a riding and racing stable had originated not long after the first child of the present Davidsons had learned to walk. They found Cynthia outside standing close to an old horse named Barg who was hitched to the wagon of a visiting friend and tied to the rail in front of the house, its head bent low nuzzling Cynthia's face. Carolyn had run outside in terror, until she realized that Cynthia was in no danger. The old horse seemed to recognize the gentle innocence of the toddler babbling away in its face. Carolyn stood a moment and watched in awe, all but certain that some indefinable bonds of creature-communication were passing between child and beast. When at length Cynthia turned to see her mother standing watching, the beaming smile of pleasure on her face brought tears to Carolyn's eyes. A lifelong love had been born.

Their first purchase of what might be called recreational horseflesh came with Cynthia's fifth birthday—a chestnut Welsh Cob mare whom Cynthia called Cobby.

Cynthia was an expert in a man's saddle by eight, and more horses followed. They all took to riding together, and some breeding was the inevitable next step. As with most things Richmond Davidson undertook, he threw himself into it with wholehearted zeal and gusto, learning everything he could about various breeds, which were more suitable for what sorts of work and riding, what were their various temperaments, and which they should make the dominant focus of their energies at Greenwood. His father Grantham was pleased when he saw his son expanding the plantation's resources.

One thing led to another. Stables and a new barn were added dedicated to the horses, certain fields and pastures were either cleared or converted from other uses to more equine pursuits. Perhaps the greatest development of all was the discovery of Alexander's special gift. It happened altogether by accident. One of a team of four pulling a wagon loaded high with cotton had suddenly gone wild for no apparent reason. The horse reared and bolted, frightening the other three. They darted out of control and upset the wagon, throwing off two slaves from its bench seat. The horses broke free and tore across the field. They circled in a wide arc, eventually slowing as they began to tire. All around was a commotion of ropes and whips and shouts, the senior Davidson yelling out orders to subdue the wild creatures.

In the midst of the pandemonium, they saw the slave of Richmond's father slowly walk out toward the team, heedless of the ears laying back and the glint of danger still in the eye of the instigator of the madness. He walked straight toward the horse, speaking in gentle, barely audible tones, putting his head up next to the wild creature and slowly stroking its nose. He found the yellow jacket that had caught under the harness, removed it, and soothed the spot with a bit of mud.

A few minutes later he was leading a calm team back.

"Dey be all right, Massa Dab'son," said Alexander to Richmond's father. "He jes' tol' me he gots him a pain where dat bee stung him, but he be fine by'n by. He jes' need a little rest, dat's all."

"Of course, of course, Alexander, whatever you say," said Grantham Davidson.

Alexander unhitched the team from one another, led away the red Bashkir, and moments later was refitting the harness as the horse stood by with the docility of a child.

From that day on, Alexander had been given charge of any special equine needs about the place. More recently, in Richmond's and Carolyn's time, Alexander had seen to most of the breaking and training, whose secrets and mysteries Richmond would have given anything to learn but about which he still confessed himself mystified. When he tried to model his words and movements exactly after Alexander's, horses reacted in a completely different way. The only other individual at Greenwood who possessed a similar knack for communicating in the invisible equine language of subtlety, nuance, and whispers of love and command, was Seth, who grew up loving the animals as much as had his sister.

The carriage passed a large fenced corral on their right as it approached the house. A few horses cantered toward them as they passed.

Carolyn again turned pensive as their stately red brick home drew into view amid the trees. There were moments she almost imagined that Greenwood was of another time and place when life moved slower and things were simpler than they seemed determined to become nowadays. At the Beaumont estate, she had felt an urgency and haste amid the crowd. Maybe that was why she left Greenwood as seldom as she did. The drive up through the trees toward the house represented more to her than merely coming home. It always meant a slow and peaceful return to the pastoral simplicity of the lives they had carved out for themselves.

If they could not slow down the cadence of the world's drumbeats, perhaps at least they could find a corner of that world to be a refuge where they could live their own lives. They had determined that serenity and calm would be the undergirding foundation of their existence. The only way to achieve this was to steadily refuse to allow the world's pace to dictate their own. They hoped, in some small measure, to be able to offer that same serenity to any and all who chanced to come to Greenwood.

At length they emerged from the trees. The house that came into view had been entirely constructed out of classic old orange terra cotta brick, with tile and slate roof. The architecture was German, unassuming yet stately in its own way, and typically Virginian at the same time, with tile and protruding ornamental brickwork bordering windows and doors. There were two full floors of living quarters, though a cellar as well as a mostly empty loft beneath the roof essentially made it a structure of four floors. Behind the main house and connected to it stretched what had once been a cattle barn but was now mostly used for the storage of machinery, wood, and for the drying of tobacco. Several other smaller barns stood parallel and at right angles with the main house, all also of orange brick and slate or tile roof.

Thirty-four

*T*he train ride between the Virginia border and New York City was one Cecil Hirsch had made dozens of times once he got old enough that conductors didn't put him off at the next stop after discovering he was just a kid traveling alone. In recent years he had even been able to afford a ticket.

His low-level schemes had taken him from Atlanta to Boston and everywhere between. He knew all the cities, all the hotels, all the important sites, and enough gossip to get him by. But on this occasion his mind was filled with ambitions of a more political nature than usual. This was no hotel hustle, no nickel-and-dime con to impress tourists. This time he had the feeling he may have stumbled into the big time. He had gathered enough information to keep his devious brain busy for weeks. Whether any of it would do the senator any good, that he'd have to find out when he got to New York.

Frankly, he could care less about politics, Hirsch thought to himself. Yet something about yesterday's gala at the Beaumont estate sent his brain reeling in new directions. Suddenly it dawned on him that these people of the South would *never* relinquish what they believed in.

That's when the realization broke in on him—there was only one way this conflict could end.

In war.

As he sat looking out on the peaceful countryside of Pennsylvania, Cecil Hirsch knew that an armed conflict between the Northern and Southern states of the so-called *United* States of America was on its way. The handwriting on the wall was not so difficult to read.

The thought, however, filled him with no angst, no sense of fear or dread. Rather, a light burned in his eyes and his mind spun with the possibilities. Conflict always brought shifts in power . . . and profits to those who knew how to exploit them. The greatest benefits would go to those who knew how the game was played. Wars not only meant death and destruction, wars created wealth and power. War meant *opportunity*.

Furthermore, as he had moved about, drink in hand, smiling and donning his most affable nondescript tongue and gracious plantationesque demeanor, he had discovered another powerful secret—*women* rather than men could well be the key to the subterranean flow of clandestine information.

As he had learned long ago on the streets of New York City, he could easily make a buck telling the wives of visiting businessmen or tourists what they wanted to *hear*. Yesterday, however, the opposite truth—and one potentially far more potent—had gradually come clear as he had watched and listened and glided in and out of small cliques of wives and belles and mothers and grandmothers of all ages. Opportunity might come to one who was a good *listener* even more than to one who merely possessed the gift of interesting gab. By giving the wives of politicians and dignitaries the chance to *say* what they wanted to say, unseen vaults could be opened. Most of them were annoyed at their husbands—he could see it in their faces and mannerisms and the snide comments to one another about "the men"—for treating them like political and intellectual lightweights. They did not like being ignored.

When another man showed a woman the courtesy and attention she felt was lacking from the man she slept with at night, she ate it up. When a decent-looking guy like himself turned on the charm, employing just the right flattering obsequiousness, it took very little to loosen a woman's tongue. Best of all, no one ever knew—the woman herself least of all—that the lock had been picked and the informational vaults raided.

Yesterday's conversation with Lady Daphne Beaumont, for instance, had proved a veritable gold mine of tidbits about nearly everyone on the guest list, not to mention having secured him an introduction to her daughter.

He had just been glancing about and had seen a familiar face. It took him a few seconds to place it, then he remembered—Boston . . . a journalist called Waters. He hadn't expected to see anyone from the North, especially New England, and the fellow had looked at him a little too keenly. Where had they crossed paths before?

Then a few yards away Hirsch had spotted the opportunity he had been waiting for. He moved in its direction.

"Would you be the Lady Daphne Beaumont I have been hearing about?" he said, sidling up in one of those ambiguous moments of conversational transition that characterize the social ebb and flow of such gatherings.

"Why . . . yes, I am," said Lady Daphne, turning toward the question, blushing with pleasure at the underlying implication of its wording. "I don't believe I have had the pleasure."

"Cecil Hirsch, ma'am," said Hirsch, taking Lady Daphne's offered hand and drawing it to his lips, where he let it linger just a second longer than was customary. "I cannot tell you how happy I am to finally make your acquaintance. It seems that everywhere I've gone today I keep hearing your name."

"Really, Mr. Hirsch? I can't imagine why," said Lady Daphne, her blush deepening.

"Oh, it's obvious, isn't it—you're the hostess. Your husband may be the center of attention with all those politicians over there," he said, nodding his head in the direction of an earnest discussion in progress on the other side of the lawn, "but everyone knows who makes an event like this possible, and successful I might add. If you want my opinion—"

Here he paused slightly and glanced around, lowered his voice, and drew close in affected confidentiality.

"—if you ask me not one of these men would be worth a thing without their wives. The women do everything for them behind the scenes, yet what thanks do they get? None. That's why I always find women far more interesting than men."

"Why, Mr. Hirsch, you are a naughty one!" laughed Lady Daphne.

He allowed his lips to curl slightly into a coy but knowing smile.

"I mean it," he said. "And you . . . I mean—after what I have seen today, goodness . . . your parties will be the toast of the capital!"

"Oh . . . !" exclaimed Lady Daphne, nervously bringing up her fan and flapping it a time or two.

"Promise me, please—you must promise now, before you become the social hub of Washington and forget such people as me—that you will invite me to at least one of your parties after you arrive."

"I shall never forget you, Mr. Hirsch," laughed Lady Daphne. "And you shall have invitations to all my parties!"

Hirsch laughed as if it were the wittiest thing he had ever heard.

"Thank you so much," he said suavely. "I cannot tell you what that will mean to me."

"Are you really from the capital?" asked Lady Daphne.

"My work takes me there occasionally."

"What is your work, Mr. Hirsch?"

"News, Lady Daphne."

"Oh, how simply marvelous!"

"That is why I had heard of you before I came. No one in the news business has failed to hear of the former Lady Daphne Downes MacFadden of the Charleston MacFaddens. It is already setting certain circles abuzz in Washington that the granddaughter of Sir Richard MacFadden, knighted by the king of England himself, is in all likelihood already packing her bags for the capital, where she will soon be the wife of Virginia's newest senator."

Hirsch had not added that this information had been given him in a brief dossier on Beaumont by his rival in the campaign, who had in fact sent him here for the express purpose of making sure Beaumont never made it to Washington at all.

By this point in the conversation, nearly drowning in pleasure under the weight of Hirsch's blandishments, Lady Daphne's reserves were completely gone.

"You are really too kind, Mr. Hirsch!" she said, employing the fan again to breeze away her reddened cheeks. "To think that you had actually heard of me . . . I don't know what to say!"

"It is no more than a woman of your social prestige deserves."

"I only hope we get to Washington," she said.

"There is little doubt of it, from what I hear," said Hirsch.

"I don't know. . . . Sometimes I think my husband is too pro-slavery even for a slave state like Virginia."

"How could that be?"

"It's just that he says things, that, if they got out, I'm not sure people would understand."

"But surely he wouldn't say anything to put himself in a negative light."

"Oh, but you don't know my husband. He has a dreadful temper and things come out. Sometimes he becomes so angry with the slaves—"

She paused just long enough to lower her voice.

"—when they don't work hard enough I've overheard him speak of hanging them!" she whispered. "People would not understand that kind of thing."

"But he hasn't actually has he—hung any of your slaves?"

"No. But I truly think he could. If he ever does, I just hope I don't find out about it."

"What can you tell me about this rumor I heard somewhere that the Negroes on one of the plantations near here are being taught how to behave like whites?"

"Oh, it's true, Mr. Hirsch. I don't know how you heard about it way up in Washington, but it is definitely true. They are being taught to read, how to buy things and use money. And not only that," she added, lowering her voice and drawing near him with a confidential tone, "they are being taught all these things by the wife of an important plantation owner."

"Lady Daphne!" gasped Hirsch in a shocked whisper, as if it was the most scandalous thing he had ever heard, "you don't mean—"

He allowed his voice to trail off significantly, catching her eyes as he did and holding them with his own. Slowly his eyebrows raised as if he were just now grasping her intent.

She nodded with a look of playful cunning, thoroughly enjoying having such a juicy secret, as she thought, with such an enchanting young man. The moment lasted but a second or two.

"—Oh, here comes Veronica," she said, glancing away. "You must meet my daughter, Mr. Hirsch. . . . Veronica, dear—"

As Lady Daphne proceeded to introduce the two who had noticed one another earlier, Hirsch immediately knew that Veronica Beaumont was nothing like her mother. A single glance into her eyes and he knew she was cut of the same cloth as he. She was shrewd, and a user.

"Miss Beaumont," he said, now lifting her hand to his lips for a lengthy kiss.

As he let her hand down and allowed his eyes to drift upward into her face, he found her staring straight into his eyes.

"Why, Mr. Hirsch," she said playfully, batting her eyelashes, "you do flatter a girl with your eyes!"

In that moment he knew that an unspoken understanding had passed between them. Her occasional glances in his direction throughout the rest of the day, and the subtle smiles that accompanied them, even over the shoulder of her beaux as they danced, told him well enough that she recognized the affiliation too. He knew they would meet again.

Cecil Hirsch walked into the restaurant of the Fairmont Hotel two days after the Beaumont shindig.

Why Hoyt wanted to meet him so far north was still a mystery. No one knew his face. They could have conducted their business on the streets of Washington, D.C. in front of the Capitol building and no one would have suspected what the senator was up to. But the senator insisted that the meeting, like their first, must take place away from prying eyes.

As soon as they each had a Scotch in front of them, the senator got down to business.

"Did you get anything for me, Mr. Hirsch?" he said.

"I don't know," replied Hirsch. "I suppose you will have to be the judge of that. I spoke with a lot of people."

"Did you talk to Beaumont himself?"

"I did."

"And?"

"He played it close to the vest. He's a cool customer, knows what he's about, doesn't reveal much. Platitudes mostly, states' rights, the need to keep a balance of slave and free states so that the senate is split and the country is regionally balanced, good for the economy . . . all the standard Southern arguments."

Hoyt nodded. "Yeah, that's the trouble about trying to be a moderate in Virginia. People are too easily swayed by all that. It sounds good, but it will kill our country's future, not preserve it. What else?"

"I spoke with Beaumont's wife. She said her husband occasionally talks of hanging their rebellious slaves."

"He's a U.S. Commissioner—that's a serious charge!"

"I'm only telling you what I heard."

"Has he ever done it?"

"Not that she is aware of."

"That may yet do me some good. Tell me more about it."

Cecil recounted the details of the conversation. At one point, the senator suddenly sat forward.

"He actually said that?" he said.

"According to the man's wife."

A twinkle came to the senator's eyes. "We might just have him with that," he said. "If we could get another secondary source, we would definitely have him."

"There was considerable talk about a friend of Beaumont's, a neighbor who, as I understand it, set his slaves free a couple of years ago."

"Right, a plantation owner named Davidson."

"That's the one—I heard his name all afternoon," nodded Hirsch.

"Did you speak with him?"

"Actually, no. As I was picking it up, though they used to be close friends, there is now a rift between this Davidson fellow and Beaumont. I didn't want to spoil my chances of earning Beaumont's trust, or that of his wife, by getting too friendly with the enemy, so to speak."

"Fair enough. When they were talking about him and his past association with Beaumont, was anything of interest said?"

Hirsch recounted fragments of several conversations he had overheard throughout the afternoon, including one item that seemed to interest the senator more than all the rest, Lady Daphne's comments on the education of local Negroes.

"You don't actually think she was referring to herself?" asked Hoyt.

"I doubt that," replied Hirsch. "The lady's a wingding. I don't think she's smart enough for one thing. For another, Beaumont himself would never stand for it. It's got to be the Davidson fellow and his wife. It's the only explanation."

"But the way you have recounted the conversation, the implication *could* be drawn that it is this Beaumont lady."

"I suppose."

"And if we exaggerate a little—well, it's politics!"

They continued to talk and Hoyt continued to ply Hirsch with questions about the gathering for another twenty minutes. At last he stood.

"My boy, if all this information does what I hope it will," said Hoyt at length as he prepared to leave, "you may have just saved my political career and given the Senate back to the Union. Believe me, I won't forget it. I never forget a favor."

He withdrew a small packet from inside his coat pocket and handed it to Hirsch.

"I think you will find this satisfactory for your efforts," he said.

As he turned to leave the restaurant, a man rose from a nearby table, stared at them a moment, then approached.

"Senator Hoyt, isn't it?" he said.

"Yes," nodded Hoyt.

"I'm James Waters. I write for the *Globe* . . . up in Boston. We met last year in D.C."

"Ah, yes . . . Mr. Waters, now I remember. You wrote that piece on the reaction of the western states and territories to the slavery-abolitionist debate."

"That was me."

"A decent piece, Waters."

As they spoke, Waters glanced over the senator's shoulder at the young man still seated at the table where the senator had just left him. He couldn't be sure, but he had the distinct feeling he had seen him at the Beaumont estate two days ago.

"How do you like your chances against the slavery advocate Beaumont in November?" he said, returning his attention again to the man standing in front of him.

"On or off the record?"

"Both," smiled Waters.

"On the record . . . I think my record speaks for itself, and I have every confidence that the good people of Virginia will return me to the Senate for another term working hard for the interests of our state in the nation's capital."

"And off the record?"

"To be honest, Waters," replied Hoyt, a serious expression passing over his face, "the fellow has had me more than just a little worried . . . until a short time ago. So off the record," he added with a smile, "I am now more confident in victory than ever."

Thirty-five

The envelope delivered to Oakbriar by a black messenger who had ridden up in a small white man's carriage bore the simple imprint, "Greenwood Acres."

It was taken by the Beaumont house butler straight from the front door to the luncheon room where Veronica Beaumont sat with her mother whiling away the leisurely hours of early afternoon.

The moment it was handed to her, she tore at the envelope and read the simple message on the sheet inside.

> *To Miss Veronica Beaumont,*
> *With your permission I would like to call on you this afternoon.*

It was signed, *Seth Davidson.*

"Oh, Mother," she exclaimed, "it's from Seth. He is coming to call this afternoon!"

She glanced up. Their black butler still stood at the door.

"Who delivered this, Jarvis?" she said.

"Da Dav'son's groom, Alexander, Miz Veronica."

"Is he still here?"

"Yes'm. He said he wuz to wait fer yo' reply."

"Good . . . give him this!"

She jumped up and ran to a small writing desk that sat in the corner, where she dashed off a hurried note. Stuffing it in an envelope, she walked across the floor and handed it to the black man. He turned and disappeared through the house.

Half an hour later, in her room fussing with dress and hair, Veronica heard the sound of horse's hooves outside. She ran to the window. Two horses pulling a wagon were coming up the drive!

The next instant she was flying down the stairs.

"I'll open it, Jarvis," she said as she hurried toward the door.

She pulled it open and ran out onto the porch just as the wagon was slowing in the dirt entryway. Slowly the smile of anticipation faded from her face.

"Oh . . . oh, it's you, Scully," she said slowing to a walk.

Riggs reined the horses to a full stop, set the wheel brake, and jumped down.

"Hello, Miss Veronica," he said. "I got a delivery from the station for your father. I was hoping I'd see you too."

"Well, now you've seen me," said Veronica, turning to go back into the house.

"I heard you had a birthday," said Scully at her back.

Veronica paused and turned. "Yes . . . what did you hear?" she said.

"Just that you had a big party."

"Yes, I did. And if you're real nice, Scully," she added in a teasing tone, "I just might let you give me a present."

Again she turned toward the house.

"Do you have to go so soon?" he said. "I don't have to be back to the station for two hours. I thought maybe you'd like to go for a ride in the wagon with me."

"No, thank you, Scully. Seth is coming over this afternoon. I have to get ready."

The words plunged into Scully Riggs' heart like a cold knife.

"I'll get one of the slaves to go tell your father you are here," said Veronica, then spun around just fast enough to make sure her dress twirled up around her knees.

"The delivery's for *Mister Beaumont*, if you please," he called after her a little irritably.

"Suit yourself!" she answered without turning around. "But he won't want to see you."

Scully watched Veronica's back disappear into the house, then turned and walked to the wagon to wait. In fact, neither of their fathers appeared, but two sullen black slaves who unloaded the wagon silently, then left Scully to turn the horses around and start back into town without another word to anyone.

An hour and a half later, Seth Davidson rode into Oakbriar in a one-horse buggy pulled by a spirited reddish thoroughbred. The differences between the two young men was like night and day, a fact lost on neither budding socialite daughter, nor her ambitious father. Both chanced to see his arrival from their respective windows. But how different were their reactions. The man who hoped to be the junior senator-elect from Virginia come November, and then the *senior* senator of national prominence as soon as aging Senator Everett decided to call it quits, merely mumbled a few words to himself and returned to the papers on his desk. In her own room, however, Veronica shrieked with delight.

"He's here!" she exclaimed as she continued to watch from a corner of the window. A moment later she pulled back so he would not be able to see her, then ran from the room to find Lady Daphne.

"Now, Mother," she said, "here is what I want you to do. . . . "

A minute later her mother descended to the ground floor. By the time the knocker sounded below, Veronica had calmed. She heard indistinguishable words from where she listened through a crack in her door, then she sat back to wait. A minute later her mother knocked on the door of her room, then poked her head inside.

"Seth is here, dear," she said.

"Is everything ready?"

"Just leave it to me."

Veronica had studied boys and their mannerisms since before the coming of her twelve-year-old molars. Now she left Seth for just

enough time for him to cool his heels and fret nervously, so that he
would be putty in her hands. After about five minutes, Veronica
descended the stairs and walked into the parlor where he stood alone
in the middle of the room.

"Hello, Seth," she purred, "how nice of you to call."

Carefully scripted, almost the same moment Lady Daphne walked
in behind her.

"Why don't you two young people sit out on the porch?" she said.
"I always find it far more romantic there than in a stuffy old parlor. I
will have Jarvis bring you some lemonade."

Veronica looked at Seth with a big-eyed inquiring expression,
fluttering her eyelashes a time or two before glancing demurely
away.

"Uh, sure . . . that sounds great, Mrs. Beaumont," replied Seth.

When they were seated alone, Seth glanced out toward the stables,
then turned to Veronica. "I thought maybe you would like to go for a
ride," he said.

"In your buggy—oh, yes . . . that sounds wonderful."

"I meant on horseback. I brought a saddle with me, and that's why
I came with Red Flame."

"Who's that?"

"The thoroughbred there," said Seth, pointing to his horse where she
stood tied to a rail. "She's my favorite riding horse. Almost the minute
she was born, my father knew there was something special about her.
You can sometimes tell about horses that way. And he was right."

Jarvis appeared with their drinks.

"Well, I can't tell one horse from another," said Veronica when the
butler disappeared. "I can't see why people give them such odd names.
A horse is just . . . a horse. No one goes around naming their cows or
their pigs."

A look of shock came to Seth's face. How could anyone compare
horses to cows and pigs!

"A horse isn't *just* a horse," he said, "it's a *horse*—one of the most
noble and magnificent creatures that walks the earth. I love horses.

That's why people give them such personal names, because they love them."

Veronica shrugged and sipped at her lemonade. It all sounded rather juvenile and rustic.

"So . . . do you want to?" Seth asked again.

"Want to what?"

"Go for a ride . . . on horseback."

"Oh, ugh . . . no. I don't like to ride horses. It's so smelly and sweaty and they make such foul noises and messes."

"That's all part of what makes it so wonderful!" laughed Seth. "We'll go real slow and I'll show you how to enjoy riding. Your father must have a horse you like better and feel more comfortable on than the rest. Come on!"

Seth rose enthusiastically and tried to encourage Veronica to her feet.

"Seth," she said firmly, "I really *don't* want to change my clothes, after I went to all this trouble to dress up because I knew you were coming, and then go get on the back of a horse just to ride around for no reason. I don't like it. I've only been on a horse twice, and then because my father made me when I was a girl. I hated it and I told him so. I'd much rather sit here and talk. What did you want to come visit for—to see our horses, or to see me?"

"Well . . . to see you, of course," said Seth. He sat down, feeling a little mystified. "I just thought—"

"That's all right. I forgive you," said Veronica playfully. "You didn't know."

Seth took a gulp of his lemonade.

"Do you like my dress, Seth?" asked Veronica, trying to catch his eye with a smile intended to make him forget horses and concentrate on what quiet talks on porches between young men and young women were supposed to be about.

"Yeah . . . yeah, it's great."

"It's the latest fashion. It's from Paris."

"Yeah . . . it's really nice. All the way from Paris, huh?"

"So is my bonnet . . . and my shoes. Mother and I bought them down in Charlotte last month. They were very expensive."

"What were you doing in Charlotte?" asked Seth.

"Shopping."

"Nothing else?"

"Of course not, silly. Mother takes me shopping twice a year."

Seth took another drink from his glass. Veronica glanced inside. What was keeping her mother? Seth was starting to look bored.

"Do you like this color on me, Seth?" said Veronica, trying to keep the conversation going the only way most people know how, by talking about themselves. "Daddy says red makes me look pretty. What do you think?"

"Uh . . . yeah, sure—it looks great on you."

"Do *you* think red makes me look pretty, Seth?"

"Uh, yeah . . . sure."

The sound of the door opening from the house brought inner sighs of relief to both, though for very different reasons.

"I am sorry to bother you, dear," said Lady Daphne, "but poor Mildred is just getting well and I wanted to take some fresh bread to her, but I am not feeling well. Would you mind terribly, Veronica, taking it down to their place?"

"Of course not, Mother," said Veronica sweetly. "Seth, why don't you come with me? We can walk by the river."

"Uh . . . sure, I guess that would be fine."

"I will get it," said Veronica's mother, then disappeared again into the house. She returned a moment later and handed a basket to Veronica. A brief glance passed between them, though Seth did not see it.

As Veronica and Seth left the porch, Seth spoke up.

"Here, let me carry that for you."

"Oh, thank you—what a gentleman you are," Veronica replied, batting her eyelashes again.

"Who's Mildred?" asked Seth as they walked.

"One of the slave women."

"It's nice how you treat your workers," he said. "That's the way my parents are too. This is just the kind of thing my mother would do."

Meanwhile, a mile away on another part of the estate, Denton Beaumont walked toward the scene of labor where his assistant overseer was supervising ten or twelve slaves in loading several wagons. He watched for a minute or two, hardly satisfied with what he saw, then approached.

"I see Gibbons isn't doing much better," he said.

"How do you mean, Mr. Beaumont?" said the white man.

"You know good and well what I mean, Riggs," retorted Beaumont. "Look at him—he's the slowest of the lot by half. Have you been using the whip on him?"

"I haven't beaten him again, no, sir," replied Leon Riggs. He thought it best not to add that he didn't have the heart, and that the man had still not seemed to fully recover from the merciless whipping Beaumont had inflicted two years before that had been so unceremoniously cut short by the intervention of his neighbor. Leon did not consider himself a particularly compassionate man where darkies were concerned, but there was a point beyond which the whip was useless. Nor did he want murder on his conscience.

Beaumont, however, sensed the reason for the man's hesitation. Whenever a man couldn't return his icy stare he knew he was getting soft. He had seen it before.

"Give me that whip!" he yelled, snatching it from Leon's hand. "No sense you holding it if you can't use it. There's only one thing lazy niggers like Gibbons understand."

He stomped off. The next sounds Leon Riggs heard came from the stinging lashes of the tiny leather thong-ends of the whip slicing into Nate Gibbons' shoulders and back with devilish precision. Riggs did his best to close his ears to the cries of pain and screams for mercy, but he could not. For a few moments he stood like a statue, eyes on the ground. The vicious sounds of the whip, however, proved too much even for his iron stomach. Finally he swallowed hard and took a few steps away.

Within a minute or two the flogging was over.

Beaumont instructed several of the slaves to carry Gibbons to the

creek, wash him off and revive him, then get back to work, him along
with the rest of them. That Gibbons was hardly in any condition to
lift his own legs, much less hundred-pound sacks of grain up onto the
wagon, was a point neither they nor Riggs himself felt like raising. It
was as painful to the overseer as it was to those under his charge to
watch Nate Gibbons struggling for the rest of the day to carry the
sacks to the wagon and hoist them up when it was all he could do to
keep from collapsing.

But Riggs dared not intervene for fear Beaumont could well appear
again unannounced and take the whip to him instead if he saw
anything he didn't like.

As they walked beside the river, Veronica slipped her hand into Seth's
arm and drew close to him. His pulse quickened. He knew his parents
wouldn't approve of his being alone with her like this. But since they
were doing a good deed, he hoped it would be okay.

Seth noticed a few trout lazily swimming in the shallower parts of
the river. Gradually Veronica slowed their pace yet the more.

"What will you do, Seth," she said, "when *you* become master of
Greenwood?"

"What kind of a question is that?" he laughed. "I am only eighteen.
I won't worry about that for another twenty or thirty years!"

"But you will take over sometime."

"I suppose, but—"

"Will you have slaves, or will you . . . " She allowed her voice to
trail off.

"Do you mean will I continue my father's policies or become a slave
owner myself?"

"It is something a girl, even one who has just turned eighteen
herself, might like to know if she . . . "

Again Veronica let him guess what she had been about to say. She
glanced down momentarily, then peeked out at him from the corners
of her eyes with a bewitching smile.

"As for my father's former slaves," he said, "they are free now and there is nothing I could do to change that even if I wanted to. But to answer your question, I would not buy new slaves and I have no intention of becoming a slave owner. I think what my mother and father did took great courage and I support their decision entirely. I only hope I can learn to be as courageous a man as my father."

What she thought of such a soupy sentiment, Veronica chose to keep to herself.

"And your mother?" she asked.

"What about her?"

"They say she spends as much time with the slaves as she does at home. That hardly seems right."

"She is trying to help them, improve their lives, teach them to read and do things for themselves that they have never learned to do."

"My father says it is illegal to teach slaves to read."

"I know, but it shouldn't be."

"Isn't your mother afraid of being arrested?"

"I've never heard her mention it. No one would dare."

"It still doesn't seem proper or dignified."

"My parents don't just want their slaves to be free, they want to help them mature as people who can live at a higher level, and who can grow and develop . . . as *people*."

Veronica listened with a blank expression. What on earth was he babbling about with those words—*mature* and *grow* and *develop*? She tried to listen politely, but *this* was certainly not what she had contrived to get Seth alone beside the river for!

"My mother is a natural-born teacher," Seth was going on. "She was always teaching Thomas and me things. No matter what would come up when we were young, she would use it as an occasion to give us a little insight or a tidbit of history or something. It was wonderful. My mother made life so interesting that it could never be boring. She is the same with the black ladies and their children. If she doesn't help them learn things, who will? They will never learn to read otherwise. She can teach *anyone* to read! There are few things that give her so much joy as to see the light of learning come alive in a child's or an

adult's face. And when the coloreds read the Bible for themselves . . .
it gives them such a feeling of worth. Maybe that's the answer to your
question of why she is at the colored village so much of the time.
There is so much exciting and important work for her to do there."

"*Exciting?*" repeated Veronica with a bewildered look on her face.
"What in the world are you talking about, Seth?"

"Don't you think learning and teaching and discovering new things
is exciting?"

"I've certainly never thought of it that way. I think it's boring.
Surely God didn't intend for coloreds to read, especially read the
Bible."

Seth looked at her in disbelief.

"What are you saying?" he said. "Why not?"

"The Bible is for white people. Everyone knows that."

"The Jews and Arabs, who are the people of the Bible, were people
of the desert. They had dark skin. Jesus himself might have been more
dark than white. The Bible is for everyone."

"But surely . . . Negroes are *different.*"

"How?"

"You know . . . they don't have . . . they're not as smart. They're
inferior to whites. They're not *supposed* to learn and read and do all
the same things we do."

The look of disbelief on Seth's face grew to incredulity. He stopped
and stared at her for a few long seconds. Unconsciously Veronica
removed her hand from his arm. She could hardly return his stare.

"Veronica," he said after a moment, "that's absurd. It's absolutely
untrue!"

Her eyes flashed. An angry reply rushed to her lips, but she had the
presence of mind to stifle it rather than make this momentary breach
between them more serious.

There was a long and somewhat tense silence. Gradually they began
walking again, this time a little apart from one another.

"Do you support everything your parents do?" Veronica asked after
a minute or two.

"I support *them*," replied Seth, "the people they are. I consider my father a wise man. I consider my mother a wise woman. To me, that says everything. I may occasionally disagree with something one of my parents says. That doesn't change my respect for them."

"What have you disagreed with?" asked Veronica.

"I don't know. I can't think of anything at the moment. I don't look for things to disagree with them about, but to agree with."

"And you agreed with his freeing of the slaves?"

"Absolutely!" replied Seth. "The same will come to every plantation eventually, even your father's. Slavery cannot possibly survive much longer."

Veronica took in his words without further comment in that direction. She was going to have to make more changes in Seth than she had realized.

Thirty-six

The night was black and silent.

Suddenly Lucindy Eaton felt a big fleshy hand clamp down over her lips. At the same instant a voice sounded at her ear.

"Lucindy, hit's time," whispered Amaritta. "You gots ter git yo' young'un wifout makin' a soun'. Da two bigger chilluns is already gone. Be down ter da washin' place by da creek in five minutes. You come wif da baby. Git one change er clothes fo' you an' dem an all what da baby needs an' dat's all."

On noiseless feet the housekeeper left the tiny cabin and was gone. Again it was black and silent. As Lucindy came further awake she wondered if it was a dream. But feeling about, she found that Broan and Rebecca were gone. With heart pounding, she rose quietly and gathered what Amaritta had said. Three minutes later, clutching her still-sleeping two year old to her breast, she stole from the cabin into the night.

When she reached the creek, Amaritta stood with her two shivering and confused older children. But after Amaritta's stern adjurations to silence, neither uttered a peep.

"I's leab you here now, Lucindy, chil'," said Amaritta. "You 'member dat da good Lor' is wif you, and' dat he guides all his chillun to da promised lan'."

From the shadows a figure now appeared. Lucindy could not at first even tell if it was a man or a woman.

"Who dat?" she asked.

"Dat be yo' conductor," replied Amaritta. "You be gittin' on dat train now an' you don't need ter know nuthin' mo' dan ter do what he sez. He'll take you ter da firs' station. An' 'member, chil', effen anythin' happens an' you lose yo' way, you jes' look up—you see dat pan dere, an' dat handle up in da sky? Dat's da drinking' gord, an' dat star at da en' er its handle, dat's da Norf Star, an' hit's always pointin' norf. So effen you gits los' you just keep walkin' tard dat star like da ol' song sez."

She leaned forward and kissed Lucindy on the cheek.

"Good-bye, chil'," she said, then turned and disappeared, tears in her eyes that Lucindy would never know about, leaving Lucindy and her three children alone with the mysterious conductor in the night.[*]

---

[*] "A Tobacco planter named Colonel Hardy in the District of Columbia had lost five slaves . . . and although 'they were pursued by an excellent slave catcher,' they disappeared. . . .

"The experience of Colonel Hardy's slaves was a kind of textbook study of the way the Underground Railroad functioned. Jo Norton, one of the fugitives, told the story of the escape to a reporter for an abolitionist journal. Norton had been determined for some time to try to escape north with his wife and child. One night Norton met on a dark road a man whom he identified by his voice as a Northerner. Several weeks later he met the man again and told him of his desire to escape and was informed of the facilities of the Underground Railroad. He was told to return in three weeks to a certain spot late at night. At the rendezvous he met his 'conductor' and four other slaves—two men and two women—of Colonel Hardy's, all terrified at the prospect of going under the ground. They were to follow the road some thirty miles in the direction of the north star until it came to a railroad and walk along the tracks until they encountered a man. If he said 'Ben,' they were to accompany him. They found Ben just as dawn was breaking, and he hid them in bundles of cornstalks. That night someone appeared and led the two women to a road where a carriage waited to take them to Baltimore, where they were hidden. The men were fed by Ben, a free black, and remained concealed in his corncrib. Meanwhile the item in the abolitionist journal describing their arrival in Albany was printed and sent to Colonel Hardy, who called off his slave hunters on the assumption that their quarry was out of reach. Only then did the flight continue. In Baltimore the fugitives were supplied with pocket money and told to behave naturally, mingling with the crowds and keeping track of a thirteen-year-old black boy who was to act as their guide. The boy led them to the edge of the city just at nightfall and from there they traveled by night, staying during the daytime at the homes of Quakers along the route. From Philadelphia they went by fishing boat to Bordentown, New Jersey, and from there on a train to New York, the women dressed in handsome clothes with veils to conceal their faces and riding first class, the men hidden in the baggage car. Jo Norton returned later to lead his wife and child to freedom."—Page Smith, *The Nation Comes of Age*. New York: McGraw Hill, 1981, pp. 628–29.

Thirty-seven

*D*inner at Oakbriar several days later had to be delayed for thirty minutes while they awaited the return of husband and father, along with Wyatt, who had been out all afternoon with several of their men. Denton Beaumont had been unsuccessfully looking for a runaway who had been gone for six hours. He was dirty and tired, and consequently when he sat down his mood was surly.

As the family sat down and two silent attendant house slaves began to serve them, the discussion took an unexpected turn.

"What would you think, Mother," said Veronica, "of you and I going down to our slave village and teaching the colored women to read?"

There was a twinkle of fun in her eye as she sneaked a glance at her father to see his reaction.

"Whatever for, dear?" responded Lady Daphne.

"To help them mature and develop as people, Mother," replied Veronica in an earnest tone, her face staring across the table with a wide expression of innocence.

Now the heads of the three male Beaumonts also turned toward her. She stared back blankly at her father, than glanced innocently at Wyatt, as if to convey, "What . . . why are you looking at me so?"

"What kind of nonsense are you talking about, Veronica?" said her father at last, looking out from under cloudy black eyebrows.

"I only wanted to know what Mama would think of us trying to help the slaves improve themselves."

"Why . . . I think it's a wonderful idea, dear," said Lady Daphne at last. "But I don't know the first thing about teaching someone to read. We'd have to find out what to do."

"Don't take her seriously, Mother," said Wyatt in his deep bass voice. "She's making sport of us. I can tell. She doesn't mean it for a minute."

At that, Veronica burst out in a giggle.

"How did you know, Wyatt!" she laughed.

"Well, for one thing, it's the stupidest idea I ever heard. For another it's against the law. Father would be sure to get defeated if we did something like that. And for another, I know you wouldn't lift a finger to help anyone else unless there was something in it for you."

"That's a mean thing to say!" she shot back, pretending to pout, although in truth she did not see anything so derisive in his assessment.

"That doesn't mean it isn't true," rejoined her brother.

"Now, now, children," chided Lady Daphne. "We don't want to argue around the table."

"Mother, when are you going to stop calling us children!" said Veronica. "Cameron's the only one who's still a child."

"I am not. I'm fifteen."

"Exactly," said Veronica with snooty superiority, "—*a child.*"

"Quiet down, all of you," said the master of the household. He had been stewing over his daughter's little game and now intended to get to the bottom of it. "Veronica—I want to know what put an idea into your head like teaching the slaves to better themselves."

"Nothing, Daddy."

"Something put it there. I've never heard you use a phrase like *help them mature and develop as people* in your life. I don't even know what it means. It's not you, Veronica. I want to know where you picked up such a notion."

"Just from Seth, Daddy."

"*He* said that?"

"Yes, Daddy."

"Where did he get it?"

"His mother is teaching their coloreds to read."

"I thought as much—has that whole family gone mad! Is the woman as big an imbecile as her husband? I've a good mind to bring charges against her. The law would be on my side. What a thing that would be," he added with a laugh, "—Carolyn Davidson in jail!"

Lady Daphne glanced at her husband, shocked to hear such words of ridicule toward a woman come out of his mouth. She wisely kept her own mouth shut.

"Veronica," said Beaumont, leaving the delicious thought for the moment, "when are you going to give up this childish infatuation with that Davidson boy?"

"He's not a boy, Daddy. He's older than I am."

"Not much. And however old he is, he's wool brained. No good can come of it. It sounds like he is as big a fool as his father."

"Well, I like him," retorted Veronica playfully. "I might even be in love with him. I think he will change."

"Why would he?"

"Because he loves me too and would do anything for me? I'll *make* him change."

"Look, Veronica," said Beaumont in a stern tone, "I want you to stay away from him. No good can come of it. We've had nothing but trouble with our slaves since the Greenwood niggers became so uppity and are going spreading their notions around everywhere. Nothing but trouble, I tell you, and I'm sick of the whole thing! It's time some people around here started listening when they're spoken to and doing as they're told!"

Veronica took his bluster in stride, knowing that their father would do nothing to them. Only Cameron was still young enough to be intimidated by his father's tirades, although given what Denton Beaumont was capable of, this hardly qualified as even a mild one. But it was sufficient to silence him if he had had any thought of saying anything further.

Wyatt soon excused himself and went outside. He had been break-

ing a year-old mare whom he hoped to train to race one day. He had
been out on the hills with his father's men looking for Gibbons who
had disappeared, and was now anxious to return to his mare. Veronica, too, neither humbled nor worried, also soon excused herself and
went up to her room.

"What are you so upset about, dear?" asked Beaumont's wife when
their eldest son and daughter were gone.

"What do you mean?" he snapped.

"You seem tense. There's not really anything so wrong in her seeing
Richmond and Carolyn's boy . . . is there? Seth is a nice boy. He
always treats me with courtesy."

"A fool can be courteous, Daphne. It means nothing. I don't like
him."

"There . . . you see. Something is bothering you. This isn't like you."

He lifted his glass and took a long soothing swallow of after-dinner
port, then let out a sigh. "One of our troublesome slaves has disappeared," he said. "We've been out looking for him but can't find him
anywhere."

"You've no idea where he's gone?"

"He's in no shape to go anywhere," retorted Beaumont. The calm-
ing effect of the port had lasted about ten seconds. "He's hiding out
on the land somewhere. We'll take the dogs out tomorrow. He won't
get far. Believe me, once we haul him back, there will be a lesson none
of the others will soon forget."

Before he could say anything further, Leon Riggs walked in holding
a coiled strand of rope. He nodded to Lady Daphne and Cameron,
then turned to Beaumont.

"This strong enough?" he said.

Beaumont turned away from the table to face him, and took the
rope and examined it briefly.

"It ought to do fine," he said. "And you remember the oak . . . the
one we used before?"

Leon nodded and left the house. Involuntarily Lady Daphne shuddered, glancing toward Cameron and hoping that he did not grasp
what the brief conversation between his father and his man was about.

"Don't be too hard on them, dear," said Lady Daphne, who had no
idea that her husband had already beaten the missing slave to within
an inch of his life. "Remember, you are running for office now. People
have to think of you as a gentle man toward your slaves."

"Keep to your own affairs, Daphne!" he snapped. "No man ever
succeeded growing tobacco and cotton who was gentle to his slaves.
That's why God put men to rule over both slaves and women, because
women don't have the stomach for what's necessary."

Upon reflection, however, Beaumont had to admit that his wife was
right. He'd have to take care of Gibbons at night. He wanted the
slaves to know, as a lesson. But no sense stirring up the rest of his
men. He and Riggs would take care of it themselves . . . tomorrow
night . . . as soon as the dogs found the cur and they could drag him
out of his hiding place and sit him high enough on a horse to slip the
noose around his neck.

He poured himself another half glass of port, drained it in a single
swallow, then rose from the table and followed his assistant overseer
outside.

"Leon," he said after him, "there's still two or three hours of
daylight left—let's turn the dogs loose after him now. His trail will be
too cold tomorrow."

"Don't see much sense in it, Mr. Beaumont," replied Riggs, who in
truth was exhausted from the day's search and did not relish another
three hours trying to keep up with the hounds. Unlike several other of
Beaumont's men who were single and who lived at Oakbriar, he had a
wife and son and lived in town. "We've already been every place close
by he could have got to. He'll have to move again tomorrow, and
that'll be the best chance the dogs have to pick up—"

"Curse you, Riggs!" Beaumont exploded. "You're as fainthearted as
my wife. I gave you an order—if you can't carry it out, just tell me
and I'll find someone who can."

"Yes, sir, Mr. Beaumont," said Riggs. "I didn't mean it like that. I only meant—"

"I know what you meant, Riggs," interrupted Beaumont. "Now go get the dogs and get back out there on the ridge."

Thirty-eight

The visitor to appear in the middle of the night on Greenwood's doorstep in early June had hoped to see the face of Moses answering his gentle but persistent knock.

But Moses' hearing, along with his gait, was not what it once was. Furthermore, he had been blessed with that gift not given to all during their advancing years, of being able to sleep soundly for eight or more hours every night. The visitor made his cautious approach to the Davidson plantation house somewhere between two and four in the morning, with such canny step, though impeded with a painful limp, that not even the dogs asleep at the side of the house awoke to give herald to his presence. All the while, Moses slumbered on dreamless and dead to the world in his room on the ground floor.

Richmond Davidson had always been a light sleeper. Was it that his mind was too active, even at rest, or that his active physical constitution simply kept brain and body moving a little too rapidly to enter the full depths of sleep which others enjoyed? Regardless, the fact was that after dropping off quickly and thoroughly most evenings between nine and ten o'clock within moments of head hitting pillow, the master of Greenwood considered himself fortunate to obtain more than four or five hours of sleep before fitfulness began to intrude. Thence the remainder of the night passed tossing about and doing his best not to disturb the wife at his side, who could sleep as soundly as Moses. He usually patiently waited until an hour fit to be up should tediously draw near, though typically still long before daybreak.

During these slow-moving predawn hours of semidozing wakefulness, every sound for a mile came to his ears—every low of sleepless cow, every drop of rain, every distant bark of nocturnal fox, every rustle of occasional breeze in the giant oak next to the house, every frog, every cricket, and, in winter, every crack of thunder far and near. Thus it was on a night so still that not a blade of grass or stalk of grain moved, that within seconds of the first creak of intruding step on the porch below, he was slippered and robed and creeping down the main staircase of the house with rifle in one hand and flickering candle in the other.

As he tiptoed toward the door, again came a rapping of knuckles against it, not loud but obviously intended to rouse someone inside. Someone of ill intent would hardly thus announce his presence, or stand waiting in front of a door well known never to be locked. Davidson set his rifle aside, put his free hand to the latch, and slowly opened the door to the width of about a foot.

The light from his candle fell on the most miserable-looking face he thought he had ever seen, a Negro man, his face perspiring and covered with dirt and grime. His clothes were torn and ragged and it was obvious from the splotches of what could only be dried blood that there were wounds on arms, legs, and shoulders. At the sight of a white face staring back at him from inside the house, looking fearsome as shadows from the candle danced about it, the man's eyes grew wide with terror.

For an instant, it looked like the black stranger would bolt. Doubtless he knew he wouldn't get very far very fast in such a condition.

"What do you want?" said Davidson somewhat apprehensively, for a visitor at this hour looking as this man did boded no good.

"Ah wuz hopin' ter see Moses, massa," said the man in a trembling voice.

"Are you a friend of his?"

"No, massa. Ah neber laid eyes on da man in mah life. Ah jes' knowed he libbed here wif y'all."

"What do you want with him? You are obviously running from something . . . what are you afraid of? What has happened to you?"

"Mah massa dun whupped me good, massa. Ah dun run away, but now ah's feared turrible ob what he's gwine do ter me effen he fin's me, spechully after ah dun hid out from him fo' a day an' a night."

"But where are you from and what—"

He paused and lifted the candle a little closer to the man's face.

"Wait a minute," said Davidson. "I recognize you, don't I? Though faintly, because the only other time I saw you, you were unconscious. You're from Oakbriar? You're Mr. Beaumont's slave?"

"Yes, suh, massa."

"Has he been whipping you again, like before?"

"Dat he has, massa."

"That's why you ran away?"

"Yes, suh, Massa Dab'son," said the man, and once his tongue was loosened, the whole story was not long in coming out. "One ob da nigger boys," he went on, "he herd massa talkin' 'bout roustin' me outta bed one night an' takin' me ter sum oak tree, an' massa wuz sayin' he cudn't wait ter see me swingin' in da breeze. An' when ah herd dat, ah waited till hit wuz dark an' den ah run, though ah cudn't run much on account er da whuppin', but ah snuck outta dere an' ah limped ter da trees an den up into da hills. Ah went in an' out ob da riber ter keep da dogs from sniffin' me out, an' ah hid up in one er dem caves up on der ridge by da peak where dey're all feared ter go on account er da stories ob ghosts an' bones an' dem ol' Injun legen's dat's nuffin but superstishun effen you ax'd me. Eben dose dogs cudn't fin' me dere, an' den w'en ah figered hit wuz safe, ah cum down here on account er what ah dun herd 'bout you, massa, an' dat you's a kin'ly man ter yo' slaves an' from what dey tol' me you did ter keep massa from killin' me las' time. An' ah knowed dat a nigger man called Moses libbed in yo' house as a man-slave like, wifout bein' a slave no mo', an' dat's why ah cum ax'n fo' him."

At last, he stopped for a breath. His short speech had given Richmond a great deal to think about, and presented him with a serious dilemma. The full ramifications of it, however, were not immediately apparent to him as he stood in the dark pondering what to do. What was clear was the fact that he had been unwittingly presented with a situation that, if he followed his conscience, would inevitably widen the gap between himself and his neighbor all the more.

Yet what could he do but render aid? The man was obviously desperate. He had come seeking refuge. Richmond did not doubt for a moment that the man's life was now in more imminent danger even than before his flight from Oakbriar. He had seen enough on the previous occasion to recognize that hanging a man would not lie outside the scope of what Denton might do if sufficiently roused. There had been evil stories through the years among the slaves about things that had happened at Oakbriar. He had not wanted to believe them. Now he began to wonder if there might be more truth to them than he had been willing to admit.

He would consider what to do in more detail later. Right now this man needed help, and had come to *his* door seeking it.

"Come in," said Richmond, swinging the door the rest of the way back.

The man hesitated, as if he had not heard correctly.

"In ter da big house, massa?" he said, the huge whites of his eyes in the darkness revealing his astonishment.

"Yes . . . come in. We don't stand on ceremony here. We treat all men as God's children. Are you hungry?"

"Yes, massa . . . ah be par'ful hungry. Ah ain't had nuffin t' eat fo' two days."

"Then let's get you washed up and into a clean shirt and trousers—I'll wake Moses and see what he can find for you while you're washing up. Then we'll get you something to eat and drink and find you a bed."

"Bless you, massa—dat be 'bout da kin'est thing a man cud do fo' a nigger man . . . thank you, massa. Ah's neber fo'git dis, no suh."

"What is your name?" asked Davidson.

"Nate, suh," answered the black man. "Nate Gibbons."

Around ten o'clock that morning, a caller came asking for Thomas.

"Dere's a young man ax'in 'bout Massa Thomas," said Moses as Richmond, Carolyn, and Thomas sat at the breakfast table together. The elder two had eaten hours ago but were sitting at the table with their youngest son.

"It's Jeremy!" said Thomas, jumping up and running through the house to the door. Carolyn glanced toward her husband with a questioning glance.

"Jeremy McClellan," said Richmond, "William's son."

Less than two minutes later Thomas came hurrying through the kitchen again, this time with a rifle under his arm. This time Carolyn's expression was one of alarm.

"Is it all right if I go with Jeremy?" he said. "His father promised to take us shooting. Don't worry, Mother, only for rabbits," he added, turning toward Carolyn.

"That's fine, son," replied Richmond. "This will be the first time you've gone shooting without me. You remember everything I've taught you?"

"Sure, Father."

"The gun's not loaded?"

"Not till we reach where we're going."

"You've got shells?"

"Here in my pocket."

"Good boy. All right, have fun. Greet Mr. McClellan for me."

"I will! Bye, Mother . . . bye, Father," said Thomas, leaving the kitchen again. A few seconds later they heard the front door slam.

Carolyn glanced at her husband. "It sounds like you and he had already talked about this," she said. "You're sure he's all right with the gun, going off with Jeremy alone?"

"I've taught him all I know about gun safety. There comes a time when we've got to let them test their wings. I think he's ready. William and I spoke briefly at Oakbriar about him getting together with Thomas and Jeremy."

Further conversation was interrupted by Moses with a question, followed on its heels by the appearance of Mary and Nancy from the village to see Carolyn.

⌒

Richmond had not planned to keep news of their midnight caller, who was now sleeping peacefully on a makeshift cot he and Moses had assembled in the cellar, from his youngest son. But a strange sense of relief swept over him the moment Thomas was gone. Somehow, he knew Thomas would not be pleased with what they had done. He was just glad remnants of the poor man's smell—before he and Moses had managed to get him bathed and his wounds dressed—had not lingered in the house to give away the uninvited secret.

What to do now was the question. He and Carolyn had hardly had a minute to themselves since the strange morning began several hours ago.

About half an hour after Thomas's departure, they walked out of the house onto the veranda together. Carolyn had a watering can in her hand and proceeded to water several potted geraniums and a hanging fern, then sat down beside her husband.

"It would seem we have a situation on our hands," she said.

"Indeed it would!" rejoined her husband.

"Did you adjure Moses and Maribel to silence with the other blacks, until we decide what is to be done?"

"I did, although I doubt it was necessary. They both recognize what is at stake should word get out that we have one of Denton's runaway slaves under our roof. It would likely go as badly for us as it would for that poor man down in the cellar."

"Not quite so bad," said Carolyn. "He would be hanged—you would only be put in jail for harboring a runaway."

"Of course. I only meant that it is a serious matter. We must tread carefully. It is especially serious in that we know full well who the man's owner is. That only adds to our guilt in the eyes of the law."

"If you returned him now, there would probably be no charges brought against you for giving him a meal and a few hours sleep. But for us to keep him for even a day . . ."

"Carolyn, you're not suggesting that we return—"

"No, not at all. I was only thinking out loud. Obviously, we know what Denton is liable to do. Neither do I like the idea of my husband in jail."

"It won't come to that."

"Men have been jailed for less. The times we live in now can easily drive men to great evil. I do not like to think what could happen."

It fell silent a moment.

"Why didn't you tell Thomas?" asked Carolyn, glancing toward her husband.

He did not reply immediately. "I'm not sure," he said at length. "Until you and I decide what is to be done, I had a feeling that the man's safety could be jeopardized further by Thomas being party to it. I would rather he didn't know at all than for us to make him promise to keep it from anybody else, especially Jeremy and Cameron. That might be intolerable for him."

Carolyn sighed. "I know what you are saying. Sometimes I think Thomas is more in sympathy with Denton's views than ours."

"I've noticed it too," nodded Richmond. "Yes . . . somehow Thomas complicates this whole thing."

"Is that why you sent Seth down to the colored village before Thomas was up?"

"One of the reasons. I knew Seth would say nothing until we decide what to do."

"We'll have to talk to him before Thomas gets back from town. Do you think he will understand us not wanting him to tell his brother?"

"He is the older and more mature of the two. It is an unfortunate position to put him in, but he will see that it is for the best."

"He trusts us—that counts for a great deal."

"Well," said Richmond, "we had better make some preparations while Thomas is away."

"What *are* we going to do, Richmond?"

"I don't know. But I am not going to send him back to Denton."

"We cannot keep him here and hope he blends in with our Negroes. Word would leak out eventually. Denton would come and claim him and probably bring charges of theft against you, and there would be nothing we could do."

"No, we can't keep him. He's got to go . . . but where?"

"The only place he would be safe is in the North, and even there not absolutely safe as the runaway of a Commissioner."

They contemplated Carolyn's words for a minute or two.

"That is probably the only solution," said Richmond at length. "We will have to try to help him get to the Pennsylvania border. I'll ask him if he knows anyone up there, or has any free relatives."

"Until then?"

"He will have to stay in the cellar, and we will have to have Moses sneak food down to him when Thomas is in another part of the house or outside."

"I don't like the sound of acting behind our own son's back."

"It's for the man's safety, and we've got to keep him here long enough to get him healthy enough to travel."

"What about . . . ?" Carolyn's expression said clearly enough what she was thinking.

"I'll set up a chamber pot and stool down there," replied her husband, rising.

"Not very sanitary," grimaced Carolyn, "though I don't know what else to suggest."

"My main concern is keeping the man alive and news of his presence limited to Moses, Maribel, and Seth and the two of us. It will only be for a few days."

A week later, under the light of a three-quarter moon, a white man and a black man quietly led two horses away from Greenwood's stables. When they were far enough away that the sounds of their hooves would awaken no light sleepers, either at the big house or in the Negro village, and invite unwanted inquiry, they mounted and rode quietly away.

Keeping to little-known back roads, they pursued a generally northerly course for most of the night, until they were well beyond the point where anyone connected with the plantation called Oakbriar might see them. By then the greatest danger was past. Anyone seeing them now would assume the Negro to be the slave of the white man accompanying him.

When one of the men returned midway through the afternoon, a day and a half later, both man and his beast were fatigued from their journey of nearly two hundred miles. Yet as anxious as he was to get home, he made sure to take the long way around so that he would approach his own plantation from the west and thus avoid the risk of being seen by anyone from neighboring Oakbriar.

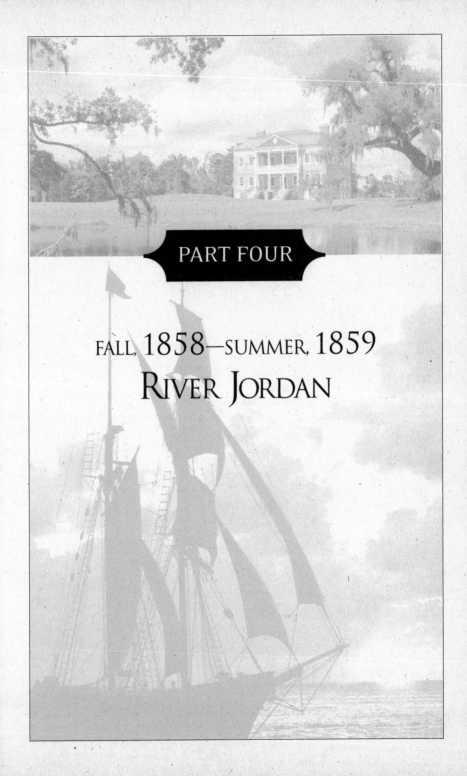

PART FOUR

FALL, 1858—SUMMER, 1859
RIVER JORDAN

Thirty-nine

$\mathcal{F}$ear and uncertainty accompanied Lucindy Eaton's every step during her first week away from the only home she had ever known. She and her three young ones walked to a new destination every night, she carrying the youngest as much as she was able, the two older ones, though only four and six, like their mother, on foot.

People whose names she never knew led them from station to station, sometimes alone, sometimes with others. On some nights only one conductor appeared. Occasionally there were others to help with Calebia. Sometimes the toddler was given a warm milky potion. Lucindy didn't know what was in it, but it made her sleepy and, more importantly, quiet. Lucindy could not help wondering if she had made a mistake and ought to turn back. By the time two weeks had passed, she went forward as if in a dream.

By night, they traveled from station to station. By day, they slept—in barns, cellars, haylofts, many times under the stars. Food and water were provided by unseen hands of ministration which she never saw again.

Night faded into night until the weeks became a sleepy and confused succession of new people and places—of cold and dirt and dampness and smells and hunger and fatigue. She could not now have found her way back to the plantation of Miles Crawford in South Carolina even had she wanted to. She knew so little about the larger

world of which the slave states of the American South were a part, she
had no idea when they passed into North Carolina nor would even
have known what the words meant had she been told.

Now that she was a runaway, she could never turn back. At every
station, there was talk about the increasing number of bounty hunters
scouring the countryside for slaves to return to their masters. Though
she had never heard of the Fugitive Slave Law, she knew that
runaways had even fewer rights than regular slaves and that they were
punished severely when they were caught. She had watched too many
mothers silently endure the terrible agony of seeing their children sold
away from them, never to set eyes on them again. She would die
before turning back, knowing that to be caught would surely mean
lifelong separation from her three precious ones for whose freedom
she was risking all four of their lives.

The months of the summer on that invisible nighttime railroad
passed both slowly and quickly in an endless blur. On some evenings
Lucindy now began to feel a chill in the air.

How far was the promised land called Pennsylvania?

It already felt like she had been walking forever. In fact, her journey
had still only just begun. In the first four months, zigzagging across
the map, she had only progressed a hundred and seventy-five miles
toward the North. How many miles more than that had she actually
walked she had no idea. There were over three hundred miles ahead of
her, and as the U.G.R.R. moved anything but as the crow flew, she
might have to walk more than twice that far before she reached her
destination. A single man might take an express train and travel much
faster. But no passengers were slower than young mothers and children without husbands. Progress was always slower in winter.*

As their steps took them farther north, she had a difficult time
understanding the speech of some of the white people helping them.
Instead of the rough shouts of her master and his men, these whites

---

* "To avoid the danger of blacks being employed as spies, each fugitive slave had to deliver a note from the
conductor at the previous station to the conductor of the next. Needless to say, the 'trains' on the Underground Railroad ran irregularly. A light tap on a door or window any hour of the night or early morning
might announce the arrival of a new 'shipment of black wool.'"—Page Smith, *The Nation Comes of Age,* New
York: McGraw-Hill, 1981, pp. 628–29.

spoke slowly and softly, using strange expressions and words like *thee* and *thy* and *thou*. But the language of kindness is universal, and she soon learned that these gentle people called themselves Friends, while others referred to them as Quakers.* Black freedmen usually guided them through the night, but often the homes they were led to were those of these "Friends." Sometimes they traveled for several nights without a station or depot to sleep in at all when the previous night's conductor left them, huddled alone with blankets out of sight. Lucindy was told at such times that they were in unfriendly country where depots were far between. The children had an easier time sleeping during the day than did their mother. Though exhausted to tears, Lucindy often sat wide eyed all day, jumping at every sound, terrified they would be discovered by dogs. When another conductor appeared the following night, handing them hard biscuits and getting them to their feet to lead them stealthily away into the night, she hardly knew whether she could face another long trek.

Ever the waking dream began anew, night after night . . . walking . . . walking . . . walking through the blackness. But whenever the voice whispered, "Follow me," Lucindy did not hesitate, but rose and obeyed. They were the words that led to freedom.

Lucindy awoke suddenly after a long day hidden in some bushes where she had been told to wait.

Something had awakened her out of a sound sleep. Now she knew what it was—the stink of a polecat. It smelled like it was close!

The sound of baying hounds seemed to be coming from three directions at once!

---

*"Levi Coffin was a North Carolina Quaker who moved to Newport, Indiana, where he became a prosperous businessman, president of the town bank, and one of the most active conductors on the road—so much so, indeed, that he became known as 'the President of the Underground Railroad.' He turned his business talents to improving the organization of the escape routes. His home in Newport became a kind of switching yard for refugees coming up from the South as well as those moving east and west seeking refuge in New York state or Canada. One night seventeen runaway slaves were brought to his home in two wagonloads by agents. They had hardly been fed and sent on their way before word reached Coffin that fifteen Kentucky slave hunters were on their track. Coffin arranged for the fugitives to be scattered across a number of tracks and the slave hunters, after three or four fruitless days, gave up and recrossed the Ohio."—Page Smith, *The Nation Comes of Age*, New York: McGraw-Hill, 1981, pp. 628–29.

Quickly she picked up little Calebia and put her to her breast to keep her quiet. But the little girl sensed her mother's terror and could not settle down. By now, Broan and Rebecca were stirring.

"What dat stink, Mama?" said Broan, rubbing his eyes.

"Shush!" she said in a loud whisper. "Dat's a blamed skunk—but dere's houn's out dere too . . . we got's te be still as er mouse!"

Rebecca and Broan crept closer and huddled to her side. Eyes wide, they waited.

Suddenly a rustling sounded next to them. The smell of skunk became almost intolerable. Out of the brush appeared the arm of a black woman. Lucindy nearly lept out of her skin at sight of it. The woman reached for the baby, and before Lucindy could object, placed a rag over the tiny nose. Immediately Calebia quieted and conked out.

"Lor', protec' us here from dose confound dogs," prayed the newcomer, sitting down beside them and handing the two older children hard biscuits. She gave Lucindy a chunk of roast turkey to eat with hers.

The sounds of the dogs gradually receded in the distance. Lucindy and the children remained silent. Broan slowly put the fingers of one hand to his nose and squeezed his nostrils shut. They were accustomed enough to bad smells. Traveling as they did, they knew that people smelled bad. But never had they known anyone to stink like this woman!

"Dey'll likely be back," said the black woman as she rose from the ground. "Dem houn's is a real nuisance. We gots ter git cross da stream an' confuse dere noses so dey don't know w'ere you been. You git goin'—dat way dere," she added, pointing. She handed Calebia, who had gone out like a light after one sniff of the woman's rag, back to Lucindy. "I's jes' got a little bizness ter ten' to firs'."

She disappeared back into the woods, returning a few seconds later clutching a burlap sack by its neck.

"I brung along dis ol' dead polecat," she chuckled. She began rubbing it about the ground where they had been sitting. "Y'all keep goin', I's tell you w'ere, an' jes' let me foller behin'."

They did as she said, following her instructions as they went while she brushed the smell of skunk back and forth over the trail behind them. Finally they came to the creek and waded across. The chill of the water woke up whatever of their senses the polecat hadn't.

"Now, jes' walk straight up da water," said the woman, "'bout a quarter mile, den by sum rocks, turn inter da woods. Dere'll be sum folks ter meet yer by'n by. Meantime I'll move 'bout on dis side wif my bag er tricks. Now git goin'."

Lucindy did as she said. Two or three minutes later, she glanced back. There was the old woman, grinning from ear to ear, still dragging the skunk behind her all about the shore of the water in both directions from where they had been.

They reached the bend in the creek beside a big pile of boulders. Before they even were out of the water, two black men appeared. Without a word, they scooped up Rebecca and Broan and walked away from the creek, while Lucindy struggled to follow. Not a word was said for five or ten minutes. The men walked fast through trees and around big rocks. Gradually their way opened out of the woods where a small river flowed by. The men did not slow their step. Still holding the two children, they plunged into the water and waded across. A little frightened, Lucindy followed, her arms tiring but holding Calebia up out of the water as best she could, even as it came up to her own waist.

Climbing cold and dripping out on the other side, from somewhere one of the men produced dry clothes for her and the two older children and told them to change into them. The men disappeared and returned in five minutes. They took the wet clothes, stuffed them into a burlap sack, threw a few big rocks into it, tied its neck, and heaved it into the middle of the river.

"Follow me," said one of the men as the other now disappeared for good.

They followed him for the rest of the night and reached their destination sometime when the moon was high. Lucindy was so exhausted she hardly noticed the ministering hands that cared for them. She was nearly asleep even before she lay down on the floor in a corner where several blankets were waiting for them.

As the small band slowly moved in a general northeasterly direction following the contour of the coastline and the Appalachians, and as the months of fall progressed, gradually the weather began to change. Rain came now more frequently and the nights grew colder. Progress slowed too. Conductors did not come every night.

A dreadful storm in late November, followed by the flooding of every river and stream in North Carolina, made travel impossible. Lucindy and her three children found themselves living for a month in a Quaker barn. Mercifully, it was a warm storm and they did not suffer much except from boredom. The kindly Quaker mistress of the place did what she could to make their prolonged stay comfortable, gave the children candy at Christmas, and when they finally left in the first week of January gave Lucindy a waterproof oil cloth that they could huddle under if caught in the rain.

Two weeks and several stations later, again they found themselves waiting in a barn without a conductor. The following night more passengers arrived. When the conductor finally came several days later, a black woman from the North, and walked into the barn, exclamations of joy accompanied her greetings of the others, by which Lucindy gathered that he was her brother, and this was the family she had come for.

"Well, den, let's go," she said.

Lucindy gathered up her children and things to follow. The woman glanced at her, then over at her brother.

"Who dis?" she asked.

"She wuz here w'en we cum."

"What she thinkin'? Dis weren't da cargo I came fo'. I cum ter bring *you* out, not every slave in da Souf."

"She gots no conductor ob her own."

The woman sighed. "More chilluns," she said to herself. "Dey'll slow us down fo' sho'."

"We can't jes' leab'em, sis."

"All right, den—come along. But you gots ter keep up."

Lucindy remained with the same party and its conductress for the next six weeks, moving northeast along the southern ridge of the Appalachians through North Carolina, eventually passing into southern Virginia. Imperceptibly winter now began to loosen its grip on the land and give way to spring.

Forty

$\mathcal{M}$alone Murdoch sat staring into a cold, half-empty, bitter cup of coffee.

Most nights were the same. As the flames of his campfire slowly died into embers, their haunting shades and movements drew his memory back to that horrible night that had marked out his fateful destiny. In spite of the ghastly images it always brought back, he enjoyed peering into the flames. For the searing pain of that night had long ago found relief in hatred, as unresolved personal agonies often do. That hatred grew to feed on itself, and in a twisted way became its own reward. Now he almost looked forward to each night's campfire, for it caused the morbid pleasure of hate to burn the hotter in his heart.

A rustle of wind in the leaves above him disturbed his reverie. He glanced up and about him, his hand unconsciously seeking the revolver at his side, then slowly returned his attention to the sheaf of papers in his hand. Descriptions of runaways were always sketchy at best. Nevertheless, he went through the complete list every night. It was uncanny how often one particular detail led to apprehending one of the runaways. He made his living by knowing how to use the details, and he mustn't overlook a single one.

Here was one, for instance. He perused the description a second time:

Runaway from Phillips plantation in central Georgia near Macon.
Answers to Jack or "Pig." Male, 38 years old, approximately six feet,
medium build, strong arms, ugly wide face, mule-headed, easily
provoked, last seen wearing stolen riding boots and white man's
leather jacket. Reward $125 alive, $75 dead.

On the surface, it didn't seem like much. But to a man like Malone
Murdoch, this brief notice was fraught with opportunity. Within
minutes of an encounter with a group of runaways, he might recognize half of them from just such an outline. They were such an ignorant lot. Most never knew him for a bounty hunter. A few questions
to get them blabbing and he might easily be able to secure half of
them on the spot from the descriptions in his hand. That's why he
went over the pages every night beside his campfire.

The loneliness of such an existence did not occur to Malone
Murdoch, nor the eternal effects of hatred upon his own soul. This
was the life he had chosen for himself—a life of vengeance, to atone
for the sins visited upon the fathers. White fathers. *His* father. The
money was all right. He had several thousand stashed in a bank in
Atlanta. He would have quite a bit stored away someday. It wasn't the
money that lured him. He did it to feed his hatred, but it was a
hunger that could never be satisfied.

He continued to stare into the fire, the reflection of the flames playing upon the hard angles of his chin and cheeks and dark eyes that
knew neither remorse nor love. A wide, bushy brown mustache was
the chief characteristic of a face that might once have been handsome.
Instead, it had grown permanently expressionless. Malone Murdoch
had not smiled in years. In his face one saw only silent fury and the
slow burning lust of unrequited vengeance.

The year had been 1831. Malone Murdock was eleven when the slave
uprising led by Nat Turner broke out in Virginia.

Turner's own master at the time, by all accounts, had been a good man who had treated his slaves with more than ordinary kindness. Nevertheless, Turner felt commissioned by God to lead the slaves out of bondage. His spiritual fervor grew as he preached to Negroes, while he himself was sold from owner to owner, about rising up against their white taskmasters.

After murdering his own master, Turner then moved from plantation to plantation gathering more black followers as they went, killing and burning and calling upon slaves everywhere to unite in the insurrection for freedom.

Malone's mother was in the final stages of pregnancy and had taken to her bed only two days before the slave rebellion reached his own father's plantation. The first he knew of it he was being shaken awake from a sound sleep.

"Get up, boy!" cried his father. "Get up . . . on with your trousers!"

Waking up, all he heard at first were ominous shouts coming from somewhere. He saw strange lights from outside eerily playing upon the walls of his room. A faint smell of smoke was in the air though he hardly noticed it at first. He did not know that his home had already been set ablaze, only that his father's voice contained a fear and urgency he had never heard before.

"Run, Malone!" said his father, hurrying him into his boots. "Down the back stairs, into the cellar, out the coal door, then make a dash for the woods."

"What about you, Papa?" said the terrified boy.

"I've got to get your mother. I'll have to carry her. She can't make it down the stairs alone. We'll meet you in the woods. Now go!"

Emerging into the night air a minute later, smudges of coal on hands and knees, eleven-year-old Malone could not imagine why it was so light out. But he did not hesitate as he tore across the open space behind the house. When at last he turned from the cover of a tree to look back toward the house, his mouth and eyes gaped open in stunned disbelief. Fire already engulfed the barn and rose fifty feet in the air. The entire building was consumed in bright red and orange as the flames shot high into the night sky. The house he had just left was not far behind.

A mob of twenty or thirty blacks was running about and shouting

*wildly, carrying torches aloft and setting everything alight that would
burn. Half he recognized as his father's most decent and trusted slaves.*

*What was happening! Hadn't his father always been kind to them?
Why were they doing this!*

*In terrified panic he watched helplessly as the flames slowly took over
more and more of the house.*

*The mob now spread around back by the way he had just made his
escape, eventually surrounding the house. He crept farther back into the
shadows, watching in confused horror, the triumphant and frenzied faces
of the wild black mob forever etched in his memory.*

Suddenly he heard a woman's scream. He knew it was his mother.

Choking down his own sobs, still he looked on.

*His father appeared briefly in an upstairs window. He knew he was
looking for him, to see if he was safe. He stepped from behind the tree and
raised one hand in mute appeal. That his father saw it was evidenced as
he began to raise his hand in reply.*

*An explosion of gunfire sounded and one of the black men emptied his
rifle into the window. His father's silhouette slumped over and disappeared below the window frame. Within seconds the house was swallowed
in flame. A few more screams in a woman's desperate voice drifted across
the night, and then were gone.*

*Only the shouts of triumph from the black men remained, and the
crackling of the huge conflagration that lit up the night sky for five miles
in every direction.*

～

A few faces stood out in his memory from that night, glistening,
sweating, black faces, the reflection of the flames dancing in their wild
eyes as the light of his campfire flicked in his own at this moment.
Malone Murdoch had vowed to track them all down if it took him the
rest of his life. Ever since, he had devoted his life to the capture of
runaways, and in the process had gradually, one by one, hunted down
some half dozen of his father's former slaves. All were now dead.

Murdoch tried to tell himself that he didn't hate all blacks. He had

no quarrel with law-abiding, obedient, submissive slaves who knew
their place. But the distinction of his prejudice was not always easy to
draw. In his eyes all coloreds were related, and all slaves would revolt if
given the chance.

Here is an interesting one, he thought as he continued to sift through
his papers:

> *Runaway slave mother, light complexion, late 20s, thin of build,*
> *medium height, two children, boy 6 called Broan, girl 3 called*
> *Rebecca, and 2 year old. Woman answers to name Lucindy Eaton.*
> *Reward for return of all three—$95, offered by Miles Crawford,*
> *Aiken, South Carolina. No reward for baby.*

They would be easy to spot, said Murdoch to himself. Mothers and
kids usually were, though the rewards often weren't worth the trouble.
He usually didn't bother with kids unless he had several bound for the
same place and could tie them all up as a group in a wagon. Whether
this $95 would be worth trying to haul a couple black brats and their
mother back to South Carolina, he'd decide that at the time. If they
were too far north when he caught them, he'd probably just kill them.
But if he had more cargo going the same direction, he might bring
them along for the extra hundred.

Their underground network of supporters and routes and hiding
places was still a mystery to him. If he could just crack it, he could put
a stop to the whole thing. If his success curbed his livelihood as a
bounty hunter, that was fine with him. He wasn't doing this for the
money. Malone Murdoch was on a mission of righteousness to put an
end to slave rebellion.

In the meantime, he would continue to follow what leads came his
way. When necessary he usually rounded up half a dozen local thugs
with the promise of ten dollars for a night's work. But this fellow he'd
been following for the last two days was apparently helping only small
groups. He ought to be able to handle it alone. Six or eight runaways
had been spotted three nights ago heading this way. He had no idea

yet which descriptions they might fit. Once he had them tied up, he would figure out who they were and what to do with them.

He tossed what remained of his coffee sizzling into the fire, then sat staring into its depths another thirty minutes until the flames had died away and only glowing coals remained.

Still he sat . . . alone with his thoughts.

Forty-one

A few more travelers joined the brother and sister train as they went, mostly single men, though there was one aging woman who kept to herself. Occasionally they were met by other conductors, though the sister who had come for her brother seemed to know the way by herself, and know every station along the way. It was clear she had made this trip before.

One evening just before dark, disaster struck. Having no idea his movements were being watched, a black freedman appeared as the shadows of night had begun to fall. The freedman and the sister who had come for her brother seemed to be acquainted. They spoke together a few minutes, then the party, now eight or ten strong, set out to follow him.

They had not gone far before they heard the sound of horses' hooves galloping toward them.

"Scatter!" yelled three or four voices at once.

Instantly they fled for the surrounding woods. Seconds later a single rider came into sight and bore down upon them. His eyes flashed with fire at the sight before him of fleeing runaways. In one hand a twirling rope was poised above his head.

Lucindy dove into a thicket of thorns and brush, frantically pulling and pushing Broan and Rebecca with her. Behind her the rider's coiled rope found its prey. A cry sounded as he tugged on it and one of the single men toppled to the ground with a grunt and a thud.

From her hiding place, Lucindy nearly crushed Calebia's face to her.

"Not a peep, Broan . . . Rebecca!" she whispered as they huddled close. "Dat man dere's fearsome! He look like da kin' er man dat'd kills us ef he fin' us. So shush yo' moufs!"

Her assessment, though she had but caught a glimpse of his face, was accurate enough. For the first time since they had set out, they were truly in mortal danger. Lucindy watched through the brush as the white man secured the rope to his saddle horn, then yelled down at the black man.

"Get up, nigger!" he cried. "Get up and face your betters!"

Slowly the man climbed to his feet, the rope tight around his chest. He began trying to loosen it.

"Hold on just a minute!" said the white man, yanking back viciously, nearly pulling the man to the ground again. "I don't recall saying anything about that rope. You leave it just where it is until I ask you a few questions!"

He sat on his horse looking the man over, squinting as he let his eyes wander up and down. He was obviously thinking.

"Where you get them boots?" he asked.

"Offen a dead white man, massa," said the trembling black.

"Mighty fine-looking boots for a colored man."

"I figured he din't need dem no mo'."

"You're lying, Pig! I think you stole them from your master before you ran away, just like you did that coat."

"Why you call me dat?" said the black man.

"That's what folks call you, ain't it?"

"But how you know?"

A grin spread over the bounty hunter's face.

"That's all I wanted to hear," he said. "You're as stupid as you are ugly. Well, Pig, your running days are over."

He turned his horse around, then lashed him mercilessly. The sudden movement pulled the slave off his feet. Murdoch tore off on his mount the way he had come, dragging the man over the bumpy ground behind him.

The instant he was out of sight, Lucindy heard a voice behind her.

"Git da kids an' cum . . . hurry. We gotter git deeper into da woods afore he's back!"

Struggling out of the thorny thicket, heedless of pricks and scratches on hands, face, and arms, they ran to follow.

And not a moment too soon. In less than a minute they heard the horse galloping back toward them, their companion still dragging behind. They stopped and crouched low, a little farther away than before but still able to see as the poor man's captor galloped back and forth several more times, pulling the man tumbling and twisting over the rocky and uneven ground.

At last the galloping slowed. Lucindy moved a few leaves with her fingers. She could just barely see the black man's broken body attached to the rope behind the horse. To her eyes the bloody and battered lump of humanity must surely be dead.

"You see this, all you other niggers!" yelled Murdoch. "This is what is coming to you when Malone Murdoch gets his hands on you!"

He dismounted and walked to where the black man lay on the ground. "All right, Pig, get up."

There was no response.

"Get up!" he repeated, kicking the body over with his booted foot.

"Well, don't matter to me," said Murdoch. "You're worth seventy-five dead and it'll make my job easier getting you back."

Suddenly a crack of pistol fire echoed in Lucindy's ears. The black body jumped slightly at the shot then lay, if possible, more still than before. She leaned back into her hiding place, stomach lurching at the murder she had just witnessed.

Five minutes later they heard the horse walking slowly away. They waited where they were until it was pitch black. Thirty or forty minutes went by. Then by means of a few low whistles and birdcalls, the group, minus one, managed to gather together some distance away in the woods and continue by a different route, in horrified silence. Death had touched them closer than ever and fear now guided their every step.

Several days after the killing, Lucindy awoke in the attic of the house where they had arrived the previous night. She heard voices below her. The man and woman she had been traveling with were talking about where they were bound and the rest of the family waiting for them there. She listened a while longer as they discussed the route toward their destination, which would soon take them eastward up into the mountains and across toward Ohio. She then climbed down the ladder to join them.

"Where dis Ohio y'all's been talkin' 'bout?" she asked.

"Dat's where dis train's boun'," replied the conductress.

"I don' want ter go ter no Ohio."

"Why not? Hit's across da Jordan," said the man.

"What difference it make where you go," added his sister, "jes' so long as you be free?"

"I gots me a man waitin' fo' me," replied Lucindy. "He sent fo' us."

"Where you gwine meet him?"

"I don' know."

"Den you ain't neber gwine fin' him no how. You can' jes' go fin' somebody out in the middle ob the whole worl' like dat."

For the first time the thought entered Lucindy's brain, what if she never did find Caleb? What would she do then?

"I's gots ter go ter sumplace called Pennsylvania," she said hopefully.

"Den sumbody brung you ter da wrong station at dat place where we first met," said the man.

"Why you say dat?"

"Cuz dis train's boun' fo' Ohio."

"Dey's right nex' ter each other," said his sister. "Where you gots ter go in Pennsylvania?" she asked Lucindy.

"I don' know, near a place called York," Lucindy answered. "Dat's what dey tol' me—sumplace called Hanober."

"Dat's way ter da eas'. Den my brudder's right—you don' want ter be comin' wif us. Dat be da other direkshun from where we's boun'.

Once we head ober dose mountains, we be goin' da wrong way altogeder. You gots ter take anuder train."

"How I gwine do dat?"

"We's talk ter da stationmaster at da nex' depot an' see what he sez."

When they did so two nights later, however, the man's answer was not what Lucindy had hoped to hear.

"No conductor comes through this station bound that direction, miss," the man said. "You'll have to get there on your own."

"But how I fin' it alone?" she asked, her voice starting to tremble. "What ef dat white man be out dere—dat bounty hunter dat killed Jack? What ef he's follerin' us?"

"He ain't or he'd er dun sumfin afore now," said the woman.

"Don't worry," added the stationmaster. "I'll tell you where to go. You'll be safe. It's the only Quaker house for miles. You'll find it all right."

Forty-two

Two nights later, fearful but trying to summon courage from her travels thus far, Lucindy and the children set out alone.

The stationmaster gave her food for a few days, but with the baby, the tarp, and their few other clothes, she couldn't carry much. They were tired and weak and gradually growing thin. Broan was too small to be of much help.

The first long night on their own passed safely. When daylight began to dawn, however, the farmhouse the man had described was nowhere in sight. Unknowingly they had already passed the station an hour before daybreak. Lucindy found a place to sleep and they passed the day safely, then continued on the following night in the same direction. But with every step they now moved farther and farther from the railroad. After three more nights, out of food and growing desperate, Lucindy knew they were lost.

The train to freedom had derailed.

At last she sat down and began to cry. All she could think of was the evil face of the white man she had seen pulling Jack behind his horse. If he found them he was sure to kill them all.

The night was windy but clear. Maybe it was time to start praying, thought Lucindy.

The words she had heard so many times came back to her. She would try to say them.

Our Father, she began, *dat art in heab'n, hallered be dye name. Dye kingdom cum, dye will be dun, on erf as hit is in heab'n. Gib us dis day are daily bred . . .*

She stopped and started to cry again. It was no use. What good did it do to pray to someone called *Father*? Her own father carried a whip and punished anyone who disobeyed. The words meant nothing but evil in her mind. Her father and the bounty hunter were just alike. Were all white men besides the Quakers cruel? How could she pray to someone like *that* for help!

God was a white man's God, the God of the plantation masters—a white *master*, a white *father*. When they went to church, the preachers preached from the pulpit that the only way to please God was to obey their masters.

Was there a different God in the North? Lucindy wondered. Might there be a different kind of God who cared for people like her?

God must not be like a father, he *must* be something else. Maybe the God for free people was a woman, like a great big mammy to everyone in the world. She wished God could be a *mother* instead of a father. Her mother had been so kind and good before she died.

Finally she stood and gazed up into the sky. "Help us, God, whoeber you is!" she cried into the wind. "We's los' an' we don't know what ter do!"

As if in answer to her desperate plea, Lucindy remembered Amaritta's words: *Effen you gits los' you just keep walkin' tard dat star like da ol' song sez.*

She continued to look up into the cloudless sky. There it was, the shape of the stars just like Amaritta said.

Softly she hummed the familiar tune, then slowly began to sing:

> *Step by step keep-er-travelin' on,*
> > *Foller da drinkin' gord.*
> *Sleep in der holler 'til da daylight's gone,*
> > *Foller da drinkin' gord.*

Singing gave her a little hope. She picked up Calebia and began to walk again.

"Norf . . . keep goin' norf," she said. "Dat's where we's boun'. We jes' foller dat dere star."

Broan and Rebecca followed as Lucindy continued to sing, gathering more courage with every step. The faint sound of the children's voices now joined in.

> *Think I hears da angels say,*
> *Foller da drinkin' gord.*
> *Stars in da heabens gwinter show me da way,*
> *Foller da drinkin' gord.*
>
> *Foller dat riber 'til da clouds roll by,*
> *Foller da drinkin' gord.*
> *Keep on er movin,' an' lookin' ter da sky,*
> *Foller da drinkin' gord.*
>
> *We's gwinter foller da drinkin' gord,*
> *We's gwinter foller da drinkin' gord.*
> *Keep on travelin' dat muddy road ter freedom,*
> *Foller da drinkin' gord.*

"Lor'," said Lucindy as she finished and looked up into the night sky again, "You dun brought us dis far an' we ain't gwine ter go back no how. Eben effen I don' know how ter pray, I'd rather be on dis road wif my chilluns an' maybe die tryin' ter git ter Caleb an' freedom den ter go back ter da whip an' dose chains ob Master Crawford. Whoeber you are, you be da one dat put dat drinkin' gord up dere in da sky like dat as a sign fo' folks like me. So we's gwine ter foller it till sumfin happens. Cum on, chulluns," she said to Broan and Rebecca, "we's goin' on—jes' keep lookin' up at dem stars, dey'll show us da way ter go."

They walked north all that night until the stars began to give way to the kind of darkness that precedes the dawn. Finally they sat down and huddled together near a clump of trees to wait.

"I's hungry, Mama," said Rebecca.

"We's all a mite hungry, chil'. But sumfin good's gwine happen by'n by. We'll git sum sleep now an' dream 'bout dat good stew we dun eat at dat las' station—y'all member, where you played wif dem nice w'ite chilluns dere."

When the sun came up the children still slept. Lucindy sat up, rubbing her eyes and staring at their surroundings. A barn and farmhouse sat only a stone's throw away. A rooster crowed, then was joined by another as they set about trying to awaken the rest of the place. They were lucky not to have been discovered already! In the darkness they had nearly blundered right into a farmyard!

As Lucindy turned to wake the children and move farther out of sight, a woman dressed in gray stepped onto the porch and went to empty a chamber pot in the outhouse. Lucindy remained still and watched. When the woman came out and walked back toward the house, Lucindy shook Broan awake.

"'Member all dose nice w'ite folks at da stations?" she whispered.

Broan nodded sleepily.

"See dat lady yonder," she went on. "I think she might be one er dem. I's want you ter go ax her effen she cud spare sum food fer sum train trab'lers. Don' be feared. Effen she say no, den you walk 'round da barn and cum back ter me. If she say yes, den you tell her you ain't alone an cum back an' git yo' little sister. Now go on—don't be feared. She be dressed like sum ob dem other station folks dat took care ob us."

Too sleepy to be afraid, and his stomach too empty to argue, Broan left the cover of the trees, glanced back only once at his mother and sister, then continued on toward the house.

Forty-three

*I*t had been almost three years since the visit to the Waters' home of the three friends of her mother. But Cherity Waters had not forgotten her father's words from that day: *Your mother was very faithful to church . . . you are free to go anytime you like.*

She had been thinking about her mother a lot lately. She was the kind of girl who made the best of what life gave her with as optimistic a spirit as possible. But it was difficult growing up without a mother. As much as she loved her father, and hadn't a regret in the world about anything to do with him, there was a lonely corner of her heart that he alone couldn't satisfy.

She had been thinking about her mother ever since that day in her room at school. The desire had grown in recent weeks to know what her mother had found at church and in her black Bible that had given her life meaning. Cherity could not know her mother's heart. But perhaps there she could in some way draw into closer contact with her spirit.

"Daddy, what church did you and Mama used to go to?" asked Cherity one Friday morning as she and her father were seated together at the breakfast table. "You know—the one those three ladies who came to visit were from?"

"The Congregational Baptist Alliance Church," replied her father. "Why . . . are you thinking of going?"

"I am. Would you like to come with me?"

"Thank you, but no. I had my fill. I think you would perhaps be able to respond more personally without me there anyway. If you find something you like, I won't be the one to discourage you. Your mother went every Sunday. It certainly meant something to her . . . and I thought it did to me," he added with a peculiar expression.

"I know, Daddy—you've told me that," replied Cherity. "I guess maybe it's time I found out what it is."

Two days later, at about ten minutes before eleven o'clock on a Sunday of late October, Cherity Waters—against her natural predisposition as it might have been, wearing a bright pink and yellow dress and matching hat—made her way through the doors of the Congregational Baptist Alliance Church on the heels of a man and woman who had walked up seconds before. She cast one last glance back to her father's buggy disappearing down the street, then continued the rest of the way inside.

Cherity was both nervous, and curious to see how this church would differ from chapel at the boarding school. Odd incongruous images of what to expect crowded her imagination. Mostly she envisioned dowdy old people wearing black clothes and solemn expressions, stiff-backed seats, lifeless songs, organ music, flies buzzing about, boring sermons, stained-glass windows, and mingled ever and anon with these mental pictures clung the faint aroma of mildew that, in its spiritual rather than corporeal sense, seemed to hover about the memory of the three ladies who had called at her home. Her father was so interesting and gay. She imagined her mother the same. How could such musty specimens have been her mother's friends? Maybe today's experience would help her discover the answer.

She followed the elderly couple inside, through a darkened vestibule where a few people were gathered speaking in hushed tones, and on into a large room of high-vaulted ceiling and open beams. Organ music was playing softly and reverently.

Cherity paused to get her bearings, then continued following the man and woman down one of the aisles, the floor creaking beneath their feet. As she went she slowly took in her surroundings. There were the colored windows behind the organ where a lady sat pumping her feet as she played. The black clothes and solemn expressions were in ample evidence too, as she noted from glances to her right and left. There were no chairs, only long pews with upright backs that stretched from aisle to aisle.

The man and woman turned into one of the rows and made their way to the center. She followed and sat down beside the man. For the first time he seemed to notice her and gave a slight nod. Finally seated, she could relax. She glanced about for any sign of the three ladies who had known her mother. She thought the back of one head several rows in front could be one of them. But from where she sat it was hard to tell.

Ten minutes later the organ music stopped. A slight commotion in front turned her attention to the door of a side entrance. Through it a man walked expressionless, very tall, balding, and dressed in black nearly from head to foot. He took a place in front of a giant lectern. Slowly he lifted both hands. As if on command, everyone in the church stood. Without an idea what had been about to happen, Cherity was still sitting on the pew when suddenly she found everyone else in the place standing. She leapt to her feet as a great blast from the organ shook the building. A scuffling followed, from somewhere books were produced, and around her everyone began to sing. About halfway through the hymn the man at her side noticed her still standing with hands at her side. He nodded with his head, then pointed to her left, where at last she realized a book like she saw in everyone else's hands was located in a wooden tray attached to the pew in front of her. She smiled at the man, then took the book and opened it, but soon realized she had no idea where to turn. She tried in vain to sneak a glance to her left, or between the two ladies in front of her to catch a glimpse of the page to which their book was opened—the man beside her was too tall, held his book too high, and apparently felt that one good deed for the day was enough. The hymn concluded with a rousing "Amen" before she had been successful in finding the page.

The pastor now raised his hands again, then ceremoniously and slowly lowered them. Not realizing the opposite signal had been given, and at that moment distractedly taking in some of the people around her, Cherity suddenly found herself the only person, save the black-clad man in front, in the entire church still on her feet. Quickly she sat, pink rising to her cheeks. A few heads turned in her direction, then slowly returned forward.

Now that she had survived a rising, a sitting, and the first hymn, Cherity had drawn two very important conclusions that would enable her to get through the rest of the hour without calling further undue attention to herself:

One—everyone acted in unison. If she did what they did, she would not stand out.

Two—there were cues to these uniform actions, such as the raising and lowering of the minister's arms. She must be on her toes to watch for them.

Little did Cherity Waters realize that within five minutes of entering the church, she had laid hold of the mighty truth of religious conformity, a principle so pervasive and potent that it dictated not only matters of correct behavior in nearly every Christian community in the land, but also of what comprised correct theology. Deviation and individuality were the great sins such modes of conformity, and many like them, were designed to combat. One must never stand when others sat, or sit when others stood. And one must always recite—whether hymn, reading, doctrine, or creed—ever and always . . . in *unison*. Conformity must be preserved at all costs.

Cherity thus got through the service without further gaffes. However, she could decipher not the slightest meaning out of the sermon, which comprised the final thirty-five minutes of the hour—during which she indeed found the pew back straight and its bottom hard. The man conducting the soliloquy was speaking in English. She heard individual words she recognized. But he somehow managed to string them together in such a way as to utterly obfuscate any hope she had of gaining whatever meaning he might have been trying to convey.

Recognizing the cues by now well enough, and aided by a loud benediction which could have served no salient function other than to punctuate with dignified finality the closing of the service, Cherity turned with everyone else toward the aisle. Following the lead of those in front of her, she began inching her way toward the rear of the church amid the slow-shuffling crowd of fellow worshippers.

She had not quite reached the door when she felt a tug at her elbow and heard her name.

"Cherity, my dear," said a woman's voice, "I hardly recognized you!"

She turned to see the woman whose head she had been staring at throughout the service. "You look lovely, my dear—I am Harriet Filtore, one of your mother's friends . . . we called on your father some time ago."

"Yes, ma'am—hello," said Cherity.

"Come with me, please, dear—I want you to see the others too! Oh, this is just too exciting!"

She tugged Cherity along against the flow of the human stream. "You have grown so, my dear," said Mrs. Filtore as they went. "You've turned into a lady. And a lovely one. I am so glad. Mabel, Sarah . . . you'll never guess who I found in our congregation! Look, it's Kathleen's daughter Cherity!"

"Oh, my goodness!" exclaimed Mrs. Foxe. "And in a dress! Cherity . . . how good of you to come."

"Hello, Cherity," said the third member of the trio, Mabel Bledsoe. "I am so delighted to see you!"

"Let's go sit down somewhere and have a nice talk," said Mrs. Foxe.

"Do you suppose pastor would let us use his study, Sarah?" asked Mrs. Filtore.

"Or one of the Sunday school rooms?" suggested Mrs. Bledsoe.

"We will find a suitable place where we can be alone," said Mrs. Foxe. "Come, Cherity, dear—we shall get away from all this bustle. We want to find out how you have been!"

Without much opportunity to do otherwise, Cherity smiled and

followed. She soon found herself seated in a small musty room smell-
ing vaguely of children, mothballs, damp plaster, chalk, and week-old
stew. The faces of the three women stared eagerly into hers with smiles
of mingled delight and anticipation to find Kathleen Waters' daughter
temporarily free from the clutches of her backslidden father. They
might not have another opportunity like this to win her soul, and they
intended to make the most of it. Whether the Spirit was moving in
anyone's heart in the room they did not pause to inquire . . . *they*
intended to move and do so with vigor. They meant to insure that this
girl did not leave the building until the Spirit had gotten off his
haunches and done his business and had brought salvation to this
poor lost soul.

Slowly the smiles faded and the tone became serious.

"Cherity, my dear," began Mrs. Foxe, "we believe the Lord brought
you here today so that you might find faith in him. Tell me,
Cherity—do you know what sin is?"

Having no idea his daughter was about to undergo the spiritual grill-
ing of her life, James Waters had stopped into one of his favorite
haunts in Boston, which sat not far from the church, to pass the hour
while enjoying a cup of tea and the Sunday *New York Times*, the only
edition of the *Globe*'s competition he allowed himself, chiefly for the
purpose of the crossword puzzle. Strangely, he found himself unable
to concentrate. His thoughts kept wandering to what Cherity might
be hearing back within the hallowed walls of Baptist Alliance. He
knew the pastor had changed two or three times since his days of spiritual activity with wife and older daughters.

His feelings concerning Cherity's church visit were oddly mixed.
For one with such marked personal antagonism to what he now
considered the humbug of ritual, dogma, and pat answer, he was
strangely neutral concerning how his daughter might respond. There
lingered love and fond memories of his wife such that, in spite of the
harsh words he had spoken to Richmond Davidson concerning his

own thoughts about God, if their daughter was able to find any solace or meaning in the church, out of respect for Kathleen, he would have been glad. It might serve as a bond, however slight, between mother and daughter, and he would have welcomed it . . . so long as nothing involving what he would consider outright falsehood were involved.

After forty minutes or so, he rose and returned to his buggy outside.

Even as the intense interview involving the daughter of James Waters was taking place, four hundred fifty miles to the southwest another equally unexpected, though far briefer, interview was about to take place at the Virginia plantation called Oakbriar, where a knocker had just sounded on the front door.

Denton Beaumont was sick of his overseer's assistant, Leon Riggs, pussyfooting it around his slaves. Riggs hadn't been his old self ever since Nate Gibbons' disappearance. Beaumont harbored more than half a suspicion that Leon had had a hand in the affair somehow, though not the slightest evidence had ever come to his attention and nothing had been seen or heard of Nate again. Now more than ever the slaves needed an iron hand, not a velvet glove. He himself tried to maintain a bravado around his men, assuring them that Nate was dead and "good riddance to bad rubbish." He knew well enough what was going to happen to him, and he had crawled off like the coward he was to die alone in some cave.

But he knew the slaves didn't believe it. They all thought Nate had escaped and was now free in the North somewhere. Whether they possessed any reliable information to corroborate their hope, he had no idea. But they believed it. And Gibbons' successful flight made them all tense and jittery. He knew the single black men especially were looking for their chance to follow him. Now was no time for Riggs to turn soft.

Meanwhile, downstairs, his daughter had just answered the front door. She had run to it eagerly with a gleam in her eye, hoping she would find Seth on the other side of it.

There stood the hugest black man she had ever seen in her life.

The gleam faded from her eye as soon as she saw that he was black. Yet the fact that he did not appear too many years older than herself kept the hint of a playful smile on her lips. She had been trying to wile and seduce young men for so long with her subtle use of beguiling expression that she could no longer help herself. It came out whether she was conscious of it or not.

"Hello," she said coyly.

"You Miss Bowmont?" said the black man.

"That's right." She inched a little closer and let her eyes flutter a few times.

"I come to see yo' daddy. He here?"

"Maybe . . ."

"Veronica, honey," said Lady Daphne, approaching the door behind her, "who is—"

She stopped in midsentence and gasped in terrified astonishment. "Goodness!" she exclaimed under her breath, "he is a big one. . . . Jarvis!" she called behind her.

Even as upstairs Denton Beaumont's thoughts were brooding on Leon Riggs' incompetence, his black butler appeared at the door to his study.

"Massa Bowmont, suh," he said softly. "Dere be a man downstairs come fo' to see you, suh."

Beaumont glanced up irritably. "What kind of man, Jarvis?" he said. "Who is he?"

"Don' know his name, Massa Bowmont. He didn't say. He's be a colored man, suh."

"One of ours?"

"No, suh."

"I have no interest in seeing some nigger. Send him away."

"He says he be a free colored, suh. He be a mean-lookin' one."

"And he wouldn't tell you what he wanted?"

"No, suh—just dat it be somefin you'd want ter hear."

His curiosity finally getting the better of him, Denton Beaumont rose and descended the stairs to the front door. By then wife and

daughter had disappeared. There stood the man exactly as advertised—big, black, mean.

"My butler says you're a freedman?"

"Dat's right. I's got me a paper to prove it."

"I'll take your word for it . . . for now. What do you want?"

"I's be lookin' fo' work, Mister Bowmont."

"I've got more than fifty slaves that I don't have to pay. Why
should I take on one more that would expect a wage?"

"'Cause I knows dere kind. I knows how ter make dem work harder
dan any w'ite man can. Effen I don't, after a week, you kin git rid ob
me an' you won't owe me nuthin."

Beaumont eyed the man carefully. He had made him an offer
almost too delicious to refuse. This fellow could prove useful. This
might be just the answer he had been looking for to the dilemma of
what to do about Leon Riggs.

"What's your name, freedman?"

"Slade, suh . . . Elias Slade."

Beaumont took in the information with heightened curiosity. Now
he remembered the fellow. He had heard about him. Suddenly this
man's showing up on his doorstep had become filled with all the more
interest.

"You do know, do you not," he said after a moment, "that I could
enslave you myself, right now? It has been more than a year since
Davidson freed you and you are still in Virginia. That makes you
available to any white man who wants you."

"I knows it, Mister Bowmont. But maybe you shud be sayin', any
w'ite man who *can* put his chains on me. I figger you's smarter'n to
try dat, an' dat I can do more good fo' you da way I am."

⟨⁓⟩

The question that had been posed to Cherity Waters about sin came
so unexpectedly that for a moment she sat speechless, blankly returning the woman's earnest gaze. At first she thought perhaps it was a
joke. But the look on Mrs. Foxe's face displayed no hint of humor.

"I . . . *think* so," replied Cherity at length. "But I really didn't come here to talk about that."

"Nothing is so important, dear."

"There was enough about sin and hell and judgment in the sermon. I could make little of it."

"Then why *did* you come here today, dear?" asked Mrs. Bledsoe.

"I wanted to see if I could learn what my mother found so important that this church played such a large part of her life. I want to know more about her. This seemed like a good place to begin."

"We think that is wonderful, Cherity," smiled Mrs. Foxe. "Everyone in the church loved your mother a great deal. To understand your mother's faith, dear, you must first come to understand sin. The gospel begins there."

"What does 'gospel' mean?" asked Cherity.

"Has your father taught you nothing of such things?" asked Mrs. Filtore.

"He has taught me to be a good person, to treat people with courtesy, kindness, and respect, always to tell the truth, to say what I mean, and to be the same person on the outside as I am on the inside. But I have never heard him use the word *gospel*."

Three glances were exchanged. They indicated clearly enough that the views of the assembled committee were unchanged regarding the suitability of poor Kathleen Waters' husband as a father, despite finding the girl in church in a dress. They still, however, had no idea how thorough was Cherity's ignorance in the learned ways and means, taught phrases and clichés, and ingrained prescriptions and recipes of their fundamentalism. As is often the case with such types—having never considered in depth for themselves the intellectual rigors involved in the transition from unbelief into belief—they assumed a greater universal understanding of the salvation formula than was the actual reality.

"Gospel means good news, dear," said Mrs. Foxe.

"The gospel of Jesus Christ," said Mrs. Bledsoe, "is the good news that Jesus came to save us from our sins."

"That is why the gospel begins with sin," added Mrs. Filtore.

"And sin is . . . *good* news?" said Cherity. "That doesn't sound very pleasant to me."

"Sin isn't the good news, dear, but that Jesus saves us from sin. That's what it means to be saved—to confess one's sin and accept the atoning blood of Jesus as the propitiation for our sin."

Cherity nodded. "Yes," she said slowly. "I've heard things like that, though I've never heard that word. But I want to know what it *means* . . . in real life."

"To find out what it means, one must enter into the saving life of grace," said Mrs. Foxe, taking up the banner again to press home the victory. "Are you ready to confess your sin?"

"I don't know," said Cherity. "What do you mean exactly?"

"Admit the wickedness in your heart before God, so that the blood of Jesus can make you clean."

The words jarred against Cherity's brain.

"My *wickedness*?" she repeated slowly.

"Yes, Cherity, dear . . . your sin," nodded Mrs. Foxe.

"In order to repent," said Mrs. Filtore, "the first thing one must do is recognize his sin."

"I don't feel like a sinner."

"The heart is deceitful and wicked. You mustn't listen to what your heart tells you. We all must repent. To do so we must acknowledge our sinful state under the curse of Adam."

"What is the curse of Adam?"

"Original sin, dear—what Adam and Eve did in the Garden by disobeying God and trying to trust in their own righteousness to save them—"

"Our own righteousness is as filthy rags," added Mrs. Bledsoe, on cue.

"—Which is why Adam and Eve died under the curse of sin," Mrs. Filtore went on. "But Jesus shed his blood as the atoning sacrifice to pay the price of our sin and take our place under the curse of death. By repenting of our sin and receiving his precious blood, the curse is lifted and we are made righteous unto eternal life."

Cherity sat staring, her eyes wide.

"I am very sorry," she began. "I do not mean to sound either stupid or rude, but I'm afraid I didn't understand much of what you just said. What does paying a price have to do with sin?"

"The wages of sin is death," interjected Mrs. Bledsoe from her mental cue cards.

Cherity glanced at her, still confused. The ever vigilant Mrs. Filtore saw the look and was ready with the appropriate reply.

"Death is what all sin deserves," she said. "That is simple enough to understand, is it not?"

"I think so," replied Cherity. "Badness doesn't deserve to live . . . is that what you are saying?"

The good Harriet Filtore would have preferred one of the more stock phrases. It took her a moment to translate Cherity's unrehearsed response into the lexicon of her vocabulary to see whether it was acceptable or not. After a second or two she concluded that it would pass.

"Something like that," she nodded slowly. "And since sin deserves death," she went on, "a sacrifice must be made . . . to atone for that sin."

Again, Cherity's expression went blank. "What does *atone* mean?" she asked.

"To make up for the sin."

"To wash the sin of scarlet as white as snow," added the helpful Mrs. Bledsoe.

"And so a sacrifice must be made for sin," now said Mrs. Foxe, coming back into the forefront of the discussion.

"Why?" asked Cherity.

The enormous significance of the question was so stark in its simplicity, that momentarily it silenced all three women. The fact was, the single-word query—which should have stood front and center as the foundational and most vital of all inquiries throughout the nineteen-hundred-year history of Christianity—was one none of the three had ever considered. Nor had it even been hinted at in all the years of their catechistic training to meet every so-called "objection" that might be raised against what they called "the gospel."

They sat for a moment in bewildered silence. At last Mrs.
Filtore—ever on her toes with a response from the stockpile of platitudes she had memorized for such occasions, although she did not
have one which *quite* fit the present dilemma—spoke.

"Because God established the sacrifice in the Old Testament to be
the remedy for sin," she said. "His holiness cannot abide in the presence of sin. Sacrifice is the only possible atonement for sin."

"But *why?*" repeated Cherity.

"Because the death of an innocent must pay the price for sin."

"The death of an *innocent?*" said Cherity.

"Yes, dear, it is not only a sacrifice that must be made for sin, but
the perfect laying down of an innocent victim, shedding his blood in
the sinner's place, thus paying the price instead, and atoning for the
sin."

"That sounds dreadful—killing an innocent victim so that a guilty
sinner can go free. That doesn't make any sense at all. Who would
dream up such an awful arrangement?"

"A loving and holy God, dear. The sacrifice makes it so that we
don't *have* to die, but can have eternal life."

At last a little light began to break through. "Oh . . . you mean
heaven?" said Cherity.

Mrs. Filtore nodded. "The atoning sacrifice, where the debt for our
sin is paid by another, the innocent Christ Jesus who is willing to pay
the debt for us, standing in our place to incur the judgment and wrath
of a holy God against sin, which cannot abide in his almighty presence, allows us to enter eternal life rather than suffer the wages of sin
which is eternal death and hell."

Cherity's face fell. "I'm sorry," she said, "You must think me terribly stupid. But again I simply cannot understand how that could be.
The innocent dying for the guilty makes no sense."

"Not to our sinful minds perhaps. But God's ways are higher than
man's ways."

"The way of the cross is foolishness to them that are in darkness,"
interjected Mrs. Bledsoe.

"But you still haven't answered why," said Cherity. "If it's true, it *has* to make sense. All truth must make sense, that is something my father says and I agree with him."

"It does make sense, dear, but only to the spiritual mind."

"Many are called but few are chosen," said Mrs. Bledsoe. "The way is narrow that leads to life, and few there are who find it."

"I am truly sorry," said Cherity, "but honestly . . . it doesn't make sense to me."

The three women glanced about hopelessly, silently inquiring of one another, *How are we going to help her understand? She is such a babe. Her mind is so darkened by the ways of the world. What can we say that will help her see?*

And well might they ask. Had they but known the Father of Jesus Christ one-thousandth as well as they knew a hundred formulas concerning the work of his Son that they had contorted to fit into their bag of responses, their own hearts might have been opened a chink to receive a flash or two of light reflected from the wonderful, glorious, honest, humble, truth-opening, wisdom-producing, God-discovering, and growth-*necessary* question that had just been posed out of the mouth of a babe . . . the single question, *Why?*

But they could not see because they would not. They had been so thoroughly schooled in the recitation of pat phrases that they had little practical awareness indeed of the great truths to which those phrases pointed—nothing less than the brilliance of the high Fatherhood of the universe. Nor did they grasp that, in their present form, the axioms by which they tried to enclose those truths actually *hid* the light of them from shining into the hearts of men—the so-called saved like themselves, along with the unsaved whom they were so anxious to redeem with their blueprints for salvation.

But the Spirit of God, whom Cherity had come that day seeking without knowing it, had heard her humble cry. And he—her Father and Creator and Savior—would make provision, through the pain of loss, to draw her into his lap and satisfy the thirst she barely knew she had.

"I am sorry," said Cherity at length. "I think perhaps I ought to go."

She began to rise.

"But don't you want to know the joy of salvation that your mother knew?" asked Mrs. Foxe, nearly pleading now. "Your mother had eternal life, Cherity. Don't you want to know it too?"

"Perhaps another time," said Cherity. "My head is swimming right now. I can't think straight."

She left the room, glanced about to reorient herself, tried a couple of the empty corridors, then managed successfully to navigate her way out of the church. There was her father waiting in the buggy.

"What took you so long?" he said with a smile. "I saw everyone leaving thirty minutes ago. I thought maybe you had decided to stay and have the pastor to baptize you or something!"

"It wasn't that," said Cherity with a sigh of mental exhaustion. "I never exchanged a word with the pastor."

"What kept you, then?"

"Those three ladies wanted to talk to me," replied Cherity sitting down next to him on the leather seat. "I think they were trying to get my soul saved or something, but I couldn't make sense of what they were talking about."

"What did they say?" asked James, giving the reins a flick.

"They were talking in circles about sacrifice and debt and atonement and all sorts of other things," said Cherity as they bounded into motion. "But they never answered why it was as they said. It was like whenever I asked a question, they went into a special language or something."

Waters laughed to hear his daughter's description of the religious parlance that made up so much of church orthodoxy of which he had once been a part.

"And hell?" he said with raised eyebrow, glancing toward her.

Cherity nodded. "Yes, hell came into it some too."

"It always does. It has always mystified me why the proponents of a religion based on the love of God are always so anxious to talk about hell. Maybe it bothers me now because for so long I spoke that jargon myself without ever pausing to ask if it made sense."

"They wanted so badly for me to understand them," Cherity went on. "I felt bad that I couldn't. But they just kept going into that incomprehensible way of talking full of so many odd words and explanations that didn't make sense."

Forty-four

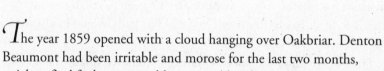

The year 1859 opened with a cloud hanging over Oakbriar. Denton Beaumont had been irritable and morose for the last two months, quick to find fault, more ruthless toward his slaves, given to bursts of temper at the slightest provocation. His change in mood stemmed from two devastating blows to his prideful sense of invincibility.

First, a slave he despised had successfully run off and apparently made good his escape. No matter what he said in public, he had serious reservations that the man's bones were really lying up in one of the caves on the ridge that the children of the region feared. His insistence on it, however, would doubtless add yet more to the spooky tales of Indian ghosts and burials and sacrifices that, like a magic elixir of gleeful terror, spread among the young. Now there was a real man who had never been found, whose skeleton or half-rotten corpse they might stumble on at any time. It kept the younger children well away from Harper's Peak, while drawing to it, always with a friend or two, the more daring of their older fellows.

The fact was, the man was gone. The reminder enraged Denton Beaumont every time he thought of it. He was worried where it might lead. Always in the back of his mind was the awareness that other of his slaves might gain courage from what Gibbons had done and that before long he could have a rash of escape attempts on his hands.

But worse than all that, after considering his victory almost automatic—he had not actually begun to put anything away in a traveling chest, but almost—two months before the election things had begun to take a nasty and unexpected turn. From out of nowhere a series of articles had appeared that, over the course of eight weeks, had devastated his campaign.

His lead had vanished. When November of 1858 came, his advisors were secretly not optimistic.

Hoyt had, in fact, trounced him. Not by a landslide, but by enough to make the defeat sting. Now the fool had begun another six-year term, Senator Everett would not come up for reelection for four, and even if he decided to run in '62, now he had a humiliating defeat to headline his résumé, not to mention having been passed by two years earlier in favor of Davidson and Everett. The party would hardly look upon him as a favorable candidate.

His brief rise into the political limelight had been quashed before it began.

Within a few short weeks of his hiring, the Beaumont slaves came to hate Elias Slade more than any white overseer. A turncoat of one's own kind was worse than an outright enemy.

Slade had, in a sense, nothing to lose. He could not be flogged or disciplined—if Beaumont tried it, Slade would turn his back and leave, for he was a freedman. And a Negro of his strength could easily find work in either the North or the South, despite his sketchy past. Someone was always willing to pay for raw brute strength. If he got too out of hand, they could, of course, shoot him or hang him. But none of Beaumont's men relished the thought of tangling with Slade. He could have put any three of them on the ground unconscious in ten seconds. He was a goliath of a man, with massive biceps and forearms and shoulders and legs almost superhuman in size, and a neck as thick as a tree trunk. The steely glint in his eye made it clear from one look that he would have little compunction about the shedding of human blood. He had done so before and, if challenged or roused, would not hesitate to do so again.

Nor was Slade stupid. He had decided to try the Beaumont estate after bouncing around for a couple of years at a half dozen menial jobs, not more than half expecting much to come of it. He knew Beaumont had no affection for coloreds. But somehow he sensed more opportunity would come his way than at the nearby McClellan plantation where he had spent several of his early years. So as things had turned out, he knew that he had fallen on his feet. He had no intention of provoking an incident. He knew which side his bread was buttered on, and could follow orders well enough when it suited him.

Furthermore, the inhuman flogging that poor Nate Gibbons had endured—and not one of his fellow slaves would forget the sight of his open gashes and slow-oozing wounds—had had its effect. Despite rumors to the contrary, half of them thought Nate dead, and took no pleasure in the thought of suffering Nate's fate, either whipping or death. Slade would not take the whip to one of them himself. Whether it would be called an ethical scruple, it would be hard to say, but at the point of picking up a whip against a fellow black man, Slade drew the line. Beaumont seemed almost to respect him for it. Yet one word from him was sufficient to put the whip into the hand of one of the white men who would be more than happy for an opportunity to prove to their boss that he had none of Riggs' qualms in the matter of severity.

Slade's addition to the Beaumont coterie of slaves, hired white men, and overseers had precisely the effect Denton Beaumont had desired. Grumbling and discontent among the slaves, to all appearances, settled down. At least they kept any grievances to themselves.

Now that Riggs had ingloriously been sent back to town and was working along with his son at the depot for pennies, whatever grumbling went on came from the white quarters, whose occupants were less than happy to see a big "free nigger" usurp the position of leadership several of them had hoped to get after Riggs' firing. Their position was complicated by the fact that from the start of the new arrangement, Beaumont seemed to take, if not a liking to the man-beast, then a certain evil pleasure in having him around and knowing everyone was terrified of him, blacks and whites together. As often as not these days,

Slade could be seen at Beaumont's side whenever the latter went out on the estate, a hulking bodyguard and team of oxen all rolled into a single man. In time it almost seemed like Slade had an invisible power over his master as well as his fellow slaves.

Whether loss of the election had diverted Denton Beaumont's lust for power into a need to make yet more visible the iron grip of his rule at Oakbriar, or whether Slade's constant attendance stemmed merely from the practical desire to maintain control in the best and most efficient means possible, the fact was, his presence changed things. A few of the white men spoke amongst themselves of quitting. But where would they go? Beaumont paid them decently and they knew well enough that neither the Davidson nor the McClellan plantations needed men. So most remained where they were and kept their grousing to themselves.

If her husband's mortification was keen, at least he had plenty to keep himself busy. But Lady Daphne's world had crumbled around her at his loss of the election the previous November. True to what the young man Cecil Hirsch had intimated, she *had* begun to pack her bags for Washington. And while Denton was away voting on election day, she had spent the morning making out a preliminary guest list for her first party, which she planned to host within a month of their arrival in Washington.

Her grief since that time was deepened in the knowledge that certain damaging reports and quotes had been published about her husband which, it was thought, had begun to turn the tide in Hoyt's favor. There were several damning accounts but two worse than all the rest.

The first alleged that, as recently as during his candidacy, Beaumont had been on the verge of hanging one of his slaves. Lady Daphne was not in the habit of reading newspapers, especially political articles. But in the months leading up to the election she had perused anything having to do with her husband, secretly hoping to find her own name mentioned, even some reference to the enhanced social prestige of the capital that was sure to accompany their arrival the following January.

To discover instead, not at first her name but evidence enough, in her own mind, of things she had said, was so shocking as to send her into a near faint. She groped for a chair and sat down, hoping against hope that an untimely word from her own lips would not cost Denton the Senate seat.

Denton ranted at first. But after some time had passed he thought little more of the disparaging articles that had begun to appear in Virginia's newspapers throughout the fall months, nor of selected quotations here and there that, taken in their implied context, cast him in an unfavorable, even at times an unseemly, light—presenting the image of a man who did not seem the genteel sort to represent the good people of Virginia in the august chambers of Congress.

But as the tide had begun to turn back in Hoyt's favor, he had taken them more seriously, fuming and cursing, and turning his attention toward what—more importantly, *who*—could be the source of such-and-such a quote that had been so twisted and contorted and made him appear so much different than he really was.

But then, just a week before the election, had come the most crushing blow of all. A front page headline in the *Gazette* read: "Is Candidate's Wife Secretly Teaching Slaves To Read?"

Beaumont stormed up the stairs, paper in hand, to confront his wife in a wrath of scarcely suppressed fury.

"What do you know about this!" he demanded, throwing the paper into her lap where she sat. Stunned by his tone and expression, Lady Daphne took the paper, trembling, found the article with the help of his finger jabbing at it in her face, and proceeded to read the incriminating words:

> *Rumors have been circulating for some time in Spotsylvania County, Virginia, of a clandestine school for slaves. Now information has recently come to light linking such reports with the wife of a prominent landowner in the region of Dove's Landing.*
>
> *According to reliable sources, when asked about the rumors, Lady*

Daphne Beaumont was quoted as saying, "It is definitely true. They are being taught to read, how to buy things and use money."

Could the mysterious teacher of slaves be none other than the wife of senatorial candidate Denton Beaumont himself, whose plantation Oakbriar is located just two miles from the town where the rumors began, and who seems intimately acquainted with the details of the affair?

If so, it would seem to cast strange light on the candidate's role as county Commissioner, in which his chief duties entail tracking down runaway slaves and returning them to their rightful owners.

Has a case of conflict of interest and illegality surfaced just a week prior—

The words on the page before her eyes began to blur. Lady Daphne's face went ashen. She glanced up. Denton was staring straight into her face with a look more threatening than any she had ever seen.

"But . . . but . . . ," she stammered, ". . . it's not true, Denton."

"Of course it's not true!" he thundered. "It's an outright lie. And I want to know how it comes to have your name associated with it!"

A choking dryness in Lady Daphne's throat made an immediate response impossible. As she struggled to find something to say, her husband rescued her from her plight.

"It obviously originated at Greenwood," he growled. "The double-crossing hypocrite! All Davidson's talk about supporting my candidacy! I was a fool not to see something like this coming. And so close to the election when it's too late to head off the damage. How did Hoyt possibly manage such a story? What I want to know is how they come to have a quote from—"

He stopped, suddenly recalling the conversation around the dinner table from some time before.

"Of course!" he said to himself. "That day Veronica came home from Greenwood with all that tomfoolery about teaching slaves. Were they using her to bait you?"

"I . . . I don't know what you mean, Denton."

"Did you talk to anyone about Davidson's wife and all her nonsense with their darkies? Did you and Veronica ever discuss the matter again?"

"Uh . . . no, Denton," answered Lady Daphne.

"Where is Veronica?" said Beaumont, concluding that his wife could have had nothing to do with it. "I'll see if she knows anything."

He grabbed the newspaper back, turned, and strode from the room, leaving behind his trembling wife who realized that only a technicality in her answer to his questions had prevented a lie escaping her lips.

Beaumont succeeded in getting no more information out of Veronica than he had her mother, other than confirmation of the fact that she had heard straight from Seth that it was indeed Carolyn Davidson who was teaching Negroes to read. Beaumont's obsession with the untruth of the basic charge of the article kept him from looking further into the matter of the incriminating quote, which he took also for a fabrication. Lady Daphne was thus left as the only one who knew the full truth of the affair. And such she left it.

It turned out that Virginians wanted their elected officials neither too *harsh* toward slaves, for the sake of their national influence and reputation, nor too *lenient,* for the sake of proudly protecting the bastion of the South. Now reports were swirling that Beaumont might be both. Worse, he might have skeletons to hide in closets that pointed in both directions at once. Confusion and uncertainty about a candidate, especially concerning an emotionally charged issue like slavery and the treatment of Negroes, and just a week before the election, could prove lethal.

And such it did. It was far too late for most of Beaumont's denials even to reach the state's newspapers, much less turn the tide of his now plummeting support.

When news reached Oakbriar by special messenger two days after the election that the first results were going badly, and then the day following that Hoyt's reelection was assured, the blow had been devastating to the Beaumont household.

Lady Daphne hardly knew what to do with herself after that dreadful day. Ever since, she had guiltily guarded the terrible secret that she had blabbed to a stranger about her husband's temper toward their darkies and Carolyn Davidson and her slaves. The personal blame she carried added a horrifying sense of sickening dismay to the death of the Washington dream . . . the knowledge that *she* had been the cause of it.

"But, Mama," said Veronica one day, trying to cheer up her mother after she had bemoaned that they would never become part of the Washington social scene, "we shall just substitute a wedding for your Washington party. You can still invite all the same people. I will let you invite whomever you want!"

From where she sat, Lady Daphne glanced up at her daughter.

"Whose wedding, dear?" she said in a faraway voice.

"Mine, Mama!" giggled Veronica. "As soon as I can arrange it."

"That's nice, dear . . . of course," said her mother. In her mind, Veronica was still a little girl playing little girl games with nice little boys. She had no idea just how serious those games were about to become.

Forty-five

Scully Riggs had just finished loading a wagon full of supplies from the afternoon train when he glanced up to see Seth Davidson ride by in a buggy pulled by an auburn thoroughbred.

The thought that Veronica Beaumont was so friendly with the son of a nigger lover drove him into a frenzy of angry jealousy every time he saw one of the Davidsons.

Riggs stood up, straightened his back as he wiped the back of his hand across his sweating forehead. He stared after the buggy making its way down the street with Seth inside it like he thought he was the most important person in the world.

The high-and-mighty Davidsons . . . he hated every one of them!

The day would come, he thought, when he would make Veronica his one way or another . . . and get rid of Seth Davidson for good.

Seth rode on, pulled up in front of the Dove's Landing Bank, got down, and went inside.

Scully Riggs cinched up the ropes over the load, hitched up the team, then climbed aboard. Suddenly his pulse quickened. There were Veronica and her mother coming out of Baker's mercantile! He flapped the reins and yelled to his team.

"Hello, Miss Veronica," said Scully a minute later, reining the two workhorses to a noisy and dusty stop alongside the sidewalk.

"Oh, Scully . . . ," said Veronica, looking toward him blankly.

"Afternoon, ma'am," he added to Veronica's mother, then turned again to the object of his primary attention. "I'm just on my way out to Oakbriar with a delivery. Weren't scheduled till tomorrow, but the train come in a little early so I got it all loaded. Maybe I could call on you later, Miss Veronica, since I'll be out your way."

"I don't think so, Scully," said Veronica, disgusted at the very thought of Scully Riggs coming to call on her. "We're going to be in town for a while."

"How is your father, Scully?" asked Lady Daphne. "Why do I never see him anymore around Oakbriar?"

"Uh . . . he got fired, ma'am. I figured you knew."

"Oh, no . . . my goodness—I am sorry. What is he doing now?"

"He's working at the depot like me, ma'am. He don't care for the work much, but like he says, it's a job."

"Give him my regards, then, Scully."

"I will . . . thank you, ma'am. Bye, Miss Veronica."

Veronica said nothing. Scully whacked the leather against the backs of his team, and jostled off down the street.

⌒

"Why did you say that, Mother?" said Veronica when he was gone.

"What, dear?" asked Lady Daphne.

"All those questions about Scully's daddy. Who cares about him anyway? And to give him your regards—goodness, Mama . . . what if someone heard you!"

"I don't see what's wrong with it, dear," said Veronica's mother. "The man worked for us for years. He sat in my kitchen and ate with us many times."

"They're trash, Mama, that's what's wrong with it. You can't be too friendly to their kind—people will get the wrong idea."

They continued along the boardwalk.

"Oh, Mama, there's Seth!" Veronica suddenly exclaimed, then dashed off in the direction of the bank as quickly as femininity and her long dress would allow.

Seth paused momentarily outside the bank. Now that he had conducted his father's business, he had forgotten what it was his mother had asked him to do for her in town. Then he remembered and turned toward Auburn Flame. As he reached the buggy, he saw Veronica walking hurriedly toward him.

"Hello, Seth," she said.

"Hi, Veronica," Seth replied, glancing about behind her. "Are you in town alone?"

"No, Mother and I—"

Suddenly she stopped and put the back of her hand to her forehead. "Oh . . . I'm . . . I'm feeling faint!"

"It's probably the sun," said Seth, taking her arm as Veronica clutched and leaned against him. "Let me help you to my buggy. I'm sure you'll feel better in the shade."

"Oh . . . thank you, Seth," sighed Veronica weakly.

He led her to where the buggy sat, then helped her step up and inside. "Oh, yes . . . this is much better," she said, drawing in a breath. "I think I will recover now . . . how can I ever thank you, Seth . . . except I do think I feel a headache coming on," she added.

"Stay here as long as you like," he said. "I have another errand to do for my mother. Do you mind going along with me?"

"Not at all, Seth."

"Good," he said as he jumped up and sat down beside her. Moments later they were bounding along the street.

"There's your mother," said Seth, glancing up the street.

"Yes . . . I'll meet her later," replied Veronica. "Right now I just want to sit here in the shade."

Veronica gave a little wave as they passed. Lady Daphne's eyes followed Seth's buggy with a look of bewilderment. Where was Veronica off to now?

Five minutes later Seth came out of Baker's holding a small package. Veronica still sat in the Davidson buggy looking very pleased with herself. As Seth walked back to join her, he saw three of her friends walking away from the buggy tittering, casting glances back as they went and giggling amongst themselves. He climbed aboard.

"My headache is getting worse, Seth," said Veronica, her expression showing suffering. Again she put a hand to her forehead. "Would you mind terribly . . . I hate to ask, it's such an imposition, but Mother is going to be in town much too long, and . . . and would you mind taking me home?"

She paused and glanced into his eyes with a pained but innocent expression. "But of course," she added, "if you're too busy . . ."

"Oh, no . . . sure, I guess," said Seth. "I'm done with both the things my mother and father asked me to do. I don't suppose it will matter if I'm a little late getting back. What about your mother?"

"I told Sally to tell her I wasn't feeling well and that I was going to ask you to take me home."

Satisfied, Seth called to Auburn Flame and the buggy bounded into motion. As they approached her friends, Veronica scooted a little closer to her squire, gently slid her arm through his, and leaned her head against his shoulder. As they passed, she stole a glance at the three girls out of the corner of her eye and cast them a wily smile.

<hr>

As soon as they were out of town, Veronica's faintness disappeared. No more mention was made of her head, though she continued to sit close and lean against Seth as if for support. They arrived at Oakbriar some fifteen minutes later. Seth pulled the buggy in front of the house, jumped down, then turned and offered Veronica his hand. She took it daintily, then stepped to the ground. He led her up the porch to the front door.

"I, uh . . . guess you'll be all right now, huh?" he said, turning to walk back down the steps.

"Oh, Seth," said Veronica, "please don't go just yet. Mother is still in town and . . . I need someone—"

She glanced up into his face with big, sad, drooping eyes, then let them flutter a time or two as if she were fighting back tears.

"—to take care of me," she added.

She turned the latch and went inside, leaving the door open behind her and Seth standing where he was.

"Beruriah," he heard her call, "would you bring us two plain juleps—Seth and I will be on the back porch."

Tentatively Seth stepped inside. He saw Veronica's dress just disappearing from the other side of the entryway toward the kitchen. She paused and turned back.

"Come, Seth," she said. "Come through the house with me. We'll sit on the back porch."

Three minutes later they were seated on the porch swing, gently rocking back and forth.

"This is much better," said Veronica, giving her face a few swishes of her fan for effect. "I am starting to revive."

Beruriah appeared with their drinks. Veronica took them without thanks.

"I am so content when I am with you, Seth," said Veronica when the house slave had returned inside. She let out a long sigh, sipped at the edge of her glass. "You are so good to me. It is almost like all my dreams have come true. And see—my headache is gone already."

"Uh . . . good, that's great," mumbled Seth.

"Just think," Veronica went on dreamily, glancing toward him and batting her lashes, "when I am your wife I will be able to make you just as happy."

Seth's eyes opened wide in dumbfounded silence. For the first time, all Veronica's hints and playful suggestions he had allowed himself to ignore and laugh off as mere childish talk—she had talked about marrying him since they were children and he had ignored it just as long—culminated into the stark realization that she was serious! He had thought about it too, just like when Thomas overheard him talking to Demon, but it had never seemed quite so close . . . so real!

He took a nervous swallow of julep to keep from having to reply. Yet even as he did so, it could not be denied that Seth Davidson was under Veronica Beaumont's spell, and had been, without knowing it, for some time.

After a few more minutes of light chitchat, Seth excused himself,

over Veronica's objections, insisting that he had to get home with his
mother's package. The truth was, he needed some fresh air himself,
and a chance to think. Now *he* was the one getting a headache!

The ride home plunged Seth deep in thought. As soon as he arrived
back at Greenwood, his parents knew something was on his mind. For
the next two days he kept to himself and remained uncharacteristically
quiet.

The next day, Saturday, the same three friends who had seen Veronica
in town were visiting at Oakbriar. As always their talk centered around
young men. As was usually the case, eventually Veronica's love life
came to dominate the discussion as they clustered about her and tried
to fix her long black curls into one or another of the different styles
they had seen in a fashion magazine.

"You and Seth are simply always together!" giggled Sally O'Flarity,
daughter of a plantation owner south of town.

"How do you think I should wear it for my wedding?" said Veronica with serious expression.

"Veronica, you didn't tell us!" exclaimed the youngest of the group,
seventeen-year-old Brigitte McClellan who looked upon Veronica
Beaumont as the authority on everything about winning the affections
of a young man.

"Tell you what, silly?"

"That you and Seth are going to be married!"

"*Are* you really engaged?" asked Marta Perkins, daughter of the
manager of the Dove's Landing Bank.

"No, silly!" laughed Veronica. "Don't you think I would tell you if
I was?"

She cast a glance in the mirror, admiring the handiwork of her
friends and fiddling with a curl or two with her fingers. Slowly she
became serious.

"Well . . . ," she said after a minute or two, drawing her words out
teasingly, "I suppose you could say we are *sort of* engaged. I am easing

him into it," she added with a wicked smile, "I just haven't made his mind up yet."

"Well, you had better make sure before you lose him," said Marta.

"He wants to marry me, I know it."

"Why doesn't he ask you, then?" said Brigitte.

"He's too shy."

"You'd better make sure you nab him before he gets away," said Sally.

"What does she have to worry about?" said Brigitte. "Who else is Seth Davidson going to look twice at?"

"Maybe one of you!" laughed Veronica.

"Don't be silly. We would never steal him from you."

"He is so handsome," sighed Brigitte.

"I still think you ought to make up his mind for him as soon as you can," added Marta. "He will be rich when he inherits Greenwood. You have to do *something*, Veronica. You don't want to wind up as the wife of a shopkeeper or day worker or something horrible like that."

"You three worry about yourselves, not me," laughed Veronica. "I have no intention of being anything except the mistress of Greenwood—just so long as Seth's father doesn't go broke first . . . at least that's what my father says could happen."

"I hear they are making more money than ever," said Marta, "and that the slaves have to give them back all the money they pay them anyway."

"Where did you hear something like that?" asked Sally. "It can't possibly be true."

"From my father. He knows about everybody's money. He thinks I'm not interested, but I listen to every word he says."

"If half the things they say about Seth's father are true, he must be crazy," said Sally.

"I am going to marry Seth, not his father," laughed Veronica. "Within ten or fifteen years we will own Greenwood anyway. By then his father will have nothing more to do with it. As soon as we are married, I will make sure of that."

Forty-six

One Sunday afternoon in March, Seth wandered into the kitchen at Greenwood. Maribel was elsewhere in the house and Carolyn was opening a jar of peaches canned from the previous season when Seth sat down at the table. His father and brother were out at the stables working with a new horse they had just bought for Thomas.

Carolyn could always tell when Seth wanted to talk. Sometimes he was reluctant to share and at other times he seemed to want to tell her everything. This day proved to be the latter.

Carolyn had always been the listener with whom he had shared all his life's dreams and troubles, anxieties and ambitions, frustrations and triumphs as he grew from a boy, through his early teen years, and toward manhood. Her thoughts and suggestions were always sound, and now that Seth was indeed nearly a man, he relied more than ever on her common sense and wisdom.

To the outside world, Carolyn Davidson appeared a dutiful wife, perhaps too eager to put her husband on a pedestal, never engaging in the subtleties of critical innuendo that bound so many women of her station together in common exasperation with their men. Because she carried herself with a graceful deportment that did not find it necessary to speak her mind on every topic raised, as many women feel to be their solemn duty, there were many who never perceived the depths of intellectual currents in which Carolyn Davidson's brain swam.

But Seth recognized it. He had plumbed those depths through the years. In them he had discovered the wisdom that comes with years of prayerfully absorbing truth, along with obedience to that truth which—and *only* which—has the capacity to bring potential wisdom alive. For until it is enlivened by obedience, all knowledge and insight are but dead things, not yet living truth.

In short, Seth and his mother were friends of both heart and mind. He not only loved her, he trusted her, and was eager to receive from and be fed by her. He saw in her what she would always be in this life—his spiritual elder.

As they chatted casually, gradually he began to talk about Veronica. Soon, without the slightest embarrassment to confide such things to his mother, he told her everything that had happened two days before.

"I don't know, Mother," Seth said after a while, "sometimes I think I really like Veronica, and at other times she seems like she's about ten years older than me and from a different world altogether. I can hardly believe that I am actually older than she is. When we were children it was different. But somewhere along the way, she seemed to pass me by!"

The kitchen fell silent for a minute or two. At length Carolyn spoke up. Her tone was thoughtful, serious, her words carefully chosen. She knew her son's future was at stake.

"There are young women," she began, "who feel a sense of power when they can control young men, especially when they can control how those young men feel about them. But I would hardly call that passing you by. I would call it becoming skilled in the ways of the world."

"Is that why girls are always flirting, Mother?"

"One of the reasons, I suppose," smiled Carolyn. "But it's also simply from self-centeredness. Girls of character, who are thinking of others rather than themselves, don't flirt. It has always seemed to me that flirting is nothing but self-preoccupation."

"It always makes me uncomfortable," rejoined Seth. "Some boys like it. I suppose it makes them feel good to have a girl make over them. I wish Veronica would do less of that to me. She doesn't have to, so why does she do it? Was it that way when you were young too, Mother . . . I mean, girls flirting with young men and all that?"

"I suppose it was," replied Carolyn. "But I grew up in the west of the state in a church where girls were not allowed to be forward and immodest. It was very strict, so you didn't see as much of it. If my father had even once seen me making eyes at a boy, he would have taken a switch to my bottom and given me blisters. After I married your father and came to this part of the state where the Southern plantation influence is stronger, I was shocked at first. In this culture it seems that most young girls are trained from birth how to flutter their eyelids, and taught a hundred sneaky little ways to set traps for boys to make them notice them. I couldn't stand it at first."

"And now?"

"I still can't stand it, especially when I see it directed toward you and Thomas. But I have learned to laugh it off a little more than I once could. Everyone has to decide what kind of person one wants to develop relationships with—self-absorbed people or others-centered people. It's a dilemma we all have to resolve for ourselves—what kind of people will we surround ourselves with? If young men are attracted to young women who flirt at them, then I suppose they will get what they deserve. If young women are attracted to young men who make eyes at them, they too will get what they deserve."

A silence fell.

"If you and Dad didn't play these little games," said Seth at length, "how did you notice each other and get to know one another? How did you realize that you loved each other?"

"A long story, Seth," smiled Carolyn.

"Tell me."

"Are you sure you want to hear it?"

"Sure . . . yeah, I do."

⁓

"When your father walked into a small church in Norfolk where my father was supply preaching," Carolyn began, "I didn't notice him and

I don't think he noticed me. I was sitting up front playing the piano for the service, though my heart wasn't in it. I just stared at the hymnal and played the notes. I hardly looked up and heard nothing of my father's preaching during those months after I had returned from the West.

"It was the low point of both of our lives. I was a young widow. I felt abandoned by God and didn't care about anything. And you know about your father's first marriage—"

Seth nodded.

"Well, Richmond was still reeling from the series of blows it had dealt in his life. He wasn't a Christian and had had no spiritual background, except the few ideas people pick up here and·there, mostly wrong ideas, just because they think this is a Christian country founded on the puritan values of the pilgrims. But like most people, Richmond had no idea of the practicality of a personal walk of faith. Though I had been raised in the church, I really had no conception of such myself. I called myself a 'Christian' and my father had baptized me when I was ten. But I had no idea what it meant either, which is why my first husband's death shattered me so and left me spiritually desolate.

"For whatever reason, Richmond wandered into that little chapel one Sunday evening for the service, and sat down in the very back row. I don't know what he expected—"

"Was he searching for God?" asked Seth.

"Of course, in the way everyone is searching for God inside without knowing it. I don't think he was consciously saying, *My life is a mess. I'm lonely. I'm miserable. Aha . . . God must be the answer—I shall search for him and find happiness and peace!* It isn't usually so definite. Circumstances come in our lives, God makes his presence felt, sometimes subtly and at other times loudly and visibly, and then in one way or another we begin to look up to say, *I will arise and go to my Father.* But when Richmond walked into the chapel, I think he was just starving for some kind of human contact in the midst of his desolation. The singing of the opening hymn drew him as he walked along on the street outside. He paused, then came inside and sat down. God was drawing him, but he didn't know it at the time."

"Then what happened?"

"He sat through the service staring ahead blankly, and I sat through the service staring ahead blankly. After the closing hymn was done, and while my father stood outside greeting people as they filed out, I got up from the piano and began gathering the hymnals from the chairs to put them in the box where we kept them. It was what I did after every service as the church emptied out.

"So I picked them up one by one and carried a stack to the box to one side, then went back for another handful. When I was about half-way done I looked up, and there was a man sitting in the back row staring at me. I'd thought I was all alone and it startled me to see someone else there . . . and looking right at me."

Carolyn paused and smiled as she recalled the incident.

"'Would you like some help?' said the man, standing up and beginning to gather the hymnals from the last row of chairs.

"'Sure,' I said.

"And silently we finished stacking the hymnals in the box. Then I looked up and smiled and said, 'Thanks.'

"He smiled back. I expected him to leave. I turned to walk back to the piano to gather up my things. But when I turned around again, he was still there.

"'Do you mind if I ask you something?' he said.

"'No, go ahead,' I said.

"'Is that true, what the man said a little while ago . . . you know, about God knowing each one of us personally, really knowing us, and wanting the very best for us if we will just let him give it to us . . . is that really true? I've never heard someone say anything quite like that before. I mean I've been to church plenty of times, but I've never heard anyone make it sound so personal—just between us and God, if you know what I mean?'

"'To tell you the truth,' I answered with a shrug. 'I don't know if it's true. A year ago I would have said it was. Now I don't know.'

"He nodded, but didn't ask me what I meant. I guess he thought it was my own business. He had troubles of his own.

"'All right then . . . thanks,' he said, smiling at me in a sad way. I could tell he was disappointed in my answer. I wish I had something more positive to say. But I couldn't lie. Right then I didn't know if it was true. I didn't know if anything was true. But the poor man looked so dejected as he walked out of the church, I felt sorry for him. He met my father coming back inside. They shook hands and exchanged a few words, then the stranger walked out and away into the night."

"That doesn't sound anything like Dad," said Seth in surprise.

"You've got to remember, at the time he wasn't much older than you are now. He was only twenty-four and was miserable. Remember, he had recently returned from England where he'd been married and then went through a terrible divorce. His older brother had also recently died and he had come back to help your grandfather with Greenwood, something he had never planned to do. His whole life had been turned upside down, just as mine had. So I had nothing to offer by way of encouragement."

"It doesn't sound like the two of you were in very good shape," said Seth.

"We weren't," laughed Carolyn. "But God was at work."

"What happened next?" asked Seth.

"I didn't think too much of the incident all week, until the next Sunday evening. About halfway through the service I happened to glance out into the small congregation and there was the same man sitting there listening intently to my father. This time when the service was over, he didn't wait for me to pick up half the hymnals alone. As soon as most of the people were gone and I got up from the piano, he stood up from his chair and started collecting the books in back and carting them to the box. We met about at the middle of the church.

"'Thanks again!' I said, I suppose with a little more friendly expression than I'd been wearing the week before.

"'Don't mention it,' he replied, smiling too.

"'Have you figured out the answer to your dilemma?' I asked.

"'Not yet,' he said with a little laugh. 'But I'm still trying. Actually,' he went on, then sat down in one of the chairs in the front row like he was in no particular hurry to leave, 'I have been thinking about it a lot. That's why I came back, hoping I would hear something tonight to shed a little more light on it. But to tell you the truth—,' he added, lowering his voice and glancing back toward the door, 'I thought tonight was a snoozer. That was one of the most boring sermons I've ever heard!'

"I couldn't help laughing. I had been listening to my father three or four times a week since I had been old enough to keep quiet through the service. I had heard some of the same sermons a half dozen times. He didn't have to tell me that sometimes they could be boring!

"'But,' the man added, 'I have not been able to get out of my mind that phrase from last week, that God knows us, and will do his best for us . . . if we will let him. Do you realize what a remarkable thing that is? It would be the most revolutionary news ever in the history of the world. All through the centuries, men have expended such effort and expense, not to mention bloodshed, in the name of religion, supposedly to find the truth about God. Yet here is the simplest formula imaginable that would explain the entire human affair. That is why I must find out if it is true. Do you think this man knows, this pastor here? You work for him . . . at least you play his piano and pick up his hymnals, you must know something about the man—do you think he really believes what he said last week?'

"'Why don't you ask him?' I suggested.

"'I don't know,' he said. 'I suppose because I would rather hear it from you. I would rather find out from someone like myself, a regular person who had to discover God for himself, or herself,' he added with another smile. 'I would rather hear it from you than from a preacher who gets paid to believe it, if you know what I mean.'

"'But I already told you,' I said, 'I don't know. I'm struggling with the same thing myself—whether it's true or not.'

"'Yet here you are in church from week to week, playing the hymns and picking up the hymnals. That seems a mystery to me. Why are you here if you don't believe it?'

"'I suppose I would say because I have to be,' I said. 'I don't suppose I really have to be, it's just that I've got nowhere else to go.'

"'What do you mean?'

"'Actually, Reverend Peters is my father, and . . . I lost my husband about a year ago.'

"'Oh . . . I am very sorry.'

"'It happened suddenly and tragically, and threw me into such a depression that all I thought I had believed was suddenly gone. I haven't known what to believe ever since. I really had no where else to go but to come back here.'

"'I understand,' he nodded. 'My own life's circumstances of the past year have thrown me into a tailspin as well, though not a spiritual one. I have no spiritual beliefs to speak of. For months I have been wondering what is to become of me.'

"'That is exactly how I would describe it!' I said.

"'In my case,' he said, 'my wife turned suddenly into a different person than I had married . . .'

"A far-off sad look came into his eyes as he spoke as if he were reliving the pain.

"'Then I received papers of divorce and there was little I could do to contest it. I was shattered. And, still shattered, I walked into this little church a week ago and heard that startling statement about God.'

"We sat for a few minutes, just the two of us together in the front row of the church. Then I heard the door open and my father come back in.

"'By the way,' said the man beside me, 'my name is Richmond Davidson.'

"'I am Carolyn Peters,' I said, and we shook hands.

"And that," Carolyn added, smiling at her son, "is how I met your father."

"That's quite a story, Mother!" said Seth. "And then after that, did Dad get his question answered?"

"You know your father," laughed Carolyn. "What do you think!"

"I see what you mean!"

"We both got our questions answered. We started seeing more of one another, going on long walks and talking and talking and talking. We became friends . . . best friends. We shared our questions and doubts, and I shared with him about the fundamentals of the Christian faith. Just being around him helped my own faith gradually come back. I guess you would say we searched for God together. After a while we started praying together, asking God to reveal himself to us and help us in our search to know him. Eventually we fell in love with each other. I certainly never expected to marry a twenty-five-year-old divorcé, and your father never expected to marry a twenty-three-year-old widow, but that's what happened."

Carolyn sighed contentedly and smiled.

"Thanks for sharing all that," said Seth. "I never knew exactly how it came about before. That's the kind of romance I'd like to have—friendship. I think I should talk to Veronica about these kinds of things, don't you think? I need to know what she thinks about God and everything."

"I think that is a good idea."

"In fact, I think I will ride over and see her today or tomorrow."

Before Seth had the chance to do so, however, an unexpected turn suddenly came to Greenwood that would postpone his plans a few days.

Forty-seven

*I*t had been nine months since the Beaumont slave, fleeing for his life, had appeared on the doorstep of the Greenwood plantation house. Once getting him safely over the Pennsylvania border, with ten dollars in his pocket and an aging horse to get him wherever he needed to go, as nothing further had come of the incident, Richmond Davidson found it gradually receding in memory. Fortunately his neighbor had not come asking if they had seen his runaway, for that would have presented Richmond Davidson a very difficult ethical dilemma indeed.

Just when the episode seemed about to disappear into the forgetfulness of the past, suddenly it seemed that the runaway Nate Gibbons had sprouted human roots that had begun to grow more runaways just like himself.

Nancy Shaw appeared at the house one April morning not long after daylight. Richmond and Carolyn were in the parlor reading their Bibles and chatting as they enjoyed a second cup of coffee together. An urgent knock sounded on the front door. Maribel was in the kitchen and Moses still slept. Richmond rose to answer it.

"Please, Mister Dab'son, is da missus here?" said Nancy. "I gots to talk ter her."

Carolyn heard Nancy's voice from where she sat and detected an

unusual tone of urgency. Her first thought was that some crisis with
Phoebe's two-year-old little girl had arisen.

"Hello, Nancy," she said, approaching behind her husband. "What
is it?"

"I's got ter talk to you, Miz Dab'son," said Nancy. "You gots ter
come wif me."

"Right now, Nancy?"

"Yes'm. Dere's somefin' you gots ter see."

Carolyn glanced at Richmond, then disappeared for a moment,
returned with her shawl, and walked outside. Nancy led the way back
toward the Negro homes, walking so quickly Carolyn could hardly
keep up with her. None of Carolyn's questions succeeded in drawing
out answers that shed any further light on the reason for Nancy's early
morning visit.

When they arrived, Carolyn greeted five or ten others who were
gathered around the Shaw home, waiting. Nancy led her up the porch
and inside. There sat a black woman and three children whom Carolyn
had never set eyes on before. Malachi, Phoebe with her baby, Isaiah,
and Aaron all stood silently waiting to see what the mistress would say.
On the woman's face was an obvious expression of trepidation. She did
not know this mistress and had no idea what to expect. Despite reports
to the contrary which had driven her here, Carolyn was white, and this
was not like the many Quaker stations where she had found refuge in
her long journey. This was a plantation with a white mistress and a
feared white master. That was enough to cause any black to tremble
who was doing something she wasn't supposed to.

"Dis be what I wuz tellin' you 'bout, Miz Dab'son," said Nancy.
"Dey jes' 'peared 'bout an hour ago. I kep' 'em here till it wuz light
an' I knowed you an' da massa'd be awake. I din't want ter cum
sooner, though I di'nt know what to do wif her. Dey gots no place ter
go. She said dey come here cuz dey herd you help black folks what's in
trouble. I don' know what she mean by dat, Miz Dab'son, but dere
she be, big as life, wif dem three chilluns dat's somebody's gotter feed
cuz dey look like dey ain't been eatin' nun too much. I tol' 'em dey

cudn't stay here—we ain't got room fo' da likes er dem. But dey got no place ter go, Miz Dab'son."

Carolyn listened attentively, then turned to the black woman.

"What is your name, dear?" she asked.

"Lucindy, missus," she answered.

"Are these your children?"

"Yes'm."

"How old are you?"

"Can't rightly say, missus. I think sumfin' like twenty-five er sumwhere 'roun' dere."

"Are you from nearby here?"

"No, missus."

"Where are you from?"

"Souf Car'lina, missus."

"What are you doing so far from home?"

"My man, he got sol' an' da massa was gwine marry me ter sumbody else an' den a message dun cum dat my man had excaped ter da Norf an' den dey cum ter take us too."

"Who came?"

"Conductors, missus."

"Were you the master's slave, or are you a free woman?"

"No, I's jus' a slave, missus."

"How did you happen to come here?"

"I wuz on da railroad fo' mumfs an' mumfs an'—"

"What railroad? Did you have money to actually—"

"No, missus, da undergroun' railroad. Hit don' cost nufin'. But den I gots los' an' no conductor cum ter fin' us, an' we jes' follered da Norf Star, an' by'n by I ran into sum other coloreds, an' dere was talk 'bout a nigger man dat sumbody named Dab'son helped git ter da Norf . . . a slave man dat run away on account er his massa was gwine kill him. An' he run ter dat massa Dab'son an' he helped him."

"I told her dere weren't nuffin' like dat wif our massa," said Nancy. "I tol' her she dun got da wrong place effen she's lookin' fo' dat kind er help. Dere ain't been no nigger cumin' here gittin' rescued like dat. Tell her, Miz Dab'son."

Carolyn was still reeling from the young runaway mother's story and hardly heard what Nancy said afterward.

"How did you hear of this?" Carolyn asked, still looking at the girl. "Did someone on your plantation talk to the man?"

"No, missus. Nobody knowed him. I tol' you, hit wuz after I missed my train."

"If the man went North, how did you hear of it?"

"Dere wuz jes' talk, dat's all. I don' know where it cum from."

"What did you do then?"

"We hid out out an' kep' walkin' mostly at night, an' w'en we'd see a group er niggers out workin' in da fields wif no w'ite men, we'd go join 'em an' dey'd gib us sumfin' ter eat, an' after I heard dat talk an' den foun' out dat folks said we wuz in Virginia, I ax'd where be da Dab'son plantashun."

"And what did people say?" asked Carolyn.

"Everybody, dey'd herd da name an' dey'd point dis way er dat 'cause dey all knew which direction ter tell us ter go, an' den finally w'en we cum here dis lady, she say *dis* be da Dab'sons."

"Well, I suppose that's right because we are the Davidsons. I am Mrs. Davidson. But whether this is the place you are looking for, I don't know. You heard what Nancy said, that she knows about no runaway slave from here going to the North, do you, Nancy?"

"No, Miz Dab'son. I don' know what she cud be talkin' 'bout, 'ceptin' it be Joseph—he went Norf."

"You see, Lucindy," said Carolyn, "some of our own slaves have gone North. But we let them go. They weren't runaways."

"Dey said dese Dab'sons dun set dere slaves free," said the girl.

Nancy and Malachi looked at each other, and all the rest who had clustered around the open door also exchanged looks.

"You understand, Lucindy," said Carolyn, "that it is against the law for us to harbor a runaway slave?"

"Yes, missus. But I had ter try ter fin' my man. He ain' neber even seen his own baby. An' effen we's from da kings er da ol' books, I don' want ter hab ter tell her 'bout dose five ribers where we all cum from in da ol' days wifout my man."

At the words, Malachi's eyes shot wide. Had he just heard what he thought he'd heard!

He had completely forgotten about the five rivers and the kings and the old books. He hadn't remembered those tales his mother used to tell them since he was a boy, not even realizing that his own mother had also passed along the legend to his wife!

Unconsciously Malachi glanced down at his palm, not thinking what hearing the strange but familiar old words meant—that he and this pilgrim runaway who had landed on their doorstep came from the same ancient African roots.

"Well, Nancy," said Carolyn, interrupting Malachi's thoughts, "do you think you and Mary and the other women can give Lucindy and the children something to eat and drink and make them comfortable until I talk to Mr. Davidson and we decide what is to be done?"

"Yes, Miz Dab'son," replied Nancy. "We's do dat, all right."

Carolyn returned to the house with much to think about. Her husband took in the news with grave expression.

"I don't know that this bodes well, Carolyn," he said seriously. "That Negroes five hundred miles away are talking openly about us having given comfort and aid to a runaway slave, when our own blacks know nothing about it—a slave belonging, technically by law *still* belonging, to Denton Beaumont . . . if this escalates, it could land us in a lot of trouble."

Carolyn nodded.

"What did you tell them?" he asked.

"I told her nothing other than that I would talk to you. I was vague about the Gibbons affair and didn't address it. But how could anyone have found out, Richmond? No one knew but you and me and Seth. I'm pretty sure Thomas never knew."

"And Moses," added Richmond. "But I'm confident he said nothing."

"Maribel didn't even know," added Carolyn.

"There is only one other possibility," sighed her husband. "Gibbons himself must have had a loose tongue. In all the haste and secrecy of that night and my ride north with him, I never considered that he might tell people what had happened once he was safely over the border, nor the implications. I said nothing to him about remaining silent. It simply never occurred to me."

"Well, it's too late now. He must have talked. I sincerely hope Denton never hears of it. It would not be beyond him, Richmond, to bring charges against you."

"Let's don't add to our worries with concerns that aren't there. From my impression of such things, Negroes tend to be tight-lipped and talk only amongst themselves."

"I just hope it stays that way. What are we going to do, now that our own people know? They may not know about Gibbons, but they know about this girl and the things she's saying. If we help her, Richmond . . ."

Carolyn's voice trailed off. It was a difficult dilemma. They both knew well enough what happened to runaways who were returned. Denton's role as local commissioner made him the chief legal authority against runaways. They were made examples of, often ruthless examples, to discourage further rebellion—women as well as men.

"It would seem we need to seek the Lord's mind," mused Richmond thoughtfully. "And quickly. I know what I usually say about God moving slowly and the Spirit's never being in a hurry. But there are times when one does not have a great deal of time and when one must act decisively. The woman and her children are sitting down in the Shaws' house right now. So it would seem that this is one of those times. I know the Lord can reveal his will anywhere, but I fancy a prayerful walk in the arbor . . . care to join me?"

They rose and left the house together. Within three or four minutes they were walking in the depths of their garden sanctuary, to all appearances silent yet inwardly lifting their hearts to the throne of divine will where they attempted, as much as they were able, to place all decisions until a direction was made known to them.

They walked several of the pathways, tossed a few crumbs to the fish in the pond, smelled a few blossoms, wandered into the great oak and beech wood, encircled it, returned to the arbor, and then sat down on one of their favorite benches in its midst. Carolyn was the first to speak.

"Two things occur to me," she said. "The first is simply a reminder of the Lord's words, 'If any man asks of you . . . give.' It is a simple enough principle that has helped us in many situations before. I know the woman hasn't really *asked* anything of us as such. But we're not trying to find some way to wriggle out of the spirit of the command by trying to find a loophole in its letter. We are seeking the Lord's will. The fact is, she has come and, in a sense, placed herself in our hands. Is that how you see it?"

"Clearly," nodded her husband. "Like it or not, we are under divine orders concerning the woman—divine orders to help her, to do the best we can for her. What that *best* might be . . . that is the sticking point. Is it to *follow* the law of the land, which says we must return her to her rightful owner . . . or to *break* the law of the land? This would seem to be one of those infrequent moments that occasionally come in life when God's way may indeed be contrary to the law of the land. Even though we are told to obey the law of the land, when is it right to break that law?"

"As you always do," laughed Carolyn, "you take everything to its fullest possible implication."

"How else can we discern God's mind than to look at it from all angles and ask him to reveal the direction we are to go? But you're right," he laughed, "I was going on and on, and you said you had two things that came to you. I am anxious to hear the second."

Carolyn was silent a long while before answering his inquiring gaze.

"The second is simple enough," she said at length. "It too is one that has many times shown us light in some darkness. The dilemma is difficult, as you say—the Bible commands us to obey those that are in authority over us, yet there are times when to do so places such obedience in direct conflict with some other scriptural command. Is this one of those occasions? I don't know. Therefore, the only question I can think to ask that, in a sense, nullifies all other analysis and reduces every decision to its essence for anyone calling himself a Christian, is simply this: What would Jesus do if he were facing this situation that we are facing?"

Richmond nodded, almost as if he had been expecting his wife to say exactly what she had said. In truth, the two thought so much alike that even as she was speaking, the very same words had come to him.

"I know," Carolyn went on, "of the common tendency to dismiss such an inquiry with absurd explainings away such as, 'But Jesus was not married,' or, 'But Jesus would never have owned a plantation,' or, 'But Jesus never spoke to the social order of his time.' All I am saying is this: If Jesus could come right here and now, and sit on this bench, and he were facing *this* precise dilemma, with a woman lost and afraid down there in Nancy and Malachi's house, a slave woman with three innocent little children, a woman who is terrified and wondering what is to become of her, and if, with that woman to deal with, Jesus knew that a law existed in the land compelling the return of runaway slaves to their owners . . . were Jesus to face *this exact situation*, here and now . . . what would he do? What would Jesus really and truly *do*?"

Again it was silent a long while as husband and wife considered the question Carolyn had posed.

"Are you asking me what I think?" said Richmond at length.

"I suppose I am," replied Carolyn.

"He would be to her just like the father of the prodigal. He would open his arms to her as our Father will one day welcome all his lost, wayward, tired, and fearful children into the bosom of his home."

"But practically, Richmond . . . what would Jesus actually *do*—here and now, if he were in our shoes?"

Richmond thought a moment.

"Well then," he said, "I think he would take her in his arms, wipe away her tears, say, 'Fear not, my child, you are safe now. You have a Father who loves you, and I love you, and I will always do my best for you.' Then I think he would bathe her and bathe her children, put them in clean clothes, give them something to eat, and put them to bed between warm blankets where they could sleep and not be afraid.

After that," Richmond added with a smile, "I don't know what he would do."

Carolyn Davidson returned to the Shaw home about an hour after leaving the four vagabonds in Nancy's charge. She found the situation much as she had left it, though Nancy had gradually begun to warm a little more to her temporary guests.

"All right, Lucindy," said Carolyn, "I would like for you and your children to come with me. Here, hand me the youngest," she added, taking the sleeping little girl in her arms.

"Where's you takin' dem, Miz Dab'son?" asked Nancy.

"To the big house, Nancy," replied Carolyn. "Just for now."

Carolyn led the way with Lucindy following, each of her hands clutching the small trusting hands of her big-eyed silent youngsters.

Nancy watched them go. As much as she had wanted to get rid of her unwelcome visitor such a short while ago, the dear woman's old nature now came to the fore and feared what the master might do.

Nancy had never in her life seen the master be other than kind to anyone, white or black, horse or dog. Yet all too easily does the serpent tell us that he who planted the tree of life is evil. And how readily, against all evidence to the contrary, does the old Adam believe it. Thus, the race of men has still, after all this time, refused to look up and behold the face of its Father in every loving provision that is made. But Carolyn knew both the Father and the heart of her husband, whose earthly agent he was for the transmission of that truth to these simple people. Like the Son before her, she would take the hand of this little one, as that Son takes ours, and lead her to him whom she could trust to do his best for her. And Nancy, too, would find again, as she had so many times in the past, that her master would always choose the way of kindness.

"What are your children's' names, Lucindy?" asked Carolyn as soon as they were away from the Negro homes, where twenty sets of eyes were still staring at their backs wondering what "Massa Dab'son" would do.

"Broan an' Rebecca an' Calebia," she answered.

"They are lovely," said Carolyn. "Did you give them their names?"

"Yes'm. What gwine happen ter me, missus?"

"I don't know, Lucindy. Right now I am taking you to meet Mr. Davidson."

"Is he gwine whip me—," began Lucindy, trembling.

"He whips no one, Lucindy. He is a good man."

"But he's da massa."

"Yes he is. He is the owner of this plantation."

"He must be sum fearsum, den."

Carolyn could not help chuckling. "Why would you say that, Lucindy? My husband is like a good father to his people, not a cruel master."

The black woman stiffened. Images of her own cruel father filled Lucindy's mind to such an extent that she could scarcely fathom what Carolyn was talking about—using the words *good* and *father* to describe the same person. "You sez he's like . . . a *father?*" she said.

"Yes—he *is* a father," smiled Carolyn.

"Den he can't be good."

Carolyn saw terror in the poor girl's eyes at the thought of encountering what to her mind was an unknown terror, as God must seem to those who do not know his true character. She looked deeply into Lucindy's eyes.

"Do you think I would whip you, Lucindy?" she asked.

"Oh, no, missus. You's 'bout as nice as you cud be. You an' dose ladies called Frien's is 'bout da nicest w'ite ladies I's dun eber met."

"What if I was to tell you that Mr. Davidson was just as kind as I am?"

"I don' see how dat cud be, missus."

"Why?"

"Cuz he's a man . . . a w'ite man. He's da massa, an' my own father whupped anyone who wuz bad."

"Well, you shall find Mr. Davidson just as I say, Lucindy, and more besides."

So thoroughly foreign, however, was anything in Lucindy's experience resembling a loving father that she could not grasp the existence of a loving Fatherhood at the heart of the universe. Despite all Carolyn had told her, she still trembled as they walked up the steps, into the veranda, and through the front door into the house. She had never been inside a plantation house in her life. Though some might have taken one look inside such a lavish home and concluded that they had been given a glimpse of heaven itself, poor Lucindy was still terrified of the awful presence who dwelt within.

But like Lucindy, many will one day enter that Presence to discover something quite different from the fearsome Almighty whom they envision anxious to wield bolts of vengeance against them. Instead, on that day they will indeed meet a Father—and what a Father . . . the Father of Jesus Christ himself!

A tall man came from somewhere within to greet them. Contrary to every expectation of fierce judgment, he approached with wide smile and outstretched arms.

"Is this Lucindy?" he said in a great welcoming voice.

"This is Lucindy, Richmond—Lucindy, I would like you to meet Mr. Davidson. And these three dears with her are Broan and Rebecca and Calebia."

Davidson stooped down and gazed first into the little boy's face.

"Hello, Broan," he said. "How old are you?"

"Almost seven?" answered the boy timidly.

"Well, that is a fine age. And how about you, Rebecca . . . how old are you?"

"She's five," said the boy.

"I see," said Richmond. "What do you think, Rebecca . . . is Broan right? Is that what you are?"

"Yes'suh," said the girl shyly, then hid her face in her mother's dress.

Davidson stood and once again faced the mother. "You seem to have a fine young son and daughter, Lucindy. I want to welcome you all to my home."

He opened his arms again, and, notwithstanding her hesitation, stretched them around Lucindy's thin shoulders and bony frame and embraced her warmly. When he stepped back, there were tears of wonder in her eyes. What kind of man was this who would treat slaves like his own children!

He took a clean white handkerchief from his pocket and handed it to her. She dabbed her eyes with it. Then he gazed earnestly into her eyes.

Carolyn handed him the youngster, who was coming awake. He took the child in his arms. "And this seems like a fine young daughter," he said, "who will soon be as big as her sister!"

"I want you to try not to be afraid, Lucindy, my child," he went on. "You and your little ones are safe now. You have a Father in heaven who loves you, and because we are his, we love you too and we will try to do our best for you. Now while Carolyn was fetching you, I have prepared a room for you, with clean white sheets and a white robe for you to wear. I prepared it just for you, so you mustn't be afraid or nervous. While you are with us, this will be your room. And Maribel has been warming water on the stove and pouring out a nice hot bath and finding some clean clothes for your son and daughter. After Carolyn and Maribel have helped you bathe, we will give you something to eat and then put you to bed between warm blankets where you will be able to sleep and not be afraid."

The morning was still relatively early and neither Seth nor Thomas had yet made an appearance. As it was, Thomas was the first to walk into the breakfast room. He found Maribel bustling about and his parents seated at the table with four coloreds he had never seen before.

"What are they doing here?" he asked.

"They are traveling, Thomas," answered his mother. "They came to the Shaws sometime during the night. We thought they would be better off here."

"Why here? Why can't the Shaws keep them?"

"We thought this was best. But we have to keep anyone from knowing. People have different ideas about blacks, you know, and it could be unpleasant for all of us if word of it spread. Would you like some breakfast?"

"No . . . I'll get something to eat later." He turned and left the room.

Ten or fifteen minutes later, Seth appeared.

"Good morning, Mother . . . hi, Father," he said. "Hi, Maribel."

"Massa Seth, you want sum eggs an' hot biscuits?"

"Sure, Maribel, that'd be great." He sat down next to his father.

"Seth," said Richmond, "I would like you to meet Lucindy and Broan and Rebecca, and Lucindy's littlest one who is Calebia. Lucindy, this is our son Seth."

"Hi," said Seth, pouring himself out a tall glass of milk, giving no appearance to thinking anything out of the ordinary at all in seeing a kitchen full of blacks.

The first order of business for the day, immediately after breakfast, was to talk to their black people. Richmond had gone down earlier, told Malachi that he and Mrs. Davidson would be back around ten o'clock to talk to all the adults about the runaway woman and her children. He asked him to gather everyone by the stream where Mrs. Davidson held her meetings. They could take the morning off from work to be there.

A little before ten, Carolyn and Richmond left the house for the five-minute walk to the cluster of cottages where their people lived and on to the small clearing by the stream. They found them all seated on the ground and waiting. Richmond walked to the front of them.

"Good morning," he said. "As you know, something has come about that concerns us all—the appearance of Lucindy and her three children. Where and how she heard that she could find refuge here, none of us knows. It doesn't matter now. The fact is, she is here. We have to decide what to do.

"You all know that it is against the law to harbor a runaway slave.
The mere fact that Lucindy and the children are up in the big house
right now, sound asleep after a nice breakfast, is enough to put me in jail
if the wrong people heard about it and decided to have me arrested."

At the word *jail*, the eyes of at least half of those black faces listening grew to twice their original size.

"My concern is not so much for my own safety," Richmond went
on, "though I am not eager at the prospect of going to jail, but my
main concern is for you. If I am arrested, things could go very badly
here. There are many who are still angry with us for giving you your
freedom. They could take Greenwood away and send you all away
too, and perhaps even take away your papers of freedom.

"The reason I am telling you this is a simple one: No one else must
know about Lucindy and her children. No one at all outside Greenwood. That is going to be difficult. You see other blacks and slaves in
town and at the church meetings. But you must not breathe a word of
this. One chance comment, and rumors could spread, and the sheriff
could ride in here and take me away. Some rumors about our plantation and your freedom have apparently already been spreading. You
must all be very, very careful. I repeat, no one must ever know about
Lucindy and her children."

He paused to allow his words to sink in.

"Do you all understand?" he added.

In unison, some twenty-five heads nodded vigorously and silently
up and down.

"I want you parents to talk to your children and make sure they
understand. Those you are not sure you can trust to keep their
mouths shut, do not take them to town and do not take them to the
meetings until they forget about it. If we are not careful, everything
we have begun here together, and the good life we all have together,
could be destroyed."

"We understan', Mister Dab'son," said Malachi. "You kin count on
us. We's say nuthin'. Coloreds knows how ter keep dere moufs shut
w'en dey hab to. But what's you gwine do wif da girl, Mister Dab'son?
You gwine sen' her back where she cum from?"

"I don't know yet, Malachi," sighed Richmond. "Mrs. Davidson and I will have to talk about it and pray about it and see what God wants us to do. But I do not think we will send her back. We will not knowingly turn away one who comes to us for refuge."

Forty-eight

When Lucindy Eaton awoke the morning following her arrival at Greenwood she wondered if she was dreaming. In nine months of travel she had never felt the luxury of such a bed. The kindness and gentleness with which she had been treated the previous day was as foreign to her as if she had somehow passed into another country altogether.

She stretched sleepily, relishing the pure pleasure of the soft clean bed. She felt relaxed all the way down to her bones. Then suddenly she remembered—she was in a white man's house, and this was a white man's bed. A renewal of terror seized her.

Hurriedly she glanced about. Where were her children?

Laughter and a few happy shouts met her ear from another room, and a second or two later Broan and Rebecca scampered in. They were followed by two of the ministering angels from her dream, a big black woman carrying Calebia, and a white lady whose face was smiling radiantly at her.

"Good morning, Lucindy," she said. "Did you sleep well?"

"Yes'm. I ain't neber slep' in no bed like dis afore."

"Well you shall sleep in it as long as you like," said Carolyn. "While you are here, it will be your very own bed."

The arrival of the Davidsons' unexpected guests temporarily pushed Seth's resolve to talk to Veronica to the back of his mind. It was therefore not until the afternoon of Lucindy's second day at Greenwood that Seth saddled Auburn Flame and rode toward Oakbriar.

Elias Slade had been watching Veronica Beaumont's none too subtle machinations to lure Seth Davidson into the center of her web with almost an inward grin of mocking humor. He knew the Davidson kid. He had spent enough time at Greenwood working under him to know that he was too soft for a girl like Veronica. He was already in over his head, and didn't even know it.

But watching Veronica play her game and spin her webs also aroused Slade's passion. She was a beautiful and well-proportioned girl, whatever the color of her skin. The fact that she was the daughter of a wealthy plantation owner, and thus forbidden to a black man like him, only made her all the more desirable.

Added to that was the fact that every female slave at Oakbriar between ten and forty was terrified of Slade and kept well clear of him. And further, after what had happened at Greenwood, their fathers, husbands, and brothers were all watching out for them vigilantly—for, if they would not willingly incur a whipping for crossing Slade while working in the fields, any one of them would fight to the death to protect the honor of their girls and women against such a beast.

Thinking of Seth and the conversation with the girls she had been with a few days earlier, Veronica wandered out of the house and aimlessly made her way in the direction of her mother's garden, passed leisurely through it and continued on. She had no particular destination in mind as she dreamed lazily how she might be able to awaken a little more of the beast in Seth and help to make up his mind for him, as she had said to Sally, Marta, and Brigitte.

She rounded the corner of the barn, now considering a walk beside the creek, even perhaps dabbing her toes in it, for the day was warm. Suddenly she nearly bumped headlong into the mammoth form of Elias Slade, standing in the shadow of the building.

"Oh!" she said, startled, "excuse me, Elias . . . I didn't see you standing there."

"No harm dun, Miz Bowmont."

Veronica paused and glanced up into the big man's face. She saw well enough that he was looking down at her chest. But rather than turn away, she enjoyed the knowledge that men stared at her. Nothing gave her a greater thrill than to stir a man's passion. It was part of the excitement. Strange as it might be to use the word in connection with one like Veronica Beaumont, in her own way she was actually a little naive. She had never been with a man and had no intention of letting her games go that far. It was only that to her—a *game* . . . a game of power, of control . . . of juvenile feminine seduction. She had been at it so long, making people take notice of her, that she almost couldn't help herself. But she had never encountered one like Elias Slade before. , . .

She blinked demurely. "What are you looking at, Elias?" she said with a suggestive smile.

"Nuthin', Miz Bowmont."

"Come now, Elias," she teased, "just because you're colored doesn't mean you can't admit that you think I'm pretty."

Slowly she lifted her hand and touched one of his arms with the tip of her index finger, then let it move up and down toward his rippling biceps where the sleeves of his blue work shirt were rolled. Taking a step closer to him, feeling the heat of fear rising from her body and spreading the intoxicating aroma of her perfume, she continued to let her finger play across the outline of his muscles, while Slade stood still as a statue.

"You're a strong man, Elias," she purred.

She let her voice grow soft, stringing out the words slowly. By now she had come to sense that what she was doing was dangerous, even recognized that she was playing with fire. But she couldn't stop herself. It was too delicious to toy with a man's affections. She had been doing it since before she could remember, in childhood ways, and now in womanly ways. Unfortunately, she hardly saw the difference. She had never yet been in a situation she couldn't handle. It never occurred to her that she would not be able to control one so far beneath her. In this present case, however, she underestimated how hot the fire inside a man like Slade burned, or how suddenly it could explode into flame.

Seth Davidson had ridden into the precincts of Oakbriar on the opposite side of the house about the same time Veronica had disappeared
around the barn. He was talking to Jarvis at the front door just about
the time Veronica's treacherous game of cat and mouse turned ugly,
and in the midst of her catty stratagems she suddenly found herself the
prey.

"Stop . . . stop it right now, Elias!" she yelled. "Don't you dare . . .
Elias—"

But there was no one to hear her cries. Elias had made sure of that.

"I don't know, Massa Dav'son," Jarvis was saying back at the house.
"Las' time I saw her, she lef' out da back door. She may hab been
goin' fo' a walk down by da garden."

"You don't mind if I just walk around back and take a look, do
you," said Seth, "and see if I can find her?"

"No, suh, Massa Dav'son. I's sure dat be jes' fine."

A minute or two later, Seth had been through the garden and was
walking in the direction of the barn. As he glanced about he wondered
where everyone was.

He heard a muffled scream. He stopped and listened, then sprinted
for the door of the barn.

Running inside, at first all was darkness. Again came a scream, then
another.

"Help . . . someone . . . get off—you big brute! Help—"

A vicious slap sounded, followed by a scream of pain. Seth knew it
was Veronica.

He groped forward. After coming in hurriedly from the sunshine,
he was hardly able to see his way in the dark barn. He bumped into a
post and tripped over a bale of hay.

"Veronica!" he called as he picked himself up. "Veronica . . . is that
you!"

"Seth!" she cried. "Seth . . . please, help me!"

The light from an upper window illuminated a corner where a stack of bales sat. As his eyes became accustomed to the dim light and he stumbled his way further inside, Seth saw two figures in the dim light.

"Seth—" screamed Veronica, struggling to get up and run to him. Another blow knocked her back to the floor.

By now Seth could see enough to make out what was going on. He didn't recognize Slade, nor even realize at first that Veronica's assailant was black. But the color of skin didn't change what had to be done. He ran forward and hurled himself with all his might toward whomever it was bent over trying to keep Veronica down.

He might as well have thrown himself against the trunk of an oak for all the effect of his attack. But at least he succeeded in knocking Slade off his balance, momentarily shoving him away from Veronica. She jumped to her feet and ran to the opposite side of the barn.

"Seth . . . Seth, I'm safe!" she cried. "Come on . . . let's get out of here!"

Seth regained his feet, just as Slade turned around and began to pick himself up. But Seth did not flee. He would not leave until Veronica was outside.

"Go, Veronica," he said. "Get out of here. Go find your father." As he spoke, from where Slade climbed to one knee, the light from the window fell on Seth's form as he stood blocking the way to Veronica like an avenging angel.

"So, hit's you, young Dab'son," said Slade angrily. "Dis ain't none ob yo' affair."

"Somebody's got to stop you, Slade. This is Miss Beaumont—have you gone crazy . . . trying to hurt *her*! What are you thinking, man?"

"What I dun's my own biz'nus. Hit's between me an' her. Now back away, w'ite boy, effen you don't want me ter hurt you real bad."

Seth's feet did not budge.

"Get out of here, Veronica!" he shouted again behind him. "Slade, you stay where you are till she's gone."

By now Veronica was paralyzed with fear, not for herself but for Seth. Not only had Elias Slade's passions been aroused, now so was his fury. He rose and took a menacing step toward Seth, then suddenly flew at him and struck wildly, intending to render him senseless in a single blow.

But in the dim light and uneven footing he was not at his best. Nor did he quite realize how nimble Seth was on his feet and how swift were his reflexes. Seth easily sidestepped the charge, eluding Slade's blow with a quick twist of his torso. At the same moment his coiled arm loosed a lightning punch. His fist struck just below Slade's left eye and immediately drew blood. Slade staggered, enraged yet further, and fell to one knee as shafts of shooting light exploded through his eyes.

By now Veronica saw how extreme the danger to Seth was likely to become. Having suffered no injuries except to her smugness and her dress, she tore from the barn, then picked up the hem of her dress and sprinted for the house, in terror for what might be Seth's fate if she did not get help. She only prayed Jarvis knew where her father was this afternoon!

Inside the barn, Slade shook his head to clear his brain, for the blow had stunned him in more ways than one. Until fifteen seconds ago, no fist of man or boy had ever succeeded in making clean contact with his face. The sensation of being felled in such a manner, and by a scrawny weakling of a white boy, was a new one. He quickly righted himself and turned again to face his foe. He came on more warily this time, like an enraged bear. Alongside his massive bulk, Seth was but a child, but apparently one whose reflexes Slade had underestimated.

The two circled one another cautiously, fists raised, muscles coiled and awaiting opportunity. But Slade had too long relied on his sheer bulk and strength to be able to learn new habits within the span of a single fight. Again he charged, and yet again Seth's quick-shifting feet and two twists of his waist left Slade grabbing at air. This time both Seth's fists found their marks in rapid succession, to the side of the big man's nose and directly into the center of his right cheek. With these blows, Slade kept his feet yet now tasted his own blood. He spun around again like a vicious wild man at last unchained.

He did not wait, but charged again with a roar of rage. This time he was able to lay a hand on an outlying portion of Seth's clothing. It was all he needed. Seth's only hope lay in footwork, and in keeping space between himself and his adversary. But Seth's hundred and seventy pounds were no match for Slade's vastly superior strength in a close fight where Seth could no longer loose himself from the huge man's grasp.

He would surely have been killed and Slade hung by a local mob had not the deafening roar of a shotgun blast a minute later interrupted the beating before it became an execution.

Slade stopped the pummeling and turned. There stood his employer, smoke rising from the barrel of the rifle in his hand, the look of unchecked wrath on his face. The two men stood staring at each other in silence.

"My daughter says you tried to rape her?" said Beaumont in suppressed wrath.

"She dun start it, suh, Mister Bowmont," said Slade, unhumbled but soft spoken.

"What happened?"

"I's mindin' my own bis'nuz, Mister Bowmont. I come back for da tools like you tol' me. She come roun' da barn an' started speakin' ter me. She started feeling' my arms an' getting' real close an' talkin' 'bout her brests an' like dat, like no wumun oughter do, like she wuz tryin' ter git ter me, not me ter her."

Beaumont listened. Though it was hard for him to believe his daughter had been that forward, he had seen how she acted around men before. Was his daughter a complete nitwit, trying her ploys on someone like Slade?

"Then what?" he said.

"I dun los' my head, Mister Bowmont. She got me all worked up. How's I ter know she wuz just funnin' an' meant nuthin' by it. How's a man ter know when a wumun duz dat ter him dat she don' mean it?"

Beaumont revolved the thing in his mind another minute longer.

"All right, Slade," he said at length. "You might be right, I can't know for sure. They say most mules get three chances. But my slaves have never been as lucky as my mules because I can't trust them as far. But since you're not a slave, I figure even a mule-ugly nigger like you gets one chance. You just had yours. When I came in here I intended to empty both these shells into your belly. I may live to regret not doing so. But if you ever so much as lay one finger on my daughter again . . . I *will* kill you. Now get out of here."

Even Elias Slade, who feared no man alive, knew that he was lucky to still be breathing and not have a shotgun hole through his chest. He had let the young vixen get to him. But though the Davidson kid just may have saved his life by keeping it from going too far, he would get revenge on him somehow. No one struck Elias Slade in the face and got away with it.

He slunk from the barn, doing his best to hide his own injuries, and disappeared.

Meanwhile, Beaumont waited until the big black man was gone, then walked forward and looked down at the unconscious form lying in the straw on the wood floor. With one foot he shoved at the limp piece of broken humanity and turned it over. It was Seth Davidson, all right, just like his daughter said—face bloodied, clothes ripped, and to appearances one arm broken between the wrist and elbow. He had hoped that maybe somehow it wouldn't be him after all.

He stared down at Seth's face a moment more, shuddered at the sight, then turned and left the barn, instructing one of his men standing outside to go into town for the doctor, adding softly, "But take your time about it."

Beaumont did not see Elias Slade for the rest of the day. But there could be no denying that the big black man occupied more of his thoughts even than did his daughter. The situation was delicate. By all rights, Slade should hang for what he had done. One word and his men would round Slade up and overpower him. If they could find a limb strong enough to hold him, by nightfall Slade might be hanging dead from some nearby oak.

But it wasn't every day someone of Slade's strength and usefulness came along. The man's power went beyond mere physical strength. He was intimidating, and Beaumont had rather enjoyed the added dimension that Slade's presence lent to his own authority and rule. On the other hand, Slade knew that his master had grown dependent

on him. He carried himself with just a little *too* much confidence that
was unseemly for a black. Maybe this incident was just what he
needed to keep Slade in his place. If the man ever stepped out of line,
he would be able to hang him without recrimination.

But if he did not hang him immediately, Beaumont reflected, he
would have to come up with some plausible explanation that would
satisfy the community and not cast he himself in an unfavorable light
for being too lenient with the man. The one result he could *not* afford
was to look weak himself. That should be easily enough managed, he
thought. Whatever Veronica told people, he would add his own
embellishment as justification for not having shot Slade on the spot.
As for the Davidson kid, he doubted he would make much trouble.
He would tell his men what had happened in his own way, do his best
to keep it quiet and not make too much of it, and then make sure his
own version of events was the one that got around.

The fact was, Beaumont admitted to himself in a jumble of mixed
but selfish motives, he didn't want to get rid of Slade. He would have
one of the men give the brute a dozen lashes, and that, along with
sketchy reports of the affair, ought to meet the case when rumors of
the fight began to circulate, as they surely would.

There was, of course, the matter of his daughter's honor to
consider. But his qualms in that direction did not trouble him for
long. Veronica's honor, he thought, was well able to take care of itself.

Forty-nine

If Seth Davidson thought going to see Veronica after talking with his mother would ease his uncertainty, he was badly mistaken. Not only had he not had the opportunity to speak with her, he had been pummeled within an inch of his life instead. Now in Veronica's eyes he was not just a good-looking neighbor boy whom she had had her eyes on since childhood, but her brave squire, her knight in shining armor. Though her father would gladly have made less of the affair, for it made him look none too good for keeping Slade on after it, Veronica made sure the entire county heard of it and knew what a hero Seth Davidson was. The subtle effect was to produce within Seth a sense of protective duty toward Veronica. Even if at first the only means by which he felt it was from the way people looked at him, it could not help but invisibly draw the strings between him and Veronica a little tighter than they had been.

The doctor set Seth's arm, wrapped his chest tightly, and gave him powders to take in water for the pain of his facial wounds and cracked ribs. Otherwise, however, he pronounced him as healthy and fit as ever. With Seth at home in bed to recover under his mother's and Maribel's watchful care, as life resumed normalcy Veronica slowly realized that the terrifying episode may just have given her what she needed, as she put it, to "help Seth make up his mind," or, failing that, to make it up for him. In her heart, she knew well and good that the whole thing had been her fault. But like her kind generally, she was not humbled by her blunder and miscalculation so much as determined not to make the same mistake again.

Meanwhile, the sordid details of the little *tête-à-tête* behind the barn would remain between her and Elias Slade. What did anything he might say matter anyway? He was black, and she had the rip in her dress to prove that it was his fault. In the meantime, as long as Seth was all right, she would use the incident to her benefit.

What was needed, of course, was for Seth to get down to business with one of those man-to-man talks with her father. Veronica knew well enough that Seth was still not ready to initiate the fateful interview. She knew equally well, however indebted he might be to Seth in the matter of the Elias Slade attack, that the bad place would freeze over, as she had heard some boys say, before her father would come crawling to Seth to welcome him into the Beaumont fold.

She would have to give things a little shove, encourage them along, so that the momentum of events carried forward all concerned toward the inevitable conclusion.

Men sometimes needed help with these things.

Accordingly, one day about a week after the ugly incident in the barn, by which time Seth was able to get up and around, though with his arm in a sling and his chest still wrapped, Veronica appeared at Greenwood in her father's fanciest buggy.

"Hello, Veronica," said Richmond, the first to greet her as the wheels of the carriage crunched to a stop at the entryway in front of the house. "Here . . . let me help you down."

She was dressed in more subdued colors than usual, and, if he was not mistaken, wearing one of her mother's hats. The overall effect was to make her look older than her nineteen years. Almost matronly.

"I came to see Seth, Mr. Davidson," she said as he led her to the front door. "I thought he might like some fresh air and would enjoy a ride."

"I see," nodded Richmond as he led her inside. "I suppose that might be a good idea—he is about to go crazy being cooped up all day long."

"Seth . . . you have a visitor," he said as they entered the house.

The animation on Seth's face to see her gave Veronica all the more hope for her little scheme. He nearly bounded out of the chair at the suggestion of a ride.

"That sounds terrific!" he said. "I can hardly stand the sight of these four walls much longer. Mother, would you get me another shirt and help me get my boots on?"

A few minutes later, Richmond Davidson was helping his son up into the buggy.

"You take good care of him now, Veronica," he said. "If I don't see you when you come back, please greet your father for me."

She nodded and smiled. "I will, Mr. Davidson," she replied, to the first of his requests at least. As for the second, she had no intention of doing any such thing. This was not a time she wanted to rouse her father's ill feelings toward anyone with the name Davidson. This was a time to let the dead past bury itself, or whatever the expression was. Let him carry his own greetings to whomever he wanted, not expect her to do it for him.

She glanced toward Seth and handed him the reins.

"You take these, Seth," she said. "It was all I could do to get this stupid horse here."

"There's nothing to it," said Seth, taking the reins with his free hand. "Look," he added with a laugh, "I can do it with one hand! Grey Pride knows the way, you just have to guide him once in a while."

"Why do you call him that?"

"That's his name," laughed Seth.

"How do you know?"

"I know all your father's horses by name."

"My father's horses have names too, just like you said yours do!"

"Of course . . . well, not all of them do, just the riding and buggy horses. But we give all our horses names, even the old plough horses.

Gid'up!" he called, flicking the reins, and they bounded into motion and down the winding drive.

When they reached town, however, Veronica leaned over and took hold of the leather straps again. "I think I can try it again," she said, making sure people saw her at the helm as they made their way through the middle of town. "I just need to make a stop at Mrs. Baker's store . . . you don't mind, do you?"

"No . . . sure," said Seth.

She pulled back on the reins a little too quickly and they jerked to a stop in front of the big sign that read "Dry Goods and Mercantile."

"Gently," laughed Seth. "All you need to do is ease back. He'll do the rest."

Veronica glanced about, then stepped down. "Now you wait right here, Seth, dear," she said as two or three passersby glanced their way from the boardwalk. "I will be right back."

The curious ladies continued on with inquisitive expressions on their faces, speaking in hushed tones.

"That's the Davidson boy, isn't it?"

"Yes . . . heard what happened to him. . . . "

". . . dreadful . . . arm looks badly hurt . . . can't believe her father kept him on. . . . "

"Are he and the Beaumont girl . . ."

They passed around a corner and out of sight. Veronica smiled to herself and went inside. As the door closed behind her she proceeded to move about, aimlessly looking at this and that, waiting for Mrs. Baker's curiosity to mount. Out of the corner of her eye, Veronica saw the proprietress move toward the window and glance out.

"Is that Seth Davidson in your carriage there, Veronica, my dear?" she finally asked.

"Oh, yes," replied Veronica nonchalantly. "He is recuperating, you know. We thought he needed to get out, his mother and I. So Seth and I are doing a few errands together."

She paused and smiled. "Dear Mrs. Davidson . . . ," she said, "she is so sweet, why she treats me . . . almost like a daughter."

Veronica stopped abruptly and covered her mouth.

"Oops, I didn't mean to say that!" she said. "Pretend you never heard a word, Mrs. Baker. Promise me you will say nothing."

The storekeeper nodded her head vigorously. But her ears were burning.

When they left town thirty or forty minutes later, after a few more trivial stops, Veronica was pleased with the day's outing. They had been seen together by enough of the town's busybodies and gossips in whose hearing she had dropped enough tantalizing tidbits to insure that tongues were set wagging.

Now all she had to do was wait, and continue to play her dutiful, responsible, concerned, supportive, wifely role.

Thereafter, Veronica took to visiting Seth at Greenwood almost every day, making sure she was seen as she passed through town, continuing to dress matronly and carrying herself with grave expression, always stopping in at some store or another for a few idle but carefully chosen words here, a few additional hints there, all designed to convey the impression of an ever closer knot being slowly and invisibly tied between the young people of the two plantations which lay to the west and to the east of town.

She made sure, as the whispers began to circulate, that no thread could be traced to her. She wanted Seth to get wind of them, and then, with a shy smile of pleasure, she would blushingly profess herself as surprised by them as he.

Oh, Seth, she would say, *but just think . . . it might be true after all, if we . . . that is . . .* as she turned away with reddened cheeks and a shy smile, as if suddenly realizing she had said too much.

The rumors regarding the second-born offspring of the two plantation owners were not long in sprouting.

The whisper, in its first germinal form, merely said, as all the ladies had noticed, that Veronica Beaumont seemed changed, and in its second stage it only amounted to this, that Seth Davidson's heroic behavior had certainly calmed her down and, others asserted, begun to make a woman of her. It was added, so people said, that Seth had nearly been killed defending her honor, and what more could a woman want in a man than one who was willing to give his life protecting her?

In the third stage of its development—as significant glances were exchanged—it was observed that the two young people were spending more and more time together after the incident, and behaving as if they were closer than ever. Some said there had been talk between Mrs. Davidson and the Beaumont girl as mother and daughter. Others said Veronica spent just as much time at Greenwood as she did her own home.

"Have the young man and the girl's father spoken together?" someone wondered.

No one knew. But even that could not change how things stood. It would certainly happen before long. It was how these things were arranged.

And slowly in ever widening circles, as March gave way to April and April gave way to May, and as the reports took on a life of their own—not a soul in town suspecting that a whole family of runaway slaves was hiding out under the very nose of the daughter of the local Commissioner—the word eventually spread so thoroughly as to be accepted as common knowledge that Veronica Beaumont and Seth Davidson were all but ready to formally announce their engagement.

⌒

Thus was deepened the involvement between the two families, entangling the two principal men in Veronica's life no less that it was occurring against their own wills. Lady Daphne picked up fragments of the rumors with ambivalent feelings. She wanted Veronica to have whatever she wanted. She could probably learn to like Carolyn if she tried.

Denton Beaumont, however, was anything but pleased when the rumors began to filter into his own hearing. His thoughts were not so congenial toward the proposed union as his wife's. The fool had probably saved him from being grandfather to a bastard black child and forever ruining his chances of holding political office. He should be grateful. But the thought of being beholden to Richmond Davidson's son nearly drove him mad. The thought of his daughter marrying the imbecile was intolerable.

Yet what could he do? Seth had become a local hero. The engagement would seem already a *fait accompli*. For him to spurn young Davidson now would make him look like an ungrateful idiot.

Bah! He could hardly stand the thought of the thing! Yet if he attempted to deny his daughter, she could make his life miserable. She would probably run off with him anyway.

Denton Beaumont knew that he was between the proverbial rock and a hard place. But his daughter held all the cards.

Fifty

~

Cherity Waters sat in her upstairs bedroom at home in Boston, gazing again at the tintype of her mother. The old black Bible lay on the desk beside her.

All her life her image of God had been fashioned by this picture of her mother in her hand—faint, distant, small, and in sepia tones rather than the colors of real life. Whenever she heard the word *God*, her subconscious called up sensations of silence, mystery, unresponsiveness. God and her mother had always been linked. Before the three ladies from the church, her mother was the only person she knew of who took God seriously. In her little girl's mind, how could God and her mother not somehow be alike?

The church service sorely disappointed her. She had gone in hope and left in confusion. She had hoped to find out that there might be more to God. Apparently there wasn't.

She picked up the Bible and again flipped through the pages. But her interest in it was gone. The underlinings and notes no longer drew her as before. They had become as lifeless as the tiny photo.

The talk with the three women had quelled her hunger to know more about this book. It was written in a language that didn't make sense to her. It wasn't merely the odd words and old-fashioned language. It was the harsh negativity of the women's hearts even as their faces smiled with pretended love. If God was so caring, why did they talk about judgment and the wages of sin and death and hell before telling people what that love might mean? In spite of their affected kindness, she had come away with the distinct feeling that the only way she, or anyone else, could be acceptable in their eyes was to admit what horrible sinners they were. Was that all they could think of? She didn't like it. It was so negative and critical.

She would like to know what God's love might mean. But how was she to find out? Who could tell her? Who could show her such love?

"Why are you dead, Mother?" she whispered, still gazing at the photograph. "I wanted to know you. Why must I live without you?"

But there was no reply. There never was. The room remained silent. The photograph revealed its secrets no more readily than did the Bible. There were no more answers from God than there were from her silent dead mother.

Slowly Cherity set the picture down.

Gradually the questions in her mind drifted in another direction, though Cherity hardly realized to whom she had begun to speak.

Why did you let her die? If you were going to give me a mother, why did you take her from me? Where did I come from? Who gave me life . . . you, Mother . . . or you, God? How can I still be alive, if I came from you, but neither of you are alive? Am I really going to go to hell just because I can't see you and hear you? Is heaven going to be full of people like those three women?

She paused and breathed deeply two or three times. The question her brain had just posed jolted her back to the present. She smiled a little morosely. *If so*, she said to herself, *maybe I don't want to go there anyway.*

Cherity hardly recognized the extent of change within her own heart since the church service. Nor was she aware that her questions were no longer those of a little girl who yearned for her mother's arms but rather were questions that reflected the growing independence of a young woman who felt the need to rise up and stand strong—knowing that it was up to her to walk beside her father in this world.

In the midst of her present confusion, little did Cherity realize to what extent the Father of both her and her father heard every word.

She had no inkling that this Father was already, in his own unique way, drawing them, preparing them to recognize his voice when he called more distinctly. For when that time came, he would speak, not in the language of cliché and religiosity, but in the language of the heart. And then they would hear.

"God, if you are listening . . . why don't you say anything?" she said one last time. "What kind of God are you, anyway?"

But still Cherity Waters heard nothing.

"Am I just talking to myself?" she said at length. "Maybe God doesn't even exist at all."

She rose and left the room. One thing she wasn't going to do was dwell on it. If there were no answers to such questions readily apparent, then she would take life as it came to her and be happy about it.

Fifty-one

$\mathcal{M}$other," said Veronica one afternoon in May when at last she was ready to spring her trap, "may we invite Seth over for dinner?"

"Certainly, dear," replied Lady Daphne. "Is he well enough?"

"He is much better now. Except for the sling no one would know what had happened. I think he needs to start getting out and socializing again. How about the day after tomorrow, Mother?"

"I think that will be fine, dear."

"Good, I will send Jarvis over to Greenwood with an invitation this afternoon. I will go up to my room and write it right now."

The handwritten invitation arrived at Greenwood only two hours after its ink had dried. Seth immediately went to show the note to his parents.

"You know, Seth," said his father, "there are rumors floating around. . . ."

"I know, Dad," said Seth. "Believe me, they're not true. I don't know why everyone else is talking about us like they are."

"People love to gossip about young people in love," said Carolyn. "I doubt Veronica does much to discourage the talk. I think she loves it."

"I know," sighed Seth. "She and those silly friends of hers!"

"*Are* the two of you in love, Seth?" asked his father.

"I don't know, Dad. I always just kind of figured . . ."

Whatever Seth's thought, he did not complete the vocalization of it.

"Figured what?" asked his father.

"You know, growing up together like we have, and then lately . . . it seemed natural, I guess, like one of those things that would just happen and . . . and I figured that someday, you know."

"That you and Veronica would marry?"

"I guess."

"But it's come on you more suddenly than you realized?"

"Something like that, Dad."

"Did you and she ever have that talk?" asked Carolyn.

"Uh . . . not really. But Veronica can be hard to talk to, though."

"It needs to be done."

"I know," nodded Seth. "I had ridden over to talk to her and ask her what she thought about God and spiritual things, but then I got trounced by Elias instead."

He glanced down at the card in his hand. "I think I'll accept this invitation, go to dinner, and then have a talk with Veronica and get some things settled between us."

When Seth arrived at Oakbriar two days later about four-thirty in the afternoon, the door was answered by Jarvis, dressed in more formal attire than usual. He showed Seth into the seldom-used drawing room where Seth waited for a minute or two before Lady Daphne appeared. She was dressed in formal evening wear.

Seth glanced at his own casual slacks and jacket. At least his mother had convinced him to put a tie on at the last minute. When Veronica walked in another minute later, the sight nearly took Seth's breath away. The long orange dress with large white bow at the hip on one side looked like it belonged at a fancy dress ball. Her hair was piled high on her head, every curl in place. She and Sally and Marta had spent three hours on it earlier in the afternoon.

"Wow, Veronica!" said Seth. "You look great. I've never seen that dress before."

Veronica beamed. It was the most enthusiastic response she'd had from Seth in her life about anything she'd ever worn.

"And here I am in a casual coat and with my arm in a sling!" he laughed.

"It's all right, Seth," said Lady Daphne. "You didn't know, and you look fine. We just felt like dressing up, didn't we, Veronica, dear?"

The drawing room door opened and Veronica's father walked in. He didn't exactly smile, but at least greeted Seth with a nod and offered his hand. Seth shook it, then winced involuntarily.

"I'm sorry, boy," said Beaumont "I thought it was—"

He glanced at the sling holding Seth's left arm.

"It's all right, sir," said Seth. "A couple of my right ribs got cracked, too. The doctor says there's nothing more to be done for them but give them time. When my arm gets in just the right position, sometimes I feel pain."

"Yeah, ribs can be slow to heal," nodded Beaumont.

Jarvis walked in, carrying a tray bearing four tall glasses.

"A glass of sherry, Seth?" said Lady Daphne, taking one of the glasses.

"Uh . . . I don't—"

"Come on, boy," said Beaumont. "You're nineteen, they tell me, and you took on the toughest cuss for miles—if that doesn't make you old enough for a sherry, I don't know what does."

Beaumont took two of the glasses and handed one to Seth. Veronica and her mother took the others and Jarvis left the room.

"A toast," said Lady Daphne, raising her glass, "to the young people, Seth and Veronica . . . and their future."

They all lifted the glasses to their mouths and sipped lightly.

This is going very well, thought Veronica. Her father was behaving himself like a perfect gentleman!

Seth, on the other hand, was squirming under his collar. The swallow of sherry burned all the way down his throat. He was starting to sweat.

"I haven't had a chance to thank you, my boy," said Beaumont, fumbling for words, "for jumping in and . . . uh, saving my daughter's honor against Slade like you did. It took a lot of courage, and I'm grateful." He had said a little more than he intended, but he let it stand.

"Thank you, sir," said Seth.

Yes indeed . . . very, very well! said Veronica to herself, not realizing how much fortitude it had likewise taken for her father to swallow the huge portion of crow required to utter the words. But he prided himself on being a gentleman, and had determined to be gracious to Seth in front of his wife and daughter.

"Well, then," said Lady Daphne, "shall we go into the dining room?"

Drinks still in hand, they entered the dining room, where a lavish table was appointed with the finest silver and linen. Two candles were burning, and two silent Negro attendants waited patiently to serve them. Seth noticed that only four places were set.

"Where are Wyatt and Cameron?" he asked.

"We sent them away," replied Lady Daphne. "We thought this would be a good opportunity for the two of you and the two of us to enjoy a nice, quiet dinner together."

Once again Seth felt the heat rising around his neck. Veronica's father and mother took their places at the head and foot of the table, then he and Veronica sat down opposite one another on the two sides. She glanced over and smiled. It was a different expression than he had ever seen on her face before. He wasn't quite sure what it meant.

Then the memorable meal got underway.

⟨⟩

An hour and fifteen minutes later, with the last of the cherries and pudding settling comfortably and warmly inside, and the two attendants clearing away the last of the dishes, Lady Daphne, who had sturdily and bravely borne the heaviest load of the dinner conversation, her husband seemingly having settled from the amiable persona he had presented in the drawing room back into the quiet and sullen man they had all grown to know and love, scooted back her chair and rose from the table.

"Come, Veronica, dear," she said, "I think the men want to be alone."

Immediately Veronica rose, smiled at Seth, and left the room with her mother, who had executed her lines, as Veronica had outlined them prior to the meal, to perfection. Seth watched them go with something akin to horror. He too had noted the gradual shift in temperamental weather at the far end of the table and didn't relish the thought of being left alone in the midst of whatever storm was brewing there.

The door closed behind the two women. Seth nervously probed the inside of his collar with a finger, and waited. A long silence followed. Inside, Denton Beaumont was cursing his daughter for putting him in this position, and at the same time cursing Richmond Davidson for siring a blasted son at all. But, he told himself, protocol must be observed. He was, after all, a Virginian. He must conduct himself like a gentleman.

Now he too slowly slid his chair back on the oak floor, and rose.

"Why don't you and I go into the parlor, Seth," he said, "and have a drink together."

He took two steps, opened a door, and called through it. "Jarvis . . . a couple of brandies . . . in the parlor."

He closed the door and motioned for Seth to follow. Seth rose and followed him through another door, through the drawing room, and into the parlor, where Beaumont closed the door behind them.

"Care for a cigar, son?" said Veronica's father, opening the lid of a box on one of the tables and removing a seven inch Havana.

"Uh . . . no, sir."

"Don't smoke?"

"No, sir."

"You ought to try it sometime. A good cigar will help your digestion."

"Yes, sir . . . but no, thank you."

Jarvis entered with a tray. Beaumont took one of the glasses and swallowed half its contents, liberally poured, for Jarvis knew his master, in nearly the same motion. Jarvis then offered the tray to Seth.

"Uh, no thank you, Jarvis," he said.

"Come on, boy," barked Beaumont. "Nothing like an after-dinner brandy to settle the stomach."

"Yes, sir . . . but I would really rather not."

"Suit yourself—Leave the tray, Jarvis," said Beaumont. "I'll have that one myself later. . . . I have the feeling I'm going to need it," he added under his breath.

As soon as the butler was gone, Beaumont took a seat in his favorite chair and motioned Seth to sit down opposite him. Seth did so.

Another long silence followed. This time it was not so painful for Beaumont, for he had the comforts of his cigar and his brandy to occupy him. Seth sat waiting.

"I want to talk to you, son," said Beaumont at length. "I have a question to ask."

"Yes, sir."

"Are your intentions honorable toward my daughter?"

"Of course, sir."

"Just what are your intentions, then?"

"What do you mean, Mr. Beaumont?"

"You know what I mean—are you and she . . . do you, uh . . . *understand* one another?"

"I think so, sir," said Seth a little hesitantly.

"Are you satisfied with how things stand?"

"I suppose," nodded Seth. "I mean, I do have a few things I feel we need to talk over, but in general . . . yes, I suppose."

"All right then. As long as there has been an understanding reached between you and that you are both satisfied, I suppose I shall not stand in the way of it—Are you sure you wouldn't like a cigar?"

"No, sir."

The conversation then began to wander, touching lightly, with Beaumont doing most of the talking, on the weather, the outlook for this year's crops, cotton prices, the laziness of slaves, and the political outlook in Washington, in that order.

When Seth and Veronica's father emerged from the drawing room ten minutes later, Seth looking bewildered, Beaumont looking somewhat haggard but resigned to the inevitable, Veronica and Lady Daphne were waiting for them in the sitting room.

Seth never did have the opportunity to speak with Veronica alone. By the time the evening ended and he began the drive home in the descending dusk, the topics that had seemed so imperative that he raise with her only a few short hours ago had grown fuzzy and vague in his mind.

Immediately after Seth's departure, Veronica pestered her father mercilessly for a report. Beginning to get a bad headache from the ordeal, he recited back to her the entire conversation more or less word for word.

Vague as it might have been at a few points, Veronica was well pleased with the outcome. It was almost as much as she had hoped for . . . and would suffice.

When Seth rode up the drive to Greenwood, it was almost completely dark.

He had been in no hurry to get home and had intentionally allowed Auburn Flame to dawdle. It wasn't that he consciously thought to avoid his parents or did not want to tell them that he hadn't spoken with Veronica as he had planned, or that, in fact, the only one whom he had spoken halfway seriously with was Veronica's father.

He was embarrassed about the evening's outcome, embarrassed, as he now thought back on it, that he had been so spineless not to speak his mind more forcefully. He was not reluctant to tell his parents from any desire to hide it. He would have shared anything with them gladly. Only in this case, he didn't know what to say.

He wasn't quite sure himself *what* had happened.

After he and his parents had talked so specifically beforehand about the need to clarify things with Veronica, that he hadn't done so, and now seemed to have become entangled all the deeper—a private talk with drinks and cigars with Denton Beaumont, for goodness sakes!—after all that . . . he just needed to think a bit before he asked his father what to do.

The buggy wheels crunched over the gravel. The house was nearly dark. He saw the lone light from the lantern in his parents' room upstairs, but he would not disturb them tonight.

He stopped in front of the barn, unhitched Auburn Flame, and took her inside. The night was clear and there would be no rain . . . he would see to the buggy in the morning.

Slowly he walked across the entryway, glancing up at the light in the window. Maybe he ought to knock on their door and talk this thing over. . . .

No, he thought. He just needed a good night's sleep to clear his brain.

Seth opened the door and went inside. With as soft a step as he could he made his way up to his own room.

Morning brought no relief to Seth's perplexities. When he awoke his father was already gone from the house. He dressed and went downstairs. There was enough commotion with Thomas eating and Maribel at the cookstove to keep him from any awkward silences.

"Good morning, Seth," said Carolyn.

"Hi, Mother," said Seth. "What's Maribel got on the stove? It smells good!"

"Johnnycakes an' eggs, Massa Seff," called Maribel from across the kitchen.

"Great! I'm starved. I slept too long."

"You were late getting home," said Carolyn. "Did you and Veronica get everything settled?"

"I don't know, Mother," replied Seth. "I hope so."

Even as he said it, Seth realized it was a stupid thing to say. He hadn't gotten *anything* settled. But he let his words stand, and moments later was diving into the plate of food that Maribel set in front of him.

The day proceeded but no opportunity arose where Seth and his mother found themselves in a setting alone where their conversation flowed naturally into the channels of open and relaxed dialogue. Nothing more was said about the previous night.

Nor did it come up the next day . . . nor the day after that.

Gradually Seth's dinner at Oakbriar slowly began to fade into the past. Life resumed its course and things settled into their former routine.

Most thought and activity around Greenwood for some time had been occupied with keeping Lucindy and her rambunctious family quiet and out of sight, especially when visitors came. How long she would be with them was still undetermined. The fatigue from travel clearly showed. Even though they realized the danger to themselves increased with every week that passed, neither Richmond nor Carolyn had any thought except for Lucindy's health and to get some substance back on her bony frame.

They did what they could to make the basement comfortable, where they hurried their young charges whenever they heard Veronica's buggy ride up, with stern admonitions to silence.

Thus the time passed, if not without certain anxieties and moments of tension, yet safely and without detection. Whether or not it had anything to do with their home being turned into a hiding place and house of refuge for runaways, Thomas receded more and more into himself. He had agreed to confidentiality, but the new situation only amplified his silent irritations toward his parents. He spoke but little. A cloud hung over his countenance, and little anyone said or did succeeded in drawing out of him the happy and carefree boy he had once been.

Veronica still came to visit the semi-invalid almost daily and behaved much the same as ever, except for an added friendliness, a discernible increase in her eagerness to engage the two older Davidsons in conversation. Once or twice Lady Daphne accompanied her and had tea and cake with Carolyn, never suspecting the secret hidden below her in the basement. Nor did Carolyn for a moment suspect the plans Veronica and her mother shared.

As yet neither Richmond nor Carolyn, whose visits to Dove's Landing were infrequent, had so much as an inkling how far things had advanced between the two young people.

Fifty-two

By mid-June Lucindy Eaton was strong enough to travel.

She had put on ten pounds and had recovered much of her strength after seven weeks at Greenwood. Carolyn sensed that she was restless and thinking of moving on.

"Where will you go when you leave us, Lucindy?" asked Carolyn one day.

"I's gwine fin' my man."

"Where is he, Lucindy?"

"I don' know, Missus Dav'son. In da Norf sumwheres."

"But how do you expect to find him?"

"I don't know—is da Norf dat big? He's in sumplace called Pennsulvania er sumfin' like dat."

"Pennsylvania is enormous, Lucindy. It has more than a million people."

"A million . . . laws almighty, Missus Dav'son!"

"Is that all you know about where he is?"

"Dere wuz anuder word dey tol' me not ter fergit—dat's Hanober, er sumfin'. Next ter dat on da message dat came wuz a picshure ob a horse's head."

"What was it like?"

"Don' know, Missus Dav'son. I didn't see it. It wuz drawed in da cake er soap—Hanober wif a horse's head, dat's what she said."

Lucindy went on to recount her brief conversation with Mistress Crawford's housekeeper.

"Dere wuz jes' a horse's head scrached in da soap."

"What it mean?" Lucindy had asked.

"Don' know, chil'. Mus' be er clue er sum kin'. When you git ter Hanober, you bes' look fo' sumfin' ter do wif horses."

That evening, Richmond and Carolyn consulted a map as they discussed the matter. Hanover lay only some five or six miles across the Pennsylvania border between Gettysburg and York.

"I think I should be the one to take her, Richmond," said Carolyn. "Traveling with three like that, the chances of discovery will be greater. It will take us three or four days just to reach the border. It would not go so badly with me if we are caught as it would you."

"I do not like the sound of that!" said Richmond.

"You know what I mean. Juries are more sympathetic toward women."

"Juries! Good heavens, Carolyn, you make it sound like robbing a bank!" he laughed.

"It is a crime, Richmond," said his wife seriously. "We will be breaking the law. It's only practical that I take her."

He sighed. "I suppose you're right. But I don't like the thought of placing you in danger."

"The danger has come to us, Richmond. By harboring and helping, we have added to it and increased our own danger. We did not seek it, but here she is under our roof, one of God's precious ones. We have to do *our* best for her if she is to experience the love of her Father-God's which will be an even *better* best for her."

"Eloquently put, my dear wife! We did not seek it, but neither can we run from it."

He smiled thoughtfully. "I wonder what are we getting ourselves into?"

"We don't know. But God knows and we can rest in that, and then take each day as it comes to us. We cannot see the next page of our life's book, but only the one open to us. As long as we let God turn the pages, the unfolding of that story is in good hands."

"All true. Yet I still do not like the idea of you traveling alone. What about Seth?"

"Would it be right to involve him? If caught, it could go badly for him too."

"One or the other of us, it seems to me, must accompany you. I simply cannot allow it otherwise. I shall talk to Seth and see if he is willing."

Taking advantage of Thomas's absence on a hunting trip of several days with Jeremy and his father, and still unaware of the maelstrom of gossip swirling about Veronica's matrimonial plans, Richmond and Seth fabricated the vehicle of journey and what they hoped would be Lucindy's escape to freedom.

Richmond contrived this carriage of subterfuge out of one of their old wagons that was still serviceable and reasonably comfortable, but which had fallen into disuse when they acquired more modern wagons and buggies over the years. Richmond chose this one because the bed behind the two-man bench seat was unusually deep, yet not more than about six feet in overall length. The carriage had apparently been designed as a small and lightweight single-horse delivery wagon of sorts, comfortable as a buckboard but with heavy springs for the hauling of moderate loads, serving both the purposes of transport or freight. Richmond concluded the depth of the bed must have had something to do with its original owner's desire to design something capable of stacking behind him two heights of hay or straw bales rather than one. He could not remember when it had come to Greenwood, or under what circumstances, and thought perhaps his father had either purchased it or had it built when Richmond was in England years before. But he did not remember its use, only its storage in one of the equipment barns after his return.

It was the extra depth of the freight box that provided Richmond Davidson the framework required for the transport of a very different form of cargo.

To their desired end, he and Seth had fabricated a second floor some fifteen or sixteen inches above the actual bed of the carriage, below which—in a cramped but utilitarian hidden chamber—the four runaway black slaves could lay virtually undetected. Above it, on the newly created false floor of the carriage, they intended to set enough boxes and crates and other items disguised to appear of greater depth than they were, so the contents of their load would give every appearance of resting on the original carriage bed. Of course close inspection would divulge the false floor and hidden chamber easily enough. But they hoped to avoid such close inspection by the appearance of innocence.

In order to facilitate their journey and make it possible to travel as many hours as they could without lengthy stops—hopefully cutting the entire journey to the border and back to three or three-and-a-half days—they had included a small mattress and blankets among the items lying on top of the false floor so that Seth and Carolyn could take turns sleeping. Also, they would hitch the carriage to two of their most dependable long-range hauling horses. The horses could not go twenty-four hours a day without rest, but they could certainly go a good portion of it.

Fifty-three

Completely oblivious to the machinations of secrecy presently in progress at Greenwood, Denton Beaumont received a letter that would change his as well as the future fortunes of everyone in his family. Which was greater, the elation of the master of the house, or the relief of its mistress to be exonerated for the stinging election loss, who could say? Though the master felt himself vindicated when he learned of the new developments, forgiveness toward those who had caused his humiliation would not be so quickly forthcoming. And though his wife did not feel completely acquitted for her hidden role in the defeat, the news certainly in large measure moderated the guilt that had accompanied it.

When Jarvis brought the day's mail up to his study, Beaumont flipped though the stack absently, hardly noticing from whom each had come. He was in a surly mood. He had only moments before chanced to overhear Veronica and her mother talking some nonsense about wedding dresses and fabric and bridesmaids. The thought of it revolted him. That he had resigned himself to Seth Davidson as a son-in-law did not make the fact any more pleasant. He only consoled himself by thinking that the marriage should, in time, afford him opportunity, if not actually to take title to the Brown land, then at least to be accorded the freedom to roam about it without compunction, and thus hopefully at last lay his hands on the fortune he knew it contained. He had waited twenty-five years. Perhaps his daughter's marriage to the son of his neighbor and nemesis was the only way to achieve his secret goal.

He picked up the stack of three or four envelopes and perused it again. His eyes fell on one name among the rest: *Frederick Trowbridge*.

What could he possibly want? thought Beaumont with annoyance, unless it was at last to apologize for shunning him in favor of Davidson and Everett three years ago!

Skeptically he slit the envelope, took out the single sheet, and began to read.

> *Dear Denton,*
>
> *I realize we have had our differences over the past few years. I have heard of your displeasure about my handling of the affair involving your neighbor Davidson, as well as the ill-advised decision of some of our colleagues that he ought to be put forward as our senatorial candidate. Perhaps my words at this point will mean little to you, but I hope, for the sake of our past friendship, that you will give me a fair hearing.*
>
> *Let me first simply apologize for those past events to which I refer. That many of us were wrong about Davidson is clear enough now to all. We should have known all along that you were our man. I regret my hand in the matter and am humbled by the recognition of my mistake.*
>
> *We are also aware of certain underhanded methods employed by Senator Hoyt in his recent election victory, not to mention outright lies circulated about you and your wife, and that by all rights you should easily have defeated him.*
>
> *Abraham Seehorn and I would like to meet with you, privately and in strictest confidence, to discuss these and other matters pertaining to your future. Please reply if you are agreeable and we will arrange a time and place suitable for such a meeting.*
>
> *I am,*
> *Sincerely yours,*
> *Frederick Trowbridge*

With a *humph* or two at the man's presumption coming to him like this, cap in hand, after the treatment he had received, Beaumont nevertheless read over the communiqué another four or five times, trying to divine every possible ounce of meaning from its words. His heart beat a little more rapidly each time as his own fancies supplied hoped-for meaning to what had been left unsaid between the lines.

It could do no harm to meet with them, he said to himself at length. He might as well hear what they had to say.

When Denton Beaumont walked into the out-of-the-way hotel tavern on the outskirts of Richmond, his two hosts rose to meet him.

"Ah, Denton," said Trowbridge expansively, as if there had never been a dispute between them, "how good it was of you to come! You know Abraham Seehorn?"

"Yes . . . hello, Abraham."

"Beaumont," said Seehorn, setting his cigar down long enough to shake hands.

They all took seats. Trowbridge ordered a new round of drinks, Seehorn offered Beaumont a cigar. In a few moments the three were chatting amiably.

"We want to talk to you about your future," said Trowbridge at length. "We have had our differences in the past, but that is behind us. We believe that Virginia's future lies with men like you."

Beaumont nodded guardedly. The words were welcome, of course, but he was reluctant to commit himself until he heard more.

"There is no sense beating around the bush," Trowbridge contin- ued, "so I will put our cards right out on the table. Senator Everett's health is not the best. Nor is he entirely in step with many in the party. When his term is up, he will not run for reelection. Abraham and I, and with our backing all the party leaders will support it, intend to make you our candidate. There will be no nonsense such as what Hoyt used against you. You should win easily."

Beaumont took in the words, heart beginning to pound a little more rapidly but still trying to maintain an outward calm.

"I am flattered and honored," he said. "And I appreciate the confidence you show in me. But 1862 is three years away. Much can happen in that time. It strikes me as a little early for any of us to be making too many predictions about any supposed victory at that time."

"Of course, you are right," nodded Trowbridge. "But as I said, Senator Everett—"

"The man's in his dotage," interrupted Seehorn, punctuating his words with a cloud of smoke from his cigar. "And with Hoyt espousing moderation in the matter of the Negroes, Virginia has lost its Southern voice in Washington."

"Abraham is right," said Trowbridge. "The situation is dire. Many of us are not at all pleased. Though Everett is the older of Virginia's two senators, he has become almost a lackey for Hoyt by his silence. But it is clear that Hoyt does not speak for our interests."

"But what can I do about it?" said Beaumont. "What can any of us do?"

"The point is," Trowbridge went on, "we do not want to wait three years."

Beaumont took in the words with confused expression.

"I . . . am uncertain what you mean," he said.

"You are correct in saying that the election is three years away," continued Trowbridge. "But we believe there are ways in which your influence can be felt immediately."

"What ways?"

"We want you to go to Washington now, as soon as is convenient, perhaps in the fall. We need a man we can trust. We will arrange for some post or appointment to give cover for your activities between now and the election."

"What would be the purpose of my going now and holding such a post?"

"What we chiefly want is simply for you to be there, to meet your future congressional colleagues, to mix with important people, to make speeches . . . in short, to be a voice for Virginia. We want to increase your visibility and stature, so that when the time of the election comes, you are already on your way to becoming a national figure and leading Southern spokesman."

At last they had succeeded in getting Denton Beaumont's attention! Now all he had to do was to keep from gushing all over himself with pleasure over the proposal. With great effort he swallowed the smile that tried to break out on his face.

"You would, I take it, not be adverse to such an arrangement?" suggested Seehorn.

"No, of course not . . . I mean, anything I can do for the party, and Virginia," replied Beaumont. "I mean . . . we must all make sacrifices, and I would be more than willing—"

"I thought so." Seehorn's lips smiled around his cigar.

"As Abraham has said, Senator Everett is losing his grip," said Trowbridge. "As soon as you are situated in Washington, we would also like you to begin working closely with him, both in preparation for your taking over his seat later, but also acting in a sense as an invisible stand-in for him. We want his policies to begin to reflect your views as soon as possible."

"Will he go along with that?"

"He will be only too glad for the help," answered Seehorn. "I have already spoken with him about it. He is willing to give you a free rein."

"What about your family?" asked Trowbridge. "Would there be any difficulties there?"

"No . . . none whatsoever," replied Beaumont. "My wife and daughter will be only too pleased to relocate to Washington. They were more disappointed than I was with the election!" he added with a light laugh. "Although my daughter is scheduled to be married late in the year—to Davidson's buffoon of a son, believe it or not!—so we will have to work around that. It may not be possible for them to join me in the capital immediately."

"But you see no hindrance to your being able to take up certain responsibilities within a few months, looking for a house in the capital, being seen socially, that sort of thing?"

"No . . . no hindrance whatever."

"Your plantation can get by without you?"

"I have enough men to keep the darkies in line."

"Good. Then we will get to work on our end as well in hopes that by midfall or the end of the year at the latest, you will be situated and on your way to becoming a recognized and respected figure in Washington."

Fifty-four

*H*earing that their neighbor was away, and desirous of using that fact to whatever advantage it might provide them, Carolyn and Seth, with their four charges, left Greenwood in the small hours of a morning when a full moon would allow them to travel and make a good distance before daybreak. Hopefully they would be many miles from the vicinity of Dove's Landing before they were seen. By then no one would know them.

They set out with Seth at the reins, Carolyn lying on the mattress in back, and, at least until they should be well away from Dove's Landing and any prying eyes, Lucindy, Calebia, Broan, and Rebecca, as comfortable as they could be made with blankets, in the hidden compartment below her.

Progress was slow. Seth did not want to push the pace too early. Diamond and Coronet had to carry them a hundred and forty miles and he must gauge their endurance carefully. By daybreak the group was well away from the region where they would be recognized. Seth pulled off the road onto a grassy flat beside a stream and reined in.

"I think it is time for a stop, some exercise, and whatever else anyone needs to do!" he said.

Behind him, Carolyn roused herself and sat up. "What time is it?" she said.

"I don't know, six . . . six-thirty," replied Seth. "You get any sleep, Mother?"

"A few good hours. You know me, I can sleep anywhere! I'll be able to take over for you."

The pounding of the floor below her and Broan's muffled voice reminded her that they were not alone.

"Just a minute," she laughed. "I'll have you out of there in half a minute."

She got up, rolled the mattress back and lifted the loose plank beneath it that served as the door for their hideaways. Light flooded the hidden chamber and two little bodies came scampering out, jumped to the ground, and scurried about. As soon as Calebia was lifted to the ground, she tried to run after her older brother and sister.

"Don't go far, children!" Carolyn called after them. "Remember what we talked about—if anyone comes you must get back into the wagon quickly."

Lucindy's head followed from beneath. With a little more difficulty, and Carolyn's assistance, she worked her way up and out.

"You poor dear," said Carolyn, "you must be so cramped down there!"

"It ain't so bad, Missus Dab'son," said Lucindy, "speshully at night. We wuz asleep so di'nt hardly know no dif'ernce, 'cept w'en I'd wake up an' start up an' bump my head. But I'll lay anywheres ter keep from goin' back, so it don't bother me none, Missus Dab'son."

Seth was just coming back from a clump of trees as the two women climbed down.

"There's a nice stream there," he said. "You can wash and drink, and I'm going to water the horses and give them something to eat. Maybe we should eat our breakfast here too. It seems safe enough. There are no towns or farms or houses anywhere nearby that I can see."

They were on their way again in an hour, Seth taking a turn on the mattress and trying to sleep, though without a great deal of success. His mind was too full of the dangers, and the commotion, wriggling, questions, and ceaseless chatter from beneath him didn't help. Lucindy may have been able to lie comfortably in a sixteen-inch dark compartment, but such did not lie within the range of human possibility for three energetic little youngsters. Eventually they drifted off to sleep again, and slowly Seth dozed off. When he awoke the sun was high in the sky, his mother still sat on the seat in front, and otherwise little had changed.

He rolled back the mattress and lifted the board.

"I'm going up front for a little while," he said. "How would you like some light and fresh air down there?"

"I gots ter do sum necessaries, Massa Seff," said Broan with urgency in his voice.

Seth laughed. "A stop would probably do us all good," he said. "I could use one myself, and I'm sure your ma would like to get out of there and stretch her legs."

Carolyn pulled to the side of the road and stopped, then climbed down and stretched.

"How you doing, Mother?" asked Seth.

"I'm getting tired. But we'll make it. How far do you think we've come?"

"I don't know . . . thirty or forty miles. We've been keeping a decent clip—which reminds me," he added, walking around to the back of the wagon where they kept the water barrel and buckets, "we need to feed and water these horses as often as we can."

Carolyn opened the food basket and set out a few things, and within ten minutes the travelers were on their way again. Seth and his mother sat on the front bench, Lucindy and her children sprawled on the mattress in back, munching on bread and cheese, in bright spirits once again to feel the sun and breeze on their faces. Seth and Carolyn chatted away and another hour passed without incident.

Suddenly Seth stopped in midsentence and scanned the road ahead.

"I think I hear someone coming," he said. "Back underneath!" he called behind him, handing the reins to his mother, then turning around. "Hurry—and not a sound."

They had practiced this several times, so the children knew instantly what to do. Broan and Rebecca scrambled through the opening, with Lucindy stuffing Calebia through and then wriggling in beside them with slightly more difficulty. The moment she was inside, Seth clamped the board in its place, folded back the mattress, and lay down. They hoped that the sling in which his arm was still bound would justify the presence of the mattress.

Almost the same instant, a buggy came around the bend in the road in front of them. Both continued on, and passed. Carolyn gave a nod and a smile but did not slow down, the man tipped his hat as they passed, and that was that. At least it gave some comfort to know that their appearance did not attract immediate and obvious attention.

They passed through several towns throughout the course of the day, always adopting the same plan—with Carolyn at the reins in front, Seth on the mattress behind, and with stern admonishments to silence below.

By late afternoon, fatigue was noticeably setting in with drooping eyes and nodding heads, even occasionally on the parts of the drivers. They continued on, however, knowing that they would have to stop eventually to give the horses a rest and wanting to make it as far as they could before then. Seth judged that by now they were within twenty miles or so of the Maryland border. From Spotsylvania, they had come through Stafford, Prince William, and finally Loudoun Counties. Only another thirty miles through the panhandle of the northernmost slave state east of the Monocacy River and they would reach the Mason-Dixon Line and Pennsylvania border south of Hanover. They were now in hillier terrain. They hoped it would not slow their progress.

"Riders!" said Seth suddenly. "Lots of them—Mom . . . Mom, wake up!"

Behind him Carolyn struggled to rouse herself to wakefulness. "Get up here, Mom!" Seth called back to her. "You've got to take over."

Still half asleep, Carolyn sat up and crawled forward. Seth slowed the horses, set the reins on the bench and hurried back to her place. He was under the blanket and Carolyn had just managed to grab hold of the reins when the dust and thunder of a half dozen horsemen came into sight ahead of them. Their leader reined in. It was obvious from the way his men surrounded the wagon that he expected her to do the same.

"Howdy, ma'am," he said with a nod and tip of his hat. "The name's Murdoch—where you headed?"

"North," said Carolyn.

"How far north?"

"Not far."

While they spoke, one of the riders made his way around the wagon, looking it over slowly.

"What's with him?" he said, nodding to Seth where he lay in the back.

Below him in darkness, Lucindy lay trembling in terror. The moment he spoke she had recognized the man's voice.

"That's my son," said Carolyn. "His arm's broke."

"Yeah, I can see that. Why's he laying on a mattress?"

"He got two cracked ribs, too. They sometimes pain him. It's more comfortable for him lying down, ain't it, Son?"

"Yeah, Ma," said Seth, looking back at the man who was staring at him.

"What happened to you, boy?" asked the man.

"He got into a fight with a black fellow about twice his size," said Carolyn, glancing back at the man.

"A slave?"

"No, a free colored."

"They're the worst," said the man.

"What about?" asked the other man.

"It was over a girl," said Seth.

The man smiled. "What color girl?" he said.

"A white girl. He was bothering her and I didn't think he oughta be."

"Well, you sound all right to me, kid. Listen, ma'am, you ain't seen any niggers on the road back there, have you, traveling alone?"

"Traveling alone, you say?"

The man nodded.

"No sir, sure haven't . . . have you seen any coloreds, Seth . . . traveling alone?"

"Nope."

"Well, there's runaways about, ma'am. Get a lot of them this close to the border. We're after a couple families right now said to be headed for Pennsylvania. You sure you ain't seen nothing suspicious or out of the ordinary?"

Carolyn shook her head.

"All right, then—best to you, ma'am. And you keep them niggers in their place, boy!"

Just as quickly as they had appeared, the riders galloped off and were gone.

Wide awake now, Carolyn breathed a sigh of relief and glanced back at Seth.

"Did you see how he was looking over the wagon!" she said. "I was sure he was going to start poking around and looking under everything."

"All the more reason for us to keep moving as fast as we can," said Seth. "That man was a bounty hunter, I'm sure of it."

"A bounty hunter!"

"There are more and more of them, Mother, with runaways on the increase. We're going to have to be really careful. I've heard they can be ruthless. Keep the horses moving along if you can, even though they're starting to tire. We'll look for a place where there's water and where we can get off the road just before it gets dark."

"He wuz a bounty hunter, 'deed he wuz, missus Dab'son," added Lucindy in a frightened voice from below. "I's neber fergit dat voice."

As soon as they had the chance, Seth sat to one side and Lucindy's head popped up and, still frightened, she told them about the incident she had witnessed with Murdoch before. Her story sobered them all the more to the extreme danger of what they were doing, and what would likely be the consequences if they were caught.

About four hours later, as Seth had suggested, they pulled well off and out of sight of the road near a small stream, unhitched the horses, and made preparations to sleep for several hours and let the horses eat, drink, and rest. Even though several hours had passed since they had seen the riders, they knew it would be imprudent for everyone to go to sleep outside in the open. Seth said he would stay awake and keep watch. Carolyn and Lucindy arranged themselves and the children as comfortably as they could, huddled together with mattress and blankets, with the board to the hidden chamber open so that the latter four could quickly hide should the need arise.

They were all so exhausted, after a quick cold supper and drink of water, that the five were asleep within minutes, leaving Seth to himself.

The next thing Carolyn knew, Seth was jostling her awake.

"Time to be going, Mother," he said. "I've got the horses hitched back up, the moon's up. If you want to stay like you are, I think it'll be fine in the middle of the night like this. Just be ready to get them below if we run into anyone."

"Do you want me to take the reins a while, Seth?"

"That's all right. I dozed off a little too. I shouldn't have but I couldn't help it. So I'm okay for a while—get some more sleep if you can."

Carolyn pulled the blanket back up around her shoulders, glanced around at Lucindy, Broan, Rebecca, and Calebia sleeping contentedly against boxes and crates and half the mattress, smiled to herself, then closed her eyes again. Seth called out to the horses, and they bounded into motion.

Encountering only a handful of riders and wagons and buggies after the gray light of dawn began to steal over the hilly Maryland landscape, they reached the Pennsylvania border—Carolyn again at the reins, Lucindy and her three hidden once more out of sight below.

For the sake of prudence, Carolyn kept Lucindy and the children where they were. They knew nothing about how safe runaway slaves actually were merely because they crossed the border. Carolyn judged it best to tell them nothing of the border sign she had seen while they slept. No harm could come from exercising added precaution all the way to their destination.

When she heard Seth stirring behind her, she motioned him forward. Seth sat up and crawled forward.

"What is it, Mother?" he asked.

"We crossed the border," she said softly. "We're in Pennsylvania."

"We made it!" cried Seth.

"Shh!" she motioned with her finger. "I'd rather keep them quiet and hidden until—'

But Lucindy was awake and had heard.

"We's cross ober dat riber Jordan!" they heard her exclaim beneath them. "Hallelujah . . . da promised lan'!"

Seth and Carolyn could not help breaking into laughter.

They rode into the town called Hanover a little over two hours later, Lucindy and the children now sitting up and gazing around them, the young mother with wide-eyed curiosity as if she expected this town of the promised land of the North to be paved with streets of gold. But it looked no different than a thousand other towns on both sides of the Mason-Dixon Line.

"Now what do we do?" asked Seth.

"I don't know," replied his mother. "The only clue we have is a horse's head."

"There's the livery stable down there at the end of the street," said Seth. "That's probably as good a place to start as anywhere."

They continued on toward it, then Seth reined in and got down.

"What's your husband's name again, Lucindy?" he asked.

She told him, and Seth went inside. Five minutes later he returned.

"No one in there's heard of him," he said. "I'm going to try the blacksmith's shop. They also told me about a man with some stables on the north side of town who sells horses."

He walked to the nearby blacksmith's shop but returned a few minutes later shaking his head. He climbed back up and took the reins. A few minutes later they were leaving Hanover by the north-bound road.

"There, that's it," said Seth, pulling up in front of one of the last houses in town. Behind it were several corrals with a dozen or more horses inside. "I'll go see what they have to say."

Again he got down and walked toward the house. While they were waiting, Carolyn and Lucindy gazed about. A few farmhouses could be seen out in the surrounding countryside. Two men were out ploughing in the distance. Mostly the land was cultivated, but one or two pastures were dotted with grazing cattle.

Seth returned again with the same news. It was obvious that Lucindy was close to tears. What good would freedom do if she and the children were alone?

"What's we gwine do, Missus Dav'son?" she said in a forlorn voice.

Carolyn thought a moment, then smiled.

"Do you remember what I have been telling you about God being our good Father?" she said.

"Yes'm."

"Because he is our Father, he knows what we need, and he wants to give us what we need. He is Caleb's Father too. God knows where he is right at this moment."

"He duz!"

"Of course. God is looking down at Caleb right now, just like he is looking at us. Imagine that—God can see all of you right now, your whole family. *We* don't know where Caleb is, but *God* does. So we have to ask him what to do."

"Den let's ax him!"

Carolyn bowed her heard and closed her eyes.

"Heavenly Father," she prayed, "we don't know what to do. Lucindy's come all this way to find her husband, but we don't know where he is. But we know that you do. So please show us where Caleb is, and what you want us to do. If he's still a spy hiding out some-where in this land of milk and honey, then we need for you to lead us to where he's hiding."

Suddenly little Broan's voice shouted out almost before Carolyn had finished, "Look, dere's a horse!"

They turned and followed his hand where he was pointing to the top of a large farmhouse about a hundred yards farther along the road. On top of its pitched roof rose a black metal weathervane displaying the head of a horse rather than a rooster.

Lucindy gasped. Carolyn glanced over and saw a look of shocked astonishment on her face. "Da win'," she said. "Da win' in da horse's head!"

Seth flicked the reins again and they bounded into motion. A couple of minutes later, trembling inside, Lucindy and Carolyn, this time more hopeful, followed Seth to the front door of the house beneath the horse's head while the three children waited in the wagon. Seth knocked on the door.

A woman answered wearing a long gray dress with white collar, a sight familiar to Lucindy from her months of travel. She looked over her three callers with a questioning glance.

"Good day," said Carolyn, stepping forward. "I wonder if by chance you might be able to help us. We are looking for a man called Caleb . . . a colored man."

"I do not know the name," answered the woman. "What wouldst be thy business with him?"

"This is his wife," answered Carolyn, nodding toward Lucindy.

"I am sorry I cannot help thee."

Disheartened, they turned to go as the door closed, and began walking back to the wagon.

"Wait," said a voice behind them.

They turned to see the woman again in the door. "I just thought thee might have interest to know of a man called Broancaleb—"

Lucindy's eyes shot wide.

"—a strange name, dost thee not think," added the woman, "but he said there wast but one person in the world who needed understand it, and when she heard, she would know the meaning."

"Is he here?" asked Carolyn. At that moment, shout though she would have, Lucindy had lost her voice.

"He is our hired field servant, good lady."

"Where is he?"

"There, in the field with my husband."

She pointed to the two men they had noticed, one white, one black, the one leading a team of oxen, the other wielding a plough behind it.

Already Lucindy had pulled her dress up above her ankles and was running away from the house over the freshly upturned earth toward the two men as fast as her legs would take her.

⌒

When Carolyn, carrying Calebia, and Seth, carrying Rebecca with his one good arm, and little Broan hurrying to keep up, reached them, the father and mother of the three children were still in one another's arms. The good Quaker farmer continued to stare in bewilderment. Hearing shrieks a moment before, he had turned to see a black woman racing toward them, then watched his man drop the plough and hurry to meet her with outstretched arms.

As they fell apart, Lucindy babbling and crying for joy, Caleb glanced about, then dropped to one knee with a big smile as the others approached.

"Dis big feller be my man Broan!" he said.

"Papa?" said Broan softly. He only faintly remembered his daddy, but it was enough. The next instant he was up in the big man's arms in the grip of a great hug, a wide smile of long-belated happiness on his seven-year-old face. This he certainly remembered! Rebecca followed, though without memory to aid her, was shy at first and clung to Lucindy's dress. Then Lucindy went to Carolyn, whose eyes were wet at sight of the wonderful reunion, and took the youngest girl from her. Lucindy turned and handed their daughter to Caleb.

"Who dis?" he asked.

"Dis be yo' daughter, Caleb," she said proudly. "I wuz carryin' her w'en you lef'. I named her after you."

Caleb took the little girl in his arms, tears now pouring down his dirt-stained black cheeks in full measure.

"Da Lor' be praized!" was all he could say. "Da Lor' be praized!"

Gradually more introductions followed, then they slowly walked back to the farmhouse, where Carolyn explained that part of the story she was personally acquainted with to the Quaker farmer and his wife, who had taken Caleb in over a year before. Within an hour Carolyn knew that in Frederick and Sarah Mueller she had indeed discovered kindred spirits.

How she wished Richmond was with them! She could envision her husband and the Quaker man glancing at one another, mutually seeking opportunity to excuse themselves, and then spending the rest of the afternoon out in the fields talking earnestly about the high things of God.

Anxious to begin their homeward journey and get as far as possible before nightfall, two hours later Seth and Carolyn prepared to make their departure.

Carolyn took Lucindy in her arms and the young woman began to bawl.

"I can't neber thank you, Missus Dab'son," she blubbered. "I's neber forgit all you dun fo' us. We owe you an' Mister Dab'son our freedom. You wuz so good ter us. An' you helped me know who my real Father wuz."

"Oh, Lucindy," said Carolyn as she held the young black mother affectionately, "that is the best thanks you could ever give me! We will never forget you, either. You are a special friend."

Full of the humility of gratefulness, Caleb shook Seth's hand. Carolyn gave each of the children a final hug, and at last, with many tears on all sides, they were off.

As Seth and Carolyn rode back into Hanover and then south toward the Maryland border, what remained of the day passed quietly in a mood of happy, thoughtful melancholy. Carolyn found herself wondering if they were now part of the mysterious U.G.R.R.

She could not help thinking that this was probably not their last encounter with it.

While his neighbor's wife and son were away on their clandestine mission of mercy, Denton Beaumont sat on the train toward home after his eventful meeting with Frederick Trowbridge and Abraham Seehorn. He was elated beyond words. Deep down it rankled his innate pride to be in a position of subservience to two men who had passed him over once before, especially in light of the possibility it might be cast up to him the moment he did something they didn't like. There was nothing he hated more than being beholden to any man. It made him feel owned . . . like a slave.

But for this prize . . . it was a price he was willing to pay. And his reservations were outweighed by the tremendous satisfaction of knowing that Virginia's party leadership had at last come to its senses and anointed him its standard-bearer for the future.

By the time the train pulled into the Dove's Landing station, Denton Beaumont was already beginning to carry himself with the dignity, and perhaps a touch of hauteur, of his new position. This was vindication indeed for last year's loss.

As he stepped out onto the platform and looked around him, it was with no small pride that he realized himself indisputably the most important man for miles—soon to be one of Virginia's most powerful and influential men, and a national figure of prominence.

How and when he would break the news to Daphne and Veronica . . . that he hadn't decided yet. They would go wild with delight! He smiled to himself. Knowing his wife and daughter, they would probably start buying new dresses and planning their Washington social calendar immediately.

If only there wasn't the idiocy of Veronica's marriage to contend with, they could all pack up and leave for Washington right now. For two cents, he would contrive to be in the capital at the time and miss the whole thing. But he knew neither Veronica nor Daphne would stand for that. He would just make the best of it he could, alternating his time between the capital and Oakbriar.

He could afford to wait another few months before beginning his new life in the corridors of power at the heart of the nation.

$\backsim\!\!\sim$

With satisfied and overflowing hearts, Carolyn and Seth rode into Greenwood the following day, having no idea that during their absence along with Denton's, news of Seth's dinner at Oakbriar had finally reached a few influential tongues and was now spreading like a brush fire. The proposed union was now on everyone's lips throughout Dove's Landing.

Within a week of their return from the Pennsylvania border, word was all over town that Denton Beaumont and Seth Davidson had *talked*. An arrangement between their families was discussed.

If the term *engagement* was not formally used, word had it that they had come to an understanding. And everyone knew well enough what *that* meant.

Fifty-five

On a black South Carolina night, with scarcely enough moon to create shadows in the woods, much less see by, a certain ticket mistress of the U.G.R.R. handed off a new passenger for whom instructions had come to her a few days before. As she turned to walk back to the big house where she managed to come and go almost at liberty, the conductor's voice behind her broke the stillness.

"Wait jes' er minute," he said. "I dun fergot—I got's sumfin' I figger you might like ter see."

He pulled a crumpled letter out of his pocket and handed it to her.

"Where'd hit cum from?" said the large woman as she took it.

"Don' know. Cum ter one ob dem Quaker depots 'long da line an' hit's been gittin' passed back'ards down da R.R. from han' er conductor ter han' er conducter eber since. Nobody know's where hit's from. Sumbody muster knowed which line ter sen' hit on. Jes' got one word on da envelope, dey said w'en hit got ter da right place, folks'd know."

"What word?"

"Jes' *Amaritta*—dat's all."

Several hours later, with the morning sun beginning to spread its warmth over the South Carolina countryside, Amaritta Beecham turned from the cookstove with a smile on her face. There stood her mistress who had walked into the room behind her only a moment before.

"What's that you just put in the stove?" said Mrs. Crawford.

"Nuffin' er no value, missus," replied Amaritta.

"I want to know what it was."

"Jes' some scraps er paper, missus."

"Then what are you grinning about?"

"I wuz jes' thinkin' what a fine mo'nin' hit is, missus, an' how happy I is ter be alive."

Muttering something under her breath which it was just as well her housekeeper did not hear, Mrs. Crawford spun around and left the room.

Amaritta turned back to the stove and opened the small door once again. She could just make out a few fading words on the paper that had traveled so far as it curled into flame. But she would never forget the words. She had read the brief message through eight times before committing it to the altar of a grateful heart:

> *Dear Amaritta. I's havin' sumbody dat kin rite put dese words down. I's hope an' pray dis fin' you sumday. Me an' my chilluns be safe an' we's wif dat spy an' you knows who I means. We dun got 'cross dat Riber Jordan an' foun' dat win' in dat horse's head. Da railroad cum off da tracks one time, but God dun pick me up an' took me eben w'ere dose tracks don' go. But I's be shure glad he did cuz I met sum good folks dat helped me mor'n I kin tell you 'bout. I's grateful fo' yo' help, mor'n I kin say too. I wish I cud see you ter tell you all 'bout hit. My man's got him er job an' we's happier den we kin be. I's neber fergit you. I's see you in heaben one day w'en we all gits ter dat big promised lan', an' I's tell you everything den. You's da bes' ticket mistress in da whole worl'. Dis be from Lucindy.*

Families in *Dream of Freedom*

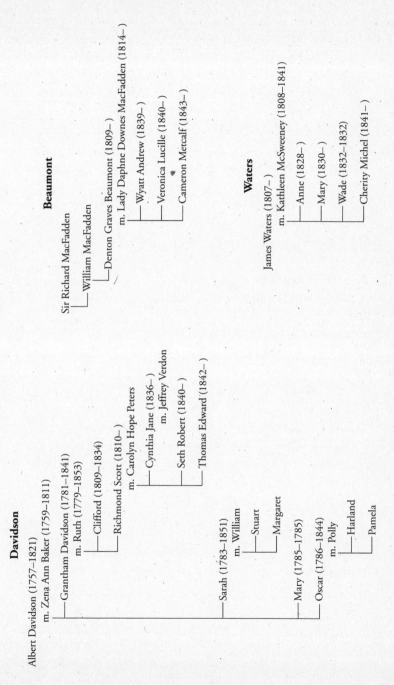

Davidson

Albert Davidson (1757–1821)
m. Zena Ann Baker (1759–1811)

Grantham Davidson (1781–1841)
m. Ruth (1779–1853)

Clifford (1809–1834)

Richmond Scott (1810–)
m. Carolyn Hope Peters

Cynthia Jane (1836–)
m. Jeffrey Verdon

Seth Robert (1840–)

Thomas Edward (1842–)

Sarah (1783–1851)
m. William

Stuart

Margaret

Mary (1785–1785)

Oscar (1786–1844)
m. Polly

Harland

Pamela

Beaumont

Sir Richard MacFadden

William MacFadden

Denton Graves Beaumont (1809–)
m. Lady Daphne Downes MacFadden (1814–)

Wyatt Andrew (1839–)

Veronica Lucille (1840–)

Cameron Metcalf (1843–)

Waters

James Waters (1807–)
m. Kathleen McSweeney (1808–1841)

Anne (1828–)

Mary (1830–)

Wade (1832–1832)

Cherity Michel (1841–)

Watch for Volume 2 of American Dreams,

Dream Of Life . . .

Coming soon!

About the Author

Californian Michael Phillips began his distinguished writing career in the 1970s. He came to widespread public attention in the early 1980s for his efforts to reacquaint the public with Victorian novelist George MacDonald. Phillips is recognized as the man most responsible for the current worldwide renaissance of interest in the once-forgotten Scotsman and one of the world's foremost experts on MacDonald. After beginning his work redacting and republishing the works of MacDonald, Phillips embarked on his own career writing fiction. Since that time he has written and co-written 47 novels and it is primarily as a novelist that he is now known. His critically acclaimed books have been translated into eight foreign languages, have appeared on numerous best-seller lists, and have sold more than six million copies. Phillips is today considered by many as the heir apparent to the very MacDonald legacy he has worked so hard to promote in our time. Phillips is also the publisher of the magazine *Leben,* a periodical dedicated to bold thinking Christianity and the legacy of George MacDonald. Combining all categories that have made up his extremely diverse writing career, *Dream of Freedom* is Phillips' 100th published work. Phillips and his wife Judy make their home in Eureka, California. They also spend a great deal of time in Scotland where they are attempting to increase awareness of MacDonald's work.